Final Cut

By
Lynn Ames

FINAL CUT
© 2016 BY LYNN AMES

ISBN: 978-1-936429-12-7

OTHER AVAILABLE FORMATS

eBOOK EDITION
ISBN: 978-1-936429-13-4

PUBLISHED BY
PHOENIX RISING PRESS
PHOENIX, ARIZONA
www.phoenixrisingpress.com

CREDITS

EXECUTIVE EDITOR: LINDA LORENZO
AUTHOR PHOTO: JUDY FRANCESCONI
COVER DESIGN: TREEHOUSE STUDIO

Dedication

To the brightest light shining in the night sky, my beautiful sister of choice, Sandra Moran. Our loss is Heaven's gain. Keep shining that light, sister. You inspire me every day to live life to the fullest. Sending you so much love in Heaven.

Acknowledgments

There are two aspects of every book I find hardest to write—the first is the back cover blurb (the synopsis). If I could adequately describe the novel in two or three paragraphs, why would I write a 300-page book? The second hardest piece is the acknowledgments. And here we are.

Although novel-writing is a singularly solitary pursuit, it takes a village to accomplish the finished product. Once I settle upon the story I want to tell, I make a list of experts in order to ensure that every aspect of the plot is possible and plausible. In this particular instance, *Final Cut* required a lot of research and a bevy of extraordinary experts. I consulted hacking experts; government officials; Washington insiders; former CIA operatives; FBI agents; Hollywood producers, screenwriters, and editors; corporate private jet pilots; and accountants. I would name all of these individuals, but, for obvious reasons given the list, there are some who would prefer to remain anonymous. As a result, I won't name any of my experts. They know who they are, and I extend my deepest gratitude to each of them.

As I write, I have a closed group of trusted readers who provide me with critical feedback. Two of these readers are former editors, two are among my oldest and dearest friends. As always, my thanks to Laney Roberts, Ruta Skujins, Jenni Levy, and Dana Francis for coming along for the journey and for turning the pages around so quickly.

Behind every great writer is a better editor. I am so blessed to have the best editor in the business. To Linda Lorenzo, may you always look forward to receiving my manuscripts and improving my work.

Now we get to the creation of the physical product. My extra special thanks to Toni Whitaker for creating the e-book versions of my work and for taking care of my publisher website so that the reader can buy directly from me.

Finally, last but absolutely not least, if a book is only as good as its cover, then I am in great luck, because I have the most talented, best cover designer in the universe. To my fabulously talented little sister, Ann McMan, Famous Graphic Designer, I have run out of superlatives to describe you and your work. Beyond that, the friendship I share with you and your lovely wife, Salem West, means more to me than words can express. I love my North Carolina family. You make me rich beyond measure.

And to you, my readers. Thank you for your unwavering support. Thank you for clamoring for more, and for supporting me as I strive to tell stories that are entertaining, deep, intricate, and enlightening. You rock.

CHAPTER ONE

"Hey, babe. Check this out." Katherine Kyle folded her copy of *the New York Times Book Review* section in half and held it out to her wife. "You know I always love the way the photographer has you cock your head to the side for these publicity shots."

"Yeah, well. It keeps me from squinting into the strobe lights and highlighting my wrinkles."

"Jamison Parker, you don't have any wrinkles."

"Really? What do you call these, then?" Jay pulled at the sides of her eyes.

"Those are laugh lines. That's different."

"You say tomato—"

The flight attendant interrupted. "Ladies and gentlemen, please make sure your seatbelts are securely fastened and your tray tables are in the upright and locked position. We'll be closing the doors shortly for departure."

Jay laid the newspaper in her lap and buckled her seat belt. She picked it up again and studied the quarter-page ad.

"From the pen of *New York Times* best-selling author Jamison Parker comes a tale of government intrigue and corporate greed that will leave you breathless…"

"Did you know Black Quill was doing pre-release publicity for the book?" Kate asked. "Isn't it a little early? The book isn't due out for another ten months."

"I didn't. But then, I'm usually the last to know."

"Nice cover art." Kate fumbled for her phone as it buzzed. "Who the heck would be texting me now?" She swiped the screen and read. "Shit."

"Shit? That's eloquent."

Kate tilted the screen so that Jay could see it.

"The Frog is on the move. Code red."

"What does that mean?" Jay asked.

"It means Sabastien is in trouble." Kate put on her Bluetooth and dialed a number.

"Ladies and gentlemen, we are now closing the cabin doors. It's time for you to turn off and stow all cell phones and large electronic devices for takeoff."

"Enright."

"Peter? It's Kate."

"I see you got the text."

"Listen, Jay and I are en route to Los Angeles, and we're just about to take off."

"What's in LA?"

"We're honorary co-chairs for the GLAAD Media Awards. What's going on?"

"You know, the usual. All hell is breaking loose."

"Can you tell me in five seconds or less?"

"Let's just say he's wanted, and not in a good way."

"For what?"

"Hacking into Homeland Security's servers and leaking classified data."

"What? Sabas... would never—"

"Ma'am, you're going to have to turn off your cell phone now."

Kate gave an exasperated nod to the flight attendant. "I've got to shut down. Quickly, what do they think he leaked? And to whom?"

"Our 1989 run-in with the Commission and all of the Hyland Commission Report, and to a reporter Jay knows well."

Kate winced. "Oh, no."

"Ma'am?"

"Peter, I've got to go. I'll call you as soon as we land."

"Fly safe."

Kate ended the call, powered down her phone, and dropped it in her bag.

"What's going on?" Jay asked.

"It doesn't make any sense."

"What doesn't make any sense? And why are you suddenly so pale?"

Kate waited until the roar of the engines was at its peak. Then she leaned over and whispered in Jay's ear. "Peter says Sabastien is wanted for treason for leaking classified documents from Homeland Security."

"What?" Jay practically screamed it, then, remembering where they were, lowered her voice to match Kate's whisper. "Why would he do that? He's saved their butts hundreds of times from hackers trying to get into their systems. What would his motive be?"

"It gets worse."

"How much worse can it get?"

Kate reached out and stroked Jay's hand.

"Kate? How much worse?"

Kate closed her eyes. Surely this couldn't be happening. She didn't want to tell Jay, but she knew she must. "He's accused of stealing the sealed materials from the Commission investigation and the plot against President Hyland."

Jay practically jumped out of her seat. "No. No, no, no." She shrugged off Kate's touch, buried her head in her hands, and grabbed a fistful of hair.

"Jay."

"Oh, Kate." When Jay looked up again, her hair was standing out at odd angles. "Who was the recipient of the leak?"

"I don't know for sure."

"Kate."

"I mean it. Peter didn't give me a name."

Jay studied her wife. "I know that look. There's something you're not telling me. What is it?"

"All Peter said was that it was a reporter you knew well."

"Oh my God! Do you realize what this means?"

"Jay, we don't know everything yet. Let's just wait until we land, then we can call Peter back and get more details."

"The book..." Jay looked down in her lap, where her face gazed up at her from the ad for her upcoming novel.

"Is a *fictional* account of something that only a dozen people know about," Kate finished.

"Knew about, you mean," Jay said, glumly.

"We don't know the extent of the leak, or what the reporter did with whatever information he got."

"Come on, Kate. If it was minor, we probably wouldn't even know about it. The FBI would have handled it, and it already would've been buried by now."

Kate stared at Jay.

"What?"

"Who are you, and what have you done with my normally sunny, optimistic wife?"

Jay heaved a sigh. "I'm sorry. You're right." She sat back in her seat. "But I've worked so hard on this book."

"I know you have, sweetheart."

"It's taken me twenty-seven years to bring myself to write about what happened."

"I know." Kate reached out again, this time intertwining their fingers. "How about if we wait until we know more before we jump to conclusions about what this means for the book?"

Jay glanced down at her lap one more time. She let go of Kate's hand, grabbed the folded newspaper, and stuffed it in the seat pocket in front of her. "Let's talk about something else."

After a moment's silence, Kate said, "Okay, what if we focus on tonight's event? How exciting is it going to be to meet Dara Thomas and her wife, Rebecca?"

"Hollywood's 'it' couple. Dara was so gutsy, coming out at the Oscars like she did."

"She was. Then again, standing up there accepting the award for Best Actress makes you the hottest property in town. It's the ideal time to do something bold if you're going to do it."

"True. But you've got to give her props. She could've lost millions in salary and some major movie roles."

"She could have," Kate acknowledged. "But to me, the coolest thing is that she didn't."

"No, she didn't. She went right back into production for the second Constance Darrow adaptation without batting an eyelash."

"Good for the studio for standing by her. What's the name of the new film again?"

"*Love Above All Else*," Jay said. "The book was exquisite. I can't wait to see the movie. It opens in theaters next week."

"I'm always leery of adaptations. Somehow, they're never as good as the books on which they're based."

"Normally, I'd agree with you. But the movie version of *On the Wings of Angels* was amazing. Then again, Rebecca wrote the script. She's the world's preeminent Constance Darrow scholar. That's how she and Dara met, isn't it, on the set?"

"I think so. You know I don't pay any attention to the gossip rags."

"But it's such a beautiful love story. It's like something straight out of a romance novel."

Kate laughed. "You're a hopeless romantic."

"Takes one to know one." Jay leaned over and kissed Kate on the cheek. "Thanks."

"For what?"

"For pulling me back from the brink. That was an excellent deflection."

"Any time." Kate reclined her seat. "It's going to be a long night. How about we try to get some sleep?"

"Honey? Have you seen my black strapless bra? I could've sworn it was in this drawer."

"No need to shout," a warm, mellifluous voice hummed in Rebecca Minton Thomas's ear, as strong arms wrapped around her naked torso. "I'm right here."

Heat flowed through Rebecca's body as she responded to her wife's touch. "Mmm."

"Did you say you were looking for this?" Dara nuzzled Rebecca's neck.

Rebecca tipped her head back. "No. But it's a nice appetizer."

"Mm-hmm."

"And if you keep it up, we'll be late." Rebecca reluctantly broke the embrace.

"Spoil sport." Dara closed the open dresser drawer. "Your strapless bras and sexy panties belong in your 'high fashion' lingerie drawer." She made a show of removing the bra in

11

question, along with a pair of black lace panties, from the next drawer down.

Rebecca raised an eyebrow. "I have a 'high fashion' lingerie drawer?" She took the bra and panties from Dara, put them on, and walked to the closet where her dress was hanging.

"You do. We have so many formal functions to attend, it only made sense to give these specialty items their own space."

"You know that's a little OCD, right?" Rebecca laughed and removed the little black dress from the hanger and stepped into it. "Zip me up?"

"You say OCD, I say efficient," Dara said as she complied, then spun Rebecca around and held her at arm's length.

"What?" Even though they'd been married for almost a year, Rebecca still marveled at the raw hunger in Dara's eyes.

"You're gorgeous, that's what."

Rebecca swallowed hard. "I bet you say that to all the girls."

"Nope. Only to the one who owns my heart." Dara ran her thumb over Rebecca's bottom lip. "I love you."

"I love you too."

The kiss was long and lingering. By the time they separated, Rebecca was completely breathless.

Dara glanced at her watch. "Oh my God! We've got to get going."

"I tried to tell you," Rebecca said. She gave herself a last once-over in the full-length mirror. In the reflection of the glass, she watched Dara slip into her shoes. The electric blue Oscar de la Renta dress hugged her in all the right places. She blushed as Dara turned and held her gaze in the mirror.

"Why are you embarrassed?"

Rebecca shrugged. "I guess I still fret sometimes that you'll feel like I'm objectifying you."

Dara came over and took Rebecca's hands. "Sweetheart, you're the one person in the world I never worry about that with. I hope you always, always look at me just like that."

"That's a given." Rebecca risked one more kiss. "Okay. Let's go before we don't."

"Right."

Together, they headed for the front door.

❦

The limo sped down Wilshire Boulevard on its way to the Beverly Hilton. Kate and Jay had barely had time to check into their hotel and change for the awards gala before meeting the driver downstairs.

"Kate? Please."

After almost three decades together, Kate understood the shorthand request without the need for further elaboration. She closed the privacy partition between them and the driver, affixed her Bluetooth to her ear, and called Peter. "Is he safe?" Beside her, Jay sat rigidly with a knee bobbing up and down and her hands clenched tightly in her lap. Kate reached out and put a hand on Jay's leg to still the nervous motion, then let go.

"He's left the building."

"Was that an answer?"

"It's what I have right now."

Kate didn't like how tense Peter sounded. It wasn't the cryptic nature of the conversation. She was well used to his insistence on secrecy. No, there was something different in his tone, something she couldn't quite identify. Yet.

"Does that mean you don't know where he is?"

"How was the flight?"

Kate accepted the change in topic for what it was—either Peter didn't have any idea where Sabastien was, or he wasn't comfortable giving the information over the phone. It also occurred to Kate that, depending on the details of the situation, she might be better off not knowing the answer.

"The flight was smooth. Jay didn't get much shuteye though. She's a little preoccupied." Again, Kate put a hand on Jay's thigh. "Surely there must be something more you can tell me?"

"The hack was catastrophic and surgical. That's why the Feds immediately focused on our guy. Whoever got in there was that good."

"Does Sabas... the Frog know who did it, or how?"

"No, and it's eating him up."

"I can just imagine." Kate pictured Sabastien, his fingers flying across a keyboard, smashing through virtual back doors to gain access to highly protected information, tracing every keystroke that preceded his. "Peter?"

"Hmm?"

"Who was the reporter?"

"I was wondering when you were going to get around to asking that. It was Niles."

"Niles Masterson?"

Jay gasped. "That was who the hacker sent the files to? Niles? Any word—"

Kate held up a hand. "Do you know what Niles did with the information?"

"I don't know everything yet. I'm still trying to get a handle on it, but I can tell you this much—he called the former First Lady to verify that her husband was asthmatic and that his inhaler was tampered with."

"He called Mimi Hyland? Oh no."

"Oh yes."

"Niles called—"

"Give me a second, honey," Kate said to Jay. To Peter, she said, "And you know this because..."?

"Because, after she alerted the Secret Service about a reporter for *Time* magazine knowing details of the incident that were never made public, Mrs. Hyland decided she should check with me to see if I had any idea what was going on."

"I didn't realize you'd remained in contact with her."

"Do you remember last June, at President Hyland's funeral, when she asked me to stay behind for a minute?"

"Yes."

"She told me she wanted to let go of the former President's Secret Service detail. She didn't feel comfortable with the taxpayers footing the bill for her safety. So she asked me if she could keep in touch with me. She asked if I would watch out for her. She said that she trusted me because her husband trusted me and because we had a history."

"That's nice."

"We don't talk often, but when something comes up and she thinks I can be helpful, she calls."

"Is that the reason that our guy managed to stay a step ahead?"

"Katherine Kyle, I don't know what you're talking about."

"Of course you don't. Anything else you want to share?"

"That's all I've got right now."

"You'll keep us posted?"

"Of course."

"Thanks. See you when we get back." Just as Kate ended the call, Jay's cell phone rang.

"Oh my God! Not already."

"Who is it?"

"My editor at Black Quill." Jay answered the call. "Jamison Parker." She listened for a minute.

"Yes, I know who Niles is. He was my fact-checking intern at *Time* before I left. I was the one who got him a job on staff as a reporter." Jay listened some more.

"He's asking you to verify that the details of my plot are based on real incidents that are still classified?" After another second, Jay asked, "What did you tell him?" Jay went pale underneath her makeup. "No, I understand. Thanks for the heads up." She cleared her throat. "Well, I'm in Los Angeles right now at a function. I can sit down with you and the publisher when I get back in a few days."

Jay turned away to stare out the window. "Yes. Two o'clock Thursday afternoon. I'll be there. Bye." She put the phone down on the seat and faced Kate. "That didn't take long."

"What did he say?"

"In light of the questions being asked, the publisher is being advised by counsel to put the book on hold until they can do more fact gathering to ensure that I haven't revealed any state secrets."

"You're kidding me?"

"I wish." Jay opened her clutch and stuffed the phone inside. "What did Peter say?"

"He said that Niles called Mimi Hyland to ask about the asthma inhaler. And that Mrs. Hyland called the Secret Service to report it. Then she called Peter to ask him about it. That's how Sabastien managed to disappear before the Feds showed up at his door."

"Peter alerted him."

"Yes. We all know Sabastien didn't do this. But someone with a similar skill set did."

"And Sabastien is our best hope to figure out who that someone is."

"Exactly."

"And he can't do that if he's locked up somewhere." Jay shook her head. "Kate, what am I going to do?"

Just as she was about to answer, the limo pulled up in front of the Beverly Hilton. Reporters and television cameras lined a red carpet. Kate took Jay's hand. "For right now, you're going to smile for the cameras and we're going to get through tonight."

"What if someone asks me a question on the way in?"

Kate considered. "I doubt word would've spread that quickly. But if someone does ask something, just act like you don't hear the question and keep moving."

The limo driver opened the door and Kate squeezed Jay's hand. "We've got this, sweetheart." She looked deeply into her wife's eyes. "Ready?"

"As I'll ever be."

CHAPTER TWO

The ballroom was abuzz with A-list celebrities, movers and shakers from the world of politics, chief executive officers of Fortune 500 companies, media giants, and assorted others, all dressed in their finest formal wear.

Dara guided Rebecca to the assigned table for honored guests and GLAAD board members at the front of the room. As she scanned the room, her eyes alighted on a striking couple striding toward them. Although she recognized them from publicity photos, she thought idly that the pictures didn't do them justice.

"Hi, Dara. I'm Kate Kyle, and this is my wife—"

"Jamison Parker," Dara said, before Kate could get the words out. She put her hand out and shook Kate's hand, then Jay's. "I'm so glad to meet you both."

"Jay, please. You know who I am?"

When Jay's cheeks turned an endearing shade of pink, Dara smiled. "I'm sorry. I wish you could see the expression on your face right now. Of course I know who you are. I'm a big fan."

"She particularly loved *Six Steps from Heaven*. Hello. I'm Dara's wife, Rebecca."

"I know," Jay said. "I loved your adaptation of Constance Darrow's work for the big screen. She's one of my favorite authors—her themes are so nuanced and complex, and you absolutely kept the integrity of the story. That was brilliant and no mean feat."

"Well, my wife is brilliant." Dara beamed proudly and slid her arm around Rebecca's waist.

"Oh, my gosh. You were fabulous in the role of Celeste, Dara," Jay added. "I should have said so, first."

"No, you got the order of things exactly right. If Rebecca's revision of the original script hadn't been so inspired, I never would've won the Oscar."

"Not true," Rebecca said. "You're a Constance Darrow fan?" she asked Jay.

Dara noted the pride in Rebecca's voice and prayed that it wasn't as obvious to everyone else. She subtly increased the pressure of her hold on Rebecca's waist in warning.

"More like a devotee. I wish my prose were half as elegant as hers. I can't wait to see what you did with *Love Above All Else*."

Before Rebecca could say anything more, Dara asked, "Why don't you two come to the premiere with us? It's the day-after-tomorrow here in LA."

Jay's eyes grew wide. "Y-you can't be serious."

Dara laughed easily, completely charmed by Jay's guilelessness. "Utterly, one hundred percent serious." She watched as Jay and Kate communicated in that silent way that only couples who had been together for a long time can do.

Kate put her arm around Jay's shoulder. "We'd love to. It's incredibly gracious of you to ask."

"Excellent. I'll put you on the list. Where are you staying?"

"Chateau Marmont."

"I'll have a car pick you up at five o'clock. Will that work for you? We can go to the premiere and then have dinner afterward."

"Pinch me, because I must be dreaming."

"Thank you," Kate said. "You just made my wife's week."

"That was easy."

"I don't suppose there's any chance Constance will be attending? I mean, she's never made a public appearance that I'm aware of, but this is her work. Surely she'd make an exception," Jay said.

"Kate. Jay. I'm so glad you're here."

Dara breathed a sigh of relief at the interruption.

"Good to see you, Jasper," Kate said. "Have you met our Vanguard Award winner yet? Jasper Lyons, Chairman of the GLAAD Board of Directors, meet Dara and Rebecca Thomas."

"A pleasure to meet you, ladies. We're so honored that you could make it."

"I appreciate the recognition," Dara said. "We love the work you do."

"I'm sorry to interrupt your conversation, but we're about to get started and I need to borrow our honorary co-chairs."

"We understand," Rebecca said.

When they were alone, Dara leaned over and whispered in Rebecca's ear. "Darling, you have got to work on your poker face. You nearly gave Constance away."

"I'm sorry. I'm just so proud of you it's hard to resist the urge to make the connection. Surely you don't think it would be problematic if we shared your alter ego with Jay?"

Dara sighed. Jay was a gifted writer and she'd been telling the truth—she was an admirer of Jay's work, as was Rebecca. More than once Rebecca had told her that if she'd still been teaching American Literature, she would have loved to include Jay's books in her syllabus. Still, the fact that Constance Darrow was Dara's pseudonym remained a closely guarded secret. Only Rebecca and Dara's agent and best friend, Carolyn Detweiler, knew the truth.

"You don't have to answer that." Rebecca broke into Dara's rumination. "I promised you a long time ago that I would never divulge anything about Constance, and I meant it. Whether you want to share all of yourself with anyone else is completely up to you, and I will always respect that."

Dara kissed Rebecca on the cheek. "I know."

"Ladies and gentlemen, if you would please take your seats," Jasper announced from the podium on stage. "Welcome to the 2016 GLAAD Media Awards, sponsored by…"

Jay cinched the belt of her robe around her waist, wiped the sleep from her eyes, and opened the door to admit the bellboy.

"Good morning, ma'am. Where would you like this?"

"Over there will be fine, thanks." Jay pointed to the coffee table in front of the couch in the living room of their small bungalow. She waited for the young man to finish, signed for their breakfast, and handed him a tip on the way out.

"Breakfast is served," she called in the direction of the bedroom. She lifted the cover off one of the plates and sniffed appreciatively as the smell of bacon wafted up toward her. "I will wait for Kate. I will wait for Kate." She replaced the lid in order to resist temptation.

A copy of today's *USA Today* caught her eye. She picked it up from the tray and unfolded it to scan the headlines.

New Hacking Scandal Rocks Homeland Security. Jay nearly stumbled as she sank onto the sofa.

"What's going on? Why aren't you eat…"

Jay barely noticed as Kate sat down next to her and wrapped an arm around her waist. "I can't believe it's already out there." She read the story, her heart sinking a little more with every word.

> Confidential sources tell *USA Today* that the FBI is searching for a single suspect who allegedly breached sophisticated firewalls and leaked highly classified Homeland Security documents to a *Time* magazine reporter.
>
> Officials with Homeland Security and the FBI refused to comment, but one anonymous, high-ranking source identifies the alleged hacker as Sabastien Vaupaul, a private contractor who reportedly has worked closely for many years with the federal government.
>
> Thus far, *Time* is withholding the extent of the information it obtained and the source of the leak, except to say the files date back decades to the presidency of Charles Hyland.
>
> Conspiracy theorists have long argued that the Hyland administration covered up crucial facts about the murky circumstances under which the President was taken hostage as part of a treasonous plot to overthrow him by his vice president and associates.
>
> This is a breaking news story. Please go to www.usatoday.com for the most recent updates.

"It's just supposition. Look at the number of times they use the words 'allegedly' and 'reportedly.'"

Jay shook her head. "For now. You and I both know they must have an ironclad source to publish Sabastien's name without corroboration from an official source. They would never risk it otherwise."

Kate took the paper from Jay and laid it aside. "Maybe. But that's not your primary concern."

"What do you mean?"

"What you're really worried about is that they'll connect the hack to you and the book."

"That's not fair. I'm truly worried about Sabastien."

"Of course. But you and I both know it's more than that."

Jay tucked her legs underneath her and folded her arms across her chest. "It won't take them a day to dig up the story I wrote for *Time* back then."

"You're right. But remember, in the name of national security, the president's staff convinced *Time* to edit out a lot of the specifics of the incident, including the existence of the Commission."

"I remember it well. And I agreed with it at the time. If anybody knew how pervasive and extensive that organization was, or how close they came to controlling some of the world's most influential governments and industries, it would have been disastrous."

"A secretive organization comprised of hundreds of operatives from all walks of life, embedded in all public and private sectors, intent on running the world its own way, by its own code, heedless of the consequences, and acting above the law. I don't know that anyone would've believed it," Kate said.

"That's why it would've made great fiction." Jay swallowed around the lump in her throat. She had worked so hard on this book. In many ways, she believed it was her best work to date.

"Don't use the past tense."

"Black Quill is pulling the plug on the book."

"Not necessarily."

Jay rolled her eyes. "Come on, Kate. Why do you think they want to meet with me on Thursday? They're not going to risk the controversy."

"Controversy sells books."

"Or ruins publishing houses."

Kate stared at Jay.

"What?"

"I'm trying to figure out when you became such a pessimist."

"I'm not—"

"I wish you could hear yourself."

Jay bit back the sharp retort. This morass wasn't Kate's fault. "You should eat before your omelet gets cold." She stood up.

"Where are you going? We both need to eat."

"I don't have much of an appetite now, thanks." Jay walked away and into the bedroom.

"Jay..."

Jay sat down on the side of the bed. She just needed a minute to get control of her emotions. Was Kate right? Was she overreacting? Perhaps, once she had a chance to sit down with Black Quill, they would move ahead with the book as scheduled.

"Hey." Kate stood in the doorway.

"Hey, yourself."

"Do you need some alone time? Or can we talk through this together?"

The uncertainty in Kate's voice cut directly to Jay's heart. All these years, they'd gotten through every crisis, every tough moment, together. She went to Kate and stepped into her welcoming embrace.

"I'm sorry. I don't know what's going on with me."

Kate pulled her closer and kissed her on the top of the head. "You've got a lot invested in this novel. This story is personal in a way that transcends any fiction you've written before. I know what it took for you to dredge up all those memories, all that emotion you worked so hard to heal."

Jay rested her head against Kate's neck and placed her hand on the center of Kate's chest. "We," she corrected. "All the emotion we, as in you and I, worked so hard to heal. It was painful for both of us, believing we'd lost each other, learning to open ourselves fully and to trust again. Thank you for letting me back in."

Kate tipped Jay's chin up and kissed her softly on the mouth. "You were my heartbeat. You still are. I stopped living the moment I got the news that your car had been forced over that cliff and that there were no signs of survivors. When you found your way home to me, it took some time for me to accept that it was real, and that you wouldn't be taken away from me again."

Jay felt Kate's back tighten and she rubbed soothing circles to ease the tension there.

"I understand that feeling. When I saw your face on CNN and they were saying you were dead, everything came flooding back for me. I'd been trying so hard to regain my memory after the accident, it was downright cruel to remember who I was only to learn that the life I was fighting to return to no longer existed." Jay caressed Kate's face and gazed into eyes that held traces of long-buried suffering. "I knew that without you, my life was over. When Peter told me you were alive and on the run from the Commission, I had no idea what to think and no way to process all that had happened."

Kate stilled Jay's hand, drew it to her mouth, and kissed her palm. "Even now, those events have power for both of us. Is it any wonder that you're off balance? I'd be more surprised if you weren't."

"What do you think is really happening with this hack?" Jay asked.

"I'm not sure. Why don't we sit down and map out what we know. We can look at synchronicities and try to extrapolate reasonable explanations. That should give us a starting point."

Jay let Kate lead her back out to the couch in the living room. She grabbed the pen and the pad of paper with the Chateau Marmont crest from the end table and wrote: Facts. Then she looked up expectantly at Kate.

"Fact: At Peter and Lorraine's anniversary party last year, after several drinks, Sabastien let slip that Homeland Security had him hacking into the personal accounts of known associates of several high profile CEOs rumored to be part of a shadowy organization he would not name."

"Fact," Jay said. "Based on that piece of information, Peter and Lorraine did a little poking around with some of their former CIA colleagues and determined that the Commission is alive and well and resurgent, and that this Administration wants to keep a lid on that information."

Kate stretched her legs out under the coffee table. "Fact: The four of us agreed that the best way to prevent a repeat of what happened in 1989 was to shine a light and expose the existence of the Commission."

Jay scribbled furiously. "Fact: We also agreed that our experiences back then put us in the best position to tell the story, and that fiction was the only viable means, since the facts of the incident remain classified."

"And here we are."

Jay put the pen down. "And here we are, with the addition of one more fact. Someone with an unknown agenda hacked into the classified files from the Hyland Commission Report and intentionally leaked that information to a reporter for a national magazine."

"A reporter who is specifically connected to you," Kate added. "Whether or not that's a lucky coincidence remains to be seen."

"You know I don't believe in coincidences."

"Me either." Kate pointed to the paper. "Now let's talk about what we don't know."

Jay made another column. "We don't know if the 1989 incident and the subsequent investigations and reports are all that was leaked, or even all that was taken."

"True. We don't know who did the hacking or the leaking, and whether those are the same parties. It's possible that the person who did the hacking handed off the information to someone else when he, or she, realized what was in the files."

"Or if the hacker was acting on his own or was hired by another unknown party to get in and access those files."

Kate nodded in agreement. "Or if the Hyland files were the intended target or collateral material."

"We have no idea if the White House is looking specifically for Sabastien based on assumptions they're making, or if he was targeted for framing by whoever the hacker or the hacker's client is."

"If that's true," Kate said, "it would be even more troublesome. We can count on one hand the number of people with knowledge of Sabastien, his skills, and his assignments."

Jay frowned. "You're right. So, if this turns out to be someone like that, the White House has a much bigger problem."

"A traitor on the inside in a classified position."

"Here we go again."

"So it would appear. But we can't be sure until we have more answers."

"Which brings us back to poor Sabastien. I really hope he's someplace he can't be found or traced, and that he can clear himself." Jay looked at Kate. "Do you think he's okay?"

"Sabastien is a resourceful guy, and he's got some powerful friends. He's got Vaughn Elliott, Peter, and Lorraine, all of whom are, or were, CIA black operatives."

"And Sedona Ramos and all her National Security Agency resources and training."

"Yep. Sabastien is probably in a private safe house somewhere with no extradition treaty, surrounded by all the latest technology toys, completely in his element."

"I really, really hope you're right," Jay said. "So, what do we do now?"

Kate lifted the lid off one of the covered plates. "We eat cold eggs and bacon, drink cold coffee, and get ready to go shopping for outfits for tomorrow's big movie premiere." She took a bite of bacon and fed the rest of the slice to Jay. "I'm sure Peter will keep us apprised if and when he's got more to tell."

Jay stabbed a forkful of her omelet. "Thank you."

"For?"

"For getting me back on track. For always knowing exactly the right thing to do and say. For not getting mad at me for being a Class-A jerk."

"You weren't being a jerk."

Jay made a face. "Yeah. I really was."

"Maybe a little," Kate admitted. She leaned over and kissed Jay gently. "I love you."

"Even when I'm being a jerk?"

"Even then."

"I'm a lucky girl."

Kate smiled at her indulgently. "We're both lucky."

Sabastien Vaupaul peeked out through the blinds for the umpteenth time. "C'est fou." He rechecked the bank of computer monitors in front of him. "This is crazy."

His fingers flew over the keyboard. He typed in a series of commands, then sat back and watched as numbers and text on one of the screens morphed into other numbers and still more text. "Non. C'est ne pas possible."

He squinted at the monitor and banged on the keys with more force, as if doing so would change the outcome. "Merde."

He nearly jumped out of his shoes at the shrill ringing of one of several cell phones on the desk. At first, he stared at it as if it was alive. After all, apart from Peter, to whom he already had spoken, nobody knew that number. A glance at the readout yielded no clues. Whoever it was had blocked the incoming phone number. Should he answer? What if the FBI had caught up with him? Then again, what if it was Peter again with some new piece of information?

Tentatively, he accepted the call. "Oui."

"I hear you're in a tight spot," said former CIA agent Vaughn Elliott.

Relief coursed through Sabastien. "It is good to hear your voice, mon amie."

"That's a first. You must really be spooked."

"This makes no sense at all. Whoever did this is a master hacker. As good as me. And nobody is as good as me."

"So you keep telling me."

"I am serious, Vaughn Elliott. And, by the record—"

"*For* the record, genius."

"Do not trouble me with the truth."

"With the facts."

"Did you call to help? Or to harangue me?"

"Unbelievable. You get 'harangue' right, but not simple American idioms."

Sabastien gritted his teeth and prayed for patience. "You are the one who got me into this mess. If you had not told the president to hire me as your government's personal counter-hacker, I would be sipping umbrella drinks on a beach like you."

"Do you want to whine? Or do you want to tell me what happened?"

"Some person must have been in the system for a very long time. He learned all my techniques. He spoofed me, and I have not been able to determine how he gained access. I have not yet found his back door."

"And if you can't prove that someone else was in there, you can't prove that you aren't the leak."

"Exactement. C'est ça."

"Do you have all the equipment you need?"

"I do."

"Are you someplace safe?"

"I hope so."

"I'm sorry this is happening to you. How can I help you?"

It was a rare moment when Vaughn Elliott showed a softer side. Although it should have brought Sabastien comfort, in truth, it scared the daylights out of him.

"Can you answer why someone would want to do this to me? And why those specific files? They could have taken anything. Yet they were very precise."

Those were the two questions that had been weighing most heavily on Sabastien's mind. The hacker could have done immeasurable damage and had access to far more sensitive materials than what was taken.

"You verified that the Hyland files were all that was stolen?"

"I did."

"I'll work on motive along with our other friends. I'll call you when I have something. In the meantime, stay put."

"Where else, exactly, do you think I would be going? For a swim on the Riviera?"

"Talk soon."

"A bientôt, Vaughn Elliott."

CHAPTER THREE

"Did you see this?" Rebecca turned her iPad so that the screen faced Dara. "*The New York Times* says Jamison Parker is connected to the reporter at the center of that new leak scandal."

"Really?"

"He was her intern when she was with the magazine."

"And their point is?"

"Jay wrote the *Time* magazine exclusive of that whole treason fiasco in the Hyland administration. Apparently, the classified data connects to when Katherine Kyle was President Hyland's press secretary. She and Jay already were together then."

"Interesting. But, unless they're intimating that Jay is the one who leaked the information to her former intern, I'm wondering why the *Times* thinks the fact that Jay and the reporter knew each other is newsworthy." Dara scrolled down. "Oh."

Instantly alerted by Dara's tone of voice, Rebecca leaned over.

"Did you get this far?"

Rebecca read the section Dara indicated. "Oh my."

Advance publicity for Parker's new book calls it, "A political thriller so real it will take your breath away." Here is an excerpt from the book's promotional blurb. "A powerful, shadowy organization wants to advance its own global agenda. To succeed, the president must be eliminated. Only one person knows the truth and can put a stop to the scheme."

> *The New York Times* contacted Parker's publisher to ask
> about the status of the book and the similarities between the
> author's real-life account of the Hyland incident and her
> upcoming fictional tale. Representatives for Black Quill Press
> refused to comment.

"Holy cow! Do you think Kate and Jay knew about any of this when we met them the other night?"

Just as Rebecca was about to answer, Dara's personal cell phone rang.

"Hi, Car. Please tell me you're not sitting on a runway somewhere and that you'll be on time for tonight's premiere." Dara listened for a moment. "Interesting. Rebecca and I were just talking about her... Yes, we read the article... Hang on, let me grab a pen."

Rebecca snatched a pen and a pad of paper off the kitchen counter and handed them to Dara.

"Okay, give me the number... Got it... Did she say anything specific?"

Rebecca wished she could hear the other end of the conversation.

"Well, I'll give her a call... I love you too. See you later. Bye."

"What did Carolyn say?"

"Jay called her. She apologized for disturbing her. Apparently I forgot to give her my number the other night. She wanted to talk to me personally, and didn't know how to reach me except through my agent."

"How did Carolyn say she sounded?"

Dara shrugged. "Like she wanted to talk to me."

"That's it?"

"If you'd let me make the phone call, I'm sure we could find out exactly what Jay wants to tell me."

Rebecca bit back her next question as Dara punched in Jay's number.

"Hello. Jay? Dara Thomas here. My agent tells me you were trying to reach me. I'm sorry. I should have remembered to give you my number the other night."

Dara was quiet for a long time, and Rebecca resisted the urge to get close enough to eavesdrop.

"No. I don't want you to do that. There's no need... No, I mean it... How about this, if you and Kate are free, why don't we meet in person for lunch and we can talk about it face-to-face?" Dara glanced at her watch. "Let's say in an hour? We'll come pick you up... Yes, I'm positive... Okay, we'll see you shortly. Goodbye."

⋙⋘

"Ms. Thomas, your table is ready." The maitre d' led Dara, Rebecca, Kate, and Jay to a secluded corner booth.

The ride over had been a quiet affair, and Dara noted that Jay looked tired, her cheeks drawn.

When they were seated, Jay said, "I'm so sorry. I'm sure you must have much better and more important things to do on the day of your premiere."

Dara waved a hand dismissively. "Nonsense. We'd just be sitting around at home, twiddling our thumbs."

"Somehow, I doubt that."

Dara didn't need to know Jay well to hear the strain in her voice. She reached across the table and put her hand on top of Jay's hand. "We wouldn't be here if we didn't want to be. We have so much respect for you and your work."

"I imagine if you hadn't already seen them, after we spoke you read today's news stories," Jay said. She licked her lips nervously and withdrew her hand. "I want you to know, the implication that I had anything to do with the leaking of classified data or hacking into secured databases is completely without merit."

"Jay." Dara waited until Jay made eye contact with her. "Rebecca and I had already seen the stories. It never occurred to us that there was any truth to it."

"Anyone who is familiar with your career and your writing knows you had nothing to do with whatever happened," Rebecca added. "You have tremendous integrity. Anyone would be crazy to question that."

Jay blushed. "I appreciate your faith in me. Still, I think it would be a mistake for me, for us,"—Jay indicated her and Kate—"to attend the premiere."

"Nonsense."

"We don't want to detract in any way from your moment," Jay continued as if she hadn't heard Dara. "This is your big night and we don't want anything to spoil that."

"You won't."

The waiter came over and took their drink orders. When he had departed, Jay said, "If the media gets wind of our presence—"

"The studio will have plenty of security on hand to keep any enterprising reporters at bay." Dara turned her attention to Kate. "I know you have extensive experience with this sort of thing. Jay has done nothing wrong and has nothing to hide. Wouldn't it be a bigger mistake to sequester yourselves away?"

Kate intertwined her fingers with Jay's. "The answer to that is more complicated than a simple yes or no. You're right that we don't want to appear to be frightened or guilty. On the other hand, we should pick our spots carefully. I agree with Jay that your premiere is not the proper venue to take a stand."

"Understood," Dara said. She paused as the server placed their drinks on the table. When he took out a pad of paper expectantly, she gave him an apologetic smile. "I'm sorry. We haven't even had a chance to look at the menu yet."

"That's fine. Just let me know whenever you're ready." The waiter retreated.

"I'm not talking about you holding a press conference on the red carpet." Dara emptied a packet of artificial sweetener into her iced tea and stirred. "My point is that carrying on with your heads held high lets the media and other detractors know that you won't be bullied or cowed by them. Maybe I'm naïve, but isn't that a good message to send?"

"True. But, if you'll pardon me saying so, attending a movie premiere when there are serious allegations and matters of national security on the line might be perceived as cavalier and disrespectful. If we were attending a major charity event or a conference on world peace—"

"No offense," Jay added. "Kate's not intimating that the movie and its debut aren't important..."

"No offense taken," Dara said. "I get where you're going with this." Dara sipped her tea. "What would happen if you addressed the allegations this afternoon, before you arrived at the premiere? Cleared the air in advance?"

Kate seemed to mull the idea over. "We could take control of the story, which is something you always want to do."

"No," Jay said, turning to face Kate. She disentangled their hands.

"Jay—"

Jay shook her head. "Not before I meet with my editor and the publisher on Thursday."

"They're not the ones whose integrity is on the line right now," Kate argued.

"Their reputation is on the line as much as mine is. They accepted the manuscript. Their due diligence process is being questioned."

"Excuse me," Rebecca said. "But wouldn't that be all the more reason to take them out of the crosshairs by proclaiming your innocence? Doesn't that take the heat off the publisher? Wouldn't they be grateful for that?"

"I would venture to guess that Black Quill's attorneys might see it differently," Kate said. "Still…"

"You can't seriously be suggesting I do this?" Jay asked.

Kate put down her Diet Coke. "Dara's got a point. Let's step back and look at this like we would any public relations situation. The first day's story focused on the leak and the suspected hacker. Today is the second day of the news cycle. In the absence of any new information about the incident itself, the media needed another angle to keep the story alive. So they dug deep enough to find a tenuous connection between you and a former intern who happened to be the beneficiary of the leaked documents."

"And they threw in the book blurb for good measure to accuse you by innuendo," Rebecca said to Jay.

"Exactly," Kate said. "So, let's anticipate what tomorrow's news story will be."

"If we do nothing and are photographed with the glitterati at the movie premiere, the media will say I have a casual disregard for a situation with national security implications." Jay ran a finger through the condensation on her water glass. "They'll skewer me."

Kate nodded. "If we stay under the radar and don't go to the movie premiere, the press likely will spend their time today digging into every story you ever wrote for *Time* because they don't have another fresh angle."

Dara sat back and observed the interchange, surprised to see Jay's fingers tremble at Kate's suggested scenario. She wondered what had caused such a visceral reaction.

"You don't think they would…"

"That's exactly what I think," Kate said, her expression grim.

"Oh, my God." Tears sprang to Jay's eyes.

Dara felt like a voyeur, privy to something private and painful. She chanced a glance at Rebecca and sensed that she was having similar thoughts.

"I didn't mean to open a can of worms," Dara said.

Both Kate and Jay blinked, as if they had forgotten that they weren't alone.

Kate recovered first. "You didn't. We're actually grateful. You've brought some clarity here. I must be out of practice. These types of considerations used to be second nature to me. I can't believe I hadn't played this out already."

"In 1987, I wrote a cover story about Kate for *Time*. She had just saved many lives during a series of explosions at the New York State Capitol. I should have recused myself from the story or at least informed my editor that Kate and I had a personal relationship—that we knew each other. I didn't." Jay hung her head.

Dara held up a hand. "You don't have to expl—"

"No. I might as well say it now, since it will probably come out in the next round or two of stories." Jay fidgeted in her seat. "*Time's* publisher suspended me over my lapse of judgment. It was public knowledge, so it's only a matter of time before that resurfaces. When it does—"

"If it does," Kate corrected.

"If and when it does," Jay countered, "the media will say I have a history of being dishonest, a verifiable track record of deceit. They'll attack my credibility."

"You were exonerated at the time," Kate pointed out. "You wrote a balanced piece. It wasn't your credibility that was questioned, it was your judgment. That's different."

"You're splitting hairs."

Kate waved away Jay's contention. "I'm going to point out here that you were the one who exposed the Hyland plot and you risked your life in the process. That's a fact. If it hadn't been for you and your exclusive, the world might never have known the truth."

"If it hadn't been for you, I wouldn't have had any facts to tell," Jay said. "You were the only one who knew the whole story. Besides, the world only read the part of the truth the administration was comfortable with us telling, and therein lies the problem."

Rebecca cleared her throat. "If I may be so bold as to ask a question here, is your new book fiction or non-fiction, Jay?"

"It's fiction, based on truth."

Rebecca smiled. "I always taught my students that the very best fiction has a basis in truth. But it *is* fiction, right?"

"It is," Jay agreed.

"Well, it seems to me that you have nothing to worry about. If the plot and main characters are fictitious, then you haven't revealed any state secrets and all this is a moot point."

Dara picked up the thread. "What advantage would there be to you to leak the documents in question? And why would you have waited all this time to do it?"

"Publicity and buzz for the book," Jay said.

"Isn't the publication date far in the future? By the time the book came out, all of this would've died down, wouldn't it?"

"Possibly," Kate agreed, "unless the situation results in a protracted criminal case or Congressional hearings, in which case it could still be going on ten months from now when the book is scheduled to come out."

"Is there anything in the book for which you could be legally challenged? Any plagiarism?" Rebecca asked.

"Of course not!"

"Exactly my point. There doesn't appear to be anything legally actionable here. This is a work of fiction. How many works of fiction are written by authors with personal knowledge of similar situations? Thousands. It happens every day. I taught about such instances every semester. We spent hours and days debating the author's true intentions and meanings. More often than not, the subtext or main text in a novel was derived from the authors' or someone else's real-life experience. It seems to me that this is no different."

Dara noticed the waiter hovering and she opened her menu. "How about if we order and then determine the best course of action to take?"

When they had placed their orders, Dara said, "So, the question on the table is how best for you to handle this situation, right?"

Jay shook her head. "The question was whether or not we should come to the movie premiere tonight."

Dara laughed. "It's gotten way beyond that, hasn't it?"

"True."

"The way I see it, there are two issues here." Kate held up her index finger. "One, is it in anybody's best interest for us to attend the premiere?" She held up a second finger. "And, two, is it in Jay's best interest to make a statement or otherwise engage the media at this point in the crisis?"

Dara looked from Kate to Jay and back again. "Although I know a thing or two about being in the eye of a media storm, I'm out of my element here. All I can offer is that Rebecca and I would very much like you both to come tonight as our guests. We would be honored to have you, and we're willing to face any fallout from that decision."

Kate looked to Jay and raised an eyebrow. Jay shrugged in response.

"Before we make a decision on that," Kate said, "let's look at question number two." She took Jay's empty water glass and replaced it with her own.

"Thank you."

"If you were my public relations client, I would advise you to get out in front of this—own the story and the next few news cycles—control the narrative before it controls you."

Jay nodded.

"Tell the media the truth—that you mentored Niles Masterson when he was an intern at *Time* many years ago, that you've had no contact with him in more than a decade, that you had no knowledge of, and nothing to do with, any leaks of classified data, and that your book is a work of fiction. You might want to throw in that you would never condone any acts of treason or terrorism or anything that threatens national security, and that you hope that the appropriate authorities get to the bottom of the situation and find the real culprits as quickly as possible. Don't take any questions, and get out of there."

The waiter arrived with their meals. When he was gone, Dara said, "So, that's settled, right? What will you do, hold a press conference this afternoon, before the deadline for tonight's newscasts and tomorrow's newspapers?"

"Either that, or we would put out a statement to all of the major news outlets," Kate said. "In any event, we should do it within the next few hours to beat the east coast newscasts tonight."

"Excellent. Then you could get that out of the way and be free to attend tonight's premiere without worry." Dara unfolded her napkin and placed it in her lap. "Bon appetit."

∽⟨⟩∾

The meeting room Dara's agent had procured for Kate and Jay in a Beverly Hills office building was packed to overflowing with reporters.

Kate stood off to one side. She scanned the room, trying to gauge the response as Jay concluded her statement.

"If you haven't done anything wrong, why did you call a press conference on such short notice?"

"You said you haven't had any contact with Niles Masterson in more than ten years. But you didn't say he hasn't tried to call you. Has he? Is it just that you haven't answered?"

"Are you going ahead with the book?"

"Has the FBI questioned you yet?"

"Have you hired an attorney?"

Kate stepped to the podium and put a hand on Jay's back. "As we said at the outset, we're not taking any questions." She guided Jay away from the sea of microphones.

"Kate, your wife has stated that she had nothing to do with the leaks, but that doesn't mean you didn't do it to benefit her career. Did you?"

Kate felt Jay's back stiffen. "Ignore it," she whispered just loud enough for Jay to hear. She increased the pressure on Jay's back. "Keep walking."

"Kate—"

"They're goading you. Don't give them what they want." Kate opened the door at the side of the room and followed Jay out into the corridor.

Jay stopped short, and Kate had to step to the side to avoid colliding with her.

"I don't care if they go after me, but when they start questioning your integrity—"

"Easy, tiger." Kate put an arm around her waist and propelled them forward.

"How can you be so cavalier about that? I resent the insinuation on your behalf."

"It's not personal, sweetheart. Did you see who the reporter was?"

"No."

"Dan Osborn from the *Star*."

"Well, that explains a lot."

"Exactly."

They turned the corner, followed the signs toward the exit, and walked out into the bright LA sunshine where the car Dara had generously hired for them was waiting.

Kate looked at her watch. "Now, we have just enough time to get back to the hotel and change for the premiere."

"Do you really think it's a good idea for us to go?"

Kate slid into the back seat and pulled Jay with her. "Dara is a big girl, she has all the facts, and she wants us to be there. I think we should oblige her."

"It's hardly a hardship," Jay said. She leaned over and kissed Kate on the cheek. "Thank you."

"For what?"

"For being my best friend, my PR person, my wife, my world."

"Wow. That's a lot of things."

Jay smiled. "You're a lot of things, in a particularly beautiful package, might I add."

"Sweet talker."

CHAPTER FOUR

Dara paused for a moment to allow her eyes to adjust to the blinding camera flashes. She reached back into the car and took Rebecca's hand to help her out.

"Are you ready, darling?"

"I'm not sure I'll ever get used to this," Rebecca said, as she straightened up.

"Well, I know I never have, so I can't imagine why you would. Smile for the cameras, love."

"You know in these pictures I always have the fakest smile."

"I have a trick for that," Dara said, as she tugged on the hand she held.

"Oh, what's that?"

"I pretend I'm making love to you." She heard Rebecca gasp. "What? That always makes me smile."

"You're wicked, Dara Thomas."

Dara chanced a glance at her wife. "Perhaps, but it seems like it's working."

She relinquished Rebecca's hand as one security guard escorted Rebecca inside while another accompanied Dara to face the throng.

"Dara, look here!"

"Dara, over here!"

"Dara, what do you think, another Oscar for you this year?"

"Dara!"

As she made her way to the backdrop where the official event photographs would be snapped, Dara smiled with practiced ease and glided along the carpet, stopping to talk to reporters for *Entertainment Tonight, E!,* and *Extra.* When she stepped on her

39

mark and struck a pose, she spied Kate and Jay making their way onto the red carpet.

Most of the Hollywood press that Dara was accustomed to seeing at events ignored them. And then it happened. One reporter broke ranks and thrust a microphone in Jay's face. That started a chain reaction, as other reporters, obviously thinking they were missing something or someone important, followed suit.

"Excuse me," Dara said. She strode purposefully back down the red carpet.

The surprised security guard hustled after her. "Ms. Thomas? Where are you going?"

"Stay with me, please. And send someone to handle those reporters right now." Dara nodded in the direction of the crowd gathered around Kate and Jay.

"Yes, ma'am." The security guard spoke into the communication device on his wrist and two of his colleagues appeared on either side of Kate and Jay.

"Kate, Jay, I'm so glad you could make it." Dara stepped in between the two women and linked her arms with theirs. "You both look amazing."

"Dara, you don't have to—"

"Oh, but I want to," Dara interrupted before Jay could finish her sentence. "Please don't take away my fun." She winked. "Smile, ladies, you're on Candid Camera."

"You're way too young to know that show," Kate said.

"One word," Dara said. "Reruns."

Both Kate and Jay laughed.

"That's better," Dara said. As flashes lit up the night sky like fireflies, she led them the length of the red carpet now surrounded by a phalanx of security guards.

The lights came up as the last of the credits rolled. The applause started somewhere toward the back and rolled in waves toward the front of the theater. Within seconds, everyone had risen to their feet.

Several people shouted, "Bravo!"

Kate felt the hair on her arms stand up as the electricity of the moment washed over her. Next to her, Jay wiped tears from her eyes. Directly in front of them, Dara and Rebecca briefly put their heads together, sharing what Kate imagined was a private moment of triumph.

When the applause finally died down, the man to Dara's left turned to the audience and spoke. "Thank you all for coming. I know I speak for all of us"—he waved his arm to encompass everyone seated in his row—"when I say *Love Above All Else* was an emotional journey. It might be once in a lifetime that you get studio backing to tell an important, modern-day story of love, loss, and redemption as complex and nuanced as this one is, a first rate script, and the great good fortune to work with such professional actors and a topflight crew like we had on this set. I'm really, really proud of this film."

Another round of applause ensued before people finally began to file out. Kate put an arm around Jay's shoulder. "You okay?"

"That was so powerful." Jay pulled a Kleenex from her purse and dabbed at her eyes.

Dara turned around to face them. "So, are you two still game for dinner?"

"Are you sure you—"

Dara didn't even let Jay finish her sentence. "Positive."

"Beautiful work, Dara." A familiar-looking, silver-haired actress whose name escaped Kate kissed Dara on the cheek.

"Thank you. Coming from you that means a lot."

"Keep challenging the establishment. Keep pushing the envelope. Keep making important work. Don't let anyone tell you there's anything you can't do. Us older broads are counting on you."

"Have I told you lately how much I love you?" Dara turned back to Kate and Jay. "Kate Kyle, Jay Parker, this is my dear friend, Sylvia Green. Sylvia, these are my friends, Kate Kyle and her wife, Ja—"

"Jamison Parker, the author," Sylvia said. She took Jay's hand in both of hers. "Enchanted to meet you. I love your work. Such integrity and grit. Tell me, dear, why haven't any of your books been adapted for the big screen?"

Jay opened her mouth to answer, but never got the chance.

"Sorry for blurting that out. How rude of me. Just know that I would love to be part of such a venture."

"I'll keep that in mind."

"Dara, dear. I must toddle along," Sylvia said. "Let's have lunch soon."

A little man waited impatiently for his turn to speak. "Dara? I know this is going to be big box office for us. I can feel it already. Great job."

"Thank you, Mr. Curtain. And thank you for your confidence in me."

"That was a no-brainer. You're the best actress in Hollywood, period. I don't care whether you're gay, straight, bi, or anything in between."

"Kate, Jay, I'd like you to meet Randolph Curtain, head of 722 Films."

"It's a pleasure to meet you, sir. Congratulations on a great film," Kate said and offered her hand.

"Thank you. I'd like to take the credit, but really, all of the credit belongs to our wonderful director here," Curtain clapped the man next to Dara on the back, "and our great cast. I just say *yes* a lot and write the checks."

"Kate, Jay, this is our intrepid director, George Nelson."

"How do you do?"

"That was a beautiful film, Mr. Nelson," Jay said.

"George, please. And it wouldn't have been possible without these two." He indicated Dara and Rebecca with a wave of his hand. "Rebecca wrote a powerful script and Dara brought it to life."

"Well, to be fair," Rebecca chimed in, "Constance Darrow is the real heroine here. Without her raw material to work with, none of this would've been possible."

"Very true," the director agreed. "Well, I'm off. As always, it was a pleasure working with you two. Let me know the next time you see a property you like. You know you can count me in."

"I must head out, as well. Here's to big box office numbers next week," Curtain said, holding his crossed fingers in the air.

"Whew," Dara said, when they'd gone. "Now we can finally get out of here. Are you gals ready?"

"Sure."

Dara led the way out a side door. As the four women emerged, camera flashes exploded in their faces.

When she could see again, Kate noted with relief that this time, the bystanders all seemed to be fans, not reporters.

Dara pointed to a black SUV idling at the corner. "Why don't you three get in the car. Carolyn is already in there, I'm sure. I'll just be a minute."

"You know I hate when you do this as much as Carolyn does, right?" Rebecca grasped Dara's hand tightly.

"It's perfectly safe. I've got plenty of security with me. Besides," Dara winked and freed her hand, "if I'd never done things like this before, we might never have met." She kissed Rebecca lightly on the mouth and walked over to the crowd surging against the barricades to sign autographs.

A beefy security guard motioned for Kate, Jay, and Rebecca to follow him to the car. As she waited for Jay and Rebecca to get in before her, Kate looked back to see Dara patiently signing autographs and posing for selfies with her fans.

Kate sunk into the leather seat. "I can't imagine what it must be like to live life under that kind of microscope all the time."

"Says the woman who spent years as the press secretary to the president of the United States," Jay said.

"That was different."

"Is that like the difference between a Molotov Cocktail and a Cherry Bomb?" The woman sitting across from Jay smiled and held out a hand. "Hi. I'm Carolyn Detweiler, Dara's oldest friend and agent to the glamour couple."

"I'm sorry. I should've made the introduction," Rebecca said.

"Not at all." Kate took Carolyn's outstretched hand. "I'm Kate, and this is my wife, Jay. I understand that you were responsible for securing the venue for our press conference this afternoon. Thank you."

"You're welcome."

Just then, the door opened and Dara climbed into the car. "Well, that was fun." She kicked off her shoes and put her head back against the headrest.

"If you're too tired…" Rebecca said.

"Not at all. What I am is famished."

"Good. I got us a reservation at West," Carolyn said.

"Oh, you're in for a treat," Dara told Kate and Jay. "West offers a spectacular view of the LA skyline and the beaches at Santa Monica."

"More importantly, it's a little off the beaten path and not quite so popular with the tourists," Rebecca added.

"Sounds delightful, but would any restaurant really be that busy at nine o'clock on a Monday night?" Jay asked.

"Yes." Dara, Rebecca, and Carolyn answered in unison.

"I guess that answers that question," Kate said.

Dara leaned forward and tapped Jay on the knee. "I haven't had a chance to ask. How did your press conference go?"

"Everything was going fine until a sleazy tabloid reporter tried to insinuate that Kate might've had something to do with the leak."

"Which bothered Jay far more than it bothered me," Kate broke in. "He was just trying to get a rise out of her."

"Well, it worked," Jay muttered.

"Do you know yet what the results were?"

"The first online reports from *USA Today*, the *LA Times*, the *New York Times*, CNN, and the *Huffington Post* were as good as we hoped. We didn't get a chance to see how World News Tonight, Nightly News, and The CBS Evening News played it on television.

"That reminds me." Jay reached into her purse. "I forgot to turn my phone back on after the movie." She had barely pushed the power button before the phone began buzzing with stored messages.

Kate peered over Jay's shoulder and frowned. "Better listen," she said quietly.

"I'm sorry," Jay said. "I don't want to be rude, but—"

"Don't give it a thought," Rebecca said. "We understand completely."

Jay pushed a button and put the phone to her ear. Her eyes closed as she listened and her face drained of color. When she'd dropped the phone into her lap, Kate took her hand.

"What is it?"

Jay shook her head.

As badly as she wanted to know what the message had been, Kate was cognizant that they were not alone. This was not a time to push.

"Is there anything we can do to help?" Carolyn asked.

"No, thank you." Jay cleared her throat. "I'm sorry. It appears I should have left the phone off."

"No need to apologize. This is important," Dara said.

"It's your big night and all I want to do is celebrate with you. Thank you so much, again, for inviting us along. The movie was amazing. I loved that book, and you really brought it to life. So many movies that are based on novels lose the heart of the story. Rebecca, you wrote a fabulous screenplay. And Dara? You truly captured the essence of the character and the underlying message of redemption and the power of love to heal. I'm really impressed."

"Thank you," Dara said. "With a great script, it's easy to make the characters come alive."

"Had you read the book?" Jay asked Dara.

Kate watched as Rebecca, who was sitting directly across from her, squirmed in her seat before looking out the darkened car window. *Wonder what that's about?*

"I did," Dara answered. "I was intrigued by the concept."

"Oh, look. We're here," Rebecca said. She reached for the door handle before the SUV had even come to a complete stop.

Kate raised an eyebrow. *Interesting.*

"You're not vegan, are you?" Dara asked her. "Because this place serves great filet mignon."

"Count me in," Kate said.

～⁂～

"I really like them," Rebecca said, as she hung up her dress and stowed her shoes in the closet. "A lot."

"Who? Kate and Jay? I like them too."

Rebecca emerged just in time to see Dara struggling with the zipper to her dress. "May I?"

"Please."

Rebecca lightly brushed her fingertips along the chiseled contours of Dara's shoulders, across her collarbones, and downward, pausing to savor the softness of the swell of Dara's breasts.

Dara's contented sigh was all the invitation Rebecca needed. She kissed a particularly sensitive spot behind Dara's left ear, feeling her own heart rate increase as Dara leaned back into her.

Several more minutes of glorious exploration later, Dara turned in Rebecca's arms.

"I thought I gave you a job to do."

"You did?"

"I did. Unzip my dress. Please." Dara said the last with her lips brushing against Rebecca's mouth.

"Right." Rebecca did as requested, easing the material off Dara's shoulders and helping her step out of the dress when it fell to the floor. Both of their bras and panties followed in short order as Dara backed Rebecca up, tumbling them onto the bed.

"Have I mentio—Oh."

"There's a time for words..."

"Ah."

"And a time for action." Rebecca flipped them over so that she was hovering over Dara. "Now would be the latter."

Kate fluffed the pillows and pulled Jay in to snuggle against her shoulder. "You okay?" She kissed her on the forehead.

Jay wrapped her arms around Kate's bare midriff. "If by okay you mean, will I live? Yes. If by okay you mean, am I all right with Black Quill reaming me out for talking to the media, essentially putting a gag order on me, and demanding that I fly back to New York immediately to meet with their lawyers..."

"We did the right thing."

Jay shifted so that she was looking directly at Kate. "Did we?"

"Of course we did. Would you rather have waited and let the media shoot at you like a fish in a barrel?"

"Nice imagery." Jay made a face. "No. But I warned you that the publisher wasn't going to like it."

Kate felt heat radiate through her body as anger boiled up within her. "Your publisher is not my concern. Your reputation and welfare are."

Jay sat up and moved away so that they were no longer touching. "They may not be your concern, but they sure as heck are mine! This is my livelihood we're talking about, not some hypothetical PR problem."

"I'm well aware of what this is, and what it isn't. Your publisher should be standing behind you one hundred percent, issuing an unequivocal denial. Instead, they do nothing publicly, and privately, they treat you as if you're guilty of something."

"This is a legal issue for them. Of course they're going to cover their asses."

"How many best-sellers have you delivered for them? How much press have you earned them? How many awards and prizes? How much money have they raked in from your books? How many top-flight authors have they been able to sign because they have you in their stable?"

Kate threw the covers off and stalked into the bathroom. She opened the tap, threw cold water on her face, shut off the water, and stared into the mirror. "What is it you're really mad about, Kyle?"

She grabbed a towel and dried off. "You're mad that you can't protect her. You can't control this. There are too many moving parts—too many unknowns."

By the time Kate returned to the bedroom, Jay was lying under the covers, her arms wrapped around a pillow, facing away from her. Kate's heart hurt. In all the years they'd been together, they'd never gone to bed angry. It was one of the keys to their successful marriage.

"Sweetheart?"

Jay didn't budge.

"C'mon, Jay. Please? I'm sorry I lost it. Can we talk about it?"

"I'm done talking." Jay's voice was muffled. "Right now, I don't want to talk, I don't want to think. I just want to sleep."

Kate slid into bed and turned on her side to face Jay. "I'm frustrated and I shouldn't take it out on you."

"You think?"

"Apparently not lately." Kate put a hand on Jay's shoulder. "Would you at least look at me?"

"Go to bed, Kate. Tomorrow's another day."

Kate swallowed the lump in her throat. What was happening to them? When had they become *this* couple?

"No." She sat up and turned on the light.

"What?"

"No. No, we are not going down this road."

"Which road is that?" Jay still hadn't moved.

"The road where we think it's okay to go to bed angry just this once. Then 'just this once' becomes once more, and so on, and so on, until we're that couple lying in the dark with nothing to say to each other."

"That's a leap."

"Not to me, it's not. Jamison Parker." Kate waited until Jay finally rolled over to face her. "I love you more than anything on Earth. You're my lover, my best friend, my wife, my world. We made a vow decades ago that we would never go to bed angry with each other. Do you remember that?"

"I do."

"And yet, here we are. I'm trying to apologize to you"—Kate held up a hand to forestall interruption—"not for the press conference, because that was the right professional decision. But my anger was directed at your publisher and the situation. I'm sorry that I took it out on you. My instinct, as you know, is always to protect you, to keep you safe. I guess I feel like I have no control over so much of this, and I'm not used to feeling helpless to help you."

Reluctantly, Jay sat up. "I love you too. But this one is mine to do, and I feel like you trampled on my instincts and pressured me into doing something I wasn't confident was the best course of action."

"I just—"

"You just went into 'I'm Kate Kyle, super PR guru mode, and I know what to do, so do what I think is best and everything will work out fine.'"

Kate recoiled at the bluntness of Jay's words. "Is that what you think this was about? My ego?"

"Not ego. No. But you were myopic. You weren't open to hearing my thoughts about it. It was as if your opinion was more important than mine."

"That's not true."

"Isn't it?"

Was it? Had she bulldozed over Jay? Kate thought back to the conversation over lunch. When she had laid out the strategy, she simply assumed that Jay agreed. Kate bowed her head.

"I'm sorry. I was sure you were on board. It never occurred to me that you weren't."

"I already had told you that I had reservations—that I was worried about Black Quill."

"I thought we'd been through that and I'd allayed those doubts."

"No. That was your perception. Actually, you dismissed my concerns and moved on."

Kate shook her head. What a mess. "If I did that, I'm truly sorry. I was wrong. I should've given you ample opportunity to make your case."

"This isn't a court of law. This is my life and my business. What I want is to have the final say over my own business affairs."

"Agreed."

"When I want your opinion, I'll ask for it."

"Even if it involves my area of expertise?"

"Yes. Even then."

"Okay."

Finally, Jay reached out and briefly laid a hand on Kate's cheek. "It isn't that I don't trust your professional judgment. But somewhere along the line in the past little while it feels like you've lost respect for me."

Kate stiffened. "Never."

"Whether or not it's true, that's how it feels to me. I'm a successful businesswoman in my own right. I deserve to be treated with respect."

"Of course you do."

"I want you to be there to support me as I would support you. But I'm through being a bystander in my own affairs."

"You were never…" The rest of the sentence died on Kate's lips when she saw the expression on Jay's face. "Fair enough."

"Okay then."

"Okay."

"Are we good now?"

Kate thought about it. Were they? She felt off balance, as if the world had tilted on its axis. "I don't know. Are we?"

"I guess we'll see as we go forward. I'm sure we both agree this is a long way from over."

"Unfortunately, you're right."

Jay leaned forward and took Kate's face in her hands. "I love you. We're going to get through this."

"Together?"

"Always." Jay kissed her, gently at first, and then more deeply. "You're my rock. But you can't save me from the world. What you can do is face it with me, by my side."

"Always," Kate said. She ran her fingers through Jay's hair and pulled her down so that they were lying in each other's arms. "You're my heartbeat, Jay."

"And you're mine. Now please turn out the light so we can get some shuteye. It's going to be a long day tomorrow."

CHAPTER FIVE

Jay was more tired than she could remember being in a very long time. She and Kate had spent most of yesterday in airports and on planes, and the three-hour time change between Los Angeles and New York wasn't helping. She'd rejected Kate's suggestion that they fly directly into New York. She wanted to sleep in their bed in Albany.

"You should've thought that one through a little better, kiddo," she mumbled to herself. She'd forgotten how much she hated taking the train to the City at the crack of dawn.

Jay checked her watch and pushed through the revolving door into the midtown Manhattan building that housed the offices of Black Quill Publishing. She was five minutes early.

She signed in with the security guard behind the large wooden desk in the main lobby, then waited as he called upstairs.

"Someone will be down to get you shortly, Ms. Parker."

"Thank you." Jay wandered a short distance away. She watched as harried men and women in business suits scurried by and impatiently pushed the elevator buttons. She didn't come here very often; most of her interactions with her editor were electronic in nature. That didn't bother her at all, as she had never been overly fond of the hustle and bustle of corporate America. Even when she'd been a reporter for *Time*, she'd much preferred spending her days in the field or writing at her desk at home.

"Ms. Parker?"

Jay started when a girl in a thigh-length skirt, tight blouse, and platform shoes touched her on the arm. The girl looked young enough to be her daughter. "Yes."

"Follow me, please."

"Sure."

The young woman led her to an open elevator. They stepped inside and the girl pushed the button for the twenty-seventh floor. Remarkably, she and Jay were alone.

"I've read all your books. I love your writing style."

"Thanks."

Silence.

"Your imagery is so vivid. I love the descriptors you use."

"Thanks."

"I want to be a writer someday."

"That's great. What's holding you back?"

"What?" The girl looked blankly at Jay.

"Why aren't you writing now?"

"Oh. Well, I've got a lot going on. I'm here eight hours a day and then my boyfriend lives across town."

"If you aspire to be a writer, you need only sit down in your chair and start putting words on the page. Otherwise, it'll always be just an unfulfilled dream."

The elevator dinged, signaling that they'd reached their floor.

"Wow. That was deep."

They exited the elevator and the girl punched in a code on a keypad and opened the glass door to admit Jay.

"Words to live by," Jay said. She followed the girl past the reception desk and down the hall. After passing three closed doors, they arrived at a glassed-in conference room.

"This is where I leave you." The girl pulled open the right-hand door. "Ms. Parker is here," she announced to the three men and a woman who sat talking quietly at the far end of a glossy, oblong wooden conference table.

Jay recognized the man sitting farthest away as Horace Fenton, Black Quill's publisher. She had met him several times over the years. No one else at the table was familiar to her. Her stomach did a flip. Where was her editor?

"Come in, Jay." Fenton motioned her to a chair next to the woman. He waited for her to be seated. "This is Thomas Ellersby, head of our legal department, Anthony Digorio, deputy counsel, and Nancy Maclin, our new editor-in-chief.

"It's a pleasure to meet you all," Jay said. She made sure to make eye contact with each of them. If they were going to mothball her book, she was not going to make it easy for them.

"Ms. Parker," Ellersby began, "we have reviewed your submitted manuscript, along with your *Time* magazine story from 1989 regarding the Hyland incident. We also requested a copy of the Hyland Commission report, and have been assured that a redacted version will be supplied to us in due course."

As Ellersby cleared his throat and focused on his notes, Jay noted that neither he, nor his deputy, nor Fenton, nor the editor-in-chief sitting next to her had looked her in the eye. Anger bubbled up from within. "I would be happy to discuss each of those documents with you." She forced herself to keep her tone level.

"There is no need." Fenton steepled his fingers on the table. "Black Quill is a business, Jay. The buck stops with me. I have to listen to, and abide by, what my attorneys have to say. I'm sure you understand."

Jay contemplated many responses. *I understand that you have no loyalty. I understand that you're a spineless, gutless...* "What are you telling me, Mr. Fenton? Are you terminating my contract?"

As Fenton opened his mouth to speak, Ellersby held up a hand. "What Mr. Fenton is saying, Ms. Parker, is that, per section G, paragraph three of Black Quill's agreement with you, the publisher has the right to nullify the contract if there are reasonable grounds to believe that the contracted work exposes the publisher to legal action. Legally speaking, and invoking the cited section, it is not in Black Quill's best interest to proceed with your title at this time."

Jay stood up. "At 'this time,' Mr. Ellersby? Or ever?" She balled her hands into fists at her side. *Don't burn your bridges. Don't burn your bridges. Stay calm. Take the high road. Remember, this isn't personal.* She could practically hear Kate's voice in her head.

Ellersby did not answer, nor did anyone else at the table.

Jay looked at each of them in turn. "I will have my own attorneys review the terms of my contract, but it is my understanding that, *legally speaking*"—she made air quotes with her fingers—"all rights to this title, including print, e-book, movie, and audio book rights, now revert back to me. In addition, I am no longer bound by your right-of-first-refusal clause, because, in essence, you have voided and/or rescinded the contract, thus nullifying that stipulation."

No one said a word in answer to Jay. Even now, no one made eye contact with her; this further infuriated her. She put her hands on the table, palms down, to hide the fact that she was shaking with emotion, and leaned forward in the direction of the publisher.

"Mr. Fenton, I have given Black Quill seven international best-sellers, including five books that hit number one on the *New York Times* Best Sellers List and remained atop that list for ten consecutive weeks."

She took satisfaction in noting the redness creeping up Fenton's neck under his starched shirt collar. "Black Quill has profited quite nicely from my writing. I am extremely disappointed that the company no longer thinks I am a good risk. Writing, as you know, is a very solitary venture. But publishing is a collaborative process. I am exceedingly proud that I upheld my end of the bargain. I submitted a compelling, well-written thriller that I would like to think would have furthered Black Quill's reputation as a publisher of quality works. I'm sorry that you didn't see fit to hold up your end of the bargain."

Jay pushed her chair out of the way and stormed toward the conference room doors. "My attorneys will be in touch to iron out whatever details remain to be handled with regard to the contract." Jay put her hand on the door handle.

"Ms. Parker?" Ellersby called after her. Jay looked back. "A reminder that you are enjoined from publicly disclosing any details pertaining to your contract or anything related thereto."

"That won't be a problem," Jay said. As she opened the door, a thought occurred to her. "By the way, where is Jeremy? I mean, the man and I have worked together on the last six books, and his initial comments on the manuscript were quite complimentary. I would have thought my editor would have been here."

Again, Ellersby held up a hand to forestall the publisher from speaking. "Mr. Taunton has been separated from the company."

Jay knew her face registered shock. "Why? Jeremy has been with Black Quill since its inception."

"We are not at liberty to discuss personnel matters."

"Of course you're not." Jay shoved open the door. "I wish you well, Mr. Fenton. Good luck, Ms. Maclin. Mr. Ellersby, Mr. Digorio, have a nice day."

Jay made sure to hold her head up as she strode down the hallway, past the reception desk, and out the entrance doors to the elevator. She was gratified to see that the elevator was only one flight up, and even more relieved when the doors opened to reveal that, again, the elevator was empty.

◈◈

"God, Lorraine, this is fantastic." Kate wiped her mouth with a napkin. "Marrying you was the best decision Peter ever made."

"If you and Jay hadn't nudged him along, I doubt he ever would've gotten up the gumption to ask me out, let alone propose."

Kate blew on another spoonful of Lorraine's homemade French onion soup and put it in her mouth. When she'd swallowed, she said, "He would've gotten around to it eventually. I think he was a little intimidated by the fact that you were a better marksman than he was."

"She was not." Peter came around the corner from the mud room. He wrapped his arms around Lorraine, who was washing dishes in the sink, and nuzzled her neck. "She was, however, a better undercover operative than anybody I ever knew, and the best cook."

"Flattery will get you nowhere," Lorraine said, shooing Peter away. "Go sit down. Your soup is getting cold."

Peter did as he was told and picked up his spoon. "This smells great."

"Wait until you try it," Kate said. "Heaven in a bowl." She took another spoonful.

"Have you heard anything yet from Jay? What time was her meeting?"

Kate checked the clock on the wall. "She's in the meeting now."

"What's your sense?" Lorraine asked.

"I don't know. I would say it doesn't bode well that Black Quill moved the meeting up by a day, but I imagine they're also paying attention to the news cycles and want to keep ahead of the curve, so this could be about plotting a joint strategy."

"She didn't want you to come with?" Lorraine set her own bowl of soup on the table and sat down.

Kate flashed back to the argument they'd had in bed their last night in LA. "This is Jay's to do. I respect that. She's tough as they come, and she's a very smart businesswoman. She can handle whatever they throw at her."

"Of course she can," Lorraine agreed.

"So how about if we focus on the bigger picture?" Kate looked pointedly at Peter. "What the hell's going on? Where is Sabastien and what has he been able to find out?"

"Last I talked to him, which was about twenty minutes ago, Sabastien was holed up in one of his off-the-books safe houses in an unnamed location that has no extradition agreement with the United States."

"He didn't even tell you where he is?"

"No, and frankly, I wasn't all that keen to know unless it becomes mission-critical. The less we know, the better."

"For now, you mean," Kate clarified.

"For now."

"Okay. I can accept that. So, you and he believe he's safe for the moment?"

"He believes he is, and that's going to have to be good enough."

"What does he know?"

"Not as much as he'd like to know. He's certain that the accessed data was specifically targeted, and that whoever stole it knew exactly what they would find."

"All of the files were related to the Hyland incident?" Kate asked.

"They were."

"Why now, Peter?"

"Good question."

"You know there are no coincidences. Jay and I discussed that the other day. The proximity to new publicity about the upcoming book and the choice of reporters are too convenient to ignore."

"Peter and I agree with you," Lorraine said.

"So, somebody went to a lot of trouble to access supposedly super-secure information within one of the presumably most technologically well-protected government agencies."

"And to point the finger at Sabastien as the source of the leak. He's positive it was deliberate," Peter added.

"To me, that's the most puzzling aspect to all this. First, how many people even know who Sabastien is? Second, why target him?" Kate asked.

"First," Peter replied, "probably fewer than two dozen people know his true identity. And second, Sabastien tells me whoever did this must've been watching his techniques for quite some time. The approach was identical to the method he was using as a white hat working for the president to assess potential breaches in sensitive agencies."

"In other words, this had to be someone with some serious skills. Otherwise, Sabastien would've known he was being cyber-shadowed."

"Yes."

"I'll ask again," Kate said, "why target Sabastien?"

"I wondered about that too," Lorraine said. "Our best guess is that they needed him out of the way. They wanted to sideline him because they were after something else, and he would've detected them and stopped them. So they pointed a finger at him to bring the weight of the government down on his head."

Kate thought about that. "But they already got in undetected by Sabastien. Why would they be worried about that?"

"True."

"Let's suppose for a second that you were right that the goal was to get Sabastien out of the way. Why pick that particular classified case? They would've had literally hundreds to choose from. Sabastien said the hacker purposely went after the Hyland case materials."

Kate got up and took her bowl to the sink to wash it. "I really, really don't want to mention this"—she finished rinsing off the soap and put the bowl in the dish drainer—"but what if Sabastien was chosen because of his friendship with Jay? Maybe it wasn't so much about him as it was a way to get to her?"

"Hardly anybody is aware that Jay and Sabastien even know each other, let alone that they're friends," Lorraine said.

"That's why I hate to mention it." Kate turned around to face her friends and leaned her hips heavily against the granite countertop.

"That would complicate things significantly," Peter said.

"This is complicated any way we look at it." Kate's cell phone vibrated in her pocket and she pulled it out to look at the display. "That was fast."

"Jay?" Lorraine asked.

Kate nodded as she answered the phone. "Hey, babe. You okay?" She walked out of the kitchen and into the family room for privacy.

"Not really, no."

"What happened?"

"They washed their hands of it, and me."

"What do you mean?"

"It was horrible. Fenton was there, and he brought his legal henchmen. They wouldn't even let him say anything. The lead counsel did all the talking."

"What did he say?"

"That the book was a risk they weren't willing to take. That under the terms of my contract they had a right to back out."

Kate closed her eyes. The hurt and pain in Jay's voice broke her heart. "I'm so sorry, honey. Didn't they give you a chance to talk them through it?"

Jay laughed mirthlessly. "They didn't give me a chance to say anything. Although, I might've left them with a parting shot or two."

Kate groaned. She could just imagine what Jay might've said.

"I heard that groan. I tried to take the high road, Kate. I really did. All things considered, I was admirably restrained. I simply reminded Fenton of all I've done for Black Quill and expressed my extreme disappointment at his decision."

"Fair enough." Kate peered out the sliding glass doors that led to a large wooden deck. Weak sunshine filtered through clouds. If Jay caught the next train, she would be home in time for supper. "Are you on your way home?"

"I was going to come straight back, but I've decided to make one more stop first."

"Oh? Where's that?"

"I'm meeting Jeremy for coffee."

"Jeremy Taunton? Your editor? He agreed to meet with you after that? Doesn't that put him in an awkward position? I'm surprised the attorneys would let him talk to you."

"He's got nothing to lose. They fired him a few days ago."

"Fired him? Why on earth would they do that? He's been with them forever, right?"

"From the very beginning," Jay agreed. "He didn't sound too sure about wanting to see me. But after I told him Black Quill was voiding my contract and wouldn't publish the book, his whole demeanor changed. He said he'd be happy to meet me."

Kate could hear the sounds of car horns honking in the background. "Are you on the street?"

"Yeah. I'm almost to the diner."

"What happened with Jeremy?"

"I don't know yet. That's what I'm going to find out. When I asked Fenton why he wasn't at the meeting, the attorney stopped him from answering me. He just said Jeremy had been, and I quote, 'separated from the company.' They had some new woman editor-in-chief. She didn't say a word the entire meeting."

"Interesting timing."

"My thoughts exactly. Listen, I'm here, so I'm going to go inside. I'll call you when I know what train I'm going to catch."

"Okay. Be safe, please."

"Always."

Kate sighed. "Jay?"

"Yeah?"

"I'm really, really sorry. We'll get through this. Together."

"We always do. Talk to you later."

"I love you."

"Love you too."

Jay loosened her scarf and sat down in the booth across from her former editor. He looked haunted.

"Hi, Jay. I would've ordered you something, but I didn't know what you wanted."

"No problem, Jeremy. Thanks for meeting me on such short notice."

"It isn't like I have anyplace else to be right now."

So much for small talk. Jay couldn't think of any way to avoid the awkwardness. She took a deep breath. "About that... What happened? I mean, you practically helped found the company."

Jeremy raised an eyebrow. "They didn't tell you?"

"Tell me what?"

"Why I was fired."

"When I asked why you weren't in the meeting, Fenton started to answer, but his attorney intervened. All he would say is that you'd been 'separated' from the company. He wouldn't even tell me when it happened."

"Figures."

At that moment, the waitress appeared at Jay's elbow. "What can I get you?"

"I'll just take a cup of coffee with cream and a plain bagel with cream cheese, please."

"You got it."

When the waitress had gone, Jay asked, "What's going on, Jeremy?"

He leaned forward conspiratorially. "Horace called me in Monday morning. When I got to his office, there were three guys in suits standing around. They were from the Federal Bureau of Investigation."

"The FBI? What did they want?"

Jeremy glanced nervously around the diner. He waited as the waitress set a cup of coffee down in front of Jay. When they were alone again, he said, "They wanted to talk about my relationship with you. They wanted to know what you'd told me about the origins of the book, where you got the idea for the plot, any background or resource materials you may have provided."

"What did you tell them?"

"I told them the truth—that you e-mailed me the manuscript, I read it, I e-mailed you back and told you it was a winner, and that I'd send you suggestions soon."

"And that got you fired?"

"No. They wanted me to provide them with a copy of the manuscript, which I refused to supply. And they essentially wanted me to spy on you, to ask you a series of questions, and to forward your answers on to them."

Jay's nostrils flared and she struggled to keep her temper under control. "They wanted you to coerce me into incriminating myself!"

Jeremy nodded. "I'm sorry, Jay."

"It's not your fault."

"As you can imagine, I refused to do what they wanted. I told them I'd worked with you on the last half dozen books and that I'd only ever known you to be professional and meticulous in your research and that I had no reason to believe that this novel was any different."

"Fenton fired you for standing up for me?"

"No. The FBI guys left. Horace wasn't happy with me, but he just sent me back to my office."

Jeremy took a sip of his coffee as the waitress set down Jay's bagel. When she'd gone, he said, "About three hours later, Horace called me back into his office. This time, there were two guys in suits. They were smaller, and a little more rumpled, but there was no mistaking that they worked for the government too."

Jay spread the cream cheese on her bagel, although she no longer had an appetite. "Homeland Security?"

"What?" Jeremy shook his head. "No. They were IRS."

"IRS?" Jay realized she'd spoken louder than was prudent, and lowered her voice. "What in the world did they want?"

"The implication was that unless I cooperated with them, they were going to make life very difficult for Black Quill, for Horace, and for me. They talked about investigating our profit-sharing program, my declared expenses, my tax returns for the last seven years, Horace's tax returns, the company's tax returns…"

Jay couldn't listen anymore. Her stomach was churning. She put her head in her hands. How could they do that? What country did they live in? "I'm so, so sorry, Jeremy."

"It's not your fault. I began to wonder if I'd fallen into a rabbit hole and ended up in Russia."

"Funny, I was just wondering the same thing."

The waitress came back and refilled their coffee cups.

"So Fenton fired you because the IRS showed up and made threats?"

Jeremy shifted uncomfortably in his seat and his cheeks turned pink. "Horace fired me because I called him a chicken shit who obviously had forgotten that one of the founding principles of our company was to give brave voices a home. Whatever happened to the first amendment?"

"Good question." Jay reached out and briefly touched Jeremy on the hand. "And thank you for standing up for me. You're a courageous guy."

"It was the right thing to do."

"Maybe so, but not everyone faced with IRS intimidation would react the same way."

"Horace ordered me to meet with you and tell you to withdraw the book. I refused. *That's* when he fired me."

"Which is why he brought in his henchmen to do the job while he sat there and said nothing." Jay allowed the disgust she felt to creep into her voice.

"Afraid so."

"I'm sorry you lost your job."

Jeremy sighed. "I'm not. I've known Horace Fenton for a very long time. I was appalled at his behavior. I believed he was a better man than that. I don't want to work for a man, or a company, for that matter, that would cave to pressure from the government when you had every right to write the book you wrote."

Jay bit her lip. "Did you really like it?"

Jeremy smiled for the first time since Jay had walked in. "I didn't just like it. I loved it. You've got a real page-turner there. It's riveting, and germane. This is important work, Jay. I would've been very proud to put my name on it as your editor."

"I would've loved to have worked with you on it. Your editing was always so precise—so sharp. You made me a better writer."

"What a gracious thing to say."

Jay signaled the waitress to bring the check. "What will you do now?"

"I don't know. I guess it depends on whether or not the Feds are going to continue to hound me, and whether or not Horace tries to blackball me."

Jay frowned. It was wrong that Jeremy should be targeted because of his association with her. "I imagine that if you stay as far away from me as possible, you'll be just fine."

Jeremy pulled his wallet out of his pants pocket.

"I've got this." Jay removed some bills from her pocketbook and waved him off, and Jeremy relented.

"You see, that's the thing about me. I have a strong dislike of bullies. I don't like to be told with whom I can associate." Jeremy winked. "What's your plan for the book now?"

"I don't know. I haven't gotten that far."

"Well, I'm just going to put this out there. If you decide you want to self-publish or shop it somewhere else, I'd be honored to edit it for you. I'd happily do it for free. That's how important I think this work is."

Jay's mouth formed an "O" but no sound came out. "You'd do that for me?"

"I would." Jeremy gathered his jacket and stood up. "If the IRS wants to come after me, let them come."

Jay stood and retied her scarf. "You're an honorable man." She kissed Jeremy on the cheek.

"Keep in touch?"

"I will."

Final Cut

64

CHAPTER SIX

Rebecca glanced up from her laptop and watched as Dara unconsciously bit her lip. She loved these quiet, peaceful early mornings where the only sounds were the call of the seagulls on their private beach and the click, clicking of the computer keys as she and Dara sat at their respective desks, creating.

"Why did you stop typing?" Dara never looked away from her twenty-seven inch iMac screen.

"You are far too observant for your own good."

"And you are far too easily distracted."

"I can't argue with that." Rebecca swiveled in her chair to face Dara. "Did you see the news that Jay's publisher dropped her book?"

Dara stopped typing and she, too, turned around. "Are you kidding me?"

"No. According to both *USA Today* and the *LA Times*, Black Quill said in a statement that they wanted to be 'sensitive to the government's concerns about national security,' and therefore made the difficult decision to cancel the book."

"Is that really how it was worded?"

"Pretty much."

"Wow. They threw Jay under the bus," Dara said.

Rebecca arched an eyebrow. "How so?"

"They might as well have said, 'We care about national security, even if our author doesn't. So we're going to do the right thing, even if our author won't.'"

"You think they're trying to damage Jay's integrity so that she can't shop the book elsewhere?" Rebecca asked. "Would they really do that?"

Dara shrugged. "I would equate it to a studio that gets spooked into backing away from a script they purchased. They may have decided the project was too controversial to make, but they want to hedge their bets and make sure that nobody else makes the movie either."

"I guess I wasn't thinking about it in those terms. That's horrible. Poor Jay." Rebecca stared out the window at the waves as an idea started to percolate in her mind.

"I know that look."

Dara slid into Rebecca's lap and swept a stray strand of hair from Rebecca's forehead. "Oh, you do, do you?"

"Mm-hmm." Dara kissed her lightly. "That's your I-need-to-right-a-terrible-injustice look."

"I have one of those?" Rebecca nuzzled Dara's cheek with her lips.

"You do."

"Huh."

"So, share."

"What if..."

"What if?" Dara encouraged.

"If you're right and the publishing industry turns its back on Jay, what if we could do something about it?"

"Like what?"

"I don't know. Couldn't we offer her a chance to adapt the novel into a screenplay without the book ever having been published?"

Dara leaned back. The sun refracting through the window glass gave her blue eyes an ethereal light. "Have I mentioned how sexy your mind is?"

Rebecca pretended to think. "Not lately."

"Your brain is your sexiest feature, and that's saying something."

"Does that mean you like the idea? Is it even feasible?"

It was Dara's turn to gaze out the window in thought. "Maybe. But I'm not certain the studios would stick their necks out any more than the publishers would."

"What if we made it as an independent?"

Dara smiled indulgently.

"What?"

"You. Two years ago, you didn't know the first thing about the film industry. Now, here you are, navigating the nuances of the business like a seasoned pro."

Rebecca laughed. "Hardly. But don't independent film companies have a lot more flexibility? Aren't they more nimble and less beholden to conglomerates?"

"They do, and they are."

"But?"

"There is no 'but.'"

"It's too far-fetched, right?"

Dara shook her head. "Not necessarily."

"But you don't think it's feasible?"

"I didn't say that." Dara tipped Rebecca's chin up and kissed her thoroughly.

"What were we talking about?" Rebecca blinked.

"The possibility of taking Jay's story directly to film."

"Right."

"The first thing we need to consider is whether or not bringing her work to the screen is something that would even interest Jay."

"Good point."

Dara started to get up and Rebecca held her in place.

"Where are you going?"

"I must be killing you. Are your legs numb yet?"

"Hardly." Rebecca wrapped her arms around Dara's waist. "Is it worth approaching Jay about?"

"Maybe. But I think before we did that, we'd need to put a lot more thought into process and practicality. I wouldn't want to broach Jay with the idea only to figure out afterward that we couldn't make it happen."

Dara gently disentangled herself and rose. "For now, might I suggest that we each finish what we set out to accomplish this morning so that we can have time for a run on the beach before it gets too hot out there?"

"Or too hot in here."

"That too."

❖❖

"Nothing? Not even a mid-range publisher?"

Kate stopped even pretending to read and put her book down in her lap. Jay's anguished expression told her more than the questions she was asking, although the questions were plenty revealing.

"Okay... Right... Let me know." Jay clicked the Off key, heaved a heavy sigh, and threw the phone down on the sofa.

Although Kate badly wanted to go to her, she wasn't entirely sure Jay would welcome the gesture. And that thought saddened her beyond measure.

"That was my agent, or should I say my new contact at the agency. Apparently, Sydney is too busy with other clients to update me personally."

Kate raised an eyebrow. "Sydney is aware how much money you've made for her, isn't she?"

"In case you hadn't noticed, that doesn't seem to carry much weight anymore." Jay flopped down on the sofa gracelessly. "It seems they can't find a single publisher that wants to touch the book."

Kate couldn't stand it anymore. She walked the few steps over to the sofa, sat down next to Jay, and pulled her close. She carefully considered what to say, mindful of overstepping. "What's the next move?"

Jay shook her head and burrowed closer. "I don't really know. I have a sneaking suspicion that Sydney might have had a visit from the same rumpled suits that got to Fenton and Jeremy."

"It's possible."

"Self-publishing might be the only way, and somehow that seems..."

"Like surrender? Like an admission of defeat?"

"Yeah. A little."

"There are lots of authors going that route. Didn't you say Jeremy offered to edit the book for you?"

"He did. But what would I do about distribution? Without a good-sized publisher behind it, I wouldn't get the push in the stores, or libraries."

Kate stroked Jay's hair. "You could release it just as an e-book."

"No." Jay shook her head. "This book is too important. It's taken me decades to write it. I want to hold the hard-back in my hands. Does that make any sense?"

"Sure."

"I can just hear what everyone would say if I published it myself. I'd feel like a failure."

Kate kissed the top of Jay's head. "First, what other people think of you is none of your business."

Jay started to protest and Kate shifted so that they were facing each other. She took Jay's hands in her own. "Second, you are many things—a failure is not one of them." She leaned forward and brought their mouths together. The kiss was long, slow, and tender. "I love you."

"I love you too."

"We'll figure this out."

"I don't see how."

Right now, Kate didn't have an answer either. What she really wanted to do was to get Jay's agent alone in a room and find out what really was going on. *Talk about overstepping, Kyle.*

ख़ॐ

"J'ai trouvé quelque chose."

"Slow down, my French is a little rusty." Peter stepped out of the restaurant where he and Lorraine were having dinner, and checked his surroundings. There didn't appear to be anyone close enough to hear him and he switched the phone call to his Bluetooth as he scanned the street for any suspicious vehicles.

"I found something. I found something!"

The more excited he got, the more pronounced Sabastien's accent became. Peter turned so that he was facing a brick wall. Old habits died hard and, despite the fact that no one appeared to be watching, he wanted to be sure no one could read his lips. "What was it?"

"A back door."

"You figured out how he got in?"

"Oui. I followed the bread bits."

"The bread crumbs? As in, he left a trail?"

"Exactement. I followed him all the way to a back door."

"That's a start."

"More than that, Pierre. I mean Peter. English, I know."

"What else?"

"I found his signature."

"He left one?"

"Bien sûr. Every hacker worth his…"

Peter endured the silence. No doubt Sabastien was struggling to remember the rest of the idiom. "Worth his salt."

"Quoi?"

"The expression is 'every hacker worth his salt.'"

"Oh. Yes. That."

"You were saying?"

"He left a signature."

"Tell me."

"You understand the ways of the hacker, yes?"

"I know enough to be dangerous, which is to say, I have some familiarity, but not anywhere near your expertise."

"Okay. To put it simply, then, the hacker left a series of letters and characters. To the untrained eye, they would mean nothing."

"But I take it that to you, they mean something?"

"They do. It is a nickname—the Black Knight."

"Night, as in darkness, or knight, as in suit of armor?" Peter asked.

"The second."

"Huh."

"You have not heard of this before?"

"Afraid not. But then, I don't run much in hacking circles. You aren't familiar with him?"

"I am not, and that worries me. I have been in this business for a very long time, Peter. I thought I knew all of the most proficient hackers. This one is new to me, and he is very, very good."

"So this moniker is all we have to go on?"

"Oui. That and the fact that he appears to be a seasoned professional. This is not some college student having fun. This is very sophisticated work."

"Okay. I'll see if I can find out anything on this end."

"I will keep looking as well."

"Are you still safe where you are, my friend? Do I need to send reinforcements?"

"For the time being, I am okay."

"Good."

"Thank you, by the way."

"For what?"

"For sending Vaughn Elliott to check me up."

Peter smiled at yet another mangled expression. "Of course. Stay safe, Sabastien. Let me know if you find out anything else." Peter disconnected the call and tapped the cell phone thoughtfully against his chin. The Black Knight. Well, it was something.

❦

"Jamison Parker." Jay used her shoulder to hold the phone against her ear as she juggled grocery bags in one hand and inserted the key in the lock with the other.

"Hi, Jay. It's Niles."

Jay's heart rate accelerated. She paused with her hand on the doorknob, but said nothing. What was there to say?

"Masterson. It's Niles Masterson."

Jay's nostrils flared. "I know who you are, Niles."

"Well, you didn't say anything. Anyway, I need to talk to you."

"It's a little late for that, don't you think?" Jay turned the knob and shouldered her way through the door.

"I know what you must be thinking—"

"Trust me, you have no idea what I'm thinking." Jay deposited the grocery bags on the counter with more force than she intended.

"What would you have done in my place? A source comes to you with the story of the century. You can't turn that down, you know? If you could just confirm details for me—"

"Absolutely not."

"Come on, Jay."

"You've lost your mind."

"Probably. I'm getting harassed by the Justice Department. They're threatening me with accusations of treason and violations of the Privacy Protection Act for allegedly participating in the crime of obtaining highly classified data. They're pressuring me for my source."

Jay wanted to know his source too, but she knew better than to ask. As it was, she never should have answered the call. She wouldn't have if she'd looked at the caller ID. But she hadn't, here they were, and Niles was inadvertently giving her a lot of information that might prove useful.

He was getting wound up, and his voice rose an octave. "They're talking about search warrants and other court orders for my e-mails, texts, and phone conversations. They're bringing the heat on the magazine too. We got summoned to a meeting at the Willard Hotel with the President's Chief of Staff, the Director of National Intelligence, and the Deputy Attorney General. At least you could make all this trouble worth my while."

When he finally paused to take a breath, Jay broke in. "I have nothing to say to you, Niles. Don't call me again." Jay disconnected the call and put the phone in her pocket. Her hand was shaking and she steadied herself against the counter.

"You okay? What's up?"

Jay started as Kate wrapped her arms around her from behind. She took a deep breath and turned to face her wife. "Niles called me just now."

"What?"

Jay noted the fire in Kate's eyes. "He wanted to talk."

"I hope you told him—"

"Easy, tiger. I told him to go pound salt and never to call me again."

"Good."

"He did tell me some interesting things though." Jay stepped to the side and began putting the groceries away.

Kate joined her. "I'm listening."

"He said the White House was leaning on him and on *Time* not to write or publish the story. He also said they threatened him with jail time if he didn't give up his source."

"No surprise there. That harkens back to the James Risen/Condolezza Rice duel a few years back. Remember?"

"I do."

Kate opened the refrigerator and made room for the container of orange juice and the eggs. "Did he tell you, or did you get the sense, of whether or not *Time* was going to go ahead and run the story?"

"He didn't say." Jay folded up the grocery bags and put them in the cupboard. "And I didn't want to risk asking him. If the Feds do collect his phone records, or if they're wiretapping him, I didn't want to give them anything."

"Smart thinking."

"I try."

"Oh, before I forget, Peter called."

"What did he say?"

"He didn't want to talk about it over the phone, but it sounded to me like Sabastien might have found something. We're going to have dinner over there tonight."

Jay checked her watch. "In that case, we'd better get moving."

∽⚭⚮

"That was a great dinner, Lorraine." Kate pushed away from the table.

"Score one for twenty-first-century husbands. Peter did the cooking."

Kate feigned shock. "I'm impressed. You've come a long way from the guy who blew up hotdogs in the microwave."

"Very funny." Peter collected his plate and Kate's. "Jay, are you finished?"

"Mm-hmm." She handed him her plate and he took the pile to the sink.

"You heard from Sabastien?" Jay asked after Peter sat back down.

"I did. He found a signature and a back door."

"Would you care to translate that for those of us who are not in the hacking business?"

"He discovered the way the hacker got in and out without being detected and the hacker signed his work with a moniker—sort of like a graffiti artist tags his art."

"So we have him?" Kate asked.

"Not exactly." Lorraine finished putting the dishes in the dishwasher and sat back down.

"We don't know who the signature belongs to yet," Peter said. "Sabastien had never heard of him before."

"What was the name?" Jay asked.

"The Black Knight."

"As in a knight in shining armor kind of knight," Lorraine added. "Peter, Vaughn, and I have used back channels, but none of our sources have ever heard of him."

"We're a little surprised and concerned that Sabastien didn't recognize the signature," Peter said. "He's been in the hacking business for a long time and knows most of the major players."

"Maybe this person isn't a major player," Kate said.

"Not according to Sabastien. This guy is very sophisticated and savvy—definitely a pro."

"Is it possible he works under more than one name?" Jay asked. "Or maybe it's a red herring?"

"I suppose anything is possible," Peter allowed.

"Maybe the nickname isn't about being a hacker at all," Kate said. She drummed her fingers on the table.

"Go on."

"What if—and let's be clear that I have no idea what I'm talking about here—but what if the nickname isn't tied to this person's hacking persona, but is something he calls himself in certain circles?"

"You're thinking about the kind of code names the Commission uses for its operatives," Lorraine said.

Kate shrugged. "I think we have to consider them at the top of the list of suspects for the hack, don't you?" She looked around the table.

"Sabastien did say that the hacker could've taken anything, but that he focused solely on the Hyland materials."

"I rest my case."

"I don't know," Jay said. "Why would the hacker leave something behind for us to find if he didn't want to get caught?"

Peter held up a finger. "Number one, hackers are arrogant and like to think that even with their signature revealed, they won't get caught."

"What about the possibility that it was put there intentionally for us to find to get us chasing our tails?" Jay asked. "I'm not ready to discount the red herring theory."

"As I said, anything is possible. Number two"—Peter raised a second finger—"The signature was purposeful..."

"That's what I just said."

74

"Easy, half-pint. Let me finish my sentence. The hacker wanted Sabastien to find the signature so that he would be focused on trying to decode the moniker rather than looking deeper into what the hack was all about. In which case, you may be right that the signature is a red herring meant to distract."

Kate sat forward and rested her elbows on the table. "Even if we do solve this mystery, it doesn't mean that the hacker isn't some hired gun."

"True," Lorraine agreed. "But once we have a name, we'll have a better shot at trying to connect the dots and find out who's behind all this."

"And that brings us back to square one. Who is the Black Knight?" Peter looked around the table. "So far, I think Kate may have the most likely answer."

"That the signature isn't strictly about the hacking? That this is a Commission code name?" Jay asked.

"Yes."

Jay shook her head. "I don't agree."

Kate watched Peter and Lorraine exchange glances. She wondered if the look signified that they recognized the strain between her and Jay.

"Why not?" Lorraine asked.

"I just think the Commission is too sophisticated to make it that easy for us to find."

"It wasn't easy," Peter said. "It took Sabastien almost a week to find it."

"I'm not convinced." Jay folded her arms over her chest.

"Well, it doesn't look like we're going to solve anything tonight." Kate yawned and stood.

Lorraine stood up as well. "I'll check with my contacts on the QT and ask if any of them can check the Black Knight/Commission angle."

"I'll keep working on it with Sabastien," Peter said, getting out of his chair. "I'll walk you guys to the door."

Jay rose and gave Lorraine a hug. "Love you."

"We love you guys too. We'll get to the bottom of this. Hang in there."

CHAPTER SEVEN

Dara removed her sunglasses and glanced around the restaurant. She checked her watch. She was on time, which meant that she was early by Hollywood standards.

"Dara, over here." George Nelson waved from a corner table.

She picked her way between the tables, acknowledging nods and waves as she went. "Hi, George." She kissed the director on the cheek. "I'm so glad you could make it."

"You know I'm always happy to see you."

Like the gentleman she knew him to be, George waited for her to be seated before he resumed his seat. His old-school chivalry was one of the many attributes Dara admired about this man. He was honorable and honest, trustworthy and forthright. That made him a rare commodity here in the land of make-believe.

"To what do I owe the honor?" George asked.

A roguishly handsome waiter hustled over to their table. Dara assumed that he was most likely an actor working on the side, trying to make ends meet.

"Good afternoon. Can I get you folks something to drink?"

"I'll have an iced tea and the chopped salad with balsamic vinaigrette," Dara said.

"I'll have the chef salad and a Coke, please."

"Very well. I'll get your drinks right out."

Dara waited until the waiter was gone. "I need to pick your brain."

"Okay," George said. "I'm not sure there's much there to pick, but I'll do my best."

"I know I can trust your discretion, and this one has to be way off the record."

"Color me intrigued. You have my word."

"That's always been good enough for me." Dara smiled. "Rebecca and I have an idea. We're not even sure she'll be interested, but on the off chance she is, we want to have all our ducks in a row before we pitch a proposal."

"I'm assuming the 'she' you mention has a name?" George raised an eyebrow in question.

"She does. In fact, you met her a few weeks ago at the premiere. She's Jamison Parker."

"The author." George nodded. "I've read some of her books. Top shelf."

"Rebecca and I both regard her and her work highly."

George narrowed his eyes. "Isn't there some serious controversy about her next novel? Something about hacking and national security breaches and other nasty stuff? Last I saw, the publisher pulled the plug."

"All true."

"Here are your drinks. Your salads will be right out." The waiter set down the beverages and disappeared again.

"There's a lot more to the story than what's been covered in the media."

"That doesn't surprise me."

"I'm not going to go into great detail here, but I can tell you this much—I've had personal assurances from Jay that she had nothing to do with the national security breach."

"If you believe her, that's good enough for me."

"I do. As I said, all is not what it seems. It's complicated and ugly."

"When is anything to do with politics not complicated or ugly?"

"Fair point."

"Your salads." The waiter set down their meals. "Fresh ground pepper?"

"Not for me, thanks," Dara said.

"I'm good," George added.

When the waiter left them alone again, George said, "What does any of this have to do with you and Rebecca?"

"You already know that Jay's publisher left her hanging in the breeze. And you've surmised that some pressure is being brought to bear by those in power to keep this novel from seeing the light of day."

"Government bullying, I presume?"

Dara nodded.

"I hate bullies."

"Me too."

"So, you said you wanted to pick my brain. What do you have in mind?" George speared some ham and lettuce on his fork and put it in his mouth.

"Rebecca and I are thinking about trying to convince Jay to bring the work directly to screen and bypass the book publication issue altogether."

George whistled. "Bold choice."

Dara took a bite of her salad.

"You haven't said anything to her yet?"

"No. As I said, we want to do some due diligence before we go to Jay with the idea."

"Have you read the manuscript?"

"No. But if it's anything like her other work, I know it will be tailor-made for the big screen. I don't know why none of her other work has been adapted."

They focused on eating for a little while.

Eventually, Dara said, "Here's what I want to know. You've worked with Randolph Curtain a bunch of times. Do you think 722 would back the film?"

George briefly stared off into the distance. "I think..." He pursed his lips in thought. "I think it depends. If you're telling me that the federal government is putting pressure on publishers not to publish the book, it would be a heck of a risk for a film production company to take it on."

"722 hired me to carry a movie after I came out of the closet."

"Yes, but you'd just won an Oscar for Best Actress."

"True. But you and I both know there are still plenty of producers out there who would've shied away from me."

"Would there be a part for you in this script?"

"I have no idea. I hadn't thought about that. We just want to make sure Jay's work sees the light of day."

"Honestly, I don't know if you could find a major studio to shoulder that kind of risk. There'd be a lot of money at stake."

"What about putting together an indie company teamed with a consortium of backers to finance it?"

George scrubbed his chin. "Maybe. What would you do, shake the trees for investors?"

"I'd create my own company and put together a syndicate of stakeholders, named or unnamed."

"Ballsy. You'd need a director."

Dara smiled at George indulgently, until he finally grinned back.

"I thought that might be where you were headed with this. I'll read it. If it's as good as you think it will be, I might be persuaded. Especially if you were going to be part of the on-screen package."

"I love you, George." She leaned across the table and gave him a kiss on the cheek.

"Do you think your author will bite?"

"Honestly, I don't know. Do you think there's any point to approaching 722 with this? I'd like to keep the whole thing closely held."

"My two cents?"

Dara nodded.

"Read the manuscript first. Let's talk after that. If I were placing bets right now, I'd say you're going to have to go the indie route. And you're going to need a strong team—folks who aren't easily intimidated."

Dara removed her napkin from her lap and folded it on the table. "I'm leery of going to Jay without knowing that I can make something happen." Almost to herself she added, "I wonder if maybe I should try feeling out her wife about it, first. See what she thinks."

"Do you know her wife?"

"We've met a few times. Her wife is Katherine Kyle. You met her the night of the premiere too."

"Tall, model-pretty, with long black hair and piercing blue eyes?"

"I see you didn't notice her." Dara laughed.

"Not at all."

"Yes, that's her."

"Didn't she work for President Hyland? She was his press secretary, right?"

"Good memory."

"Must be a helluva thing, being on the other side of the coin."

"I hadn't thought about it that way, but I would guess you're right."

"That's your next step, then? Talk to her?"

"Unless you've got a better plan."

"I've got nothing. But know that I'd like to see the manuscript if you get it and if the author will give permission for me to read it."

"I knew I could count on you, George."

"We're not there yet. There's always the possibility that you'll read the book and hate it."

"Somehow, I doubt that."

☙❧

Kate looked out the window of the train as it sped toward New York City. The sun glinted off the Hudson River as a few sailboats drifted lazily on the water. The buds on the trees opened to the warmer May temperatures. Spring was finally here.

It's a great day for a hike. Briefly, Kate wished she were with Jay and Lorraine in the Adirondack Mountains. Instead, she was spending the day with Dara Thomas in the Big Apple.

Dara hadn't said much in setting up the date—just that she was going to be in New York for a few days, and she would love it if Kate could meet with her. They'd agreed on Carolyn's midtown Manhattan office as a starting point.

Kate wondered, not for the first time, what it was Dara needed. Maybe she had some pressing public relations questions. But wouldn't a star as big as Dara Thomas have a PR rep?

It hardly seemed like an entire month had gone by since she and Jay first met Dara and Rebecca at the GLAAD Media Awards. Sabastien was still in hiding; they were no closer to knowing the true identity of the Black Knight; so far, *Time* was holding publication on any stories resulting from the leaked information; Jay still was having no luck finding a publisher for the book; and things between them... Well, it didn't bear thinking about that.

Kate was heartsick at the growing distance separating them. Nothing she tried worked. The few times she'd attempted to engage Jay in a conversation about what was happening, Jay had shut down, insisting that nothing was wrong that getting the book published wouldn't solve. She was just under a lot of pressure.

The truth was, they'd been in tighter spots both together and separately, but Kate could never remember feeling this off-balance.

The train slowed, and Kate realized with a start that they'd reached Penn Station. She checked her phone. There were no messages from Jay.

The address Dara had given her for Carolyn's office was uptown, so Kate caught the subway headed in that direction. She would find out what Dara had in mind soon enough. As for Jay... That would just have to wait.

∽⭗⭕∼

"Do you want to talk about it?" Lorraine asked.

"Talk about what?" Jay paused and took in a deep breath. The scent of pine trees and birch bark filled her nostrils. It had been too long since she'd been out hiking. She and Kate loved this time of year in the Adirondacks. The muscles in her gut tightened. She couldn't remember the last time she and Kate had done anything together either one of them would consider fun.

"Knock, knock. Anybody home?"

Jay blinked and focused on Lorraine. "I don't know what you're asking me."

"Playing dumb doesn't suit you, my friend. It's abundantly clear that you're distracted."

"Of course I'm distracted. Wouldn't you be under the circumstances?"

"Let me finish. It isn't just about the book situation. Peter and I have known you and Kate for thirty years. Both of us are concerned about you two. There's an obvious tension that we've never seen between you before."

"Everything's fine." Jay stuffed her hands into the pockets of her hiking pants and did her best to ignore Lorraine's penetrating stare.

"You know I'm a trained observer and interrogator, right?"

Jay's body suffused with heat, and she knew it wasn't from any hot flash. Anger bubbled up within her. She stopped short and turned on her friend, yanked her hands out of her pockets, and spread them wide to indicate their surroundings. "Is that why we're out here? So you can ambush me with your theories about what's wrong in my relationship? Here I thought we were just two friends out for a lovely hike in the woods. I don't know what makes you think you're qualified to judge—"

"Whoa, there. Nobody's judging you, Jay. And this was not some plot to lure you away from home and browbeat you. I *am* your friend, and I'm worried about you. You and Kate are the most perfect-for-each-other storybook couple I know. You've got the kind of soul-deep, loving relationship everyone else longs for. Which is why Peter and I are so concerned."

"Well, you needn't be." Jay started walking again, faster than before. Lorraine kept up easily, a fact that irritated Jay.

Jay told herself that she didn't care that the silence between them was strained and awkward. *Uh-huh.* Then she thought about her reaction to Lorraine's question. "More like over-reaction," she mumbled to herself.

Contrary to what she'd said to Lorraine, she was well-aware that she and Kate were struggling. She just couldn't put her finger on the root cause and felt incapable at the moment to stop the free fall.

Jay glanced at Lorraine. Her eyes gave nothing away, but Jay could imagine that she was hurt. "I'm sorry." She put a hand on Lorraine's arm and then withdrew it. "That was callous and unfair. You were just trying to help."

"It's okay, Jay. You're under no obligation to share anything with me."

"I… It's just…" Jay kicked a small rock and sent it skittering off the trail. "I don't know what to say. I don't know what's wrong. I love Kate as much, or more, than I ever have. She's my world. She always has been."

"But?" Lorraine's voice was soft. Gentle.

"It isn't so much that there's a 'but.' That's my truth. Nothing changes that."

They walked on in silence again. The occasional call of a hawk breached the stillness. "Do you ever feel off-balance sometimes? Like nothing you do is quite right? Like your whole world is off-kilter and you don't know how to fix it again?"

"Been there, done that," Lorraine said. "Yes, and we often take it out on the ones we love the most."

"Why is that, do you think?"

"I don't really know. Maybe it's because they're more understanding than anybody else. Maybe it's because they're right in front of us. Maybe it's because we trust them not to turn tail and run when we lash out."

"That's a lot of maybes," Jay said. "But maybe you're right." She vaulted over a log that was blocking the path.

"You've been under a lot of pressure. It's no wonder you're feeling out of sorts."

Jay considered. "That's no excuse. Besides, my crabbiness pre-dates the whole hacking business."

"You want to try to trace it back? Figure out what was going on in your life when you started feeling this way?"

When had it begun? What had happened before the trip to LA for the GLAAD Awards? "I finished writing the book and sent it to Jeremy in January."

"That must've felt great."

"You know? This one wasn't like my other books. Every other time I've turned in a manuscript, I've felt a sense of accomplishment and pride."

"And this time?"

The trail opened up, revealing a sparkling lake. Jay walked over to a large boulder perched at the water's edge, hopped up onto it, and scooted over to make room for Lorraine.

"This time was different. I finished self-editing, hit Send, and felt...exposed." The realization surprised Jay, but it was true.

"Exposed, how?"

"The story was so personal, so close."

A great blue heron glided across the lake, and Jay marveled, as she always did, at the magic and majesty of nature.

"You've written other autobiographical or semi-autobiographical books. I loved *Bittersweet Rhapsody*. Wasn't that all about coping with your sister's death when you were so little and the ways in which that tragedy dramatically altered the dynamics in your family?"

"It was."

"That was less personal than writing about the Commission?"

Jay pulled a bottle of water out of her pack and took a drink. "I guess I was far enough removed from my childhood that the emotional impact was less. The effect on Kate of those few months when she believed I'd been killed, what it did to her psychologically, then seeing Peter lying near death, bleeding from a gunshot wound to the chest... Those things are indelibly etched on my brain. Even though this book was fiction, to make the book all that it needed to be, I had to take myself back there, immerse myself in all those emotions all over again. I spent months reliving every detail of that time, ad nauseam."

Lorraine skipped a stone across the water. "You know Peter and I still have nightmares about the shootout at the Lincoln Monument too. At least once a month, one or the other of us wakes up in a cold sweat."

"But that was how you met. Something beautiful came of all that for you two."

"You and Kate found your respective ways back to each other in the middle of all of the mayhem. One could argue everything turned out well for you too."

"Nobody came out of that situation unscathed. I'm still haunted by so many memories."

"Then why write the book?"

Jay's eyebrows rose in surprise. "You know the answer to that. Because we all agreed that exposing the Commission, even a fictionalized version, was the only way to raise public awareness and shine light in the dark corners. The public needs to know that organizations like that really exist, that their reach is pervasive, and that they operate with impunity."

"Not at your expense, Jay. We didn't agree that the book was more important than your emotional well-being or your marriage."

Jay's heart pounded hard against her ribcage. "My marriage isn't in jeopardy." *Is it?*

"Of course not. That was inelegant phrasing. I only meant— Well, you know what I meant."

Jay took another drink of water and offered the bottle to Lorraine. "Want some?"

"I've got my own, thanks. So, let's review. Your unease started when you sent the book to your editor."

Jay scrunched up her nose. "In the interest of accuracy, my discomfort began when I started writing the book. It only escalated when I submitted the manuscript."

"No doubt all that was exacerbated by the security leak and the fiasco with your publisher."

Jay couldn't argue with that. But the truth of it didn't sit well with her. She was better than this—stronger than this. "You know, I've been through tougher times than this and not gone over the edge. Heck, Kate and I together have been through worse. It's never affected me like this before. Why now?"

"Good question. What's different?"

Jay narrowed her eyes in thought. "I'm not sure. The older I get, the more friends I lose to tragedy or illness, the more I realize how precious life really is. I don't want to waste a single day, a single minute on stuff that doesn't enrich my life. Does that make sense?"

Lorraine nodded. "It does. Would you argue that writing this novel, exposing the Commission, isn't an important and vital thing to do?"

"No. Not at all. But reliving the Machiavellian machinations and manipulations, the worst aspects of human nature, didn't personally enrich me either."

"Then what we're really saying is that you got stuck in a dark place and you forgot to come back out of the cave into the sunlight." Lorraine skipped another rock. "Nice alliteration, by the way. You get extra points for that."

"Thank you." Jay smiled and the very act of it made her feel lighter. "For everything."

Lorraine gestured to the sun and wrapped an arm around Jay's shoulders. "Time to come to the light, Jedi warrior."

The Star Wars reference startled a laugh out of Jay. "I agree." For the first time in longer than she wanted to admit, she was anxious to get home and see Kate. There was so much she wanted to say to her.

CHAPTER EIGHT

Dara gazed out over the expanse of Central Park West. Joggers moved along the trail, occasionally jumping aside to avoid being run over by impertinent bicyclists. Several softball games were underway. Here and there the lawn was dotted with colorful picnic blankets peopled alternatively by lovers and families.

The scene should have been comfortingly familiar to her. After all, Dara grew up in the shadow of this city. But it had never felt like home to her—it never was comfortable in the way she believed home should be. "That's because you couldn't wait to get out of your parents' cold, judgmental house."

"Ms. Thomas?"

Dara breathed a sigh of relief, grateful for the reprieve from burgeoning memories. She retreated to Carolyn's desk and pressed the intercom button to answer the receptionist. "Yes, Gayle?"

"Ms. Kyle is here to see you."

"Send her in, please."

A moment later, the door opened and Kate strode into the room. She was dressed casually in a pair of worn jeans, an un-tucked black button-down collared shirt with the sleeves rolled up, and a pair of scuffed black boots.

Dara crossed the room and gave Kate a hug. "Good to see you."

"Good to see you too." Kate surveyed her surroundings. "Is that you?" She pointed to a framed theater poster on the wall.

"It is. I got my first break in a play in Williamstown, Massachusetts. That was the first time Carolyn represented me."

Dara sat down in one of two wingback chairs in the sitting area near the windows and motioned for Kate to take the other chair.

"I've been to the Williamstown Theater many times. It's a great place to see a show."

"It's a great stage on which to act. I got lucky and landed an understudy role that turned into something more."

Kate laughed. "I'd say that's a gross understatement. What brings you to New York?"

"Honestly? You."

Kate's eyes grew wide. "Me?"

"Yes." Dara measured her words carefully. "Or, more accurately, you and Jay. But I wanted to talk to you alone first." She could've sworn she saw a flicker of something akin to…what? Sadness? Pain? Discomfort? Just as quickly, it was gone.

"What can we do for you?"

"It isn't anything like that." Kate crossed her arms over her chest, her unease so palpable that Dara hesitated. Maybe this was a mistake. *You brought her here, too late to back out now.* "I… That is, Rebecca and I, have a proposal for Jay. But we weren't sure how she would feel about it, and we certainly didn't want to step on any toes, so we decided that it would be best for me to run it by you first."

Kate shifted in her seat. "If whatever you want to talk about affects Jay, you should probably speak directly to her."

"We will," Dara said. "But, as I said, I don't want to bring something to her that might potentially offend her or make her uncomfortable. I hoped that you would hear me out and give me your take on it." When Kate didn't immediately answer her, Dara added, "I'm sorry. Perhaps we were wrong in our approach."

"No." Kate shook her head. "No. It's okay." She uncrossed her arms and leaned forward. "It's just… As you might imagine, Jay's been under a lot of pressure lately. We both have. She's got so little control over so much of what is happening. As much as I want to protect her, I have to recognize that she's perfectly capable of taking care of herself. That means I have to give her the space to make her own choices."

"Understood. I promise you that nothing we discuss today will take that away from her. Rebecca and I both have tremendous respect for Jay… and for you. We talk about you often and about how much we enjoyed meeting and spending time with you. We're both heart-sick over what we've read about Jay's situation with the book."

"Thank you. The whole thing makes my blood boil."

"No doubt."

"And for the record, Jay and I are equally glad to know you and Rebecca."

"Thank you. I sincerely hope we'll have a lot more time to get acquainted, which brings me to the topic at hand."

Kate arched an eyebrow.

"What if..." Dara chose her words with care. "What if Jay stopped trying to get the book published?"

"I don't—"

Dara held up a hand. "Hear me out first."

"Okay."

"What if, instead of trying to find a publisher, Jay optioned the manuscript as a film and took it directly to the big screen?"

"I'm not sure—"

"All I'm asking you is if you think Jay would be open to talking to us about going directly to film? I know you don't want to answer for her on the merits of the idea. I just want to know if you think she'd be willing to have a discussion, or if she would find it off-putting?"

Kate briefly stared off into space, her expression unreadable. Dara resisted the urge to keep talking, to elaborate. The silence lingered in the air between them.

Finally, Kate refocused on Dara. "Jay and I have been batting around all sorts of publishing options. It never occurred to either one of us to consider using another medium to get the work out."

"Is it something you think might appeal to her? Something she'd entertain?"

"Ask her."

"She won't be offended?"

"On what grounds?"

"We wouldn't want it to come off as though we don't think Jay can get the book published—like we don't have faith in her ability to rise above all this and succeed."

Kate smiled. "No. She wouldn't look at what you're suggesting that way. She'd be more likely to assume that she had really cool new friends who believed in her and her work and had her back."

Dara relaxed for the first time since the meeting started. "That's good, because we do. When do you think the two of you would be free to sit down and talk? Do you think you'd have any availability while I'm still on this coast? It might be easier to fly under the radar here than in LA."

Kate again shifted uncomfortably in her chair. "Why don't you give Jay a call and ask her? As I said, this is hers to do. I would only attend if she wanted me to be there."

Dara badly wanted to ask Kate if something was wrong. This was not the same confident, take-charge woman Dara saw in LA. That Kate would've pulled up her calendar and set the meeting. That Kate would've spoken with authority on Jay's behalf.

What had changed? *It's not your business. Leave it alone.* Belatedly, Dara realized she hadn't said anything out loud. "Right. Should I call now? Or wait until later?"

"She's off hiking with a friend today. I don't know that she'll have cell signal. I'd wait."

"Sure." Dara checked her watch; Kate had spent three hours on the train to get to New York and they'd talked for less than an hour. *Well, here's an opportunity to get to know her better.* "It's crazy for you to have come all this way just to turn around and go back. You said Jay has plans today, right? Are you hungry? I skipped breakfast and I'm famished."

"Me too."

"Lunch?"

"Sure. I've got time. You pick the place."

Dara pointed out the window. "What do you think about grabbing a couple of deli sandwiches and eating in the park? It's a beautiful day out there."

"Perfect."

⋖⋗

"I remember reading in the history books about the Hyland affair." Dara speared her dill pickle with a plastic fork and took a bite.

"Oh, my God. You have no idea how old that makes me feel," Kate said. She unwrapped her roast beef sandwich and took a bite.

Dara blushed. "I'm sorry. I didn't think about it that way. Let me see if I can dig my way out of this."

"I don't think so." Kate laughed. "How old were you in 1989?"

Dara's color deepened. "Five?"

"Five? *Five?*" Kate dramatically put a hand to her heart. "I have jeans that are older than you."

"Well, if you do, they're probably back in style now."

"Watch it, whippersnapper."

"Okay, Grandma."

"Hey! I'm old enough to be your mother, not your grandmother. Don't push it." Kate took another bite of her sandwich and wiped the corner of her mouth with a napkin. She liked Dara. She was down-to-earth, fun, easy to talk to, and clearly not impressed by her own fame.

"Fair enough. Anyway, what I was trying to say, albeit inelegantly, is that I know a little bit about your background. I know that you were the President's press secretary. In fact, I've seen television clips of you handling the media at various press conferences. You were impressive."

"Thanks. I don't miss those days."

Dara finished off her pickle. "I imagine you didn't get much sleep in that job."

Kate shook her head. "Not much. I can't remember a single night when the phone didn't ring and wake me up at least once."

"I bet. What did you do after you left the White House?"

Kate stared off into the distance and watched a flock of robins take off from a patch of grass and land in a nearby willow tree.

"I— I'm sorry. Was that a bad question to ask?"

Kate cleared her throat. "Why would you think that?"

"The expression on your face. It seemed as if wherever you just went, it was a painful place."

"Mmm."

"You don't have to answer if—"

"No. It's okay." Kate waved Dara off. What should she say? How much should she reveal? She took another bite of the sandwich, trying to order her thoughts. "Did you enjoy history in school, Dara?"

Dara eyed Kate quizzically.

"Not where you thought this was going, I take it. Bear with me."

"Actually, I love history. I took a couple of twentieth century American history classes and two political science courses when I was at Yale."

"You did?"

Dara nodded. "You're surprised."

"More like impressed."

"I didn't just want to study drama. I believe it's important to understand the world around us. Where we're going as a society is predicated on where we've been. You can't have one without first having the other."

"True enough." Kate finished the first half of her sandwich and opened her bag of chips.

"The first course was on the American presidency. The other course was titled, 'Press, Politics, and Policy.'"

"Huh. Interesting choices."

Dara swallowed a bite of her turkey, lettuce, tomato, and cheese on rye. "Would you not agree that the American presidency and politics are at the core of this country's historical fabric? That to truly understand the events of the last century, or any century since the founding of these United States, one must understand the politics of the time?"

Kate wondered how many people underestimated Dara and thought she was just a pretty face. This was a woman of depth and substance. "I completely agree." Kate licked the salt from the chips off her fingers and set aside the bag. "And in a way, that's where I was going with my question.

"You said you studied the Hyland affair in school. The truth is, you studied what the powers that be wanted you to know about the incident. The whole truth, including the nuances of the politics behind the events, goes far beyond what the public ever was told."

"I'm sure it does."

"That's primarily what this whole business with Jay's book and the leaked documents is all about. It's about shining light versus keeping secrets and allowing darkness to flourish."

"Although we haven't spoken about the substance of Jay's book, I'm assuming that the idea behind it was to shine light.

92

Hence the level of scrutiny and pressure both on *Time* magazine and the man the government is hunting with regard to the leak, and on Black Quill. That's the real reason Jay is having trouble getting the book out, isn't it? The book tells the rest of the story? The parts that aren't in the history books?"

"Jay's book is fiction with factual underpinnings."

"That was a careful way to put it." Dara finished the rest of her sandwich, rolled up the wax paper wrapping, and stuffed it in the carryout bag.

"Exercising care here is important. It is safe to say that there is much more going on here than meets the eye. I can't talk about the classified parts of what happened back then. But if you're serious about wanting to bring Jay's work to the big screen, you should know that there are those who will not like the idea. There could be backlash."

"Understood."

Kate took the last bite of roast beef and crumpled up the paper. "All of which brings me back to your original question."

Dara smiled. "I wondered, if at your advanced age, you'd forgotten."

Kate shot her a murderous glance. "Your time will come. Just when you think you're doing fine, you'll walk into a room and forget why you're there. When that happens, I want you to remember that you made fun of me."

"I'll make a note of it."

"So, before you distract me again and I really do forget, I'm going to answer your question." Kate shifted her position so that she was fully facing Dara. "What transpired during the Hyland incident deeply affected all of us. Jay and I suffered physical and emotional trauma. Both of us nearly lost our lives and each other."

Kate closed her eyes as the memories threatened to derail her. She flinched at the touch of Dara's gentle fingers on her arm.

"I'm sorry. I just— I didn't mean to cause you pain." Dara dropped her hand to her lap.

"You didn't. The pain was inflicted a long time ago. Sometimes, when the memories are fresh, it can be overwhelming. Honestly, I don't know that I could've done what Jay did, reliving so much of it in order to infuse the book with real emotion..." Kate's voice trailed off as her own words sunk in. Jay's irritability and the personal disconnect they'd been feeling hadn't started with the leak and the investigation. It had its roots in the writing of the book. How had she not seen that before? How had she not understood the depth of Jay's distress and the cause of it?

"Kate?"

"Hmm?"

"Are you okay? We really don't have to go through this. I know you're strong, and you seem to be almost as stubborn as I am, but this is not necessary."

"I'm okay. Really." Kate tucked away the epiphany for another time. "In any event, after it was all over, we needed some time away. We needed time to heal.

"Of course, we had to testify before Congress in a series of closed-door hearings. And we were required to be in court for various and sundry legal proceedings. In between, the two of us spent a lot of time in the mountains and in nature, trying to find our new normal."

"Your relationship is so strong," Dara said. "It's obvious even to the most casual observer how much you love each other. I hope that, after thirty years together, Rebecca and I have that."

"It takes work, and faith in love and each other. Jay is everything to me. I can't imagine my life without her in it." More quietly, Kate added, "I don't want to imagine my life without Jay in it." Her heart stuttered. They could fix what was wrong. Kate would go home and tell Jay what she'd figured out. They would talk through all of it, and together they would find their way back to each other. They would carve out time and space for themselves—their own personal oasis, even in the eye of this hurricane. Their love was stronger than any challenge they'd ever faced, including ghosts of the past.

"It is good to see your face, Vaughn Elliott. Yours too, Peter."

"You need a shave, Sabastien. How many times have I told you baby-faced guys and beards don't mix."

"Very funny. You do not like my goatee? I think it makes me look roguish. Maybe it is because your computer screen is too small. You cannot properly see the beard."

"Or maybe you need a shave," Vaughn reiterated.

"Peter? Man-to-man, you appreciate the facial hair, yes?"

Peter shook his head. "Sorry, buddy. It could be that Skype doesn't do the goatee justice, but I have to agree with Vaughn on this one."

"Merde."

"Now can we get down to business?" Peter asked. Despite Sabastien's repeated assurances that the connection was secured by state-of-the-art technology and techniques, Peter didn't trust it.

"Sabastien, where are we on identifying the Black Knight?" Vaughn asked.

"I have researched every major hack for the past ten years, cross-referenced all of the databases, and run every algorithm. There is not even a smell of this individual."

"A hint, or a whiff."

"Quoi?"

"There is not even a hint or a whiff. Pick one or the other of those, but 'not even a smell' is nonsensical," Vaughn said.

"Right. There is not even a whiff of anyone using that handle."

"Kate, Jay, Lorraine, and I met the other day," Peter said. "We're working the angle that the moniker might be one used by a member of the Commission. If so, the reason you're not finding anything is because the code name isn't a hacker handle at all."

"Interesting," Vaughn said. "Do you have anything to back that up?"

"Lorraine was deep undercover with the Commission during the Hyland incident. She is well familiar with their protocols and practices. Every operative had an alias. It was rare for them to communicate with each other using real names."

"Perhaps, but surely this is not the first time this person has hacked. He is too good. Why have I not found anything done by him before?" Sabastien asked.

"Is it possible this person has hacked before, just using a different signature?" Vaughn asked. "Sabastien, instead of tracing for a moniker, try looking at technique. Find something, anything, that sets this hacker apart, something that is unique to him."

"Okay. I do not know why I did not think of that first."

"In other news," Peter said, "I did some checking and discovered that Michael Vendetti, one of the key figures in the

Hyland fiasco, just got out of prison. You all know I don't believe in coincidences."

"Me either," Vaughn said. "Do you have any sources that can look into his visitors, mail, and contacts while he was locked up? Maybe there's something there."

"Lorraine is doing some digging even as we speak."

"Good. Sabastien, are you still feeling secure?" Vaughn asked.

Sabastien laughed mirthlessly. "Secure? I have not felt secure since this whole thing began. But if you are asking me if I am okay where I am, I think I am."

"Excellent. Let's reconvene next week, unless something comes up first. Keep in touch," Peter said, and severed the connection.

He opened the accordion folder on his desk and pulled out the thick file folder labeled "Vendetti, Michael." He hadn't yet told Kate that a man she once trusted as her second in command at the White House, a man who, it turned out, played a significant role in two of the most painful chapters in her life, was free. It wasn't a conversation he was looking forward to having with her. Still, he knew he couldn't put it off for much longer. He pulled out his phone and texted Kate to see if she and Jay would be free for dinner in the next few days.

CHAPTER NINE

Jay's heart leapt at the sound of the garage door opening. Kate was home. She ran into the dining room and lit the candles. The table settings glistened in the resulting glow. The smell of garlic wafted up from one of the covered serving dishes.

Quickly, Jay checked her reflection in the mirror over the sideboard. *Nervous much?*

"Jay? Honey? Are you here?"

"Right here." Jay walked around the corner and stopped short. The sight of Kate, standing in the hallway, looking impossibly beautiful, took her breath away.

"What's wrong?"

Jay blinked. "Wrong? Nothing's wrong. You look amazing."

Kate looked down at her clothes. "I look like I spent most of the day sitting on a train."

Before Kate had finished the sentence, Jay was wrapping her arms around her. "Sitting on a train never looked so good." She reached up and captured Kate's lower lip between her teeth and pulled lightly, then kissed her in earnest.

As she pulled back, she watched the pulse point in Kate's neck beating wildly. Moisture pooled in her center. "I love you, sweetheart."

Kate brushed her fingers along Jay's cheekbones. "I love you too. So very much."

Their mouths met again, tongues questing, lips melding together, the taste at once familiar and new.

Jay unbuttoned Kate's jeans, her hands trembling from desire. She ran a palm up under Kate's shirt, caressing the soft skin of her abdomen.

Her legs went weak at the touch of Kate's hands on her breasts. "I need... I want..."

After so many years together, no more words were necessary. Kate steered her down the hall, into their bedroom, and onto the bed, liberating both of them of their clothing as they went.

As Jay's naked body rose in supplication, she had a brief glimpse in her mind's eye of the candles burning in the dining room, and dinner ready on the table. Maybe they should... Then Kate shifted her weight. Dinner would keep.

✧∼

Kate pulled Jay tighter against her shoulder and breathed in her scent. These moments afterward, the warmth of their bodies fully intertwined, their hearts beating together in perfect rhythmic harmony—these were the most peaceful, happy moments Kate ever had known. She stroked Jay's hair and took another deep, contented breath. And then sniffed the air again.

"Sweetheart? Are you cooking something?"

"Hmm?" Jay stretched languorously.

"When I got home, were you making dinner, by chance? Why do I smell garlic?"

"Oh my God!" Jay disentangled herself, bolted straight up, and threw her legs over the bed.

"Something I said?" Kate gazed at her indulgently.

"Dinner. You said dinner. It's on the table." Jay gathered her scattered clothing and got dressed.

"Does this mean we don't get a second round?" Kate waggled her eyebrows.

"After dinner." Jay finished buttoning her shirt. "If it's not too ruined to eat."

Kate took her time getting out of bed. "Let me just say that if we never get to eat that meal, it will have been worth it." She wrapped her arms around Jay and pulled her close. "I love you."

"I love you too." Jay swatted Kate on the butt. "Now could you please put something on so we can salvage what's left of dinner?"

They walked into the dining room hand-in-hand. Kate surveyed the table, covered in an elegant red cloth. Jay had chosen the good silver and linen napkins that matched the tablecloth. Candles dripped melted wax onto their holders. Three covered dishes sat perfectly placed on the sideboard.

Tears pricked the inside of Kate's eyelids. She cleared her throat. "You planned this for me?"

Jay squeezed her hand. "I did. I wanted to apologize to you—to explain what I figured out today." The timbre of her voice deepened. "I wasn't planning the seduction scene until afterward."

"Too late for that." Kate kissed the top of Jay's head. "Although I'd prefer to think it was all in perfect time."

"Tell that to the cold garlic-roasted chicken and mashed potatoes." Jay went to the sideboard and lifted the serving lid off the chicken.

"I could be wrong, but I seem to remember that our state-of-the-art kitchen is equipped with a microwave."

"Good thing." Jay picked up a plate and handed it to Kate. "Fill your plate, but save room for dessert."

"If you're what's for dessert, I've always got enough room."

"Flattery will get you nowhere."

"I don't know, it's gotten me pretty far up until now."

"I'm not that easy," Jay said.

"Tell me about it." Kate filled her plate and headed for the kitchen. She microwaved her dinner and waited for Jay to do the same. Neither of them said a word until they were seated at the dining room table.

"This smells great."

"Wait until you see how it tastes before you go complimenting the chef."

"Did you make it with love?"

"I did."

"Then I know it's going to be fabulous." Kate momentarily lost herself in Jay's smile. It had been far too long since she'd last seen that light on her wife's face.

"What are you thinking?"

"How beautiful you are when you smile."

Jay blushed. "Yeah. About that." She pushed a forkful of mashed potatoes around her plate. "I realized some things today. I don't know why I didn't see them before now."

"I realized some things today too," Kate said. She put her fork down.

"Me, first, please."

Kate wanted to protest. She wanted to tell Jay what she'd figured out. Fear crept into her bones. She tried to push it away. It had been a very long time since she'd felt this unsure about where they stood. What if Jay had come to the conclusion that they needed some space from each other? *Based on what, Kyle? Why would you think that? She just seduced you. She made you a fabulous, romantic dinner. Since when did you become this insecure?*

"Kate?"

Since you completely missed the boat on what's been going on for her.

"Kate!"

Kate started and focused on Jay. "Right. You go first."

Jay covered Kate's hand with her own, then withdrew it. "Wherever you just were? Please don't go there."

"Go where?" Kate knew she was stalling.

"I don't know, sweetheart. Wherever you just went that had you looking as though your world was about to end."

Kate frowned. Jay always had been able to read her with unerring accuracy. "Let's finish eating first and then talk."

"Fair enough."

They finished the meal in silence, cleared the table, and did the dishes before adjourning to the den, where they sat on opposite ends of the sofa.

Jay tucked her feet under her. "What I wanted to tell you is that what's been happening between us—the stress and strain—it's all my fault."

"It's not—"

"Let me get this out, please. Then you can say whatever you want to say."

"Okay."

"When I chose to write this book, I knew it would be tough. I knew that I would have to relive many of the events around that time in order to properly tell the story."

"The decision to write the book wasn't only on you. We talked it over together, remember?"

"I remember. But I had the last word," Jay said. "Anyway, what I miscalculated at the time wasn't how hard it would be to revisit the events. It was what it would cost me to re-experience those emotions."

Jay's voice faltered and Kate resisted the urge to go to her.

"I—In order to make the characters relatable, in order to infuse realism into the narrative, I had to go back there and access all of those feelings I'd worked so hard to heal."

Unable to do nothing, Kate got up, retrieved a bottle of water from the mini-refrigerator in the corner, and handed it to Jay before resuming her seat.

"Thank you." Jay opened the bottle and took a swig. "So I tapped back into all of that terror, all the horror I felt, and all that I watched you endure, and Peter, and Barbara. And in the end, I nailed it. I channeled all of that pain, the suffering, the angst, and the anger into the novel. Which, of course, is what any good author must do." Jay took another gulp of water.

"The problem is, I finished writing and sent the book off to Jeremy, but I never came back out of that darkness. I never re-closed those old wounds. I've been carrying them with me since I started writing, and I've been taking them out on you. And that"— Jay paused to compose herself—"that is completely unacceptable."

Tears spilling over onto her cheeks, she looked at Kate. "I'm so, so sorry. I've been horrible and I had no right to be. I let everything about the book overwhelm me and jeopardize the one thing in the world that matters most to me—our marriage, our relationship."

Kate's heart lurched. She opened her arms and beckoned to Jay, who slid over and folded herself into the embrace.

"Sweetheart, our marriage is rock solid. I love you more than anything in the world. I can't imagine a present, or a future, without you in it."

Kate took Jay's hand and placed it in the center of her own chest. "My heart only ever beats for you. That was true thirty years

101

ago, and it's still true today. I am more in love with you than I've ever been, Jamison Parker."

"Thank God."

"Is it my turn yet?" Kate asked.

"Do you still need a turn?"

"I do." Kate tipped Jay's face up so that she could see into her eyes. "Maybe we both needed the day away to gain perspective. I came to the same conclusion that you did today—that something shifted when you started writing this book."

Kate held up a hand. "Before you interrupt me, which I know you're about to do, let me finish." She kissed Jay on the forehead.

"When I finally got that worked out in my mind, I wanted to run right back home and beg your forgiveness."

"Beg *my* forgiveness? What for? I was the one—"

Kate put her fingers over Jay's mouth. "My turn." She lifted her fingers away and kissed Jay. "I don't know how I could've been so obtuse and insensitive that I didn't see what writing the book was doing to you. How did I miss that?"

Kate shook her head. "I feel like a dolt. I'm sorry, sweetheart. I should have been there for you. Instead, I was oblivious to what you were going through. There's no excuse for that."

Jay sat up and faced her. "Stop beating yourself up. I could've said something at any time, but I didn't. As I said, I didn't understand it myself. So how could I expect you to get it? That's not fair."

"The good news is, we've both got it figured out now."

"The next question is, what do we do about that?"

Kate rose and pulled Jay up with her. "I suggest we start with the dessert you promised me."

"Dessert sounds good."

❧❦

"I'm glad you guys could make it." Peter squinted up into the sky where the sun was playing peek-a-boo with some high, scattered clouds.

"You invite us out sailing on the lake on a beautiful day, who are we to say no?" Jay applied sun block to her face and neck.

"Although you're usually more meticulous about planning in advance."

"That's because he has an ulterior motive," Kate said. "And you missed a spot." She took some lotion and rubbed it at the base of Jay's neck.

Peter wagged a finger at Kate. "I hate that you've known me so long that you know my tells."

"Do you have nefarious plans for us?" Jay asked. "Did you bring us out here like Clyde Griffiths in Theodore Dreiser's, *An American Tragedy?*"

Peter grabbed the tiller and gestured to Lorraine. "Prepare to come about." He waited for her to get the mainsail ready. "Coming about."

When he was satisfied with their course, Peter tied off the tiller. A turkey vulture swooped through the air above, capturing his attention, and Peter thought it the perfect metaphor for what he was about to say.

"I have some information to share with you and I know you're not going to like it."

"So you brought us out to this beautiful spot to soften the blow?" Jay asked.

Peter knew her well enough to recognize that the joke was Jay's way of easing the tension. "I brought you out here so that you won't kill me after I tell you what I have to say, since I'm the one who knows the way back to shore." He winked.

"You remember that Kate knows how to sail, right?"

"I'm sure he does," Kate said. She took Jay's hand and nodded to Peter. "What's up?"

There was no way to sugarcoat it, so he decided to go for the direct approach. "My sources tell me Michael Vendetti was released from prison."

Jay's face drained of all color, and she let go of Kate's hand. "When?"

"A few months ago."

"A few…"

Kate crossed her arms over her chest. "Before or after the leak?"

"Early March."

"So, before."

"Yes."

"Anybody think that's a coincidence?"

Lorraine shook her head. "It seems highly unlikely. Peter and I have someone inside the federal system scrubbing Vendetti's prison files to see who visited him, who called him or corresponded with him, and who on staff might have any connection to the Commission."

"Do we need to think about security for Kate?" Jay asked. Her voice was strained, fear written in every facial feature.

"Sweetheart—"

"No." Jay turned to face Kate. "I'm not going to lose you..." Her voice faltered and a tear spilled onto her cheek.

"No, you're not," Kate said. "Nothing's going to happen to me."

Peter sat down next to Jay and wrapped an arm around her shoulders. "I give you my word that Lorraine and I won't let Vendetti anywhere near either one of you."

"You can't guarantee that. Nobody can." Jay angrily scrubbed a hand across her face. "We know how this works. The Commission is everywhere. You can't identify every threat. If you can't identify them, you can't stop them."

"We are not giving in to fear," Kate said. "Not now. Not ever. We all know Wayne Grayson was the power behind the Commission—the man who ordered every violent action the Commission undertook over the past thirty years—and he died in prison last year."

Jay shook her head. "Somebody had to fill that power vacuum. What if it was Vendetti?"

"Jay?" Lorraine knelt down in front of her. "I've had profilers put together a dossier on Vendetti. They are convinced he's not interested in bloodlust. He's a narcissist and a schemer. He'd want to regain his stature and a place at the table, not put himself in a position where he'd be the top suspect in a murder. We never had any indication that he was actively involved in any of the violence perpetrated against either one of you."

"You're assuming he ever lost his seat at the table in the first place," Kate said.

"I don't want to frighten you, but if Vendetti's been in play all this time, and if he wanted to do you physical harm, he would've done it by now." Peter checked the horizon to make sure they were still on course.

"I know you well enough, my friend. I assume you've got someone on Vendetti right now?"

Peter smiled. Kate really did know him like a book. "I might have a person and some technology in play."

"Since when?" Kate asked.

"Since I found out a few days ago."

"So not early enough to connect the dots to the leak."

"Not yet."

"Can't Sabastien pull up his electronic footprint?"

"We talked about it. It's too risky right now."

"What do you mean it's too risky?" Jay's nostrils flared.

Lorraine stood up. "He means that if Vendetti is behind the leak and/or the framing of Sabastien, we don't want to tip him off that we're focusing on him."

"Fair enough. What's our play?" Kate asked.

Peter untied the tiller and made a course adjustment so that they were headed for a little inlet near the far bank. "We continue to work the Black Knight angle. If we can pin down who that is, we can make real headway into the question of whether the hack and the hacker are connected to Vendetti and/or the Commission."

"In the meantime," Lorraine added, "we keep close tabs on Vendetti and his known associates and we wait to hear back from our man inside the prison system."

"And we enjoy an excellent lunch courtesy of Jamison Parker at this cozy little out-of-the-way spot up ahead."

"Hey! How do you know I didn't make the lunch?" Kate asked.

Peter laughed. "In all the years I've known you, you've never once cooked for me. I think it's safe to say that whatever's in that cooler, you didn't have anything to do with it."

"Untrue," Kate mumbled. "I purchased the raw materials."

Peter peeked over at Jay. He could tell that she was far from mollified, but, at least for the moment, he'd done everything he could do to ease her fear.

◈ ◈

Kate reached across the center console and stroked the back of Jay's hand before entwining their fingers. They were nearly home and Jay had been uncharacteristically quiet the entire ride.

"Are you okay?"

"Not really," Jay answered after a little while. "How can I be? How can you be?"

Kate squeezed Jay's hand a little tighter. "I know that Peter and Lorraine are doing everything they can. So are we, so is Sabastien, and so is Vaughn. For now, that's going to have to be enough. Worrying about it isn't going to change anything."

"I can't seem to help—" Jay's cell phone buzzed and she glanced at the display. She raised her eyebrows in surprise. "It's Dara."

Kate released Jay's hand. "Better pick it up."

"Is it okay if I put it on speaker? I don't have my Bluetooth with me and you know how I hate holding the cell phone to my ear."

"Sure."

"Hi, Dara. This is Jay. I've got you on speaker. I hope you don't mind. It's just me and Kate."

"No problem. Am I interrupting something? I can call back."

"No, you're fine. We're just in the car on our way home."

"Okay."

"What can I do for you?"

"I'd like to sit down with you and have a business discussion."

Kate kept her eyes on the road, but she could feel the weight of Jay's stare. She hadn't shared her conversation with Dara, and she could just imagine Jay putting two and two together—Kate's rendezvous with Dara yesterday, and this call.

"S-sure. You mean in person?"

"I do."

"Are you still in New York? I could probably get into town tomorrow or the next day if that works for you."

"Actually," Dara said, "I'd love to come upstate to you, if you don't mind, that is."

Jay's eyebrows shot up into her hairline. "You want to come to Albany?"

Dara's laugh was rich and full. "Why are you so surprised?"

"I don't know. I just…"

After a moment's silence, Dara asked, "Would that be okay?"

Kate chanced a glance at Jay, who gestured with her hands, silently asking Kate if she had any objection. Kate indicated that it was Jay's call.

"Of course."

"I could catch the early morning Amtrak train tomorrow."

"Okay. Text me the train number and your scheduled arrival time and I'll pick you up."

"Perfect."

"Is there anything I need to do to prepare?"

"Nothing you need to prepare, no."

Again, the line went silent. "Is there anything I need to bring?"

"We can talk about it tomorrow when I see you."

"Okay. Is there anything more you want to tell me?" Jay asked.

"I'm looking forward to seeing you tomorrow, Jay."

"Good enough. Text me the details and I'll see you on the platform when you arrive."

Jay disconnected the call. They stopped at a red light. Out of the corner of her eye, Kate could see Jay tapping the phone against her chin.

"Any idea what all that was about?" Jay asked.

"Dara wants to sit down with you."

"You never told me how your day was yesterday."

Kate smiled slyly. "As I recall, we had other, more important things on our minds when I got home. And this morning we were busy rushing around getting ready to meet Peter and Lorraine at the dock."

"We're not too busy now, so how was your day with Dara yesterday? What did you talk about?"

Well, Kyle? How much do you want to say? Despite last night, Kate wasn't completely confident that they were on solid ground. Still, she always made a policy of being completely honest with Jay. Now was not the time to deviate from that.

"We had a good day. I got to know her a little better. She's incredibly smart, thoughtful, and erudite."

"You didn't answer the second question."

"What did we discuss?"

"Yes. That one."

Jay's body was stiff, her posture erect. Kate took a deep breath and forged ahead. "She wanted to know if you would be offended if she and Rebecca made you a business proposal."

"And she needed to ask you that question first, before she approached me?"

Jay didn't raise her voice, but Kate understood the importance of this exchange. What she said next could determine the difference between their new détente and a return to the discord and disconnect that had characterized their relationship over the past few months.

"She was very concerned that she didn't want to be insensitive to you. She assumed that I would know you well enough to be able to give her good advice on that front."

"And you told her, what, exactly?"

"I told her that your business affairs were yours alone and that she needed to discuss her proposal with you directly. If you chose to include me in such conversations, you would."

That answer seemed to satisfy Jay, because her posture relaxed slightly.

"So you know what she wants to talk about." It was a statement, not a question.

"I do."

"Care to share?"

Kate pulled into the garage and cut the engine. She unbuckled her seatbelt and shifted to face Jay. "She wants to talk about turning your manuscript into a movie."

Jay was thunderstruck. "She wants…"

"…to put the story on the big screen."

"B-but we haven't even been able to get a publisher yet."

Kate smiled. "I think that's her point." She waited for her words to sink in.

Jay released her seatbelt, sat back in the seat, and stared out the windshield. She made no move to get out of the car. "She doesn't care whether it gets published first."

"That's not exactly true," Kate said. "I think she wants very much for you to get your book published. She understands how important this story is to you. That's why she's offering you an alternative."

Jay scrunched her face up in puzzlement. "What am I missing here?"

"Dara and Rebecca are concerned that you're being blackballed in your attempts to find a publisher to take the novel. They want to propose that you take the manuscript in its current form directly to film instead of getting the book in print. That way, you could still get the story out and made."

Jay shook her head slowly. "Why did she think that would offend me?"

"I think she was worried that you'd perceive their offer as their having lost faith in your ability to get the work published."

"Oh." Jay tucked her phone in her purse. "What advice did you give her?"

"I told her the truth—that I couldn't answer for you. But I also told her that I didn't think the question would offend you."

Jay nodded. "All right."

"Was I right?"

"Huh?"

"Was I correct? The question doesn't offend you, does it?"

"Of course not."

"Are you upset that she came to me first?" The edges of misery crept into Kate's gut. Before this recent spate of events, such a question never would've crossed her mind.

"No." Jay took Kate's face in her hands. "Sweetheart, I don't want you to walk on eggshells with me. Not anymore. You can't control the fact that Dara approached you and not me. She asked you for your opinion. You answered honestly."

Kate kissed Jay's palm. "Let's not forget that I also told her any business discussion would have to be with you."

"No. We can't forget that." Jay leaned in and kissed the tip of Kate's nose.

"So you're not mad?"

"I'm not even close to mad." Jay let go of Kate and picked up her purse. "I would, however, like to go in the house."

"Good plan." Kate opened the car door and stood up. "What do you think?" She pulled out the house key and unlocked the door from the garage to the mudroom.

"I think I'm intrigued."

CHAPTER TEN

Dara stepped off the train at the Albany-Rensselaer station and scanned the crowd. The platform was packed with men and women in business suits. Dara gathered from the conversations on the train that they were all lobbyists or others with a vested interest, swarming the Capitol in Albany at the end of the legislative session to try to effect a favorable outcome for their causes or companies.

"Dara! Over here!"

Dara noticed a hand bobbing up and down in the air behind most of the throng. She headed in that direction. Jay met her part way, fighting her way through the bevy of taller bodies until they were face to face.

"Hi there. Good to see you again." Jay gave her a warm hug. She was dressed in a pair of stylish gray slacks and a forest green silk blouse with the sleeves rolled up.

"Good to see you too." Dara held her at arms-length. "You look fabulous. I love that color on you."

Jay smiled sheepishly. "I didn't know how formal you wanted the meeting to be, so..."

"As you can see," Dara pointed to her designer jeans and short-sleeved, v-neck shirt, "this is as formal as it gets in Tinseltown."

"My car's in the parking lot." Jay motioned for Dara to follow her. "How was the train ride? Have you been to Albany before?"

Dara was aware of several people staring at her, some gesturing and talking behind their hands. She didn't mind; she was used to being recognized and considered it an occupational hazard. Unlike so many celebrities, she made no effort to disguise herself. Such tactics rarely worked and, in her opinion, usually resulted in unflattering pictures on the front pages of tabloid newspapers.

"This is my first time. The scenery along the Hudson river was gorgeous."

"Here we are." Jay unlocked the car, a late-model BMW convertible.

"Nice wheels."

"I call it Kate's mid-life crisis car."

Dara laughed. "The other day I told Kate I'd read about the Hyland affair in the history books when I was in college. I think I gave her a coronary."

"That was cruel."

"She said as much."

"I'm not sure where you wanted to go…"

"Just someplace quiet where we can talk. You pick it."

"Okay. It's a beautiful day and it's not yet lunchtime, so how about if I take you down to the Empire State Plaza? That way, I can give you a little tour, we can sit outside undisturbed, and then, if you're hungry afterward, we can get something to eat."

"Sounds perfect." Although Dara was somewhat surprised that Kate apparently would not be joining them, she refrained from saying so. She thought back to the conversation in Carolyn's office and Kate's evident discomfort about speaking for Jay. Whatever was going on between them was none of her business.

They drove in silence for a short time until they reached an area populated by a series of larger buildings.

Jay pointed to her right. "That odd-shaped structure that looks like a flying saucer is called the Egg. It's a performing arts space."

"It really does look like something from outer space."

"The Empire State Plaza, the configuration of state office buildings and open space you're looking at, was Nelson Rockefeller's dream child." Jay slowed the car. "It's impossible to find parking around here." She scanned the street. "That building on your left is the Capitol. It's where Kate once worked and where the bombing that brought us together took place. Of course, it's long since been repaired."

"I like the archways."

"It's an impressive place." Jay sighed in exasperation. "Do you mind walking? Looks like we're going to have to find a spot a few blocks away."

"I don't mind at all. The exercise will do me good after so much time sitting on the train."

Five minutes later, they found a parking space on a nearby street. Jay locked the car and they began walking.

"I didn't realize Albany was so hilly."

"Parts of it are," Jay said.

"I love the marble." Dara gestured to the open plaza in front of them. "What are the four identical buildings?"

"Agency Buildings One through Four. Imaginatively named, I know."

"Truly."

"They house workers for the various state agencies." Jay swept her arm in the direction of a long rectangular building. "That's the Legislative Office Building, although the Senate and Assembly Chambers are in the Capitol."

"Nice that everything is so centrally located."

"It makes things handy. Better yet, there's an underground plaza, as well, so that in inclement weather, which is pretty much any time from November to April, you'd never have to go outside to get from one building to another. They're all connected underneath where we're walking now."

"Smart architecture."

"How does this spot look to you?" Jay pointed to a marble bench in front of a large rectangular reflecting pool.

"Perfect."

When they were seated, Jay said, "Kate gave me the broad outlines of what you wanted to talk about. I hope you don't mind."

"Not at all. As I told Kate, I only wanted to meet with her first because I wanted to be sure that what Rebecca and I are proposing wouldn't be offensive to you."

"Are you kidding me?" The breeze picked up and Jay tucked an errant strand of hair behind her ear. "I'm flattered."

"Good." Dara leaned forward. "I saw Black Quill's cowardly backpedal in the pages of *USA Today* and the *LA Times*. I don't know the particulars of your situation with getting the manuscript accepted by another publisher—"

"No takers." Jay scoffed. "Nobody wants to go up against the IRS and the FBI."

Dara's eyes grew wide in surprise. "The…"

"IRS and the FBI. They paid a visit to Black Quill and persuaded them that it wasn't in their best interest to pursue publication of the book."

"How can they do that? What happened to freedom of the press and the First Amendment?" Dara knew she sounded naïve, but still…

"I forget that not everyone is privy to the way politics and government can sometimes work." Jay stared off into the distance. "Unfortunately, I've had a few too many up-close-and-personal encounters."

"I'm so sorry." Dara gently put a hand on Jay's arm. "I don't know exactly what transpired with regard to you and Kate during the Hyland matter, but I gather that time must've been very difficult for you." She saw the shadow of remembered pain transform Jay's features, and she briefly regretted having brought up the topic.

"It's okay. The bogey man can't hurt me anymore if I shine the light in the dark places."

"That's what you're trying to do with the book, right? Tell the truths you weren't able to reveal back then? Set the record straight?"

"Government secrecy makes it more complicated than that," Jay said, focusing her attention on Dara, "but that's not a bad over-simplification." She stretched out her legs and crossed them at the ankle. "All of this is way off the record, by the way."

"That goes without saying."

"I've already told you more than I should have."

Dara held Jay's gaze. "I would never violate your privacy. I hope you know you can trust me." Even as she said the words, Dara felt a prick of conscience. After all, she, herself, was holding back an enormous secret. Wasn't she?

Jay laughed mirthlessly. "I didn't mean that. If I didn't trust you implicitly, we wouldn't be having this conversation. I simply meant that I've told you more than what is prudent for your own safety."

Dara's brow furrowed. "Are you in physical danger, Jay? Do you need help?"

"Oh, no." More wisps of hair fell across Jay's face and she swept them away with her fingers. "At least I don't think so."

There was something about Jay's expression just then that made the hair on the back of Dara's neck stand on end. Then, just as quickly, it disappeared.

"Anyway, the reason I'm telling you any of this is because you need to understand what is at stake and what you'd be getting yourself into if you really were serious about turning my manuscript into a screenplay and a film. It wouldn't be fair of me to let you even consider the possibility without making you aware that there are very real risks for you and Rebecca."

"We're not completely guileless, Jay."

"Oh my goodness! I would never suggest that you were. It's just that you are as high profile as it gets, and you have reputations and careers to consider."

"Fair enough. We'd go into any venture with our eyes wide open." A large gaggle of women and men in business suits bustled by them and Dara waited for them to pass. "So, would you entertain the idea of going directly to film and bypassing the publication process?"

Jay cocked her head to one side and narrowed her eyes in thought. "I'd be interested to hear what you had in mind and how you thought it could work. On the one hand, I hate to let the bastards win and keep the book I worked so hard to create from being released. On the other hand, I'm kind of excited by the possibility of bringing the message to the big screen."

"I wouldn't look at it as a victory for the bullies," Dara said. "After all, you'd have the last word."

"Maybe," Jay agreed, "but they won't go away without a fight. I can guarantee you that."

"We'll be ready."

"I don't know the ins and outs of the movie business," Jay said. "You don't know the inner workings of the publishing business..."

Dara closed her eyes momentarily as a wave of guilt washed over her. *I know it better than you'd think, Jay.* If Jay was going to trust her with her work, shouldn't Dara have an equal amount of faith in Jay? Belatedly, she realized she'd missed what Jay was saying. "I'm sorry. What?"

Jay regarded her quizzically. "Where did you go just now?"

"Why would you ask?"

"You had the oddest expression on your face."

So much for being a great actress. "First, tell me what you said that I missed." Dara knew she was stalling for time. Surely her secret would be safe with Jay. And yet... And yet, apart from Rebecca and Carolyn, not another soul alive knew, and she'd always intended to keep it that way.

"I said that if the movie industry functions anything like the publishing business, you can't be sure your backers won't turn tail and run too."

Dara smoothed an imaginary crease in her jeans. "Well, here's the thing about that. I would handpick the investors so that we would maintain maximum control over every aspect of the project." She stopped fidgeting with the denim, squared her shoulders, and turned so that she and Jay were face to face. "But before we get into the nitty-gritty of that, I feel like there's something I should tell you."

"Okay. Does this have anything to do with wherever your mind just wandered to?"

"It does." Dara blew out an explosive breath. Once she shared this, she could never take it back.

"Listen." Jay momentarily covered Dara's hand. "You don't have to tell me anything that makes you uncomfortable. And whatever this is, I can see that it clearly makes you uneasy."

Dara closed her eyes briefly again and took in a lungful of air. "No. You're about to share something incredibly personal with me—a manuscript and story that is so close to your heart, that contains your truth. That means you deserve to know exactly to whom you're entrusting such a vital piece of yourself."

Dara cleared her throat. "The fact of the matter is, I know more about the publishing business than you would likely think."

"You do?"

Dara nodded. "I do." She bit her lower lip. *Out with it, Thomas.* "Do you remember when you asked me at the premiere if Constance Darrow would be attending?"

116

"Of course." Jay pulled her legs back underneath her. "That's it! You're a personal friend of hers. I should have known—"

Dara burst out laughing, which stopped Jay in mid-sentence.

"Why are you laughing?"

"We're not exactly close personal friends, although, technically, if you think about it, maybe we are."

Jay scratched her head. "What am I missing here?"

"It's safe to say that I'm intimately familiar with Constance, since she's me and I'm her." Dara said it all in a rush, as if doing so would make the revelation less significant.

"You're…" Jay's jaw worked, but no more words were forthcoming.

"I am Constance Darrow, the author." Dara swallowed hard. "The only people in the world who know that are Rebecca and my agent Carolyn, whom you met."

Jay blinked several times. "I'm sorry. I'm still wrapping my brain around this."

Dara smiled wanly. "I know, right? I mean, who suspects a Hollywood actress of being able to put together an erudite thought?"

"It isn't that," Jay said. "You're so obviously an intelligent, articulate woman. It's that you're my literary idol."

The words were said with such reverence and wonder that Dara blushed.

"I'm sorry. I just gushed there, didn't I? I mean, I imagine you get that kind of reaction as an actress all the time, but honestly? I'm in awe of your mind."

The comment surprised a chuckle out of Dara. "You know? Of all the reactions I hoped you'd have, and trust me, I hadn't planned to share that information with you today, that reaction was about as perfect as it gets."

Jay covered her mouth with a hand. "I can't believe it. I'm friends with Constance Darrow."

"You're a geek." Dara playfully nudged Jay's shoulder. "I should have known."

"I am a geek, and I proudly own the title."

Dara's shoulders and back relaxed as a wave of relief flowed through her. "I created Constance as a counterpoint to all the objectification. I needed an outlet where I could be my most authentic self—where what people thought of me had nothing to do with my outward appearance."

Jay nodded. "I can understand that. That's why no one's ever seen a picture of Constance. And why she never makes personal appearances. Anybody with a pulse would know who you are."

"I don't know about that…"

"Don't be modest. You're probably the most recognizable face in Hollywood right now."

Dara fidgeted.

"I'm sorry. I probably shouldn't have said that, but it's true. With Constance, you have the luxury of anonymity. People have to judge you only based on your work. That's brilliant."

"Thank you." Dara watched bemused as a series of questions raced across Jay's countenance. "Go ahead. You can ask me anything."

"How weird is it playing characters you created? I mean, if the director doesn't know that you understand the character better than he or she does, that must be hard."

Dara leaned back against the marble backrest. "It has its moments."

"Well, at least you get to collaborate on the script, since Rebecca's the one writing it. You do, right? Get to have a say?"

Dara reflected back to that first night working with Rebecca…

"Boy, that sure looked like a happy memory," Jay said, breaking her reverie.

Dara shook her head to clear it. "With *On the Wings of Angels*, the original script was written by a guy who couldn't find the motivations or nuances of the characters and the story with both hands."

"That's horrible."

"It really, really was. And then a miraculous thing happened—the producers brought in a script doctor to fix it. Since Constance Darrow was unreachable and had a clause in her contract that she would not appear on set, they picked the next best thing—the world's preeminent Constance Darrow scholar—to interpret the work." Dara smiled at the recollection. "That was Rebecca."

"That's how you met, am I right?"

"Not exactly. We'd met once before, outside the David Letterman show after I'd made an appearance there. Rebecca had been corresponding with Constance for a while. Unfortunately, Dave asked Dara Thomas a question, and I used some of the same language in my response that Constance had used in a letter to Rebecca. She called me out on it and I freaked out."

"Oh, no."

"Not my finest moment. I was sure she would give my secret away."

"What did you do?"

"I ran. And I never would've looked back, except that the producers unwittingly put Rebecca back in my orbit."

"Awkward," Jay sang.

"You can say that again."

"I take it she didn't let the cat out of the proverbial bag."

"No, she never did." Dara said. "But I'd had the reaction I did, and she was quite worried that I wouldn't want to work with her. So she ferreted out Carolyn and asked her what she thought before accepting the assignment."

"That showed resourcefulness."

"It did. I was impressed. After I stopped being pissed about it." Dara laughed self-deprecatingly.

"I love a good love story. When was the moment you knew?"

"That I was in love with Rebecca?"

"Yes."

Dara allowed herself to get lost in the memory. "I fell in love with her during our correspondence, before I ever met her in person. But I think the second I knew for certain that she was my forever girl was the first line, the first scene she fixed in the script for that movie. She understood what needed to be conveyed even better than I did."

Jay heaved a happy sigh.

"So you see," Dara slapped her hands on her thighs, "I don't collaborate on the scripts. I'd only muck it up."

"That's beautiful."

A large crowd of state workers exited the closest building and Jay checked her watch. "Damn. It's just about lunch time." She stood up. "Before we get mobbed when people recognize who you are, why don't we go grab some lunch and we can finish the discussion over a meal?"

"That works for me." Dara stood up as well.

"If you'd be okay with it, I thought the most private place we could go for lunch would be our house."

"That sounds fantastic. I'd love to see your home."

"Is it okay with you if Kate joins us? I'd like her input on this."

Dara smiled, her concerns about the state of Kate and Jay's relationship allayed. "I would welcome her participation, if that's what you want."

"It is. We're a team."

"You're a great team," Dara agreed.

They walked in companionable silence toward where the car was parked. "Dara?"

"Hmm?"

"Would it be okay to share your secret with Kate? She's the most trustworthy person I know. I mean, she kept the President's secrets. I just hate to keep something from her."

"I don't expect you to keep Kate in the dark. By all means, tell her. Or I will."

"Something that good? Oh, no. I get to tell her. That way I can go all fan-girl in private and not make you uncomfortable."

"Good plan." Dara squeezed Jay's shoulder one last time and then let go. "I'm famished. What's for lunch?"

CHAPTER ELEVEN

Kate was off showing Dara around the house while Jay changed into a pair of jeans and a designer t-shirt. She needed these few minutes alone. Dara was Constance Darrow. Dara-freaking-Thomas was Constance Darrow! Jay said it again in her head. Maybe if she said it a hundred more times it would become real for her.

She zipped her jeans and ran her fingers through her hair one last time. Dara-freaking-Thomas was Constance Darrow, and she wanted to turn Jay's manuscript into a movie. *Let's not get ahead of ourselves. She wants to explore the possibility. That's not the same as a contract offer.*

"Jay? Are you ready yet? Lunch is served and Dara and I are starving."

"Be right there." Jay slipped on a pair of sandals and headed for the kitchen. Kate and Dara were seated at the kitchen island with plates of grilled chicken salad and bowls of soup in front of them.

"You have a gorgeous place. I'm in love with your library," Dara said.

Jay walked up behind Kate and put her hands on her shoulders. "Thank you. Did Kate tell you that she designed the house and every room in it?"

"She neglected to mention that." Dara wagged a finger at Kate. "You held out on me."

"You didn't ask, and it hardly seemed germane."

"She's too modest," Jay said.

"Hardly." Kate reached back and covered one of Jay's hands with her own. "I didn't pour your soup because I didn't want it to get cold."

"That's okay. I've got it." Jay squeezed Kate's shoulders and released her. She walked over to the pot on the stove and ladled herself a bowlful of the homemade tomato bisque she'd whipped up earlier that morning. To Dara she said, "I hope you don't mind soup and salad."

"It's perfect. I love tomato bisque." Dara blew on a spoonful of the soup and tasted it. "Yum. This is some of the best I've ever had. Where did you get it?"

"Jay made it," Kate said. "I married her for her culinary skills, since I can't cook."

"That's not true. You make a mean French toast." Jay leaned over and kissed Kate on the cheek.

"Breakfast is the most important meal of the day," Dara said. She took another spoonful of soup.

"What happens now?" Jay asked.

Dara swallowed. "With my proposal?"

Jay nodded.

"First, we talk about the manuscript. Can you tell me a little bit about it?"

"How about if I give you a copy to read?"

"I was really hoping you'd offer that. I promise that Rebecca and I will be the only ones to look at it for now."

"I trust you." Jay got down off her stool. "Excuse me for a second." She walked into the library, picked up the bound copy of the manuscript she'd put together after her discussion with Kate, and returned with it to the kitchen. "Here you go."

Dara reverently touched the title page on top. "I'm honored that you trust me with this."

"I'm honored that you want to have a look at it." She smiled broadly. Constance Darrow was going to read her manuscript. "By the way, I don't know what you're thinking in terms of casting, but the role of the main protagonist calls for a thirty-something actress with enough gravitas to play an accomplished, smart reporter. Do you know anybody like that?"

Dara fixed Jay with a knowing smirk. "I might. I'll have to check her availability, though. She's tough to get."

"I heard that about her."

Dara set the manuscript aside. "I'd hate to spill on this."

"I'm pretty sure I know where you could get another copy." Jay took a bite of salad. "Do you need a second copy for Rebecca?"

"We'll play nice and share." Dara winked.

"Assuming you like what you read, and what's not to like," Kate smiled at Jay, "what's the next step?"

"First, I'm certain I'll love the book—"

"You should know it hasn't yet gone through the editing process." Jay bit her lip.

"I'm sure it's in excellent shape, Jay. As I said when we met, I'm a big fan. And I know enough about your writing to know that what I've loved about your style isn't editorial—it's your talent and gift for storytelling."

Jay felt the heat in her cheeks. "You're very kind."

Dara ate the last bite of her salad. "I'm very honest." She patted her stomach. "And very full. Lunch was great. Thank you." She wiped her mouth with her napkin. "As for what comes after we read the manuscript, we'd sit down and talk about your vision for the movie and our take on it, and then talk about who we'd like to bring in to work on it. First, we'd need a script, and then we'd have to take a hard look at financing. Without money, no movie sees the light of day."

"I worry that might be an insurmountable obstacle," Jay said. "If the IRS and FBI put pressure on the publishing industry to leave this alone, imagine that magnified times ten if they get wind that we're trying to bring it to the big screen."

Dara waved a hand. "Don't underestimate me. I'm not easily intimidated, and I know lots of people just like me who'd jump at the chance to be part of this project."

Although Jay was somewhat more skeptical about how easily this might go, she badly wanted to believe that Dara was right. She needed something, anything positive, to come out of this morass.

⊷⊶

Sabastien's eyes were glazing over. He had looked at so much code that the sequences were beginning to blur together. He grabbed the bottle of Visine, tipped his head back, and squirted three drops in each eye. "C'est fou. This is crazy. It is like looking for a pin in a stack of hay."

As he stood up to stretch, one of the three computers on which he was running an algorithm, beeped. Sabastien sat back down so quickly the chair nearly rolled out from under him. He scrolled first up, and then down, and then up and down again. "Mon Dieu."

He ran a screen capture, plugged in a USB drive, and saved the search he'd executed on the drive. "I have you now, you little bastard."

He punched keys on the keyboards connected to the other two computers to cancel the searches presently in progress, initiated another custom program on each, and typed in a name: John Robie. In seconds, a series of alarms blared and a list appeared on the screen on the far right.

Sabastien nodded and dialed a phone number.

"Elliott."

"I have something."

"I'm listening."

"I know what name our hacker friend has used in the past. It is John Robie."

"John Robie?"

"Yes. I am puzzled by this, though."

"Why?"

"Because I know of no hacker who has ever used a real name. It is always a handle."

There was silence on the line.

"Vaughn Elliott? Are you still there?"

"I am. John Robie *is* a handle."

"I do not understand."

"That's because you're not a fan of old films. John Robie is the name of Cary Grant's character in the classic Hitchcock film, *To Catch a Thief*. The movie co-starred Grace Kelly. It was the last film she made for Hitchcock."

"You are a fan of old-time movies? There is something I did not know about you."

"You can't know everything."

"I have saved the search and will send it to you and to Peter."

"Make sure you translate it into English first."

Sabastien furrowed his brow. "Of course it will be in English. Your French is not that good."

Vaughn laughed, surprising Sabastien yet again. "You know how to laugh?"

When Vaughn's laughter subsided, she said, "What I meant was, explain what we're looking at in terms we can understand, not in geek-speak."

Sabastien blushed. "Oh. I see it now."

"I get it now."

"Quoi?"

"The correct expression is, 'I get it now.'"

"Yes. That." Sabastien opened a new document. "I will put this in a form even you can understand and have it to you within the hour."

"Was that a joke you just made? Because that sounded suspiciously like intentional humor."

"It was."

"Don't do it again."

"Vaughn Elliott? What is wrong with you? You are far too happy to be you."

"Don't get too used to it."

The line went dead and Sabastien held the phone out. "Goodbye to you too." He clicked on the blinking cursor and began to type.

He'd just finished and hit Send on the encrypted e-mail to Vaughn and Peter when he noticed an anomaly on the computer on which he'd revealed the hacker's identity.

"Merde! C'est ne pas possible." His eyes grew wide and his palms started to sweat. He yanked the plug on all three computers, disconnected the laptops from their monitors, hastily loaded them, along with peripherals, into a custom-built briefcase, and ran into the bedroom to pack.

Within ten minutes, he was in a car and racing down a dirt road, gravel and dust flying behind him. He keyed the Bluetooth built into his Audi. "Appel Vaughn Elliott."

When Vaughn picked up the phone on the second ring, Sabastien said one word: "Mayday."

The burner phone on his desk vibrated, and Peter snatched it up. Without even saying hello, he asked, "What's going on?"

"The Frog is in trouble and on the move."

Peter sat up straighter. "What happened?"

"Check your e-mail. You should have an encrypted folder. He called to tell me he ID'ed the Black Knight, or at least the moniker he uses in the hacker world. Fifteen minutes later he sent us the details. Less than five minutes after that, I received his SOS from a phone he and I only use in case of extreme emergencies."

"Do we need to extract him, wherever he is?"

"He didn't say. But the reason we save this phone for occasions such as this is that I have a tracker device on it. I know where he is now. I'm watching his progress."

"What's our play?"

"Digest the report he sent us, then work as fast as we can to put a real name to this asswipe and take it from there."

"And the Frog?"

"I suspect he already had another location ready in case of this eventuality. I'll continue to monitor him from here."

Peter opened his e-mail program and scanned for an e-mail from Sabastien. "I've got the folder. Lorraine and I will have a look right now."

"I'll keep you posted from this end. Let's touch base in a few hours."

The phone went dead and Peter shoved it aside. He downloaded the attachment from Sabastien's e-mail and unpacked it onto a secure external hard drive.

Lorraine, who had been sitting at her own desk across the room, came to look over his shoulder. "Sabastien's in trouble?"

"Looks like whoever he unearthed has a bead on his whereabouts. He's on the move now."

Peter opened the folder and clicked on a Microsoft Word document succinctly titled, "Summary."

> Here is what I have uncovered so far. John Robie apparently specialized in stealing classified data from governments and major corporations around the world. He then leveraged the information to extort large sums of cash. In every case,

```
it seems the ransom was paid in order to
keep    the   stolen   information   off   the
market.
     Although many tried to catch him, none
ever did. The last theft for this John
Robie took place in January of this year.
After    that,   he   disappeared   off   the
hacking scene completely without a trace.
     How do I know all this? I have included
in this folder all of the hacks in which
he used the same technique, line for line
in the code. Also, he kept a sort of
diary of the heists. He is very arrogant,
thinking no one can access it. But I did.
```

At the same time, Peter and Lorraine said, "That's probably what tripped an alarm."

Peter opened the remainder of the files, which consisted of seemingly endless lines of code. Here was Sabastien's proof. Peter pushed his chair back and swiveled around to face his wife.

"What do you think?" Lorraine asked.

"I think Sabastien's information is rock solid. What I find most interesting in all this is that John Robie fell off the face of the Earth in January."

Lorraine nodded. "Suspiciously close to the time when the Hyland data was leaked."

"Exactly. My guess would be that this guy, whoever he is, was hired by someone to do this job off the books in an exclusive contract that was too good for him to pass up."

"But, according to Sabastien, the hacker had been watching him for a long period of time, surely longer than the two months between the time John Robie disappeared and the time the Black Knight showed up."

Peter steepled his fingers. "You were on the inside. If John Robie was hired by the Commission to take on this assignment, how would it have gone down?"

Lorraine sat down and stared blankly out the window. Over time, Peter had come to recognize this as Lorraine's way of sifting through seemingly disparate pieces of information and compiling them into a scenario that made sense.

Several moments later, she said, "The Commission would have done a significant amount of homework on John Robie. If I had to guess, I'd say one or more high-value Commission members in corporate tycoon positions were past victims of Robie's entrepreneurial enterprises."

"That makes sense."

"But, as Sabastien pointed out, this guy is arrogant as hell, and no doubt greedy. He probably couldn't resist keeping his hand in play as John Robie while this long-term, probably tedious-to-him, assignment dragged on. If the Commission twigged onto Robie working free-lance on the side, they would not be pleased. You know money is no object for them and I'm sure this guy commanded a hefty price to work 'exclusively' for the Commission, which they would have required."

"So they would've stepped in and told him to shut it down, or else."

"Mm-hmm." Lorraine nodded. She chuckled.

"What's so funny?"

"Imagine if Robie stupidly and ignorantly picked as a free-lance target another member of the Commission. I can hear the ass-chewing he would've gotten from here."

"Ah. Got you." Peter swiveled back around and closed the open documents. "For argument's sake, let's assume it is the Commission behind the Hyland leak."

"I'd be shocked if that weren't the case."

"Me too." Peter faced Lorraine again. "Where would they be keeping this guy? Would they require him to be physically present at one of their black sites, as you were?"

Lorraine got up and began to pace. "I don't know. That was a long, long time ago. Technology has changed, and the major players in the Commission have likely changed too, especially with Grayson's death. I suspect their strategies might have shifted with the times."

"All true. But if you're right about how and why John Robie was still active long after the time he should have gone dark, my guess would be that the Commission wouldn't trust him. Heck, I wouldn't trust him."

"I see where you're going with this. They would've pulled him in to keep an eye on him. They'd be babysitting him."

"Bingo."

"Now if only we could figure out who in the modern-day version of the Commission would be in charge of an op like this, we might be able to narrow down his location."

Peter re-opened Sabastien's summary document and scanned it again. "It's too bad our boy didn't give us a list of governments and corporations hacked by Robie in the summary."

"If he had, we could cross-reference those companies and governments with the other information Sabastien culled and try to find a match."

"Potentially."

"Do you think Sabastien's safe? What did Vaughn say?"

"Just that Sabastien had activated an emergency protocol the two of them used and that she had a tracker locked onto him. She figured Sabastien had a backup safe house set up and that he was headed there."

"Is she going after him to protect him?"

"Not yet. She seemed content to sit tight and wait for a bit."

Lorraine stopped in her tracks and put her hands on her hips. "Sabastien's not trained to evade a tail. He doesn't have any fire power with him. He doesn't even know how to use a weapon. She's willing to leave him out there like a sitting duck?"

Peter held a hand up, palm out. "Easy, sweetheart. Remember that Vaughn knows Sabastien a lot better than we do. They've been on countless ops together. I'm sure Vaughn is well aware of Sabastien's capabilities and his weaknesses. If she thought he couldn't handle it, she'd be on a plane by now."

Vaughn settled into her seat and buckled the safety belt. The tracker on Sabastien's cell phone had last pinged him in Gibraltar. Then it had gone dark. Gibraltar was on the southern coast of Spain, but Gibraltar also was a British territory. Britain had an extradition treaty with the United States, and therefore was not a place Sabastien would pick as a destination. Morocco, on the other hand, had no extradition treaty with the United States, and was just a short ferry ride from the southern tip of Spain.

Sabastien really was a genius. She hoped that by the time she landed, she'd have news from him, but that seemed highly unlikely. Sabastien wouldn't have turned the phone off of his own volition unless someone else had hacked into the phone's tracking data. If that wasn't what had happened, it meant that Sabastien hadn't been the one to sever the connection. In either case, he clearly was in trouble.

Vaughn stowed the false passport on which she was traveling in her backpack. She'd been fortunate to catch the last flight out headed for Barcelona. From there, she would make the journey to Casablanca, the largest city in Morocco.

She should probably touch base with Peter. Because of the timing, she'd been unable to send a message securely before racing to the airport.

"Ladies and gentlemen, we'll be closing the cockpit door momentarily and we ask you to turn off all cellular devices."

Vaughn stared down at the phone in her hand. It wasn't encrypted, although she believed it was secure. Still, she was a known associate of Sabastien's. If someone was on the hunt for Sabastien and hadn't yet found him, Vaughn was a likely starting point to troll for clues as to his whereabouts.

Vaughn powered down the phone and stowed it in her pocket. When the plane landed in Spain, she'd have to find a secure connection to fill Peter in. In the meantime, she should get some rest. It might be a long time before she got another chance to sleep.

CHAPTER TWELVE

The streets of Casablanca were noisy and dusty. Sabastien checked the rearview mirror yet again. The two men who had been following him were nowhere in sight. In fact, he hadn't seen them since he'd left Gibraltar.

Grudgingly, he had to admit that all of the time he'd spent working with Vaughn had served him well today. Out of an abundance of caution, he'd booked passage via three different modes of transportation leaving Gibraltar. He settled on the chartered plane paid for with a fraudulent credit card for his escape because it presented the most controlled environment. He would've been too exposed on the ferry or on a commercial flight.

Casablanca was an easy city in which to get lost. Sabastien was grateful he'd kept the goatee. Bearded, and dressed like one of the locals, he blended in seamlessly. He honked the horn at a goat standing in the middle of the street. The goat glanced at him briefly and tossed his head in the air.

"Why do I not get any respect? Not even from a goat. This is the state of my life." He honked the horn again, and finally the goat slowly ambled to the side of the road.

Sabastien stepped on the gas. His tires spun, kicking up dirt and adding to the pollution in the air. At the next opportunity, he turned right. It had been a long time since he'd been here, but not much had changed.

An hour later, deep in the countryside, Sabastien turned off onto an unmarked, overgrown path. He was grateful for the Jeep's four-wheel drive.

A minute later, a house came into view. To all appearances, the place was untouched. Still, Sabastien wasn't about to take any chances. He stopped the car, reached onto the passenger seat, and opened a small case. Inside was a drone the size of a bee. He grabbed a tablet and a wireless joystick from the backpack on the passenger-side floor and clicked on a custom app. Then he opened the car window and let the drone fly.

He maneuvered the joystick and piloted the drone around the perimeter of the house. The video feed on the tablet was crystal clear. All the windows and doors appeared to be secure, and the drone did not pick up any heat signatures. Satisfied that his hideaway was as secure as it could be, Sabastien recalled the drone, packed everything away, and drove the rest of the way up the drive.

It was at moments like this that Sabastien was most appreciative of his inheritance and his paranoia. In his former incarnation, before Vaughn caught him hacking into her CIA operation and "acquired" him as a CIA asset, Sabastien purchased six safe houses around the globe using a dummy corporation. This place was one of them. A caretaker managed the landscaping and upkeep directly around the house, but had no idea to whom the property belonged.

Sabastien grabbed his go-bag and his backpack and headed inside. He had a lot of work to do. Top on the list of priorities was to set up a secure connection and let Vaughn know where he was and what was happening.

∽⌘∾

"Have you heard anything yet?" Jay asked without preamble when Lorraine answered the door to admit her and Kate.

"You two made it in record time."

"It might have been the urgent text saying that the Frog was missing."

"Come in. Peter tried to reach Vaughn with no success."

"Hi, you two."

"Speak of the devil and he appears," Kate said.

"Be nice, or I won't share with you the other piece of news and the reason Sabastien went silent in the first place."

Jay's ears perked up. "You've got more?"

"You know that Vaughn and I suspected that the Black Knight might have been a pseudonym for a hacker who'd previously been active under another moniker?"

"Oddly enough, I followed that," Jay said.

"Good, because Sabastien thinks he's figured out the hacker's original handle."

Peter led the way into the living room where Jay took a seat next to Kate at the end of the very comfortable leather sofa. Peter and Lorraine sat down opposite them in matching leather chairs.

"Do you have a real name for the Black Knight or just another pseudonym?" Kate asked.

Peter shook his head. "What we have is a long history of hacking governments and major corporations by a guy whose code work is identical to the Black Knight's. It's the technological equivalent of a perfect match of DNA markers in the blood. We're certain this is our man."

"Or woman," Jay said. "We can't discount that it could be a woman, can we?"

"No, but the profiler friend I contacted this afternoon strongly believes that this is a man," Lorraine offered.

"You brought in an outside profiler?" Jay's eyebrows rose into her hairline. "I thought we were trying to contain this situation—to involve as few people as possible."

Kate put a restraining hand on Jay's leg. "I'm sure this is someone Lorraine trusts with her life."

"I do and I have," Lorraine agreed. She sat forward and clasped her hands between her knees. "When I was deep under cover with the Commission, I needed to know who I was dealing with. My understanding of their psyche meant the difference between being accepted and being detected. Literally, it meant the difference between life and death. Matt was my lifeline. He was the profiler assigned to assess my Commission contacts and help me navigate their personalities, to know which buttons to push, and which to avoid."

Jay was disappointed in herself. She should've known better than to doubt Lorraine. "I'm sorry. I didn't mean to question your judgment. I know you wouldn't read anyone into the situation who wasn't ironclad on our side."

"It's okay, Jay. You're under a lot of pressure. I don't blame you a bit for being protective."

"So, before we got sidetracked," Kate said, "you were about to tell us your profiler's assessment of the Black Knight."

"The summary Sabastien provided didn't include a specific list of corporations and governments that the Black Knight targeted in his earlier incarnation as John Robie—"

"The hacker used as his alias an old movie protagonist? Who does that?" Jay asked.

"The good news is, our guy does," Peter said. "That gives us valuable information about what kind of person we're dealing with."

"It does," Lorraine agreed. "It would've been helpful if we had a list of specific targets, since that might speak to his motivation. It also would give us a way to cross-reference the entities he hacked with any known Commission members or associates. But the fact that the Black Knight has an affinity for classic movies and what he perceives as persecuted characters tells us a lot."

"He's likely someone who felt misunderstood as a child, someone who perceives himself as a sort of modern day Robin Hood or vigilante, righting the wrongs of the oppressed, exposing those who prey upon the downtrodden," Peter said.

"That would make him appealing to the Commission. I'm sure they'd fill his head with all the ways they were fighting against the establishment, creating a new world order," Kate said.

All four of them jumped as Peter's cell phone rang. He snatched it up. "Yes." He listened for a moment. "You're sure?" He nodded. "Okay." Peter grabbed a pen and a piece of paper. "Go ahead…" He scribbled on a blank page. "Uh-huh… Roger that." He listened for another few seconds. "Understood. Call me back when you can." Peter disconnected the call.

"Well?" Jay asked.

"Sabastien is safe for the moment. He lost a tail in Gibraltar and was able to get enough separation to reach his destination."

"Which was…" Kate asked.

"Vaughn didn't want to risk divulging that, even on a presumably secure line. She did say that she had eyes on Sabastien and that, at least for the moment, they were staying put. She's working on enhancing their security and will get back to me when she's satisfied that they are as protected as they can be. After that, we can work on ferreting out the Black Knight's real identity."

"What did you write down?" Jay asked.

"A set of coordinates for an equipment drop to give Vaughn and Sabastien some much-needed resources."

"But I thought you said you didn't know their location."

"I don't. This is a dead drop."

"What else can we do?" Kate asked.

"Nothing for now," Peter answered. "I'll secure them what they need and get it delivered to the designated location at the designated time."

"On another topic... Jay?" Lorraine asked. "How'd your meeting with Dara go? Want to tell us what's going on?"

✧✧

"Ma'am? Ma'am? I'm going to need you to put your seatback up and raise your tray table. Ma'am? Ms. Thomas?"

Dara's head jerked up. "I'm sorry? What?" The beleaguered flight attendant was standing over her, exasperation written all over her face.

"Your seatback and tray table need to be in the upright and locked position. We're preparing for landing."

"Oh, gosh. I'm so sorry." Dara pushed the button to raise her seat and secured the tray table. "I was so engrossed in what I was reading I didn't...hear you." By the time she finished her apology, the woman already had moved on.

Dara checked to see how many pages were left in the chapter she was reading. She tried to calculate whether she could finish it before the plane touched down.

When she felt the jolt of the wheels hitting the tarmac, she still had two pages to go. Part of her wanted to rush through and finish the chapter, but the bigger part of her preferred to savor the words on the page. She flipped the book closed and powered up her cell phone.

Rebecca answered the call on the first ring. "Hi."

"Hi, darling. I'm on the ground. Are you here?"

"Waiting for you in the cell phone lot. See you soon."

"I can't wait. I missed you."

"I missed you too."

"Bye."

"Bye."

Dara disconnected the call as the plane reached the gate, unbuckled her seatbelt, and grabbed her carry-on bag from the overhead compartment.

Ten minutes later she was standing on the curb when Rebecca pulled up.

"Hi." Dara folded herself into the passenger seat and leaned in for a long, lingering kiss. She closed her eyes. This, this was home. Home wasn't a place; it was a person. She marveled, as she always did, at the miracle of love, something Dara never thought she'd have.

"Hi, yourself." Rebecca smiled against Dara's mouth. "Now that's a greeting."

Dara sat back and buckled her seatbelt. "I love you. You're my heartbeat."

"And you're mine." Rebecca checked over her shoulder and pulled away from the curb.

When they were halfway home, Rebecca asked, "So?"

"It's incredible. The language is evocative, the plot is a page-turner, and the characters are three-dimensional. It's all that and a box of chocolates. Wait until you read it. I think it's Jay's best work yet."

"You know that's saying something."

"It is. This work is so different from anything she's written before. It's visceral and real enough that you feel as though you're running for your life along with the protagonist."

"How would you classify it? Is it a thriller? A mystery?"

Dara watched the scenery go by and pondered the question. "You know, I'm not sure it's that easy. This one has elements of both genres. It's part who-done-it and part race-against-time-to-save-the-world. It's part Jason Bourne and part *All the President's Men*."

"I can't wait to get a look at it." Rebecca took the exit ramp that led to their Malibu beach house. "Which brings us to the bigger, more relevant question of the moment. How would it translate on the big screen?"

Dara closed her eyes and leaned her head back against the headrest. She hoped she could convey what she saw as the movie running in her head as she read. "Oh, my God. This thing is tailor-made for Hollywood. It's got everything that grips an audience and pulls them in. It's got characters to root for and to fall in love with, it's got characters to boo and hiss at, it's got tension, drama, and angst. It's got more potential than anything like it I've seen in a long time."

The car cruised to a stop and Dara opened her eyes. Rebecca was staring at her, a bemused expression on her face.

"What?"

"I don't know that I've ever seen you this jazzed about something you read."

Dara nodded. "Well, I'm willing to bet you'll agree with me."

"Is there really a role in it for you?" The traffic light turned green and Rebecca proceeded through the intersection.

"The main character is a thirty-something female broadcast journalist—a workaholic White House correspondent who's got a tough-as-nails reputation and a Peabody Award for exposing political corruption in New York State."

"Perfect."

"Perfect."

They pulled into the drive and Rebecca parked the car in the garage. "Are you tired?" She waggled her eyebrows and Dara laughed.

"I'm not technically tired, no. But I could potentially be talked into taking a nap." Dara slid her hand into Rebecca's and she stroked her palm, keeping her touch feather-light. "You game?"

Rebecca swallowed hard and said, "Mm-hmm."

"Care to come inside?"

"Mm-hmm."

"Going to say anything more profound than that?"

"Nu-uh."

"Come on, professor."

Jay stretched languorously in Kate's arms. These moments—after lovemaking, when their hearts beat together as one—these were the moments she treasured the most.

Kate nuzzled her neck. "What are you thinking about?"

Jay pushed up so that they were face to face. "I was thinking how desperately in love with you I am. I was reminding myself never to take this for granted. I was counting my blessings."

Kate kissed Jay's forehead. "That's a lot of thinking."

"That's a lot of love mixed with a good dose of gratitude." Jay snuggled back into Kate's embrace.

"Did you hear anything from Dara today?"

"Oh my God! How in the world did I forget to tell you this?" Jay rolled off of Kate and sat up.

Kate scooted up so that her back was against the headboard, as well. The sheet that had been covering them fell away and pooled at their waists.

"Guess what Dara told me?"

"That she loves your book and can't wait to make it a huge Hollywood hit?"

Jay bumped Kate's shoulder. "No. I haven't heard from her since she left here."

"But you just said…"

"Oh. No. This is something she told me after I picked her up at the train station."

Kate looked at Jay expectantly.

"Aren't you going to guess?"

Kate smiled indulgently. "She's going to star in another Constance Darrow adaptation?"

"Not exactly. But you're warm."

"I give up."

"You give up too easily."

"That's not what you said a little while ago."

Jay blushed. "That's another story for another day, smart girl."

"We'll be here all day if you're waiting for me to figure it out. Tell me."

"Dara is Constance Darrow."

Kate's eyebrows furrowed in puzzlement. "I don't understand."

"Constance Darrow is a pseudonym. The reason no one has ever met her, or even seen a picture of her, is that she is Dara."

138

"Huh."

"That's all you've got to say? 'Huh?' This is huge."

"I agree. I'm still processing."

Jay waited a beat. "Are you done processing yet?"

Kate laughed. "Almost."

Jay bounced up and down. "How about now?"

Kate grabbed her and wrestled her onto her back. "Patience is a virtue."

"That's not what you said a little while ago."

"Good one. Turnabout is fair play." Kate lowered herself and Jay's breath caught at the naked expression of desire in her eyes.

"S-so you're not impressed that Dara is Constance?"

Kate kissed her. "On the contrary, I'm very impressed. But right now I'm more impressed with this beautiful, little, blonde number."

Jay's body rose in supplication as she surrendered again to the only woman who had ever owned her heart. Any more discussion about Dara and Constance would have to wait.

❧❧

"You're right."

"Hmm?"

Rebecca closed the manuscript and placed it on the end table next to her recliner. "I said, you're right. This is fabulous, and stylistically worlds away from anything else Jay's written."

Dara set aside her laptop. "I told you."

"You did. The screenplay could adhere so closely to the manuscript that we wouldn't have to do much to it. It's practically ready-made for the screen."

"I know."

"Who are you thinking for actors?"

Dara cocked her head to the side in thought. "I hadn't gotten that far. I was more focused on finding backers that wouldn't fold under pressure."

"You ought to give consideration to actors that won't succumb to scrutiny either."

"True. But first things first. We need to call Jay and tell her we love the book, then figure out a time when we can get together and collaborate on the screen treatment and the screenplay."

CHAPTER THIRTEEN

J ay was almost through with her workout. She set the weights for her arm curls and bent down to pick up the curl bar. Over the years, they'd updated and upgraded their gym so that now the equipment rivaled that of a professional fitness center.

She turned around and glanced over at Kate, who was into her fifth mile on the treadmill. Sweat dripped liberally from her face, down her neck and into her sports bra. She was completely absorbed in whatever Rachel Maddow was saying.

In the early days, they'd worked out to *Charlie's Angels* and Jaclyn Smith. These days it was Rachel Maddow and the news. What was becoming of them?

Jay, who wasn't in the mood to watch the news, cranked up "Uptown Funk You Up" on her iPod, picked up the bar, and started counting repetitions. *Twenty-one, twenty-two...*

The volume on the television suddenly turned ear-splitting and Rachel Maddow's voice reverberated off the walls. Jay whipped her head around. "What the—"

"The Department of Justice and the Director of the FBI announced today that they are beginning an official investigation into *Time* magazine and reporter Niles Masterson's acquisition of classified data from the Administration of President Charles Hyland."

Jay dropped the curl bar to the mat, ripped the buds out of her ears, and powered off the iPod.

"Sources tell MSNBC News that investigators with the Federal Bureau of Investigation descended on Masterson's apartment with search warrants and removed computers, hard drives, and several

141

boxes of files early this morning. Reached at his *Time* magazine office, Masterson refused to comment. Lawyers for the magazine say they will take their case to Federal District Court and argue that this was an illegal search and seizure.

"So far, *Time* has yet to reveal what, specifically, was leaked to them, nor have they published a story based on the documents in their possession. The plot thickens." Rachel waggled her eyebrows and gathered her papers. "Back in a moment."

Kate muted the television, walked over to Jay, and took her in her arms. "It's going to be okay."

"The Feds are escalating. Before, what they were doing was behind-the-scenes—it was all veiled threats and intimidation. This,"—she pointed at the television screen—"this is legal action."

"It's a fishing expedition," Kate said. She kissed the top of Jay's head. "They want to know what Niles has. They obviously don't know."

"Well, they're going to know soon enough."

"Maybe not." Kate stepped back and sat down on a weight bench. "Didn't you tell me when you got off the phone with Niles that day that he was frantic? And that he already was being pressured by the big guns and threatened with search warrants?"

"Yes."

"If I were Niles, I would've taken precautions. I would've moved anything valuable someplace it wouldn't be found. I wouldn't leave it sitting around in my house on my computer, or anyplace obvious, for that matter."

Jay sat down on the universal machine's seat, facing Kate. "You think he hid everything someplace that couldn't be traced to him?"

"I'm just saying it's entirely possible that the FBI won't find anything useful in the material they carted away."

"Even if that's true, I bet they won't stop there. They'll haul him in and make him tell them what he knows."

"One step at a time, sweetheart." Kate stood up. "For right now, this doesn't have any bearing on what you're doing."

"No? What if the search warrant covered his phone records? He and I had that conversation. The Feds are going to see that."

"He called you, not vice versa. And the conversation lasted less than two minutes."

"It still happened," Jay said.

"If they come knocking, you tell them the truth—that Niles called you and asked you for information, and you refused to provide him with anything."

Jay looked morosely at the cement floor. A stab of fear sent a chill coursing through her bones and she shivered. "What if the FBI comes after the manuscript? What if they compel me to turn it over to them?"

Kate knelt down before Jay and took her hands. "Look at me."

Jay lifted her eyes to make eye contact.

"Your manuscript is a work of fiction. There is nothing classified in the book. Your fictional characters deal with fictional scenarios in a fictional world. Under what grounds could they seize the manuscript?"

"I have no idea. But you and I both know that if the Feds want something to disappear, it generally does."

"The Feds are very good at intimidation, as they've proven already in this case, but we aren't easily bullied. We can ask a lawyer, if you want, but if they had the ability to compel you to produce the novel, they would've done it. They don't want a very public fight in the courts."

Kate stroked the backs of Jay's hands. "Think about it. If you had to testify in court, you'd have to talk about the ways in which your book differs from the classified truth. They can't have that."

"True," Jay grudgingly agreed. She wasn't yet ready to let go of her fear. "But they could haul me in for a closed door session."

Kate rose and pulled Jay up with her. "Sweetheart, I think it far more likely that you'd get the same treatment as Black Quill or Jeremy—the Feds would come and bluster and try to get you to back down. But that's not today. So how about if we grab a shower and have a nice, quiet dinner instead of worrying about something that hasn't happened yet?"

Jay glanced at the curl bar. She really should finish her workout. But she wasn't in the mood anymore, and, as if on cue, her stomach rumbled. "Fair enough."

"Excellent. What are you making me?"

Jay shook her head. "Are you ever going to learn to cook?"

"Why would I want to do that when I have you to do it for me?"

"Good point."

⊱⋆⊰

Sabastien finished sautéing the veal and removed it from the stove. He turned off the flame and arranged the veal on the plates alongside the rice pilaf and steamed green beans. When he looked up, Vaughn was staring at him. "What?"

"In the middle of a crisis, you're busy cooking gourmet meals."

Sabastien shrugged. "I am French. We never miss a good meal. Besides, how do we know when we will get the next one? We do not, so we enjoy now, while we can." He handed Vaughn her dish, carried his own to the table, and sat down.

"Where did you get the fresh ingredients, again?"

"I told you before, Vaughn Elliott. I had the caretaker go to the market and make these purchases before I arrived. He does not ask questions, nor has he ever seen my face. He does not know my name, and he has been in my employ for more than a dozen years. I pay him well for his discretion, and he has never disappointed me."

"Yet."

"Argh. You are such a pessimist. You think we can live on those barbaric rations you had our friend Peter send?"

"They're called MREs. The initials stand for Meals Ready-to-Eat." Vaughn pointed her fork at him. "And if they're good enough for our soldiers, they're good enough for you."

"Is this not so much better?" Sabastien closed his eyes and savored the flavors on his tongue.

Vaughn swallowed a bite of veal. "It's excellent. Enjoy it now, because you're done contacting that caretaker until all of this is resolved."

"You are such a kill switch."

"Kill joy."

"Quoi?"

"The expression is 'You're such a kill joy,' not a 'kill switch.' That's something else entirely." Vaughn took a sip of iced tea. "Peter needs the list of companies John Robie hacked. He wants to cross-reference those with known Commission members."

"I will do that as soon as I am absolutely certain that my e-mail communications are absolutely secure. I do not want to risk the Black Knight learning any more of what I know. And I do not want to expose Peter or you."

"How long do you think it will be until you can transmit again?"

"That depends."

"On?"

"On how successful we are at creating a diversion."

⤚⤙

By the time Jay's plane landed at LAX, she was three hours late.

Rebecca picked up the phone on the second ring. "Hello?"

"Hi. It's Jay. I'm finally here. I'm so sorry. My flight got diverted because of a nasty thunderstorm in Chicago."

"Unless you were in the cockpit or have some superpower that allows you to control the weather, I'm pretty sure it wasn't your fault. Do you have a checked bag?"

"I do. I couldn't decide on what I was going to need for this trip, so I brought a little bit of everything."

"Okay. I'll swing by and pick you up outside of baggage claim in about thirty minutes. Trust me, it will take you that long to get your bag. I'm driving a red Mercedes."

"See you then." Jay disconnected the call and speed-dialed Kate. "I'm on the ground."

"Are you still in the airport?"

"On my way to get my bag and then meet Rebecca."

"Are you sure about staying at their place?"

"I offered five times to stay at a hotel. They wouldn't have it. They said it would be far more convenient to collaborate if I were staying with them."

"Jamison Parker, collaborating with Writers Guild Award-winning screenwriter Rebecca Minton Thomas on a treatment and screenplay of her latest novel. I like the sound of that."

"I'm still pinching myself. I can't believe this is real."

"Believe it. I'm so proud of you."

"Thanks. Kate? They really liked it."

"Of course they did. It's brilliant."

"You're biased."

"I'm honest. Now go write a gripping screenplay."

"I love you."

"I love you too."

"Are you sure you didn't want to come?"

"What? And sit around watching you work? No thanks. I've got plenty to keep me busy here."

"Okay. I'll check in with you later."

"Don't worry about me."

"It's in my job description to worry about you. It comes under the heading, 'Other duties as assigned.'"

Kate laughed on the other end of the line.

"My bag's here."

"Goodbye, sweetheart. Say hello to Dara and Rebecca for me."

"I will. Bye." Jay disconnected the call and grabbed her bag off the carousel. It didn't take her long to spot Rebecca's car—it wasn't just red, it was fire engine red. She waved so that Rebecca would see her.

"Sweet ride," Jay said, after she gave Rebecca a hug.

"Dara said you had a thing for mid-life crisis cars. This is as close as we have to one of those."

"Very funny. I said *Kate* had a thing for mid-life crisis cars, not me. And why would you two need one of those, anyway? It's not like you're even close to middle age."

"It's LA. A status car is de rigueur."

"Of course it is."

Rebecca checked over her shoulder and pulled out into traffic. "Actually, neither one of us gives a rat's how-do-you-do about keeping up appearances. The truth is, I have a thing for red, and this was the only car on the lot that caught my eye."

"Ah. So the truth comes out."

"It always does," Rebecca agreed. "Speaking about truth, I don't know how closely your manuscript adheres to the facts of the events of the Hyland incident, but if even a third of it bears a resemblance to reality, I can't imagine living through that."

Jay felt the familiar tightening in her chest. "We almost didn't."

Rebecca glanced over at her. "I'm sorry. I didn't mean—"

"It's okay." Jay smiled wanly. "I knew what you meant. The plot is loosely based on the facts. Close enough to convey the point I wanted to make, but unique and original enough to preserve state secrets and security protocols."

"Did I mention how much I love the book?"

Jay laughed. "You might have said it a time or two when we talked the other day."

"Did Dara mention how much she loved the book?"

"She might have mentioned it a time or two as well. I'm definitely feeling the love."

"We're so honored that you would consider letting us adapt this with you."

"Are you kidding me? I'm the one who's honored. This is surreal to me."

"Been there, done that," Rebecca said as she changed lanes to get off the freeway. "Script doctoring *On the Wings of Angels* was an out-of-body experience for me."

"Speaking of surreal..." Jay knew she probably shouldn't bring it up, but this might be her only opportunity alone with Rebecca.

"Hmm?"

"I'm sure you're aware that Dara told me about Constance."

Rebecca smiled broadly. "I am. Can I just say how glad I am she did that? Now I have someone else who shares the secret. You can't imagine how hard it is for me not to shout to the rooftops that I'm married to Constance Darrow."

"I bet. How did you keep a straight face when I was gushing at the movie premiere?"

Rebecca chuckled. "I so wanted to tell you. I almost gave it away at least three times. If Dara hadn't warned me off with a look, I'm sure I would've spilled the beans."

"You must be so proud of her."

"She's amazing." Rebecca's smile lit up her face. "And I'm not saying that just because she's my wife either. I was a Constance Darrow groupie long before I knew who she was. Did Dara tell you how I figured it out?"

"She said it was an expression she used in an interview on David Letterman's show when you were in the audience."

Rebecca nodded. "I couldn't believe it was her. So I waited for her outside the stage door after the show and told her very discreetly that I'd figured it out. She bolted so fast it made my head spin."

Jay noted the pained expression as it flitted across Rebecca's features. "I'm sorry. I didn't mean to bring up a difficult memory."

"The story has a happy ending, as you know."

"As all good romances should," Jay said.

"We're here."

Jay blinked. She wasn't sure what she'd envisioned, but this glorious, sleek, modern, single-level structure took her breath away. "This is incredible. This is a beach house?"

Rebecca smiled. "Wait until you see the living room. It's got floor-to-ceiling glass that opens onto a deck and looks out over the ocean. We have our own private beach."

Jay grabbed her suitcase out of the back seat and followed Rebecca inside.

"We're home!"

"Hi." Dara came around the corner and greeted them. She was dressed in a pair of khaki shorts that accentuated her long legs and a crew neck t-shirt. "Welcome, Jay. I'm so glad you're here." She gave Jay a warm hug as Jay set the suitcase upright on its wheels.

"This place is amazing." Jay spun around to take in the state-of-the-art kitchen, the post-and-beam construction in the living room, and the afore-mentioned glass wall with the sliding glass doors in the center.

"Thanks. I kind of like it, myself." Dara grasped the handle of Jay's roller bag. "Come on. I'll show you your room. It's right down here."

As they walked down the hallway, Jay noted the artwork on the walls. "I love the beauty of these landscapes—they're breathtaking." Her heart rate accelerated and her knees buckled when they came even with a three foot by four foot framed photograph displaying the distinctive grandeur of the mesas in Chinle, Arizona. She reached out and put a hand on the wall for support. *Let it go. You're safe now.*

"Jay?" Dara's brow was furrowed in concern. "Are you okay?"

Jay regained her balance and shook her head to clear it. "I-I'm fine. That's gorgeous." She pointed at the picture.

Dara continued to stare at her dubiously. "It was a gift from my dear friend, Renée Maupin."

Jay raised an eyebrow. "I know her work. She's a friend of yours?"

"We grew up together." Dara cocked her head to the side. "Are you sure you're okay?"

"Sure." Jay realized she sounded less than convincing. Should she explain? Could she, without going into excruciating detail?

"Do you need to sit down?"

"No. Really, I'll be fine. It's just... That picture is Chinle."

"You know it?"

Jay nodded. "I spent a few months there in the late 1980s. It's complicated."

"I take it that wasn't a pleasant experience."

"Some very bad men tried to kill me there. They ran me off one of those mesas." Jay gestured to the photograph. "It took me months to recuperate."

This time it was Dara who looked shell-shocked. "I don't know what to say. I'm so sorry that happened to you."

"It was a long time ago." Jay shrugged, as if doing so would somehow slough off the memories. "It's okay. Let's keep going."

"Your room is right down here." Dara resumed walking and turned right into an airy, open bedroom that featured another glorious view of the ocean. She rolled the suitcase over to the closet.

"Wow. I'm running out of superlatives for this place," Jay said.

Dara moved into the middle of the room, her eyes filled with concern. "Why would someone want to do you harm?"

Jay sighed.

"You don't have to tell me if you don't want to. I can see this is very painful for you."

"No. It's okay. There's just no easy way to explain the circumstances. I could write a book about it and no one would believe me." Jay stuffed her hands in her pockets. "The very short version is that someone from Kate's past wanted retribution against her and decided that the most effective way to hurt her was to hurt me."

"That's horrible."

"It was the worst time of our lives." Jay wanted to lighten the mood. "But, as I said, it was a very long time ago and, as you can see, all's well that ends well."

"I feel terrible for dredging all that up for you."

"You didn't. Please, I don't want you to give it another thought."

Dara glanced out the window. "How about a walk on the beach at sunset to clear away the cobwebs?"

"That sounds perfect."

"Why don't you get settled and join us out there?" Dara pointed in the direction of the water.

When she had gone, Jay sank down onto the bed. If she closed her eyes, she still could see the guardrail, and the cliff rising up to meet the car, and... She jumped up and lifted the suitcase onto the bed, unzipped it, and unpacked her clothes. It was better if she kept busy.

Fifteen minutes later, Jay luxuriated in the feeling of her bare toes in the sand. Dara and Rebecca were at the water's edge. The sun almost kissed the horizon.

Jay paused and inhaled. The smell of the salt water, the sound of the waves beating against the shore, and the sight of the bright orange orb touching the water—all of it soothed her soul. She took several deep breaths to settle herself and joined her friends.

CHAPTER FOURTEEN

Kate glided across the water in her kayak. The sun was just peeking up over the horizon and Saratoga Lake was smooth as glass in the early morning. A deer grazing along the shore caught her attention and she paused to watch.

The shrill sound of her cell phone ringing inside the waterproof bag behind her seat startled Kate. With the three-hour time difference between New York and LA, she was positive Jay wouldn't be awake. They'd fallen into a routine of talking every night just before Kate went to bed. She grabbed the bag, unsealed it, and answered the call.

"Hello?"

"Good morning."

Kate raised an eyebrow. Peter was an early riser, but, like her, he enjoyed his solitude in the morning. Making phone calls was highly unusual. Unless…

"What's wrong?"

"Nothing. We have work to do, though, if you're available."

"Now?"

"Now would be good. I've got a Skype call scheduled in an hour, if you can make it over here in time."

Kate calculated the time difference with Spain, or wherever Vaughn and Sabastien might be. They likely were five hours ahead of New York time. She squinted into the distance. If she paddled hard, she could get back to her car within twenty minutes.

"I'll be there." She disconnected the call without saying goodbye, stowed the phone, and picked up her paddle.

Twenty-two minutes later, she hauled her kayak out of the lake and secured it on top of the SUV. Fifty-seven minutes after she'd received the phone call, she walked into Peter and Lorraine's house.

"Right on time," Peter said. He clicked the mouse to bring up Skype on his computer. Immediately, Sabastien's ID came up with the incoming call.

"Bonjour, Peter."

"Good to see you, my friend."

"It is good to be seen."

"Hi, Sabastien."

"Katherine. It is a pleasure to see you. You are looking radiant."

"I'm looking like I just finished working out."

"Well, then. That must be the glow."

"You're a smooth talker."

Sabastien shrugged. "I am French."

"Kate. Peter." Vaughn appeared on the screen.

"Vaughn," Peter said. "What's the situation?"

"For the moment, we're secure. It appears that Sabastien tripped a fail-safe when he downloaded and sent us the files. The Black Knight was able to lock onto Sabastien's location and put some boots on the ground almost instantaneously.

"That's some serious resources and connections," Peter said.

"Very Commission-like," Kate added.

"Whoever it is, they've obviously got global assets," Vaughn agreed. "Sabastien was able to lose his company in Gibraltar three days ago."

"Is it safe to know where you are now?" Kate asked.

"In one of Sabastien's safe houses outside of Casablanca."

"Smart. Morocco has no extradition treaty with the US."

"I used my marbles, Peter."

Both Peter and Kate laughed. Vaughn simply shook her head.

"Did I make a funny?" Sabastien asked.

"The expression is, 'I used my head,'" Kate said.

"Oh."

"Were you able to make any progress on cross-referencing the hacks with the affected companies?"

"Oui."

"How soon can we have it?"

Sabastien smiled. "You have mail."

At that moment, Peter's computer dinged to indicate an incoming e-mail.

"I am sorry for the delay, but it was necessary in order to throw the foxes off the scent."

"Hounds, or dogs. Not foxes," Vaughn corrected.

"They are all four legs with noses, yes?"

"Four-leggeds."

"I am hopeless."

"Sabastien? You were saying?"

"Yes. It was necessary to create a diversion before I felt it was safe to communicate with you, even by encrypted e-mail. So I reversed the tables on him."

Kate started to correct the mangled idiom, then thought better of it.

"I hacked into the Black Knight's last hack and sent him to chase his behind. While he is doing that, I was able to repair the hole and re-secure communications."

"Still, I recommend that we keep the chatter to a minimum," Vaughn cautioned.

"Agreed," Peter said. "Give the three of us time to digest what you sent."

"How long do you think you'll need?"

"I guess that depends on what we find."

"Let's plan to talk again in seventy-two hours, unless you find something that requires immediate attention," Vaughn said.

"Or unless something breaks, or breaks down, on your end," Peter said.

"Agreed."

"Be safe."

"That's the plan," Vaughn agreed.

"Au revoir, mes amis," Sabastien said.

"A bien-tôt," Kate answered.

When they'd signed off, Peter switched to his e-mail server and downloaded the spreadsheet Sabastien had compiled.

"There are two hundred entries," Kate said.

"It's going to be a long few days."

"I wish Jay was here to help us."

"How is she doing out in LA?"

"She says it's going great. She and Rebecca have really clicked. She's enjoying the challenge of writing for a new medium and Rebecca's been very patient with her. They've been writing for a solid week, and Jay says they expect to wrap things up in the next few days."

"This is the longest I can remember you two being apart in..."

"Forever," Kate finished Peter's sentence. "God, I miss her. It feels strange."

"Well, we'll have plenty to keep us busy for the next three days. It'll make the time go quickly."

"I hope you're right."

"Are you two just about done?" Dara stood in the doorway to their office. Jay and Rebecca were sitting side-by-side, staring at the computer monitor. Rebecca was completely engrossed in what Jay was saying. Jay's hair was standing at odd angles, no doubt from running her hands through it as the two of them worked out a tense scene.

They'd been at it for ten days, and Dara had watched them work long enough to recognize some of Jay's habits. She thought it was endearing.

"Earth to Rebecca? Jay? How's it coming along? We have to leave here in about twenty minutes if we're going to be on time for our reservation." Dara had secured a dinner meeting with the director, George Nelson, to give him a copy of the treatment and the screenplay and talk about possibilities and strategy.

"Huh?" Rebecca looked over her shoulder. "Oh. We're on the last few lines of dialogue right now. Give us about ten minutes and we'll have it."

"I hope you can get ready in a hurry." Dara retreated to the back deck and watched the waves lap against the sand. She'd read the pages at the end of each day. The work was good—very, very good. The material would make for an edge-of-the-seat ride for theater-goers.

Dara smiled as she imagined playing Bryce Maddox. It was a meaty role, and she would have to do a lot of research to inhabit that skin. *It's exactly the kind of new challenge I've been looking for.*

"Hey." Rebecca wrapped her arms around Dara from behind and kissed the side of her neck. "We're done. It's printing now, and I'm off to get dressed. Can you put it in a binder?"

"I might be able to manage that." She turned in Rebecca's arms and kissed her gently. "Congratulations."

"Jay gets a lot of the credit for getting it done so fast. It didn't take her any time to adapt to the differences in format and nuance. It also helped that her original dialogue was so crisp. All we had to do was bring it into Final Draft from her Word document and tweak it."

"You can tell me all about it later," Dara said. "Get dressed." She shooed Rebecca back inside, returned to the office, and put together the package they would give to the director at dinner.

They had finished the meal, the server had cleared the table, and Dara had insisted on picking up the tab, much to Jay's chagrin.

Now the three women sat quietly while George Nelson flipped through the pages of the treatment. Jay wasn't quite sure what to expect. She'd never had an Oscar-winning director look at her work before—well, not that she knew of, anyway. He said he'd read several of her books, but it was quite different to have someone of that caliber sit right in front of her reading the words she'd put on a page.

Jay had no idea how the man could make an informed decision simply by reading a five-page description of a full-length novel and a one-hundred-twenty page screenplay.

"This is engaging. It's really, really solid." George looked over at Jay. "That manuscript of yours must have been quite something for you and Rebecca to be able to put together a treatment and a complete screenplay in less than two weeks."

"Her prose is fabulous. The dialogue was pitch-perfect," Rebecca said. "And the richness of the characters and depth of the plot—"

"You can stop anytime now," George said. "I'm intrigued. I want to take this home and give it a thorough read-through. But I already can tell this is something special."

"You know some of the challenges we'd face," Dara said to George.

Jay squirmed in her chair. She wasn't certain how much Dara had shared of the situation with getting the book published, nor what the director might have read in the papers. This was where the discussion would get real for her.

Dara must have noticed her discomfort, because she subtly placed a hand on Jay's knee under the table to stop her from bouncing.

"I am aware that the book is being blackballed by Black Quill and likely other cowardly publishers, as well." George directed his attention to Jay. "I'm sorry for that. I admire your work, and I trust Dara. When she calls me to extol the virtues of a manuscript as she did with yours, I know it must be something truly special. Now that I've had a glimpse of what the screen treatment looks like, I am more inclined than ever to agree with her."

"Mr. Nelson—"

"George, please, Jay. My father was Mr. Nelson."

"George... As I have explained to both Dara and Rebecca, there are very powerful people both in the government and the private sector who do not want this story to see the light of day. If you were to decide that you wanted to move forward with this, I'm afraid you might experience significant push-back. It could get very ugly."

George leaned forward. "Jay, you don't know me, but I can assure you, I don't intimidate easily, and I especially don't cotton to the idea of being told what projects I should and shouldn't undertake."

He held Jay's gaze a moment longer, and she could see in his eyes the fire of a fighter. No, he wouldn't be pushed around. But she wondered if he really understood what the Feds and/or the Commission were capable of. Hollywood no doubt had its share of sharks, but this was a different breed of shark than he or Dara were used to.

"Thank you."

"Don't thank me yet." George winked and got up from the table. "Ladies. I'll be in touch."

৵৵

Kate stood and stretched her back. She, Peter, and Lorraine had been working on the list Sabastien provided for three solid days. They'd broken only to eat and sleep.

"What we really need is an updated roster of Commission members." Kate quickly added, "No offense, Lorraine. Your memory is fabulous and the notes you took during your time on the inside are amazing..."

"But they're twenty-five years old," Lorraine finished Kate's sentence for her. "No offense taken. I wish I still had full access."

"I'm glad you don't," Peter said. He kissed his wife sweetly on the cheek. "Let's review where we are right now."

"We have a dozen corporations on the list across every segment of technology and industry that have been known strongholds for the Commission in the past," Kate said.

"We have another ten whose functions would be too appealing to the Commission for them not to have someone on the inside," Lorraine added.

"That's twenty-two entities, down from the original two hundred. We're making real progress," Peter said.

"When are we supposed to Skype with Vaughn and Sabastien?" Lorraine asked.

"Later today," Peter said.

"I don't suppose Vaughn is still in contact with Sedona?" Kate asked.

Lorraine held up a hand. "I'm not sure you want to go there with Vaughn. She's still nursing a broken heart."

"What are you thinking?" Peter asked.

"I'm thinking that Sedona has more current contacts inside our security agencies than any of us. She might be able to save us a significant amount of time and energy. If any of these companies are on a government watch list, she might be able to ferret that out."

"I don't think we want to take that route," Peter said. "And not because of the personal issues either. If we assume, and I think we can, that the Commission still has people in key positions inside the Beltway, we don't want to tip them off that we're poking around."

"Excellent point," Lorraine said.

Kate took her seat again. "Maybe there's another way." She opened a Google search. "It wouldn't give us watch list information, but that might not be what we really need."

"What are you suggesting?" Peter asked.

"Government contracts generally are a matter of public record. We could simply do a search to see if any of these corporations have government contracts and, if so, what types of contracts they've got."

"Not a bad thought. That would at least narrow things down on one side of the equation."

Kate typed in the words, "federal government contracting." Immediately, thousands of entries popped up. She clicked on a promising website called "washingtontechnology.com."

"Well, now this is interesting," she said. Peter and Lorraine both came to stand behind her.

"All of the major players you'd expect to see received major government contracts in the past year." She scrolled down.

"Go to the 'search' tab and plug in our likely suspects," Lorraine suggested.

Twenty-two searches later, they had matched sixteen of the companies to government contracts. Kate sat back. "We didn't narrow it down much, did we?"

Peter's computer beeped. "It's Sabastien." Peter answered the Skype call.

Kate and Lorraine moved their chairs so that all three of them would be visible to Sabastien and Vaughn.

"Bonjour from sunny Casablanca."

"I take it you are still feeling secure?"

"We're fine for the moment," Vaughn answered. "I had Sabastien create some credit card and bank transactions for himself out of Brazil and Argentina to further obfuscate."

"Good thinking," Peter said.

"How is the research going on your end?" Sabastien asked.

"We've narrowed the possibilities to roughly two dozen likely Commission-infiltrated-or-owned companies that Robie hacked within the last two years," Lorraine said.

"We were just cross-referencing that list against government contracts awarded in the past year," Kate said. "That wasn't as helpful as we would have liked."

"Where were you looking?" Vaughn asked.

Kate named the website.

"And what companies did you match?"

Kate rattled off the names.

Vaughn nodded. "Those are the usual suspects for major government contracts."

"I guess we need to come up with another approach," Lorraine said.

"Perhaps not," Sabastien piped in. "I may be able to help."

"We're all ears," Kate said.

"Quoi? Qu'est-ce que c'est, 'We are all ears?'"

"We're listening," Vaughn supplied.

"When I was hacking on behalf of your government, checking the security of the computer interfaces, I was required to investigate the major contractors, of course. Those are the names you mentioned. But there was more. I also was responsible for poking into the systems of the contractors that worked underneath the major contractors."

"Subcontractors," Peter said. "It would make sense that the Commission would lurk behind the scenes where they would be subjected to far less scrutiny."

Kate pulled her laptop closer and did another Google search. "I don't see any way, by examining public records, that we could unearth all of the subcontractors." She sat back and pushed the laptop away.

"Why would you need to do that?" Sabastien asked. His forehead wrinkled in puzzlement.

"Because we need more information?" Kate countered.

"Vraiment," Sabastien agreed.

"What am I missing?"

"I was responsible for investigating all of the subcontractors with access to sensitive government information to make sure they were not compromising your government," Sabastien said. "This is no problem. I backed up for my own protection all of the work I did."

"You have the names of all of the subcontractors working for these major players?" Lorraine asked.

"Oui."

"I think I love you!" Kate said.

Sabastien's blush was visible on the screen. "Give me your list, and I will get you what you ask."

Kate retrieved her laptop and cut and pasted into an e-mail the list of the twenty-two companies. Just as she was about to hit Send, Peter put a hand on her wrist.

"Not from yours."

Kate nodded and deleted the e-mail. "How do you want to do this?"

"I'll send it to him from an encrypted account when we finish here."

"Is there anything else new to report?" Lorraine asked.

"All else is status quo," Vaughn said. She addressed Sabastien, "How long will it take to compile what we need?"

"Several hours, a day at most."

"Okay. Let's talk again in forty-eight hours. If we have something of note sooner, I'll ping you."

"Roger that," Peter agreed.

Sabastien said, "I will send the file to you with appropriate encryption, Peter."

"Thank you, my friend." Peter disconnected the call and closed Skype.

"Put that on a thumb drive." Peter pointed to the database file Kate had open on her screen.

Kate did as instructed. Maybe they really were making progress after all.

CHAPTER FIFTEEN

Dara watched Jay from a distance as she stood at the water's edge. Today was Jay's last day in Los Angeles, and Dara was surprised to realize that she would miss her friend's sparkly presence when she was gone.

"I know what you're thinking." Rebecca wrapped her arms around her wife from behind.

"Oh, you do, do you?"

"Mm-hmm. It's the same thing I'm thinking."

"And that is?"

"This place is going to be awfully quiet without Jay here. I've really enjoyed collaborating with her. But more than that, I've loved her company."

"You did know what I was thinking," Dara agreed. "It's so strange that you and I, two people who jealously guard our privacy and our space, should feel so comfortable with someone we don't know that well."

Rebecca released her hold and came to stand beside Dara at the glass. "I agree. But there's just something about Jay that puts you at ease."

They watched as Jay jumped back to keep her rolled-up pant legs from getting splashed by a wave.

"Do you think we should tell her that George is on his way over to discuss the screenplay?" Dara asked.

"Hmm. Maybe we should hear what he has to say first."

"This is Jay's baby, sweetheart."

"Exactly my point. Wouldn't it be prudent to feel George out and see what he has in mind? Jay isn't used to the bluntness of Hollywood directors. George is nice, but he can be brusque."

"Well, if his reaction over the phone was any indication, I don't think Jay has much to worry about there," Dara said. "He was practically gushing. And you know George doesn't gush."

"Okay, then. Do you want to go tell her, or should I?"

Dara opened the sliding glass door. "Why don't we go together?"

When they got close enough to see Jay's face, Rebecca pulled Dara to a stop.

"What is it?"

Rebecca gestured in Jay's direction. When Dara looked closer, she could see dampness glistening on Jay's cheek. Part of her didn't want to disturb Jay's privacy. But… She hesitated only for a moment and closed the distance between them.

"Jay? Are you okay?" Dara enveloped her in a hug. "What's wrong?"

"Oh." Jay used her sleeve to blot at her tears. "I didn't hear you coming."

Dara pulled back just enough to see Jay's eyes. "What is it?" She nodded in approval as Rebecca came up alongside Jay and wrapped an arm around her.

"Group hug."

Jay smiled wanly. "I feel like an idiot."

"Why?"

Jay lifted a hand halfheartedly to indicate Dara and Rebecca flanking her.

"Personally, we love a good cry," Rebecca said.

"We do," Dara agreed.

"I-I'm fine. Truly. I was just having a moment."

As if on cue, both Dara and Rebecca broke the hug and each took one of Jay's hands.

"Want to talk about it?" Dara asked.

Jay shrugged. "I don't know what to say. I was going over in my mind everything that's happened. It's all so crazy. All I ever wanted to do was write the great American novel. This whole thing…"

"If you don't want to pursue the film, we can drop it right now," Rebecca said. She glanced over Jay's head at Dara and Dara nodded.

162

"What? No! It isn't that." Jay sniffled. "It's just…" She gazed out at the water. "All my life I've had to fight for everything I had or wanted. As a child, I fought to survive. Twenty-some-odd years ago, in the midst of the Hyland incident, I fought to survive again and find my way home. And here I am, all these years later, still fighting for my life, fighting to survive. I'm tired."

"Jay," Dara said. "I've read all of your books. I've heard you talk about your abusive childhood on national talk shows—always with dignity, always with the aim to lift others up. Through your books and your words, you've given voice to those who have none. You've empowered them." She let go of Jay's hand and gently rubbed her back. "What I see in this situation is you once again stepping into the breach to right a wrong, to tell the truth."

"You are an extraordinary woman, a shining example to others," Rebecca added. She let go of the hand she was holding. "You are strong and resilient. You're strong enough for this fight. The great champions are the ones who keep getting up off the mat for the next round."

"We understand that you're tired. But we promise, you are never alone. Not now, not ever. Rebecca and I will fight with you. Kate will fight with you. Lean on all of us. Together, we've got this."

Rebecca got Dara's attention and pointed to her watch.

"In fact, I think in just a few minutes, you're going to see your support team grow in important ways." Dara wiped a tear from Jay's face. "George is on his way over here. He loved the screenplay. He wants to talk to you one more time before you leave."

"He's on his way here now?" Jay asked. "Oh my God! I'm a mess. I've got to change."

Dara smiled indulgently at her. "You look fine. Let's go inside so you can freshen up, if it'll make you feel better." Dara turned them toward the house. After a few steps she said, "Are you better now?"

Jay nodded. "I'm sorry. I got overwhelmed."

"It's perfectly understandable," Rebecca said. "You've been carrying a lot on those small shoulders."

"For the record," Dara said, "you've written not one great American novel, but several."

Jay blushed. "I'm no Constance Darrow."

Dara laughed. "No. You're Jamison freaking Parker and you rock."

⋸⟶⟶

Kate was in the backyard pulling weeds from in between the landscaping stones when her phone beeped. She yanked off her gardening gloves and opened the messages app. It was from Peter.

Pay dirt. How fast can you get here?

Kate typed a message back. *On my way in ten.* She pocketed the phone, ran into the house, stripped, showered, changed, and made the familiar drive in record time.

Lorraine answered the back door.

"What do you have?"

"Good to see you too."

Kate gave her friend a quick hug. "Now, what do you have?"

"Come on in and we'll show you." As they walked into the office, Lorraine said, "We heard from Sabastien."

"That's great."

"It is, and it isn't," Peter said. He swiveled around and nodded to Kate in greeting.

"What do you mean?"

"The file he sent was corrupted. So I called to ask him to re-send."

"And?"

"And it seems that someone has once again hacked into Sabastien's formerly tamper-proof servers and interrupted the data flow. From what Sabastien could tell, the hacker couldn't access the data, itself. He just prevented it from being successfully transmitted."

"Are Sabastien and Vaughn still safe where they are? Is their location compromised?"

"They don't think so. At least not yet," Lorraine said.

"But we can't take a chance on transmitting electronically anymore. Not now, anyway," Peter said.

"You said in your message that we hit pay dirt. But you never got the data."

"I was able to retrieve part of the message before the malfunction."

Peter handed a legal pad to Kate. "I wrote down from memory as many of the subcontractors as I could from what I saw on the screen before we lost it."

"Then I was able to cross-reference those names with my files of known Commission-related companies," Lorraine said. She pointed to several asterisked entries on the pad. "All of these corporations were on my radar years ago."

Kate ran a finger down the list. "Okay. But according to your notations here, these are all manufacturing companies. They do grunt work, assemble weapons, manufacture protective gear. I would think we're looking for something more high-end and white collar, like a technology company."

"Like the technology and innovation companies we saw in the list of major contractors. True. We expect that the rest of the list Sabastien sent us contains more Commission entities."

"But we can't access the rest of the list, and Sabastien doesn't have a secure way to re-send it."

"Which is why Lorraine and I are about to take a long-overdue vacation. We hear Casablanca is beautiful this time of year."

"What? You're crazy," Kate said. "You're going to go retrieve the file in person?"

"Do you have a better plan?" Peter asked.

Kate shook her head.

"Right. We're booked on a flight to Tangiers. From there we'll hop on a train to Casablanca."

"We leave in the morning."

Kate sat down. "You're serious."

"Completely. We lucked out with the flight, and anyone who might be watching for Sabastien would most likely be staked out in Gibraltar, not on the Morocco side of the strait."

Kate clasped her hands between her knees and leaned forward. "You're serious?"

"Didn't we already answer that?" Peter asked Lorraine.

"I thought we did."

"There must be another way that doesn't put either of you at risk."

"At risk? All those years in the field, and now you're worried about us being in jeopardy?"

"I know I don't have to pull the age card here," Kate said.

"No, you don't. Because it's not a factor," Peter answered.

"And this is not up for discussion. We've already made the arrangements, and we have a rendezvous point with Vaughn."

"I can't talk you out of this?"

Both Peter and Lorraine shook their heads.

"We're the obvious choice. You can't go, Kate—with the manuscript on their radar, the Feds would no doubt be curious if you and Jay suddenly left the country."

Kate sat up straight. "Do you think they're watching Jay?"

Lorraine said, "It's entirely possible."

"So they know she's in California? And potentially that she's meeting with Dara and Rebecca?"

Peter nodded, and Kate dropped her head into her hands. "Here we go all over again."

Lorraine put a hand on her shoulder. "This is the Feds, not the Commission. We don't think either one of you is in physical danger at this point."

"Gee, that's comforting," Kate said.

"You know we've got your backs, right?" Peter asked. "What happened then will never happen again. Never. Do you hear me?"

His voice shook with emotion, catching Kate off guard and hitting her hard in the heart. She cleared her throat. "I know."

"Okay, then. Let's not worry about that right now, since there doesn't seem to be a reason to do so," Lorraine said.

"Get out of here so we can get packed," Peter added.

Kate couldn't see any point in arguing further. "Right. When will you be back?"

"As soon as we can."

"Will we be able to communicate while you're gone?"

"That depends."

"On what?"

"On what we find when we get there. If we can find a way to reach out to you safely without compromising any of us, we will."

"Be safe, please."

"Always."

Kate hugged them both, as a feeling of foreboding about her friends' security washed over her. She didn't like it. She didn't like it at all. But she didn't really have any say in the matter, so she would hope for the best. The good news was that Jay would be home tomorrow. That, at least, was reason to smile.

◈◈

Jay finished packing her suitcase as the doorbell rang. She checked herself in the mirror and settled her hair. Despite Dara's reassuring words about how much George liked the screenplay, she was nervous.

"Jay?" Rebecca knocked on the doorframe. "George is here."

"Do I look okay?"

Rebecca smiled kindly. "You look fabulous. C'mon."

"I feel like I'm walking the plank."

"You'll be fine. George isn't an effusive kind of guy, but he's gushing about this script."

"Really?"

"Really."

They arrived in the living room, where Dara and George were chatting. George stood when he saw Jay.

"Good to see you again, Jay." He held out his hand and Jay stepped forward to shake it.

"Thank you for taking the time to read the screenplay."

"Thank you for trusting me with the material." George sat down again, and Jay and Rebecca took seats on the sofa opposite him.

"Let me start by saying that the material is compelling. There's a natural tension to the story, it's visually rich, and the characters are well-drawn."

"But?" Jay asked.

George looked surprised. "There is no 'but.' This is great stuff and I can easily see it on the big screen."

"Oh." The tightness in Jay's neck and back eased. "I didn't see that coming."

George, Dara, and Rebecca all laughed.

"Your honesty is refreshing," George said.

"It would certainly make you unique in this town," Dara added.

"So, what now?" Jay asked.

"Now," Dara answered, "we put together a pitch and work on getting funding for production." She turned to George. "Now that you've read it, do you think 722 will have any interest?"

"I imagine Randolph would want in. My question is whether or not he has the stomach to take on whoever doesn't want Jay to get this story made."

"Is it worth pitching it to him?"

"Aren't we getting ahead of ourselves?" Jay interrupted. "I mean, I still have two questions that I imagine need answering before we go there."

"Okay, shoot," George said.

"It seems to me I would want to know if you would agree to direct the film?"

"That's the idea."

"And, Dara, I want to know if you'd play the part of Bryce Maddox?"

"That would be up to George and a casting director, but I'd certainly audition for the role."

George shook his head and muttered, "As if that part was up for debate."

"There's a bigger question we're missing," Rebecca chimed in. "Jay has to agree to option the screenplay."

"Do you have representation, Jay?" Dara asked.

Jay thought about the way Sydney sloughed her off on a junior agent when Black Quill cut her loose. "Not anymore I don't."

"Carolyn would, I'm sure, be happy to represent you. Or, if that makes you uncomfortable because she reps me and Rebecca, I'm sure she could recommend someone else to you."

Although Jay's interactions with Carolyn had been limited, she liked what she'd seen. When she reached out to Carolyn in order to talk to Dara about the premiere in March, Carolyn had been efficient and helpful. And she'd secured the space for Jay's press conference and handled the set up with calm ease. Still, Jay would need to sit down with her first. "I'd love to talk to her about it."

"She's back in New York at the moment," Dara supplied.

"I'll give her a call when I get home."

"Okay. How about if we spend what little time we have left with Jay putting together the investor pitch? We can do the rest long distance via conference calls and Skype." Dara picked up her laptop from the end table beside her chair and booted it up.

"I'll get the snacks," Rebecca said, and headed off toward the kitchen.

⊷⊷

"Could you please not do that?" Vaughn asked. She sat at a table on the opposite side of Sabastien's work space. One of her guns was disassembled on the table in front of her.

"Do what?" Sabastien crunched down on his third cracker and cheese.

"Chew like a cow."

"I am confused. What do cows have to do with securing our communications?"

"Nothing. Could you eat more quietly, please?"

Sabastien swallowed. "Oh. I did not realize you were so sensitive, Vaughn Elliott. I will add the way I eat to my list of things about me that annoy you."

"It's a long list."

"I am aware."

"Are you getting anywhere yet?" Vaughn continued to clean her weapon.

"I believe I have discovered the Black Knight's point of entry. He is very, very good. Almost as skilled as I am."

"If it was only 'almost,' he wouldn't have gotten past you."

Sabastien narrowed his eyes. "If you are going to continue to insult me—"

"Relax."

"I should be saying the same to you." They had been cooped up together inside this space for too long. That was the problem, Sabastien told himself. He and Vaughn had worked together many, many times. Vaughn always got this way whenever she was cornered in one location for any length of time. She was not one to sit still. "Perhaps you should check the perimeter again?"

"Perhaps you should solve the leak." Vaughn rose and left the room.

"If only it were that simple," Sabastien muttered to himself. "You are a tricky bastard, John Robie. But I am smarter."

Sabastien cut and pasted another string of code and sat back. This time, he had baited a trap to lure the Black Knight in. Once the hacker took the bait, he would suffer a systemic crash. "That should slow you down."

Vaughn stepped back into the room. "It's time for me to go. I have just enough time to get to the rendezvous point and pick up Peter and Lorraine." Vaughn holstered her weapon and shrugged into a blazer that would conceal the weapon from sight. "Remember what I told you. Stay away from the doors and windows. No communications unless it's an absolute emergency."

"I know. I know, already." Sabastien made a shooing motion. "Go. Get our friends. Perhaps they will put you in a better mood."

CHAPTER SIXTEEN

J ay reached over and interlaced her fingers with Kate's. They were on the train, on the way to New York City for a meeting with Carolyn, and just pulling into Penn Station. "I love you and I'm glad you're coming with me."

Kate's smile crinkled the corners of her eyes. "I love you too, and I'm glad you asked. The idea of turning a business meeting into an excursion is genius."

"Well, I missed you. That's the longest we've been apart in twenty-seven years, and I have to say, I really didn't like it."

"Me neither."

"The idea of getting home yesterday and leaving again today for this meeting was completely bumming me out. Now I'm looking forward to a candlelight dinner and a Broadway show with my wife."

The train came to a stop and Jay grabbed her briefcase off the overhead rack.

"Subway or cab?" Kate asked, as they exited the train with the flow of commuters.

It was past rush hour, but the platform still was thick with bodies. "Do you mind if we take a cab? I really don't feel like wrestling with this much humanity today."

"Cab it is," Kate said. She led the way up to the main level and out to the taxi stand, where they queued up for a taxi to take them uptown to Carolyn's office.

Once they were settled in the backseat, Kate said, "Carolyn's office is an easy walk to the theater district. I'll drop you off and go pick up the show tickets. Call me when you're done and I'll meet you downstairs."

"Are you sure you're okay with that plan?"

"This is your work and your business. You don't need me hovering."

Jay scrutinized her wife's expression. She didn't hear any hint of hurt in Kate's voice, but... Was she telling the truth? "You know I value your input—"

"Don't." Kate cut Jay off. "We talked about this after the press conference. I heard your concerns loud and clear, and you were right."

"Kate..." Misery threatened to bubble up from the pit of Jay's stomach.

Kate turned to face Jay. "Sweetheart, I am one hundred percent behind you and fully on board with this project. This is yours, not ours. You are a fabulous judge of character. You're going to know straightaway whether Carolyn is the right fit for you. If she's not, and you trust her to recommend another agent to you, that's fine too. And if, after sitting down with her, you want to figure out your own alternative, I'll back you all the way."

Jay stared into the face she knew so well. All she saw in Kate's eyes was love and earnestness. "Okay."

"Okay," Kate agreed.

"Here you go," the cabbie announced.

Kate paid the fare as they exited the cab outside Carolyn's office. "Call or text me when you're done."

"You'd better get us the best seats in the house."

"Oh, the pressure." Kate leaned down and kissed Jay sweetly on the lips. "I love you."

"I love you too. Don't stop for any hot bread pretzels on the street. You'd better save your appetite for dinner."

"You know me too well."

Kate headed off down the sidewalk, and Jay stood still a moment to admire the view. After all these years, seeing that long-legged swagger still made Jay's heart flutter happily.

If you don't get moving, you're going to be late.

Jay pushed through the revolving door, rode the elevator to Carolyn's floor, and walked through the double glass doors etched with Carolyn's name.

"You must be Jay."

172

The woman just inside the door was petite, perky, and dressed in a crisp, charcoal gray skirt suit. Jay grasped her outstretched hand. "I'm Gayle, Carolyn's assistant."

"Nice to meet you."

"Coffee?" Gayle motioned Jay to follow her down the hallway.

"No, thanks."

"Water?"

"I'd love some."

"I'll bring it right in. Carolyn is expecting you." Gayle stopped in front of a partially closed door and peeked her head in. "Jay is here."

Jay was expecting to hear Carolyn tell Gayle to send her in. Instead, the door swung open wide.

"Hello again, Jay. It's so good to see you."

"Good to see you too, Carolyn. Thank you for fitting me in."

"Thanks, Gayle." Carolyn smiled at her assistant and gestured for Jay to come all the way into her office.

For Jay, it was always the little things that revealed what kind of person someone was. The fact that Carolyn warmly acknowledged her assistant without any hint of condescension or elitism was telling. The personalized greeting at the door rather than remaining in the power position behind the desk spoke of a woman who didn't feel the need to posture.

Carolyn led them over to a pair of identical wingback chairs and motioned for Jay to make herself comfortable. A moment later, Gayle knocked and entered with bottles of water, ice, and glasses.

"Thanks." Again, Carolyn acknowledged Gayle.

"You're welcome." Gayle left the office and closed the door behind her.

"So, Dara didn't tell me much, except that you've got a killer manuscript that she's itching to turn into a blockbuster film."

"She said that?" A warm rush of pride filled Jay's heart.

"Absolutely." Carolyn filled the two glasses with ice, poured them each a glass of water, and handed one of them to Jay.

"Thank you."

"I think Dara's exact words were, 'This film is going to set the world on fire.'" Carolyn took a sip from her glass. "And trust me when I tell you, Dara is never that effusive with praise."

Jay thought about the Dara she'd come to know over the past few weeks. Carolyn was right. Although she could be warm and supportive, Dara never was prone to hyperbole.

"You said that Dara didn't give you a lot of details, so I don't know if you're aware that it looks less and less likely everyday that the manuscript will be published as a novel."

Carolyn smiled sympathetically. Quietly, she said, "I read the papers, Jay. But I know that the papers sometimes contain only the smallest kernel of truth. I'd rather hear whatever it is you'd like me to know directly from you."

Jay nodded. She liked that Carolyn didn't offer false platitudes. "Obviously, anything I tell you must be kept confidential."

"You have my word."

Jay took a drink of water and paused. "For more reasons than I feel comfortable disclosing, the Feds are actively discouraging publication of this book. Among those to whom they apparently have reached out is my agent."

Carolyn raised an eyebrow, but otherwise her expression remained interested but unfazed.

"She essentially washed her hands of me and passed me off to one of her junior agents. I'm telling you this because, if we decide to work together, I need you to know it will likely also make you a target for intimidation."

Carolyn nodded. "I appreciate your forthrightness about that, Jay. Let me be equally blunt. If I sign a contract to represent you, it means I'm all in. I'll be your fiercest advocate, no matter who knocks on my door."

There was no quaver in Carolyn's voice and no timidity. Nothing about her demeanor gave Jay pause. She already knew that Carolyn could be trusted with confidential information—after all, she managed the career and business affairs of Constance Darrow.

"Fair enough."

"Jay, I'm aware that Dara entrusted you with her most closely guarded secret. She's given me leeway to explain to you how I work with her."

Jay furrowed her brow in puzzlement. "Why would that be necessary?"

"It's relevant so that you understand and can make an informed decision based on the extent of my involvement in Dara and Rebecca's business affairs—so that you can determine for yourself if there would be a conflict of interest in your mind."

"Oh. Okay."

"As you know, Dara and I are childhood friends. In fact, she's my best friend, and I'm hers. We've been watching each other's backs since kindergarten. When she decided to become an actress, she never considered anyone else representing her. She was my first, and still my biggest, client."

"How lucky you both are to have that kind of trust and foundation for such an important business relationship."

"I count my blessings every day, not because of the money, but because I get to work with my closest friend. And when she came to me with the idea of creating Constance Darrow, we spent weeks and months strategizing about how to carry the deception off, how to safeguard her identity, how to help her live her dreams."

"I can only imagine," Jay said.

"Dara knows that I will go to the grave carrying and respecting her secret and protecting her privacy. I'm the only one authorized to sign contracts for Constance, to negotiate terms, to appear on her behalf. That's the level of trust Dara has in me."

Jay thought of her own writing career and relationship with her agent. She had entrusted Sydney with her livelihood—with her career—and Sydney had opened doors for her. When Jay became a household name, she responded by bringing Sydney more business and clients than she knew what to do with. And now? Now, Sydney had abandoned her in her hour of need. "I'm certain that Dara's trust is well-placed."

"I'd like to think so." Carolyn took another sip of water. "Now, having said that, I'm here to tell you that what I offer Dara in terms of professionalism and service is the same thing I offer all of my clients. It's the same thing I'm prepared to offer you, Jay."

"I would never presume to question your integrity, Carolyn. I wouldn't be a very astute businesswoman if I hadn't checked with some of your other clients for their input."

For the first time during the course of this conversation, Carolyn's face registered surprise. "Bully for you for doing due diligence."

Jay shrugged. "I knew what Dara and Rebecca thought of you. I needed some input that was a little more…"

"Unbiased?"

"Yes." Jay nodded. "Unbiased."

"And?"

"And to a person, they all extolled your virtues. Your clients clearly love you."

"But?"

"There is no 'but' here. I know that I would be in excellent hands, and that you'd represent my interests with the same tenacity and level of attentiveness that you do all your other clients."

Carolyn continued to maintain eye contact without flinching. She'd handled every aspect of the discussion impeccably well, which left Jay wondering what there was to think about and why she hadn't already engaged Carolyn's services.

"You don't have to make a decision today, Jay."

Perceptive, too. Carolyn was the whole package, and she had experience with clients in the screenwriting business, something Jay knew nothing about. "Tell me what to expect in this situation."

If Carolyn minded the deflection, she didn't show it. "This case is somewhat unique, since we already know who is optioning the property. Normally, I'd encourage a bidding war for your manuscript." Carolyn smiled slyly. "I can, of course, still do that if you want."

"What?" Jay shook her head. "No. No, of course not. Dara wants it, and, unless you can give me a compelling reason to say no, I'm inclined to sell it to her."

After a beat or two, Carolyn said, "I assumed as much, but it's my job to advise you. I'd be remiss if I didn't inform you that you stand to make a lot more money if I open the project up to multiple potential buyers."

If Jay still had been wondering whether or not Carolyn's friendship with Dara would mean that she'd put Dara's interests above hers, her fears were allayed. "First, I seriously doubt that anyone else would be beating down the door for a novel with so much baggage attached to it."

"Are you kidding me? Controversy sells."

"I can believe that, but does government scrutiny sell too?"

Carolyn chuckled. "Trust me, I wouldn't have to work very hard to generate buzz and interest for an unpublished Jamison Parker novel."

"You've read my work?"

"Was that a real question?" Carolyn rose and walked over to a floor-to-ceiling bookcase behind where Jay was seated. When she came back, she was holding a complete collection of Jamison Parker hardbacks. "I really wanted to ask if you would autograph these, but I wasn't sure it was appropriate under the circumstances."

Jay's face suffused with the familiar rush of pride she felt every time someone acknowledged her work.

"You're blushing," Carolyn observed.

Jay scrubbed her hands over her face. "I tend to do that a lot, especially when people whose opinions I value say things like you just did."

"So, how about it?" Carolyn's eyes twinkled. "I mean, they're all right here…"

Jay reached into her briefcase and pulled out a pen. As Carolyn handed her the books, she noted that, although the books were in excellent condition, they clearly showed signs of having been read. She signed them all with a flourish and handed them back to Carolyn.

"Thank you." Carolyn returned the novels to the shelf. "I apologize. I know that wasn't terribly professional of me…"

"I'm happy to do it."

Carolyn sat back down. "Now, where were we?"

"You were generating hypothetical multiple bids for the rights to the book."

"Ah, yes. Okay, well, since we're not going that route, I would sit down on your behalf with the money interests and insist that, since we're giving them exclusive access to a hot property, they're going to have to compensate you accordingly."

Jay leaned forward. "I like the way you think."

"In addition to the money, I would negotiate screen credits for you, not only as the author of the source material, but as an executive producer."

"Does that net me anything more financially?"

"We'll see. At the very least, it gives you cachet, which in this business goes a long way."

"Okay." Jay drew out the word.

"We have to think of the big picture."

"Pun intended," Jay said.

"Pun intended," Carolyn agreed. "I'm hopeful this will be the first of many adaptations for you. When this movie does gangbusters at the box office—"

"If…"

"No. When." Carolyn pointed a finger at Jay for emphasis. "When this film sets the box office on fire, a lot of folks are going to be clamoring to snap up the rest of your works. Trust me when I tell you, the price is going to go up."

"I can live with that."

"Good."

"That's the first part of the equation."

"There's more?"

Carolyn nodded. "Mm-hmm. Rumor has it you and Rebecca collaborated on the screenplay."

"We did."

"That means you get screenwriter credit and compensation, as well."

Jay sat back. Her head was spinning. There was so much to consider.

"You're overwhelmed," Carolyn observed.

"Is it that obvious?"

"It might have been the deer-in-the-headlights look on your face." Carolyn's tone was gentle, and not at all condescending. "Look, film hasn't been your genre. It's the agent's job to ensure that your interests are well served. If you decide you want to engage my services, I'll take care of everything I've described and any other business issues you empower me to handle for you."

Jay appreciated the subtlety of what Carolyn wasn't saying. If Jay wanted to change representation for her novels, Carolyn would take her on as a client for that as well.

"What kind of timeframe are we looking at?"

"For…?"

"I'm sorry. I wasn't very clear. How long would it take to negotiate the rights and the rest of it?"

"That depends on who we're negotiating with. If you agree that you truly want to sell the rights to the novel, we'd be negotiating that part of the deal with Dara, since she's your buyer. After we've successfully concluded that deal, she'll put together a team of investors to produce the film. Once we know who those folks are, I can give you a firmer idea of how discussions will go."

"Fair enough."

"Jay, I've done enough of these deals on behalf of clients that I know a fair number of the players."

"I'm sure you do." Jay leaned over and unlatched her briefcase. Her mind was made up. She pulled out a copy of the manuscript and handed it across to Carolyn. "When can we start?"

Carolyn's smile lit up her face. "I'll have a letter of engagement drawn up for you and have it to you within the next eight hours. As soon as you sign that, I'll contact Dara and get the process started."

"Perfect."

They both stood and Carolyn held out her hand for Jay to shake. "Welcome aboard."

"Thank you for taking me on. I look forward to working with you." As they walked to the door, Jay said, "You did hear the part where I mentioned that you might come under an unusual amount of scrutiny from the Feds."

Carolyn's laugh was rich. "I heard you."

"Just checking."

❧❧

Peter lingered behind as the rest of the passengers disembarked from the train in Casablanca. He and Lorraine traveled from John F. Kennedy airport to Tangier and took the subsequent train ride in separate compartments, under false passports, and in disguise. He had watched Lorraine get off the train several moments earlier from two train cars behind his current location. At the moment, he was scanning for signs that Lorraine was being watched. He saw none.

When he was confident that most of the other passengers were gone, he stepped down onto the station platform and slowly ambled into the lobby using a hand-carved wooden cane. He made a show of trying to get his bearings, in keeping with the older gentleman persona he had adopted. Eventually, he wandered out to the taxi stand. Within seconds, a cab pulled up with the window rolled down.

"Need a lift?"

Peter nodded, used a shaky hand to open the back door, and clumsily climbed in. When they were well away from the station, he said, "Nice wheels."

Vaughn smiled at him in the rearview mirror. "I borrowed it from a guy who is...occupied...with a paramour at the moment. I didn't think he'd miss it for half an hour. I left my Jeep there. I figured this was less conspicuous for now. I'll have this back before the poor guy even knows it was missing."

"How was your trip?" Lorraine asked. She kissed Peter on the cheek.

"Lonely without you. It's been a while since we had to do that. Oddly enough, I didn't miss it."

"Me neither."

"If you two lovebirds are quite finished," Vaughn said, "we can get down to business."

"What have you got?" Peter asked.

"This is for you." Vaughn reached back over the seat and handed Peter a flash drive. "It's everything Sabastien has on all of the major contractors, the subcontractors, and the Black Knight/John Robie."

"Perfect." Peter handed the drive to Lorraine. "Did you bring me the change of clothes I asked for?"

"Check under the seat in front of you."

Peter did as instructed and pulled out the small backpack. He unzipped it and sifted through the items inside. "This will do the trick."

"Here. Let me hold that." Lorraine shoved the thumb drive into her pocket, and took the backpack from Peter, along with the cane.

Peter stripped off his jacket, shirt, and pants and replaced them with the pair of faded jeans, crewneck t-shirt, and hoodie from the backpack. With Lorraine's help, he removed the bald cap he'd been wearing, combed his natural hair, and added a New York Yankees hat to complete the ensemble.

Lorraine stuffed the discarded clothes into the backpack just as Vaughn pulled the cab to a stop. She reached into her pocket, pulled out the flash drive, and handed it to Peter.

"Okay. This is where you get off."

"Be safe." Lorraine kissed Peter.

"You too. See you soon."

"You should have no trouble at this time of day hailing a cab across the street to take you back to the train station," Vaughn said.

"Roger that." Peter opened his door. "You two take care of each other and Sabastien."

"Roger that," Vaughn said.

Peter exited the cab, waited for Vaughn to pull away, and crossed the street. This was the part of the plan he and Lorraine hadn't shared with Kate. Lorraine would stay with Vaughn and Sabastien to connect the dots to the Commission. Peter would head home immediately under another alias with the data and follow the leads on the Black Knight.

Kate would not have liked the idea of Lorraine staying behind, but it was not her call. Sometimes it really was easier to apologize than to ask permission.

CHAPTER SEVENTEEN

From her position across the street, Kate watched the entrance to Carolyn's office building. She was particularly cognizant of the two men in the sharp suits and shades flanking either side of the front doors, trying for all the world to look like important players conducting business on their cell phones. She pegged them for Feds.

When both men shoved their phones into their pockets as Jay exited the building, her suspicions seemed to be confirmed. She crossed the street and looped her arm through Jay's.

"Hi there," Jay said.

"Hi, yourself." Kate kissed her on the cheek and whispered, "We have company." She felt Jay's body stiffen beside her. "Nothing to worry about. I suspect they're FBI." She tugged on Jay's arm to get them moving.

"What do you think they want?"

"They haven't approached you, so my guess is they're either trying to intimidate you, or else they're gathering intelligence."

"To what end?"

"I don't know. Most likely they're building a dossier in case the Feds want to charge you later."

Jay laughed derisively. "Did you get us tickets to a controversial show? Because if not, I can't imagine how a married couple going to dinner and a show could help them build a case against me for treason or divulging state secrets."

Underneath the cavalier attitude, Kate heard the frisson of fear. "I scored us tickets to *Fun Home*. I do hope they love musicals about lesbians."

"Presumably they'll be waiting outside. In which case, I hope they enjoy people-watching."

Kate pulled Jay a little closer as they walked. "Honey, I'm pretty sure that's in their job description."

⊸⟨⟩⊱

Dara and George sat at opposite ends of the room, working the phones.

"Ivan, I know you have the capital and the cojones for this one," George was saying. "I'm telling you, it's right up your alley. You'd get to thumb your nose at the establishment, and I know how happy that makes you." George listened for a moment longer. "Right. No electronic copies of this one. This is a read-on-site-only proposition... No, I'm not kidding you. It's that sensitive... Right. Okay. See you then." George disconnected the call.

"Did you hook him?" Dara asked.

"I think so." George stood and stretched. "How many does that make?"

Dara looked down at her notes. "I count eight potentials."

"How many of those do you think we can count in the 'likely' column?"

Dara pursed her lips in thought. "I'd say we've got three solids and one definite maybe."

"Not bad."

"It was genius telling them they'd have a limited amount of time to peruse the script, and then only in our presence."

"I've done that before in a couple of extraordinary cases. It creates an air of intrigue and mystery around the project—makes folks think this is going to be white-hot."

"Very shrewd."

"I have my moments."

"Who do you see playing opposite me?"

"Good question. What about Trevor Hanscome for the president?"

"Excellent choice." Trevor was a good actor and a better man. Dara had enjoyed working with him the few times their careers had crossed. "He's debonair and suave. Plus, he's got that height

184

so that he towers over his co-stars. You'd want that in a president."

Dara's phone rang. She glanced at the display, indicated to George that she needed to take the call, and tapped her Bluetooth to answer. "Hi."

"Have you had a chance to look over the deal?"

"You do know that normal conversations start with, 'How are you? Is this a good time to chat?' Or some version thereof?" Dara imagined Carolyn on the other end of the phone, cup of coffee by her right elbow, folders open all over her desk, and a pen poised over a lined sheet of legal paper.

"If you have time for idle chit-chat, then I'm assuming you've already reviewed the contract."

"As a matter of fact, I have. It seems fair enough to me, so I signed it and returned it to you via FedEx. It should arrive to you tomorrow morning by ten o'clock."

"I do love your efficiency."

"Your new client is going to love *your* efficiency. Has she even signed the engagement agreement yet?"

"Not your business, but I just e-mailed it to her."

"You sent me the contract before you even had her on board?"

"Let's just say I'm confident she'll accept the terms. I can't wait to tell her we sold the rights!"

"You might want to"—Dara heard the telltale tones in her ear that let her know that Carolyn was gone—"wait until she signs on the dotted line first." She finished the sentence and then mumbled, "It's also customary to say goodbye before you hang up."

Jay yawned and stretched languorously. She reached beside her for Kate, hoping to sneak in one more round of lovemaking before they had to get up and start the day. She opened an eye to find the other side of the bed vacated, and that was when she smelled the unmistakable scent of cinnamon French toast and bacon wafting from the kitchen. She smiled into the pillow and drifted off for a few more minutes, knowing breakfast in bed would be served shortly. "I so love you, Katherine Kyle."

When next she woke, it was to a gentle kiss and Kate caressing her naked shoulder.

"Breakfast is served."

Jay sat up and let the sheet fall away. Diffused light was streaming in through the blinds. "What time is it?"

"Late." Kate smiled at her indulgently. "I thought you deserved to sleep in. That's what you Hollywood types do, right? Stay in bed all morning?" Kate placed a breakfast tray in front of Jay. It was laden with French toast, butter, syrup, bacon, and a side of fresh fruit.

Jay ran her hands through her hair to settle it. "That's me, the glamour queen." She accepted the glass of orange juice Kate handed her and pulled the tray higher up on the bed. "Where's yours?"

"I'm going to get it right now."

"You'd better be naked again by the time you get back here with it," Jay called after her. She inhaled deeply. A wonderful dinner and show, the e-mailed letter of engagement that Jay signed electronically and returned to Carolyn by the time they'd gotten off the train in Albany last night, lovemaking with her wife, breakfast in bed. Life was very, very good.

Kate waltzed back into the room carrying a second breakfast tray and wearing nothing but a smile. Oh yes, life was very, very good indeed.

⊰⊱

"Please do not take this the wrong way. As much as I am enjoying your company," Sabastien said to Lorraine over breakfast, "I am wishing I was back in my comfortable home, poking around in the back doors of these companies for the good guys, and not having to worry about anyone trying to throw me in jail."

Lorraine put a hand over his. "I promise you, we'll figure out all of this and have your name in the clear very soon. We're making good headway."

"What exactly are we looking for?" Sabastien asked.

"Ultimately, I'm looking for familiar names—people who I can verify are both part of the Commission and in control or in positions of power within companies holding key government contracts. These would most likely be members of the boards of directors, company executives, or owners. If you can help me trace the relationships between some of the subcontractors and the major contract holders, I'm hoping some of these names will surface. When they do, it should lead us to the end game."

"The end of game?"

Lorraine smiled kindly at him, something Vaughn never did when Sabastien got lost in American idioms. "We'll understand what it is they're up to—why they wanted you out of the way—and what it is they hoped to gain."

"Oh, I see."

"And the faster you can make the connections," Vaughn said as she came into the kitchen from the living room, "the sooner we can clear you and get out of here."

"Perhaps if you were not so on the edge—"

"On edge," Vaughn corrected him. "There is no 'the' in the expression."

Sabastien knit his brows together. Although Vaughn always had a tendency to be a little impatient and brusque, lately she had become downright surly. But anytime Sabastien mentioned it to her, Vaughn told him he was imagining things. Perhaps Lorraine could have a talk with her. He wondered, based on the disapproving expression on Lorraine's face, if perhaps she wasn't thinking the same thing.

"I guess that's our cue to get back to work," Lorraine said. "Are you finished here?"

"Oui."

She took Sabastien's plate and put it in the dishwasher.

Vaughn grabbed the car keys off the hook by the back door. "The new encrypted phones and scramblers I procured for us should have arrived at the drop by now. I'll go check on them."

When she was gone, Lorraine said, "I don't know Vaughn as well as you do, but it seems to me like she's a little..." Lorraine made a gesture with her hands to indicate that Vaughn was tense.

"She is."

"Any idea why?"

"I do not. I was hoping perhaps you could have a small chat with her."

"Woman-to-woman, you mean," Lorraine said.

Sabastien blushed. "I did not intend to... You know."

"You didn't offend me, Sabastien. I'll give it a go when the opportunity arises. In the meantime, let's go catch us some bad guys."

"Yes. Let us do that."

❧❧

"Here it is," Carolyn said. She pulled a packet of documents from her briefcase and put it on the counter in front of Jay. "I paper-clipped the check to the inside of the folder on top. I thought you might want to get a look at that first."

Jay blinked. Everything was coming together so quickly. "Can I just say, I can't believe you made the trip up here to hand this to me. You could've sent it FedEx."

"I could have," Carolyn agreed. "But then I wouldn't get the pleasure of seeing the look on your face when you open that up." She indicated the folder. "And, I wouldn't have gotten a tour of your beautiful home."

"You're very kind."

"Just honest." Carolyn looked around. "I was hoping to see Kate again."

"She really wanted to be here. Unfortunately, something unexpected came up that she had to deal with." Jay tried to keep her expression neutral. The truth was, she was worried. Kate ran out two hours ago to meet Peter, who had returned without explanation, and without Lorraine, only twenty-four hours after landing in Morocco. Kate had promised to call when she knew anything, and so far, the phone hadn't rung.

Carolyn pushed the folder closer to Jay. "You have remarkable self-control. I would've opened that by now."

"I'm savoring the moment." Jay turned the folder over and pretended to study it from all angles. She really did want to yank the cover open, but she was having too much fun enjoying the twinkle of anticipation in Carolyn's eyes; it reminded her of a parent watching a child unwrap a Christmas present.

"Oh my God! Please just open it."

Jay complied. Her eyes popped open wide at the figure on the check. "Is this for real?"

"It is."

Jay ran her forefinger over the pay-to line. This was as much money as Black Quill paid her for her last three-book deal. It made Jay want to weep—not for the money—but for the validation of her worth. The past few months, her self-esteem and self-identity had taken a beating.

"What's wrong?" Carolyn's voice sounded alarmed.

Jay sniffed and cleared her throat. "Nothing. Nothing's wrong."

"You looked like you were about to burst into tears."

Jay's hands shook as she closed the folder and replaced it on the counter. If Carolyn was going to represent her, she needed to understand her client. "Writing this book was soul-shredding. I had to go back in time and dredge up so many horrible memories and horrific events. I had to relive the worst time in my life and mine every emotion to make the story everything it needed to be."

Carolyn nodded sympathetically.

"And then, when the classified documents were leaked and the story hit the media and Black Quill bailed on the book, my world came crashing down. For months, my credibility has been questioned, along with my loyalty to this country. Without going into any detail, my friends have been threatened and harmed in real ways too."

Jay looked away to gather her composure. Sabastien, Vaughn, and now Lorraine, were hiding away somewhere in Casablanca. Jeremy lost his job—a job he loved—and his friendship with the publisher. Peter and Kate were busy hunting leads that hopefully would clear Sabastien. Niles didn't know which end was up. And somewhere out there, the Commission was having a field day.

"It's okay, Jay. Whatever it is, it's okay." Carolyn came around the island and wrapped her arms around Jay. It should have felt awkward. After all, Carolyn was her agent and this was a professional meeting. But she was also Dara's best friend, and somehow, Jay believed, Carolyn was her friend too. She was that kind of person—the kind who provided an instant sense of closeness and comfort.

"I'm sorry. I've been on such an emotional rollercoaster. To see this check—this symbolic representation of other people's trust in me and their belief in my work—it hit me harder than I thought it would. I'm usually a cooler customer than this." Jay pulled back and opened the folder again. It was time to lighten the mood. "Now, where were we?"

Carolyn clearly accepted the change in topic and stepped away as well. "We were about to toast to your first stint as a triple threat—novelist, screenwriter, and executive producer."

"I suppose that would require that we have something stronger than coffee. Hmm… Champagne in the middle of the day?"

"Why Jamison Parker, that would be incredibly decadent of you."

"True. But apparently I can afford it now."

"Touché."

కురా

"If you keep scowling, your face is going to get stuck like that. Didn't your parents ever tell you that?"

"Don't deflect, Enright. It won't work." Kate was fuming. "You should have told me the whole plan. You knew I wouldn't go along with leaving Lorraine behind like that. Don't you ever handle me again."

"I apologize. We could've gone about that differently. But the bottom line is that Lorraine is exactly where she needs to be, and so am I. Together, she and Sabastien are the most powerful one-two combination we have. They are in the best position to identify any Commission connections in that tangled web, and they can only accomplish that while they're in the same space. We've got too many information security issues to take a chance on collaborating remotely right now."

Kate hated that Peter was right. The Black Knight already had wreaked too much havoc. "Why didn't you stay with her?"

"You know why." He held up the USB drive. "We've got work to do. We need to focus on figuring out who the Black Knight is. It's the only way to clear Sabastien and take the pressure off him."

Again, Kate resented that Peter was right. Even if they could expose the Commission agents, that did nothing to get Sabastien off the hook. They would have to prove that Sabastien didn't work for the Commission and that he didn't leak the documents. Kate briefly considered checking in with Jay, whom she had promised to call hours earlier. She thought better of it. No doubt Jay was in the middle of discussions with Carolyn. To Peter she said, "Let's get started."

"I thought you might say that."

&.&

Vaughn stood on the balcony overlooking the sea. In profile, she appeared pensive. Although Lorraine would've preferred to give her privacy, time was of the essence and they could ill afford to have discord in the house. She slid open the screen door and stepped outside.

"Penny for your thoughts?"

Vaughn grunted in response. "Not sure they're worth that much."

"I'm betting otherwise. Something's clearly bothering you. Care to share?"

For a moment, Vaughn simply continued to stare out into the distance, and Lorraine wondered if she would answer.

"I hardly know where to begin." Vaughn went silent again.

"I always find the beginning a good place to start," Lorraine gently prodded.

"Fair enough. I don't know if you're aware, but I'm the one who got Sabastien his gig with the Executive branch." Vaughn pointed at her chest for emphasis. "I'm the one who put him in a vulnerable position. For all his expertise in electronics, Sabastien is, in his heart, a naïve, sweet, guileless guy. He has no idea what this predicament could mean for him."

"So your irascibility is about you feeling responsible for Sabastien?" Lorraine leaned her forearms on the railing. "You recognize that he doesn't understand that, right? To him, you're just being churlish and difficult. You're making his job here harder."

Vaughn glared at her, but Lorraine stood her ground. "We wouldn't *be* here if I hadn't pushed him to take on the contract. He said so himself in a recent conversation with me."

"If he said something to you, it was most likely in a moment of pique. Truthfully, it doesn't seem to me that Sabastien has any regrets about his employment. On the other hand, he harbors deep concern for the state of your relationship with him."

Vaughn's brow creased, but she said nothing. So Lorraine decided to push on. "What Sabastien really needs is your friendship and support. He's trying his hardest to catch this guy who's besmirched his name. It would be a lot easier for him to concentrate if he knew you had his back."

"Of course I have his back," Vaughn hissed.

"I know that. But he doesn't." Lorraine gestured back toward the house. "He thinks your problem is with him, and it's tearing him up. You're the only one who can fix that, Vaughn. And, for all of our sakes, especially Sabastien's, I really, really hope you find it in your heart to do that."

Without another word, Lorraine turned on her heel and stalked back inside.

CHAPTER EIGHTEEN

Dara and Rebecca sat side-by-side, their feet in the sand, as they enjoyed their morning coffee. Jay's project was moving at lightning speed, and this was the first opportunity they'd had to enjoy a moment of downtime together.

"I heard back from the casting director. They locked in Trevor Hanscome to play the president."

"Shh." Rebecca's head was tilted back and her eyes were closed. "Listen to the sound of the waves and take advantage of the peace and solitude while we have it. We can talk business later, can't we?"

Dara leaned over and kissed her wife lightly on the lips. "Mm-hmm. We sure can." She drew back and gazed lovingly at Rebecca's profile.

"Why are you staring at me?"

"How do you know I am?"

Rebecca smiled. "I can feel it."

"Aren't you the sensitive one."

"Sometimes." Rebecca reached out and linked their hands together.

When she opened her eyes, the depth of love reflected there made Dara want to weep with joy. "I love you."

"I love you too. Sometimes, in moments like these, I still can't believe I'm here, with you, like this." Rebecca indicated their joined hands.

"I know. I hope we always feel this way."

"Me too." Rebecca caressed Dara's hand with her thumb. "Do you think Kate and Jay still have this kind of love, this sense of wonder about it?"

Dara reviewed in her mind the times she spent with Kate and Jay, both together and individually. "I do. You can see it in the way they gaze at each other, in the respect they show for each other. It's present in their body language and the way they talk about each other when they're apart."

"I hope we have that thirty years from now."

"I hope we never have to deal with half of what they've been through, but I'd like to think whatever hardships and experiences we go through will bond us more closely too."

The shrill sound of a ringing phone pierced the peacefulness.

"You brought your phone with you?" Rebecca asked.

"Sorry. I know this is our time, but we've got a lot of balls in the air between the location scouting, the casting, the backers..." Dara glanced down at the display and her eyes widened in surprise.

"Who is it?"

"Carolyn. She never calls this early."

"Better answer it."

"Hello?"

"I'm sorry to bug you. I know it's early out there."

"Rebecca and I were enjoying a few moments of alone-time at the beach. What's up?"

"Now I feel even worse. But this is too important to wait. *Variety* posted a piece online about the film an hour ago."

"What? How could they know..."? Dara tried to gain her composure. Everyone involved in the project was required to sign a strict confidentiality agreement. "Can you read it to me?"

"It's just a brief teaser...

> The hottest, most hush-hush rumor in Hollywood has A-list star Dara Thomas snapping up a controversial property from *New York Times* best-selling author Jamison Parker. Parker, you might recall, has been embroiled in a real-life thriller over leaked classified government secrets. So far, book publishers have been unwilling to take a chance on Parker's novel. It looks like Thomas has no such reservations. Stay tuned as this one unfolds.

"That's all it says, but my phone's been ringing off the hook with calls from reporters looking to confirm the story."

"What are you telling them?"

"I'm not."

"Good."

"I sent them over to your public relations reps to take care of it."

"Okay. I'm sure that means I'll be getting a call from them shortly."

"Most likely. Who do you think talked?"

Dara had been wondering the same thing. "It'd be easier to tell you who definitely didn't talk. That would be me, Rebecca, you, Jay, Kate, and George. Beyond that..."

"Okay. Well, I'm in crisis mode over here, so I'm going to run."

"Wait!"

"What?"

"Does Jay know? I don't imagine she subscribes to *Variety*."

"She was my next call. I'm not looking forward to it. That poor woman has been through enough. I hate to give her one more thing to worry about."

Dara stared out at the horizon. Jay was Carolyn's client now; it should fall to Carolyn to make the call. But Dara's relationship with Jay went beyond professional collaboration.

"Are you still there?"

"Yes," Dara said. "I'd really like to talk to her. I feel responsible for this. I'm the one who approached her with the idea."

"I understand that. But she's a new client, sweetie, and having a discussion like this falls within my purview."

"I know. It's just..."

"How about this. I'll make the initial call, and text you to let you know when we're done. Then you can give her a buzz and follow up."

"Fair enough."

"Later."

"Good luck." Dara disconnected the call.

"That didn't sound like good news," Rebecca said.

Dara opened the web browser on her phone, navigated over to variety.com, and handed the phone to her wife.

"Oh my." Rebecca continued reading. When she finished, she handed the phone back to Dara. "I thought everyone involved in this signed the confidentiality agreement?"

"They did."

"You don't think it was anyone who signed on to the project."

It was a statement, not a question. Rebecca's astuteness was one of the many qualities Dara most admired about her. "No."

Dara had a thought. "On the other hand, some of the initial potential investors we approached were under no such constraints." The more she considered that scenario, the more likely it seemed to her that was what had occurred.

"Makes sense," Rebecca agreed. "In which case, it really was a stroke of inspiration to make them read the script in person. At least the script won't be circulating anywhere."

"Thank God." Dara stood up and reached out a hand to Rebecca. "We'd better get going." First, she would talk to Jay. Then, Dara would have to have the lawyers draft up additional confidentiality agreements for everyone involved with the film to prevent them from sharing the contents of the script or any details of the screenplay or story with anyone.

Jay sat down heavily on a stool at the kitchen island. It was only a fluke that Carolyn caught her on the phone. Usually at this hour, she was out running with Kate. But this morning, her hamstring was tight, and she'd decided to use the opportunity to write instead.

Now she was waiting for Kate to return so she could share the news with her. The doorbell rang and Jay furrowed her brow as she jumped up to answer it. She could've sworn Kate took her key with her. *Maybe she didn't bother since she knew you'd be here.*

"What happened? Did you forget your...key?" Jay's heart hammered and she stammered the last word, as she came face-to-face with the same two men who had been shadowing her in New York.

"Jamison Parker?"

"Yes."

"I'm FBI Special Agent Timothy Alexander and this is my partner, Special Agent David Welch. We'd like to have a word with you."

Jay scrutinized the credentials the agent showed her. She kept the door halfway closed behind her and stood ramrod straight in the doorway. "What can I do for you?"

Agent Alexander removed his sunglasses. "May we come in?"

Jay willed her heart rate to slow. What should she say? She and Kate had talked about this scenario in the abstract, but... What would Kate say if she were here? "I don't think so."

The agent seemed taken aback by that. "Fair enough. Ms. Parker. Can I call you Jamison?"

She recognized the technique—he was trying to ingratiate himself with her. "Ms. Parker is fine."

"Okay, Ms. Parker. I don't want to waste your time, so I'll get right to the point. We are aware that you have written a book that you are trying to get published that appears to contain details specific to some top secret information vis-à-vis the Hyland Commission report."

Idly, Jay wondered if all FBI agents were trained to use poor sentence structure. The agent's brow was raised, and Jay realized he must've thought he'd asked a question. She decided to wait him out.

"We know that you have a connection to Niles Masterson. We also know you were the reporter who broke the story in the Hyland incident. We want you to know that we appreciate that you need to a make a living now. We're sure cashing in on that experience could be quite lucrative."

Jay bristled at the insinuation, but said nothing.

"We are also sympathetic to the lure of the spotlight. We have verified that you signed a contract selling the rights to this story to Hollywood."

Again, the agent paused, and Jay maintained her best poker face.

"This could go very, very badly for you, Ms. Parker. If you, even accidentally, divulge top secret information, you will go to prison." He emphasized the word, "will."

"Is there a point to all this, Agent Alexander?"

"Look, Ms. Parker... Are you sure we can't come inside and discuss this with you?"

"Positive." Jay leaned against the doorframe and crossed her legs at the ankle, trying for all the world to appear confident and at ease.

The agent held his hands out to the side as if trying to gentle a skittish colt. "We're not the bad guys here. We just don't want to see you get mixed up in something that won't end well for you. If your work compromises national security, we won't be able to assist you."

Jay's nostrils flared in anger. *How dare you patronize me.* She wanted to scream it at him. Instead, she prayed for calm and remained mum.

"I've got an idea I think might help you out. How about if you share a copy of the manuscript with us? We could have our experts vet it, and if there's anything that would be problematic for you, they could tweak it—"

"No!" Jay said it louder than she intended, as she shoved off the frame. "I'm not giving you access to anything. If you want to have any further discussion, you can talk to my attorney."

Agent Alexander cleared his throat. "Now just slow down here a second, Ms. Parker. I'm not so sure it's in your best interests to invoke an attorney. First, we're not charging you with anything, yet. This is just a friendly visit..."

"Uh-huh."

"Second, any attorney you hire is just going to be trying to get a whole bunch of money from you. He might not have your best interests at heart. It's his wallet he'll be thinking about."

Jay stepped back so that she was fully inside the house. She wrapped her hand around the door and started to close it.

"Ms. Parker, you might want to think twice about shutting that door in our faces. If you go forward with this, be aware that your significant other had full access in the Hyland administration to top secret-level information that absolutely would compromise national security. A strong case could be made that she is the one who gave you the information for this book. She herself could be in a lot of trouble. You don't want that, now do you?"

"That 'significant other' you reference is my wife. And to suggest that she would do anything to harm this country that she served so valiantly..." Jay balled her hands into fists. "Get out. Now. And don't ever come back here. You can deal with my attorney."

At that moment, Kate came into view. She rounded the corner and sprinted toward them. "What's going on here?" she asked, as she skidded to a stop inches from the agents.

"Nothing. These gentlemen were just leaving."

"Here's our card, Ms. Parker. In case you change your mind."

"I won't."

"That would be very foolish on your part, but if that's the case, please have your attorney contact us at his earliest convenience."

"Her," Jay said pointedly. "I'll have *her* contact you at *her* earliest convenience." She reached out, tugged on Kate's sleeve to get her to come inside, and closed the door in the agents' faces.

"What was that all about?"

Jay threw herself into Kate's arms.

"Hey. Hey, sweetheart. You're shaking." Kate tightened her grip and pulled Jay closer. She brushed her lips over the top of Jay's head. "I've got you."

"Those sanctimonious assholes!" All the pent up fear, anger, and rage Jay had been feeling poured out of her body and she yielded to the comfort of Kate's embrace.

"Why don't you tell me how you really feel?"

Jay felt, rather than saw, Kate's smile, and accepted the lightening of the mood. "Well, since you asked..."

"Uh-huh." Kate pulled back and swept an errant lock of hair off Jay's forehead. "You okay?"

"I am now." Jay took Kate's hand and led them into the kitchen.

"Why did they approach you directly? That's a change of tactics."

Jay scrunched up her face in puzzlement, and then she remembered—Kate didn't know about the piece in *Variety*. So she explained about the story, the call from Carolyn, and then shared the gist of the conversation with the FBI agents.

"I leave you alone for one hour and all hell breaks loose."

"That's the last time I let a little hamstring strain hold me back."

Jay's phone, which had been sitting on the kitchen counter, rang. "Now what?" She checked out the display. "It's Dara," she said to Kate. "What should I do?"

"Take the call, sweetie. I'm going to grab a shower anyway." Kate kissed her on the forehead.

When she'd gone, Jay tried to settle her emotions and turned on her Bluetooth to take the call. "It's awfully early in the morning for you to be working. I thought you Hollywood types slept in. At least, that's what my wife keeps telling me."

"You spent almost two weeks here. Did you ever see me sleep late? Oh, and good morning to you too, Jay." Dara's voice was warm like honey, with an undercurrent of tension.

"Touché. I take it you got a call from Carolyn too?"

"I did. I'm so, so sorry, Jay. I know this is the last thing you need—"

"Don't, Dara. This isn't on you. I'm positive you didn't leak the story, and you certainly didn't authorize the hack that started this whole mess, so you're off the hook." Jay tried to keep her voice light and playful.

"All true, but I am the one who suggested going directly to film, which puts you in the crosshairs again."

"Again?" Jay questioned. "I wasn't aware that I'd ever been out of the line of fire." She swallowed the lump in her throat. She didn't want to tell Dara about her encounter with the Feds, at least not yet. She still needed time to process everything.

Something the agent said niggled at the back of Jay's mind, working its way into her consciousness. "Dara?"

"Mmm?"

"Would the fact that I sold you the rights be recorded in any public document? You know, like the sale of a piece of property gets recorded at the county assessor's office?"

"No. What you and I signed is a private contract. In most cases, we'd want the public to know we'd purchased the rights to something this fabulous and we'd task our publicity departments with getting the word out. But because of the sensitive nature of this project, I never made that call. Nor did Carolyn." Dara laughed mirthlessly. "You can bet I talked to my PR reps after the *Variety* tidbit hit, though. I instructed them to say nothing."

"Okay."

"*Variety* didn't get its information from a public document, Jay. I suspect that one of the potential investors who didn't come on board leaked it."

"Gotcha. I wasn't asking for that reason." After she'd said the words, Jay winced. Dara was too astute to let that slip by.

"You weren't?"

And there it was. Jay bit her lip. She wished she and Kate had had time to talk through the ramifications more thoroughly. She wished she'd had more time to gather her thoughts.

"Jay?"

"I'm sorry. I'm here." It was decision time. "I-I'm a little rattled this morning."

"What's wrong? I mean, apart from the obvious." Dara's voice was filled with concern.

"The FBI paid me a visit a little while ago."

"The..."

"FBI. Yeah."

"What happened?"

"Kate was out running. I should've been out there with her, but I had a tight hammie, so I stayed behind." *Get to the point, Parker. You're rambling.* "Anyway, I still need time to process it all, but mostly I think they were trying to rattle me. The reason I asked you the question was because the agent said that he was aware of the contract you and I signed. I wondered if he really did know, or if he was bluffing and had read the same *Variety* article the rest of the world can see."

"Ah. I see. He was bluffing, Jay. Short of asking me a direct question or accessing my banking records or yours, he would have no way of knowing that."

"Okay. Well, he would need a subpoena to get to either of our bank accounts, and I'm pretty sure we'd know if he'd done that."

"I would hope so," Dara said.

"Dara?"

"Yes?"

"They were trying their best to get me to give them a copy of the manuscript. It wouldn't surprise me if, having struck out with me, they would try to intimidate you into cooperating or backing away from the project."

"I told you at the outset. I'm not easily scared and I'm certainly not giving them access to either the manuscript or the screenplay."

"But if you want to walk away, I could refund you every penny. I would understand."

"Are you kidding me? That's never going to happen. We're going to make this movie, and it's going to be spectacular."

Dara didn't waver. She sounded strong, resolute. "If you're sure."

"I'm positive. If the FBI has something to say to me, they can talk to my attorney."

Jay closed her eyes and thanked Heaven for bringing Dara and Rebecca into her life.

"Jay? Are you still there?"

"I am. If I haven't said so lately, thank you."

"For what?"

"For wanting to take a chance on this—on me."

"I'm the one who should be thanking you—for trusting us with something so important and personal. We won't let you down, Jay."

Warmth suffused Jay's body as the sincerity of Dara's words sunk in, bringing her comfort. "I know."

CHAPTER NINETEEN

I know I've been a little testy lately," Vaughn said. She was peering over Sabastien's shoulder as he parsed some data on one of the companies they'd flagged as a likely Commission target.

Her proximity made Sabastien so nervous his palms were sweating. Unsure what to say, he said nothing and continued to focus on the task at hand.

"Look, I'm trying to apologize here. Can you at least take a second to stop what you're doing and look at me?"

Tentatively, Sabastien twirled his seat around. "I am seeing you."

"Thanks." Vaughn pulled up a chair and sat with her hands clasped between her knees. "I want you to understand that my displeasure isn't with you, exactly."

"No?"

Vaughn shook her head. "The truth is, I feel completely responsible for putting you in peril yet again. It seems being around me isn't good for you."

"I do not understand." Sabastien raised his hands and let them fall to his sides. "You are here protecting me. You have stopped your life, again, to look after me. How is this putting me in danger?"

"I wouldn't be here looking out for you, and you wouldn't be watching over your shoulder for bad guys, if I hadn't gotten you involved with the White House in the first place. You said as much yourself."

Sabastien scrunched up his face. He wanted to understand what Vaughn was saying and why she appeared to be so exasperated, but it made no sense. "I am convoluted."

Vaughn burst out laughing.

"I made a funny?"

"You *are* convoluted, my friend. But in this instance, what you mean to say is that you are confused."

"Oui. C'est ça."

"I'm listening."

"I was in need of a job. You spoke with the president of your country on my behalf and he engaged me—me!" Sabastien pointed at his chest. "Sabastien Vaupaul, to watch his behind and ensure the security of your government's electronic communications. This is unbelievable. I am living my dream. What I said to you I said out of fear. I did not mean anything by it."

"This is living your dream? Being on the run and holed up in yet another foreign country, with the US government convinced you're a traitor and the Commission wanting you out of the way?"

"Well, perhaps not exactly this moment, no. But in general, I am happy, Vaughn Elliott. I am doing what I love to do and getting paid a lot of money for it. I live in the most important city in your country. I never imagined such a life before I met you. Such excitement!"

Vaughn growled low in her throat.

"You make this sound and I think that you are frustrated with me," Sabastien said. "I want to understand. Truly, I do. But I do not."

"No. You don't," Vaughn agreed. "In some ways you are the smartest man I know. Nobody is better when it comes to computers. But as a human being, you are so innocent and naïve. I just want to protect you from the world you don't see. There are very real threats to you out there, Sabastien." Vaughn gestured in the direction of the window.

"I am aware. But you did not create the hack that makes this trouble. The Black Knight, or whoever he is, did this. Not you." Sabastien pointed a finger at Vaughn. "Not you. You remind me of those cowboys I see in your old movies. The ones with John Wayne and Gary Cooper."

"You watch old westerns?"

"Oui. Bien sûr."

"Why?"

"It is part of your culture. I am curious."

"You never cease to amaze me." Vaughn stood up. "In any event, I'm trying to apologize to you here. I want you to know I'm not angry with you. I'm angry with myself for getting you into this mess in the first place—for making this mess possible."

"Okay. I accept your apology, Vaughn Elliott. And I am grateful that you will maybe stop being so nasty. But please do not be a cowboy. I understand what is happening and why I am here in Casablanca. We will fix this, and we can all go home soon, yes?"

"Okay."

"Now, I am on the verge of something important here. If you could get Lorraine for me, I think I have found something meaningful."

"Roger that." Vaughn left the room in search of Lorraine.

Sabastien smiled to himself. He would have to give Lorraine a big thank you when next they were alone. Vaughn Elliott apologizing to him. Who would have figured that?

❧

"I've already apologized twenty times for not telling you Lorraine was going to stay behind," Peter said. "How many more times will I have to say mea culpa before I'm off the hook?"

"It's not like you forgot to mention that you bought a new television," Kate answered.

"Definitely not," Jay agreed. "Have you spoken to her?"

"I have not. We agreed that we would only make contact when we had something significant or actionable to share."

"How romantic."

"Did you invite me over here to browbeat me, or are we going to get down to business and figure out who John Robie is so we can clear Sabastien and bring our friends home?"

"Yes to both," Kate said.

"Fantastic." Peter opened his laptop, booted it up, and inserted the USB drive Vaughn gave him. "By the way, your FBI buddies are parked around the corner."

"I am painfully aware," Jay said.

"Honestly, I'm surprised they'd expend the manpower to tail you. That's unusual."

"I feel so honored."

"I'm sure you do." He put a hand on top of Jay's hand. "The scramblers I put in place will prevent them from being able to eavesdrop on anything that is said in this house. Your privacy is assured."

"That's something," Jay said morosely.

Peter withdrew his hand. "Let's catch the bad guys and get you your lives back." He clicked on the spreadsheet containing all of the companies and government entities John Robie had hacked within the past five years.

Kate and Jay maneuvered their chairs so that they could see the screen. "What are we looking for?" Kate asked.

"Patterns. We need to know more about this guy. We have to get inside his head. Then we can build out a more detailed profile on him."

"Even if we can do that, trying to ID him is like looking for a needle in a haystack," Jay said.

"You're unusually pessimistic today."

"Being grilled by the FBI will do that," Jay said.

"Point taken. But here's the thing." Peter opened a new spreadsheet and set up a series of columns. "This guy is prolific and arrogant. He has to have been on somebody's radar before now. If so, it's likely there's a paper trail on him—possibly a criminal record or at least an investigation. If so, we'll find it. We just need to organize what information we have into a cogent format so we can see what's right in front of us."

"That's it," Dara said. "We've got the last of the major parts cast and the contracts and confidentiality agreements signed." She turned the laptop screen so that George could see it.

"It's a good cast. One I can work with. Are you pleased?"

"I am. These are all seasoned actors with significant film credits and reputations for being dedicated to craft. There's not a diva or difficult personality in the mix. These are all actors with integrity."

"I agree. I'm sure you explained to them the unusual circumstances of the project?"

"I did. I wanted to make sure no one would back out if the going gets tough."

"You told them they would have to sign out their scripts and pages everyday? And that the scripts and pages would be tracked electronically?"

"Yes. They were mostly intrigued by the prospect of working on something this tightly controlled. Very James Bond-ish."

"I've been blocking the scenes with an eye toward ensuring that we can be nimble and versatile if we have to change shoot locations."

"Any word from the location scouts?" Dara asked.

"We've narrowed it down to several possibilities. I'm awaiting cost estimates for each to present to you and the other investors."

Dara's phone buzzed and she picked it up from the table so that she could read the display. "Huh."

"Huh?"

"My attorney." She rose and took the phone with her. "Sorry, George. Give me a second?"

"Sure."

"Hello? This is Dara."

"Dara? Ross Takada here."

"What can I do for you, Ross?"

"I got a call from an agent with the Federal Bureau of Investigation. He would like to sit down with you and discuss a project he alleges you're working on. You know, the one you had me draft the confidentiality agreements for."

Dara's heart rate accelerated. *That didn't take long.* She was glad Jay told her about her earlier visit; it lessened the shock. *At least the FBI didn't knock on your door like they did with Jay. They went through your lawyer.* Even so, the fact that the FBI wanted to chat with her was unnerving. "What did you tell the agent?"

"I told him I would talk to you. Want to tell me what's going on? Confidentiality agreements are one thing. This is something completely different."

Did she want to give Ross the details? "Are you better off not knowing?"

"Not if you're in trouble."

"I haven't done anything wrong, Ross. The FBI would prefer that the film the agent referenced not be made. I intend to go ahead with it."

"I see. What can you tell me about the film? Why are the Feds interested? And why all the extra secrecy and security protocols for the principals involved?"

"Everything I tell you falls under attorney-client privilege, right?"

"It does."

"Okay. I bought the rights to Jamison Parker's unpublished novel."

Ross whistled. "The one I keep reading about in the papers?"

"Yes."

There was silence on the other end of the line.

"Ross? Did I lose you?"

"No. That's the project the confidentiality agreements were for?"

"Yes."

"I can see why the FBI wants to speak with you."

"I'm assuming I'm under no obligation to do so."

"Correct."

"And I'm also assuming you'd advise me not to."

"Correct. But you and I ought to sit down and talk this through."

"The FBI already tried to lean on Jay."

"Jay?"

"I'm sorry. Ms. Parker."

"Well, she'd be the likely place to start. Without her, you'd have nothing to work with and they wouldn't be calling me. I would guess she was less than cooperative?"

"I don't know what exact words she used, but I can tell you the gist of the message was for them to go pound salt."

"Dara, I'm obliged to advise you that if there is anything top secret that will be revealed in the film—if national security could be compromised as the FBI intimated—you could be in legal jeopardy."

Dara pursed her lips in thought. "In order for me to be in trouble, would I have to know specifically that I was revealing classified information? I mean, if it was classified, how would I know?"

"I wouldn't want to have to cut it that fine, if I were you. Do you believe the manuscript to which you purchased the rights and/or the subsequent screenplay contain anything top secret?"

"No." Dara thought about it. "Jay's work is a fictional account based on true events. But it *is* fiction."

"You trust her?"

"I do." Dara didn't hesitate. She truly did trust Jay. Jay would not intentionally put her or Rebecca in harm's way, of that she was certain.

"Okay then. I'll let the FBI know that you have declined a sit-down and that if they have any additional business with you, they'll have to go through me."

"Perfect. Thank you, Ross."

"Don't thank me yet. And we really should get together and have a more in-depth conversation about this."

"Soon," Dara promised. "Soon. Goodbye, Ross."

"Bye, Dara."

⊰⊱

Kate finished brushing her teeth and flossing. In the reflection of the mirror, she could see Jay sitting up in bed, reading. Although judging by the faraway look in her eyes, Kate doubted Jay was retaining much of what was on the page.

"Good book?" Kate asked as she came to bed.

"Hmm?"

"The book in your hands. You know, the one you're pretending to read. Is it any good?"

Jay sighed, closed the book, and placed it on the night table next to the bed. "I have no idea."

"Want to talk about it?"

"The main protagonist..."

"Very funny."

"It's the best I can muster at the moment."

Kate wrapped her arm around Jay's shoulder and pulled her in close. "I'll give you points for trying. But don't quit your day job."

"Excellent advice." Jay rested her head on Kate's shoulder. "Does it surprise you at all that the FBI is being this aggressive? Trying to intimidate me is one thing, but Dara is one of the most recognizable celebrities in the world."

"That's probably why they used the softer approach of going through her lawyer instead of contacting her directly. You don't just knock on Dara Thomas's front door and not expect it to make a splash."

Kate ran her fingers through Jay's hair. "How did Dara sound when you spoke with her?"

"Remarkably calm. She was more worried about me." Jay gazed up at Kate. "I really, really like her. I hate that she's coming under scrutiny because of me."

"This is only the beginning. If the Feds are as serious as we think they are about keeping this story from seeing the light of day, they'll find other ways to make your lives hell."

"That's a comforting thought."

Kate could feel the tension in Jay's body. "Just the truth."

"What do you think they'll do?"

"I don't know, sweetheart." Kate kissed the top of Jay's head. "I guess it depends on how scared of you they really are."

"They were frightened enough to cost Jeremy his job and to blackball me in the publishing industry. A movie has so much wider reach, I can just imagine how they'd feel about the prospects of that going forward."

"You still have time to change your mind and pull back if you want to."

Jay sat up. "What do you mean?"

"Apart from a gossipy item in *Variety*, nothing is public yet. You could cancel the contract and take back the rights to the manuscript."

"No. I always honor my commitments. Dara has the producers on board, the cast in place, and the screenplay is finished. She's already invested significant capital and put her reputation on the line. It would be incredibly unprofessional of me to back out now."

Kate nodded. "Then that's your answer."

"But I'm putting innocent people at risk."

"You're an innocent person," Kate pointed out.

"I'm the one who chose to write the story. I knew what I was doing."

"And all of these folks are willingly attaching themselves to the project."

"They don't know everything we know."

"They know enough to make informed choices. Dara is a big girl. She knows what she's doing. You were clear and honest with her, and she opted to move forward. Not only that, but making the movie was her idea. She knew when she approached you that the Feds were applying pressure on you and others to drop this."

"Why doesn't that make me feel any better?"

"Because you're one of the most empathetic, kind, compassionate human beings on the planet." Kate turned out the light. "But if we don't get some shuteye, you're also going to be one of the crabbiest people on the planet."

"I love you."

"I love you too, sweetheart. We'll get through this together."

"I don't know what I'd do without you."

"Fortunately, you'll never have to find out."

Dara stretched her legs under the coffee table. Her laptop was open, but she hadn't looked at it in so long it had gone to sleep.

"Still thinking about today?"

"Mm-hmm."

Rebecca got up from her chair and went to sit next to her. "You thinking about scrapping the project?"

"What? No." Dara adamantly shook her head. "Why would you think that?"

Rebecca shrugged. "It's one thing to hear in the abstract that the federal government doesn't want a manuscript to be published. It's quite another to have the FBI contact you and ask for an audience."

"The FBI can kiss my keister."

"Very alliterative."

"Very true."

"You're not scared?"

"No. I'm petrified. But I made a promise to Jay and I intend to honor it. She was forthright about the potential for adverse attention. I chose to move ahead anyway. I told her I wouldn't be cowed or intimidated, and I meant it."

"What does Ross think?"

"He didn't say I'd lost my mind, but he clearly was perplexed why I would open myself to this kind of attention."

"I can see that. It isn't like you need to do this for publicity or the paycheck. Why would someone of your stature invite this kind of scrutiny?"

Dara turned fully to face her wife. "Are you having second thoughts? You think I'm making a bad decision by going forward?"

"No. I'm with you all the way. Jay's work is brilliant and deserves to be seen by the public. As I said at the outset, this is a work of fiction. Stories like this that are based on truth get made everyday. There's ample precedent for it."

"But this isn't a hypothetical scenario we're talking about. This is our lives and our reputations."

"All true. I'm willing to take the risk if you are."

"I am."

"One more of the many reasons I love you so much. You're brave."

"Don't forget smart." Rebecca leaned over and kissed Dara thoroughly.

"And sexy. Don't forget sexy."

"Never."

CHAPTER TWENTY

Lorraine stared at the data until her eyes blurred. The government issued thousands of contracts and the major recipients of those contracts, in turn, hired hundreds of subcontractors. Somewhere in here was the key to whatever the Commission was up to now. But where?

"Need some help?" Vaughn asked. She was standing in the doorway, leaning against the frame.

"I could use a fresh perspective. I've been culling the contractors, dividing them into groups according to industry type. But there are so many of them, I feel like I'm spinning my wheels."

Vaughn came the rest of the way into the room and sat down in the chair opposite Lorraine. "Let's review what we know. The Commission is most likely operating in more than one of these companies, correct?"

"No question in my mind."

"And we assume they were behind the leak of the Hyland files."

"Yes."

"We know that Jay has a history with the Commission. So that would explain why she'd be a target. So, the question in my mind is, why would it be so important to them to set up Sabastien to take the fall?"

"Good question."

"As far as we know, there's no personal reason why the Commission should go after Sabastien. So they must have wanted him out of the way for professional reasons."

Lorraine flipped the pages of the document she held in her hands. "That was something I wondered about early on. What did Sabastien know that posed a threat to their plans?"

"He said part of his job was to vet all of the cyber interfaces between the government, the main contractors, and the subcontractors to make sure they weren't jeopardizing national security or government systems. Right?"

"Yes."

"What if he discovered something the Commission didn't want him to find?"

Lorraine shook her head. "This is where I keep getting stuck. If Sabastien had found something truly damning about the Commission, he'd be dead, not discredited. They wouldn't have spent months of manpower shadowing him in cyberspace in order to frame him. They would've taken him out before he even knew what was happening. Not only that, but we've already surmised that the Black Knight had been shadowing Sabastien's cyber-movements for months without doing anything overt."

Vaughn jumped up and started to pace. "Okay. Assuming you're right that the Black Knight had been keeping an eye on him for a longer horizon, what changed? Why make a move when they did?

"What if Sabastien was about to find whatever it was the Commission was protecting or was getting too close?" Lorraine asked.

Vaughn stopped pacing. "Where is Sabastien, by the way?"

"He was falling asleep at the computer, so I made him go take a nap." Vaughn took a step toward the door and Lorraine held up a hand. "Let him sleep. He really needs it. He's been working nonstop for days."

Although Vaughn seemed as if she wanted to object, she sat back down. "When he wakes up, we need to know what contractors and subcontractors in particular he was testing at the time of the leak."

"You're right. If we can pinpoint the timeframe and match it with the companies in question, we just might have our answer."

⊰⊱

As they rounded the last corner and headed toward home, Kate felt Jay tense beside her. The black sedan sat across the street, in plain view. The agents hadn't tried to engage either of them since Jay invoked her attorney, but their presence outside the house cast a pall over their lives.

It was time to lighten things up. "Race you. Loser buys dinner." Kate started to sprint.

"No fair. You got a head start."

"Catch me if you can." Kate held back just enough to let Jay come even with her, and then sped ahead again.

"Razzzmfrazzm long legs."

Kate laughed. "Not my fault."

"Not mine either."

At the last second, Kate pulled up and let Jay pass her.

"You let me win." Jay bent over and put her hands on her knees, straining to catch her breath.

"First, you accuse me of cheating by getting a head start. Then, you complain because I let you pass me."

Jay patted Kate on the cheek. "It's a tough life." She took off up the driveway, leapt up the front steps, and touched the front door. "Now I won, fair and square."

Kate followed, lifted Jay into the air, and spun her around. "Yep. You're the champ. Dinner's on me." She lowered Jay to the ground and kissed her. "You do have a key, right?"

"Very funny." Jay bent over, untied her shoe, untangled the key from the laces, and unlocked the door.

Kate's phone buzzed. She unhooked it from the waistband of her shorts and glanced at it as she trailed Jay into the house and closed the door. "Damn."

"What is it?" Jay stretched her hamstrings.

Kate finished reading the *New York Times* breaking news alert. Briefly, she considered not showing the story to Jay. *You can't protect her from everything.* She turned the screen so that Jay could see it and waited for the reaction.

"Oh my God!" She looked up at Kate. "They're charging Niles with intent to disclose classified information?"

"Looks that way. Read the rest of it." She waited for Jay to get to the part of the story where Niles reportedly had disappeared and his attorney commented that he'd been unable to reach his client.

"No way! He wouldn't…"

"Sounds like he did."

"What could he be thinking? He's only going to make it worse for himself. He hasn't published any story yet. He could fight this and win."

Kate nodded. The charge was troublesome. Would Jay be vulnerable under the same statute?

As if reading Kate's mind, Jay said, "You don't think they could…?"

Kate pulled Jay into her arms. "We'll call the attorneys and ask whatever questions we need to ask. Niles is dealing in classified documents. You're writing fiction. There's a big difference. Nothing you've written divulges top secret information. Even if they wanted to charge you, they couldn't make it stick."

Jay tightened her arms around Kate's waist. "We're doing the right thing, aren't we?"

Kate leaned back and tipped Jay's chin up to make eye contact. "What you're doing is important. If you have any doubt—"

"I don't."

"Okay, then. I'm with you all the way." Kate kissed her on the forehead. "Want to conserve water and shower together?"

"I thought you'd never ask."

"Have you seen the latest story in *Variety*?" Carolyn glanced surreptitiously around at the other diners to make sure she and Dara couldn't be overheard and that no one was paying them undue attention. She and Dara were situated in a corner booth, having lunch at a small, exclusive restaurant overlooking the beach in Santa Monica. Confident of their relative privacy, she slid her phone across the table.

Dara expanded the screen to enlarge the size of the text on the screen and read. When she was done, she returned the phone to Carolyn, closed her eyes, and pinched the bridge of her nose between her thumb and forefinger. "Well, they got the details of the cast and the location for the filming right. I was hoping we could keep this quiet a bit longer."

"It's Hollywood, Dar. Something this juicy was bound to get out there."

"I know, but I thought we could get the location nailed down and the table read under our belts before everything hit the fan."

"Too late for that now."

"Apparently. I can understand word of the cast leaking. That was bound to happen sooner or later, but I only talked to the other investors and gave George the green light to shoot outside of London a few days ago. I can't believe that's already out there."

"Why'd you pick England?

"The UK gave us the best incentive package. Our guys started roughing out and building the sets yesterday."

"So who's feeding *Variety* the intel?"

"I have no idea. I don't think that's the most pressing question, though."

"No?"

"No. I'm wondering how long it's going to take for Ross to call me again and tell me the FBI is making another request to interview me."

Carolyn put a hand on top of Dara's. "You're sure about this project?"

Dara withdrew her hand as if she'd been slapped. "Why would you ask me that? You're the one who negotiated the contract." She took a deep breath and reined in her annoyance. First Rebecca, now Carolyn. "You read the screenplay and the manuscript, right?"

"I did. They were brilliant."

"Exactly. Nothing's changed. Jay fully disclosed the potential fallout to you and to me. We both acknowledged and accepted the probability of government scrutiny when we signed on the dotted line. End of story."

Carolyn sat back. "You're awfully touchy for someone who's fully on board."

Dara bit off an angry retort and counted to five in her head. It was rare for her to lose her cool, especially with her best friend. So what was this really about? "I have no qualms about the movie. Excuse me if I'm not crazy about the FBI inserting itself into my business."

Carolyn held her gaze, but said nothing. Dara was well familiar with the tactic. After all, she and Carolyn had known each other since they were little girls.

"This is not grade school, Car. You're not going to win a staring contest with me. Say what's on your mind."

"All right. I think you're scared, and I know you. When you're afraid, you dig your heels in and become intransigent. I just want to be sure you're making this movie for the right reasons, that's all."

Dara rubbed her neck to release the tension there as she considered her answer. "Fair enough. It's true that I've been known to be stubborn."

Carolyn raised an eyebrow. "You think?"

"Sarcasm will get you nowhere."

"So you keep saying." Carolyn smiled as she said it, and Dara accepted that the familiar banter was meant to diffuse the situation.

"Mostly because it's true."

"I'm waiting. You were admitting your pig-headedness."

"Stubbornness."

"You say potato..."

"Big difference. Stubbornness is one degree shy of pig-headedness."

"Now you're just stalling."

Dara had to concede that Carolyn was right. "Okay. I confess that this whole thing with the FBI makes me nervous. But more than that, in my heart of hearts, I believe in Jay and I believe in this movie. Car, this film has the potential to be a huge blockbuster. And it's a game-changer. It won't just entertain the masses, it will give them something to think about. It will educate them and force them to question what they think they know about the way the world works. It's important, and meaningful, and I really, really want to see it through."

"And?"

"And I'm afraid that this is going to become a clash of wills between our government and us, about creative freedom and truth-telling."

"And?"

"And I'm not sure who will win in the end."

Carolyn nodded. "Okay. For the record? My money's on you and Jay."

"Thank you."

"You're welcome. Now can we order some food?"

❖❖

"I'm sorry, ma'am. Your credit card has been declined."

"That can't be." Jay took her MasterCard back from the store clerk. "My balance is paid in full every month." She checked the expiration date on the card; the card wasn't due to expire for another two years. "Okay. Well, I'll get that straightened out. In the meantime, use this card." She handed over her American Express card for the clerk to swipe.

"I'm sorry, ma'am. This card has also been declined."

Deep crimson stained Jay's cheeks. Never in her life had she had a problem with credit. *And I shouldn't have one now.* She checked the total amount due on the cash register and counted out cash, instead. "Here. Good, old-fashioned money ought to work."

"Thank you, ma'am. Have a nice day."

"You too." Jay hustled out of the store with the packages in her hand. When she'd loaded them in the car, she called Kate.

"Hi."

"Can you think of any reason our credit cards would be declined? Did you pay the bills last month?"

"Of course I did."

"Two of our cards just got declined for $38.88."

"That's impossible."

"I thought so too."

"Hang on. I'm in front of the computer. Let me check our accounts. Which cards?"

"MasterCard and AmEx."

"Okay."

After a minute of silence, Jay asked, "Well?"

"I don't understand it. The accounts show that our bills were paid in full, but the credit cards have been frozen."

"What do you mean by 'frozen?'"

"I don't really know. There's a red exclamation point and it just says, "A hold has been placed on this account until further notice.""

A chill ran through Jay and goose flesh popped up on her arms. "Both accounts show the same thing?"

"Yes. And so does the Visa."

"That can't be a coincidence."

"No, it can't."

"What do you think—"

"Hang on. Peter's calling in on the other line."

Kate disappeared and Jay started the car. She'd been planning to run the rest of their errands while she was out, but something told her she needed to go home instead.

When she got there, she dropped the shopping bags on the counter and headed directly for the office. Kate was sitting at her desk, one hand in her hair, the other holding the encrypted phone Peter had given her when he'd returned from Casablanca.

"Okay... No... You did that?"

"Who did what?" Jay asked softly.

Kate held up a hand to wave her off. Her face was ashen, and Jay's stomach twisted in a knot.

"Okay... Where would I pick that up...? Right. Got it." Kate scribbled something on a piece of paper. "Okay. Thank you, Sabastien. I had no idea you'd done that. That was smart thinking... Right... Okay, then. Thanks. Goodbye." Kate disconnected the call, dropped her face into her hands, and cried.

Jay couldn't remember the last time she'd seen her wife shed tears. "What? What is it, babe?" She knelt in front of Kate and pulled her hands away from her face. "Come here." Jay wiped away the tears with her fingertips. "What's all this?"

Kate cleared her throat. "The IRS." Her voice caught and she swallowed hard.

"What about the IRS, Kate?" Jay's own throat constricted.

"They say we have a bank account in Switzerland with $5 million dollars in it and that the money came from Yemen. They've frozen all of our accounts and they're auditing us."

Jay's heartbeat hammered in her ears and the world around her tilted. She sat down on the floor. Words tumbled around in her head, but none of them made coherent sense. Finally, she

220

managed, "They can't do that, can they? We don't have any foreign bank accounts. They can't just make one up and plant false evidence, can they?"

Kate stared straight ahead and said nothing.

"Kate? They can't do that, can they?"

Kate shook her head.

"Who were you just talking to?"

"Sabastien."

"You broke protocol?"

"No. He did. That was why Peter was calling. He had an urgent message for us from Sabastien and he wanted to be sure we had the phone ready to receive the call." Kate's voice sounded hollow.

"I don't understand."

"I didn't either at first. But apparently, when all of this started and you said that agents from the IRS showed up threatening your publisher, Sabastien set up a system of silent alarms on our bank and credit card accounts."

"Why would he do that?"

"So that if the IRS ever tried to threaten you or me, personally, or do anything to harm either of us, he would receive an early warning." Kate ran her fingers through her hair to get it out of her face. She blew her nose on a Kleenex she fished out of her pocket.

"He did that?"

"Yes."

"Wow."

"A little while ago, an alarm was tripped on our accounts. Sabastien was at his computer, working with Lorraine when he got pinged. He was able to follow the trail and figure out what was happening. So he went into our bank accounts and our retirement accounts and moved the money out of there right before everything got frozen."

"He..." Jay thought she must've heard wrong.

"He moved our money into a couple of accounts in the Cayman Islands he set up for us and put our retirement monies into sheltered retirement funds offshore as well."

"He..." Jay still was trying to wrap her brain around it when her phone buzzed.

"Hello?"

"Jay? This is Amanda Fishel."

"Hi." Jay put a hand over the phone and mouthed to Kate, "It's our accountant."

"I just got a call from a representative with the Internal Revenue Service. According to them, you recently received a large denomination check originating in Yemen. The monies were deposited into a Swiss bank account held jointly by you and your wife. Do you know anything about that?"

"It's not true. We don't have any accounts anywhere but here in the US, and we haven't received or sought any foreign money. You know about every account we have."

"I figured as much, but unfortunately, the IRS just sent me the alleged paperwork they say they received from the Swiss, who flagged the account."

"This is all bogus, Amanda."

"I know."

"What can we do about it?"

Amanda sighed on the other end of the line. "At the moment, we're hamstrung. They're saying that they suspect you took money from foreign sources to leak classified documents. The money you allegedly were paid counts as undeclared income, or undisclosed income. That gives the IRS the right to freeze all your assets and look into every aspect of your finances."

Jay's head spun. "This can't be happening."

"They're freezing all of your bank accounts and credit cards and opening an audit of all your finances going back seven years. I'm sorry, Jay. I'm compelled by law to turn over everything they ask of me."

"I understand. It's not your fault."

"Jay? This could get pretty ugly."

"How much uglier can it get?"

"A lot. The IRS is a powerful entity. You won't be able to do any online banking, or get a loan. If you have any outstanding loans, including mortgages, cars, etc., they can be called in. You'll have no credit. Your auto insurance costs will likely go up… You get the idea."

"I do." Jay closed her eyes tightly. "We're screwed."

CHAPTER TWENTY-ONE

S crew that," George screamed into the phone. "You tell them they can't do that. We have a deal. They agreed. We have the paperwork and all the clearances and they gave us assurances that everything was a 'go.' They can't back out now."

Dara watched the dark clouds swirl in his eyes and was glad she wasn't on the receiving end of that anger.

"Yeah? Well, fix it!" He disconnected the call and hurled the phone into the couch cushion.

"What the heck was that all about?"

"The Brits. Now they're saying they awarded us all those incentives and bonuses in error and our costs are going to go through the roof. Not only that, but they're withdrawing the permission to film in our main location. You know, the one where we just spent millions building the elaborate replica of the White House."

Dara's knees went weak and she clutched the back of the chair for support. Money was flying out of the movie's dedicated bank account at an alarming rate. When she and her accountants put together the budget for the film, they used conservative cost estimates, but even with that cushion, a major shift in venue would be catastrophic.

"We have to solve this. We're too far down the road to fold up shop and move the sets elsewhere."

"We'll figure this out." George scrubbed the stubble on his face. "I promise you, we'll figure this out."

Dara wasn't as sure. "The cast will be here any minute. What do you want to tell them?"

"I think we do the read-through and see how it goes. We don't need to tell them anything yet. We're not scheduled to leave for another week."

Rebecca appeared in the doorway. "Is this a private party?"

The brightness of her smile was a balm to Dara's soul. "Come on in." She hoped her distress wasn't obvious. What would she tell her wife? Not only had Rebecca invested a significant share of her own personal savings to co-produce the movie, but she had refused payment for co-writing the script in order to offset the production costs. Now... She didn't want to talk about this with Rebecca. Not just yet.

"I'm going to make sure the room is all set," George said. "I'll see you both in there."

Dara nodded at him, grateful for his recognition that she needed these brief moments alone with Rebecca in order to compartmentalize what had just happened and to transition from businesswoman to actress.

"Hi, beautiful." Rebecca stroked her hand down Dara's back and pulled her in for a kiss. When she released her she said, "Sorry. I just couldn't imagine going hours watching you work without doing that first."

"You never need to apologize for that, sweetheart."

Rebecca's brows knit together. "What's wrong?"

"What do you mean?"

"I don't know. You just seem..." Rebecca studied her face. "Distracted."

Dara shrugged nonchalantly. "I've got a lot going on."

"Okay." Rebecca drew out the "o."

"We should get going."

"Right."

Dara could tell Rebecca wasn't really mollified. Hopefully the next few hours would provide enough of a distraction to make her forget her concerns. She led the way into the big conference room.

"I wish Jay could be here for this," Rebecca said to Dara as they watched the actors file in. "She should be on hand for the table-read. It's her film and the first performance of her work."

"I know, sweetheart. I wish she could be here too. But with the FBI sitting outside her front door, she was adamant that it would be detrimental to us and to the project for her to expose all of us to

224

that level of scrutiny. Her presence here would give the Feds confirmation of the movie deal she didn't want them to have."

"Speaking of which, it doesn't feel right to me that I get the only visible credit for the screenplay. Whose idea was it to hand out the scripts without Jay's screenwriting credit on it?"

"Jay's. Again, she insisted on keeping any mention of her to a minimum for as long as possible."

"But the actors know whose work it is."

"Yes, we disclosed that to them upfront because we needed them to understand what they were signing on to do. But this way, there's nothing overt to connect the script to Jay."

"It feels wrong to me," Rebecca said.

"I know. I'm not crazy about it myself. But this is the way she wanted to play it, so I think we're obligated to go along with her wishes. At least for now."

"Okay. Take your seats everyone." George shouted to be heard over the din of conversation.

"Time for me to go to work," Dara said.

"Break a leg."

Dara took a seat at the table next to Trevor Hanscome, the actor with whom she would share the bulk of her screen time. She closed her eyes and took a deep breath to settle her emotions. She wished Rebecca hadn't mentioned Jay. What would Dara tell Jay if the obstacles to making the film became insurmountable? *You have to find a way to see this through. Whatever else happens, Jay deserves to have her story told.*

George passed the scripts around the table. "Okay, let's get started."

Sabastien let the script run in the background. It was just a matter of time until this algorithm would yield the names of the companies he'd been vetting at the time of the Hyland files leak. In the meantime, he was very troubled by his friends' predicament. Surely there was more he could do to exonerate Jay and Kate and restore their good names. The government's deception should not be allowed to stand. But, given his current status as fugitive and suspected traitor, no one would care what Sabastien thought.

"Earth to Sabastien?" Lorraine took the seat opposite him. "You're a million miles away. What's on your mind?"

"Your government."

"Ah. That's complicated."

"I do not understand how they can black hole upstanding citizens such as Kate and Jay. This makes no sense to me."

Lorraine chuckled.

"This is funny somehow?"

"No." Lorraine shook her head. "You meant to say blackball, not black hole. A black hole is an abyss. Blackball means to unfairly tarnish someone's reputation to adverse effect—to exclude them."

"Oh. I am mangled again, yes?"

"I find it endearing."

"Thanks to God."

"To your point, things that are unjust rarely make sense. In this case, there are those in positions of power who feel very threatened by what Jay knows, and what she might do with that knowledge. As a result, they are doing their best to intimidate her—to silence her."

"But what they are doing is illegal."

"It is most assuredly unethical, and yes, now they've crossed a legal threshold."

"We must help the girls."

"You've already taken great strides in that direction by moving their money. That certainly will ease the financial stress on them."

"We must do more."

"I agree. Peter is calling in markers from some of his Washington connections even as we speak to bring pressure to bear on the Feds to back down."

"Good. I have wired the girls cash."

"You're very sweet, Sabastien."

"These are my friends. I take care of my friends."

Lorraine narrowed her eyes in thought. "Are you certain that the Swiss deposit came from within the IRS?"

"What? I am certain that it did not."

"What do you mean?"

"The Internal Revenue Service is one of the many agencies I was charged with monitoring. I would recognize their cyber fingerprints anywhere. The deposit we are talking about originated from an account I have seen before connected to, but not within, your Central Intelligence Agency."

Lorraine's eyes got big as saucers. "Shit. Can you show me what you saw?"

Sabastien's eyes lit up. "Of course."

"Do it."

Sabastien swung around in his chair and booted up yet another laptop. When he had the information on screen, he turned it to face Lorraine. All the color drained from her face.

"Are you sure that's the right account?"

"I am."

"Can you trace the deposit to a particular IP address?"

"I can and I did."

Sabastien inputted another command and again showed Lorraine the display.

Lorraine buried her head in her hands.

"Did I do something wrong?"

"No, not you." When she looked up at him again, Lorraine's eyes were haunted.

Sabastien rushed on, "But this person did not act alone. He was in cohorts with someone from the Internal Revenue Service.

"Cahoots."

"Quoi?"

"Cahoots. Not cohorts. That's something entirely different."

"Oh."

"How do you know that?"

"Because I was able to trace electronic correspondence from that address to an IP address in the IRS."

"You were?"

"Of course." Sabastien proudly puffed out his chest. "I can do practically anything."

"Let me see." Lorraine said.

Sabastien's hands were a blur as he closed and opened windows on the laptop. "I have saved everything I found so far." He handed the computer to Lorraine. "This is what I collected right after my alarm went off."

Lorraine's expression was grim as she scrolled down. "Are we able to transmit data to Peter securely yet?"

"Alas, no. I cannot be certain that our transmissions will be free of interference. Not yet."

Lorraine sighed heavily. "Okay. Let me know the second you think we're secure."

"I will. Lorraine?"

"Yes?"

"I am sorry."

"Why? About what?"

"You seem very upset. Like you saw a ghost. Do you know who these people are?"

"No. But I know what they are. And the sooner we can get this proof to Peter, the better."

"I could put it on a thumb drive and you could go home, no?"

"No, my friend. Our primary job remains solving the riddle of the leak and what the Commission's objective is. I can't leave until we have all the answers and the proof we need on that front."

"But our friends... We could fix their reputations and finances with this information I collected, no?"

"I hope so, Sabastien. But not today. Today, we find out the Commission's end game."

Kate and Peter walked up the hill on sun-splashed Connecticut Avenue. It was a mild day for Washington, D.C. in the middle of summer, and the sidewalk was filled with pedestrians taking advantage of the rare low humidity.

"It's been a long time since we've been back here, my friend," Peter said. "You okay?"

"I'd be lying if I told you this brought back pleasant memories."

"We could've taken a cab instead of the metro."

"We could have, but it's incredibly rare for it to be this pleasant in D.C. in the summertime. I needed the walk to stretch my legs and settle my emotions. It's time to exorcise old demons."

They passed the Washington Hilton. Not far ahead of them was the Russian Trade Representatives Building. Kate's heart pounded in her chest and beads of sweat dotted her brow.

"You're sure you're okay?" Peter put a hand on the small of her back to steady her.

Kate shook him off. Her breathing was shallow. In her mind's eye, she saw herself running for her life from the Russian Ambassador's reception, past the Hilton, and toward the DuPont Circle Metro station.

"Katherine Ann Kyle!"

Peter's voice snapped her back into the present.

"That was then. This is now. Focus on the now, sweetie. Nothing bad is going to happen to you. I'm right here and you're safe."

"I know that." Kate didn't mean to snap at him.

"I know you do. But I've been there, done that with PTSD myself, and I understand the illogical nature of the disease. It's okay to feel fear. It's not okay to give in to it or to dwell too long in that space."

Kate swallowed hard. She lengthened her stride and picked up the pace. "I'm fine."

Peter tentatively reached out, squeezed her shoulder once, and let go. "Yes, you are."

It's time to change the topic. "You really think Mimi Hyland can help us?" Kate asked.

"Former first ladies still have connections, and she carries weight in some circles. She always liked you and Jay. She's principled and I trust her. She may be the best shot we have at convincing the IRS to de-escalate this situation. Unless, of course, you enjoyed paying cash for your flight and getting patted down by the TSA."

"Very funny."

They turned the corner and arrived at 2122 California Street NW.

"Here we go." Peter led the way up the front steps and opened the door into the main lobby. He motioned for Kate to go first.

"Nice digs." Kate's gaze took in the columns, the marble, and the ornate details of the foyer.

"Peter Enright to see Mimi Hyland," Peter told the security guard at the desk.

"Yes, sir. One moment, please." The guard picked up a phone and pressed a button. He murmured into the receiver, waited, and then hung up. "You can go right up. Take the elevator on your right."

"Thank you."

Kate and Peter took the elevator to Mimi's floor. When the doors opened, they stepped out, and the doors closed behind them. As they did, a big ball of fur bounded at her and Kate stumbled backwards.

"Rufus! Get back here this minute."

Kate recovered, knelt down, and hugged the gorgeous golden retriever. She rubbed his ears as his tail wagged furiously. "Good boy, Rufus."

"I'm so sorry. This boy has no manners and no sense of decorum."

Kate stood up. "Mrs. Hyland, it's wonderful to see you again." She held out her hand, surprised when the former first lady pulled her into a warm hug.

"It's been too long, Kate." She jerked her thumb in Peter's direction. "This guy keeps me up to date, but it's not the same as seeing you." She pulled back and held Kate at arm's length. "Tell me, how is Jay holding up?"

The former first lady's eyes were filled with compassion and concern, and Kate was deeply touched.

"She's doing the best she can under the circumstances, ma'am."

"You did not just 'ma'am' me."

Kate raised an eyebrow.

"Please, call me Mimi. I insist."

"But—"

"No buts." Mimi waved Kate off. She wagged a finger at the dog, who was sitting ramrod straight and staring up at them with a goofy grin. "As for you, young man, that is not the way we introduce ourselves to guests."

Kate laughed as Rufus licked Mimi's hand. "He's adorable."

"He's a handful. Nowhere near as regal and gentlemanly as your Fred was."

Kate's heart jolted. "You remember Fred?"

"Of course I do, dear. He was lovely." Mimi led the way inside. "Did you ever get another dog?"

Kate shook her head. "Fred was one of a kind. After he died, neither Jay nor I could bear the thought of going through the trauma of losing another dog. Not only that, but we were both doing so much traveling, we knew it wouldn't be fair to bring another dog into the house."

"I understand. But life is so much richer with a companion, don't you think?"

"I do."

"After Charlie passed, Rufus was about the only thing that kept me going."

"I can imagine." A memory of lying on the floor with Fred while Jay was missing and presumed dead tugged at Kate's heartstrings, and she shoved it away.

"Anyway, let's get down to business, shall we? I've fixed some cheese and crackers for us, and some tea. Peter has given me the broad outlines of the situation. I want to hear the rest from you and then I'll tell you what I think I can do to help."

Mimi led the way into a richly appointed living room and indicated that they should sit on the sofa. She listened intently as Kate detailed the history of the leak; Jay's meeting with her publisher; the sudden frosty reception from Sydney, Jay's longtime agent; the federal agents' intimidation tactics with Jeremy, Black Quill, and the agent; the plans for the movie; and their own and Dara's interactions with the FBI and the IRS.

As Peter had instructed her on the flight to D.C., Kate omitted any reference to the Commission, to Sabastien, Vaughn, and Lorraine, and to the Black Knight. When she was finished talking, Mimi sprang up and strode over to the window.

"I stand here often and gaze at the Washington Monument in the distance. I love this city and what it stands for. I love this country and our system of government. I am not naïve—far from it. Charlie never insulated me from the seedier side of politics. When he was troubled by it, we would talk through it. When he questioned his own ethics and the motives and ethics of others, we discussed it. But what you describe is beyond the pale, and as you are aware, I'm painfully familiar with that."

Mimi turned back to face Kate and Peter. "You should know that I hear what you're not saying. Those people—that organization—took my Charlie from me and played God. They nearly killed him and they damn near destroyed this nation. I never bought the idea that putting a few of the bad actors away meant the end of it. And what you're describing has their fingerprints all over it." Her voice shook with anger.

"I argued with Charlie at the time. Oh, it was a battle royal. I wanted him to expose them for all the world to see. He was the one who argued that acknowledging the existence of the Commission would compromise national security. I lost the argument then. God help me, I won't lose it now."

Kate had forgotten how strong and perceptive Mimi Hyland was. She had joined them occasionally when Kate dined with the president. "I appreciate that, Mimi."

"I'd like to read this oh-so-dangerous manuscript of Jay's. May I?"

"Of course," Kate said. "Jay asked me to give you a copy." Kate reached into her briefcase, pulled out a bound copy of the manuscript, and handed it to Mimi. "She was so sorry she couldn't be here."

Kate chanced a glance at Peter. The two of them and Jay had debated it extensively; the idea that they might lead the FBI to the former first lady's door was just too much of a risk to take. So Jay drew the surveillance away while Peter picked up Kate for the trip to the airport.

"I'm sorry too. I have a great affection for your wife, Kate. She's one of the nicest, most genuine people I know. What she's being put through is a travesty. And I intend to do something about it."

"Mrs Hy... Mimi. We have no desire to put you in a difficult position—"

"Nonsense. Charlie would be appalled at these shenanigans. I may not have much of a bully pulpit left, but what I have I will use to set this right."

"What is it you have in mind?" Peter spoke up for the first time.

"A press conference." Mimi's eyes gleamed.

"A-a..." Kate stammered.

"A press conference. I believe you're familiar with how those work, Kate." Mimi winked at her. "I'm going to read the manuscript and tell the world that there is nothing in here that violates state secrets or national security, and that if Charlie were still alive, he'd say the same thing."

"Mimi, I appreciate what you're trying to do, but if I was your PR representative, I'd have to advise against getting publicly involved in something this volatile."

"Well, then it's a good thing you're not my PR rep, isn't it?"

Kate smiled at her. "Touché. But there's a big difference between making private phone calls to contacts within the government or in positions of influence, and holding a press conference where every word you say will be measured and dissected. You could be inviting a lot of trouble you don't need."

"My life isn't nearly exciting enough these days, my dear. I could do with a little trouble."

"Still—"

"My God, you're stubborn." Mimi gestured to Peter. "Is she always this obstinate?"

"I'm afraid so."

"Look. Almost three decades ago, I nearly lost my husband, and you very nearly lost your life. We all picked up the pieces and soldiered on. Congress held its closed-door hearings, a report was generated, and it was buried behind an amorphous top secret designation."

Kate opened her mouth to say something and Mimi held up a hand to stop her.

"I'm not done yet. Several horrible characters were locked away, and so was the documented evidence of the Commission. It's way past time to shine light and send the rats scurrying. If I can help get that done, and clear Jay and restore your lives to you in the process, so much the better."

Again, Kate opened her mouth to speak and Mimi cut her off.

"My mind is made up. Not another word out of you."

Kate laughed. "I was just going to say, 'thank you.'"

"Oh. That I'll allow. Now, if you both don't mind, I've got some reading to do. I'll be in touch."

CHAPTER TWENTY-TWO

Lorraine read down the list Sabastien had printed out for her of the last ten contractors and subcontractors he'd been investigating in the days and weeks before the Hyland Commission Report was leaked.

She tried hard to push aside the information about Kate and Jay's IRS troubles. If only she could get the evidence to Peter... *If you do and the transmission alerts the Commission or the Black Knight, you risk exposing everything, giving them a chance to cover their tracks and disappear into the darkness.*

Lorraine growled in frustration. The most she could do was alert Peter via scrambled call. That wouldn't give him the solid data he'd need to back up any accusations. "Let it go for now," she muttered to herself. "Keep your eyes on the main objective."

Lorraine returned her attention to the stack of papers in her hand. She recognized all the major players on the list, but it was the subcontracting companies that caught her attention now.

She grabbed a highlighter off the table and marked several of those companies for closer scrutiny.

Vaughn knocked on the doorframe. "I fixed some lunch. Are you hungry?"

Lorraine's stomach rumbled and she blushed.

"I'll take that for a yes," Vaughn said.

"I feel like I'm on the verge of a big breakthrough. I should keep going."

"You won't be able to hear your own thoughts over the sound of your stomach gurgling. Bring whatever you're doing with you."

Much as Lorraine hated to admit it, Vaughn was right. She gathered up the printouts and followed Vaughn to the kitchen.

Along the way, Vaughn said, "Sabastien tells me you've got some leads on the sources behind the girls' financial woes."

"I do, if only I could do something about it from here."

"Too risky."

"I know. But that doesn't make me feel any better."

Vaughn nodded sympathetically. "Soon. We'll have the bastards soon."

When they arrived in the kitchen, Sabastien already was sitting at the table eating. "Ah, Lorraine. Glad that you have joined us. Interesting reading, no?" He pointed to the papers in her hand.

"Very. I'm particularly fascinated by these three subcontractors here." Lorraine tilted the page so Sabastien could see it. "For some reason, the names ring a bell."

Sabastien scrunched up his face in a way Lorraine had come to recognize when he was trying to work out the English. "What is this, 'ring a bell'?"

Lorraine smiled. "They are familiar to me somehow, but I can't quite place the context."

"Ah. I see. Well, if you want, I can help with that."

"I was hoping you'd say that."

"Give me one second. I will have Veronique access all of the important characters at those companies."

"Who's Veronique?" Vaughn asked.

Sabastien puffed out his chest. "Veronique is my girlfriend."

"You have a girlfriend?" Lorraine and Vaughn asked simultaneously.

"Oh yes."

"How do I not know this?" Vaughn asked.

"When do we get to meet her?" Lorraine piped in.

Sabastien threw back his head and laughed. "You both already have met her. In fact, you've been living with her."

Vaughn looked at Lorraine and shrugged. "Got me."

"Sabastien, explain yourself," Lorraine said.

"Of course. Veronique is my main computer. I make love to her everyday and she rewards me with answers to our questions."

Vaughn wadded up her napkin and threw it at Sabastien.

"Hey!"

"That's for getting us going."

Sabastien's smile lit up his face, making him look even more youthful and elfin than normal. "I got one underneath you."

"That's over on you," Lorraine corrected. "And yes, you did."

"Anyway, I will get Veronique working on this now, and by the time we are done with our meal, we will have the answers we seek." He rose and left the kitchen.

"Who's got your attention?" Vaughn asked.

Lorraine slid the list with the highlighted names across the table. "Vector Research, Innovative Solutions, and Secure Technologies, Inc. They're all tech companies subbing on a major contract belonging to Techtronic Industries. Techtronic was owned by a known member of the Commission until a few months ago when it went public and the new board of directors ousted him."

"But you think Techtronic still has ties to the Commission?"

"I think it's worth exploring."

"Okay," Sabastien said. He sat back down and tucked a napkin into the collar of his shirt. "Bon appetit."

When they'd finished eating, they adjourned to the office. Sabastien sat down at the computer and stroked the side of the keyboard. "Okay, Veronique. What do you have to tell us?"

Lorraine and Vaughn stood behind Sabastien.

"I have asked Veronique to give us the details of these companies, the names of their principles, their titles, how long they have been with the company or on the board of directors, and what specific contracts these companies hold both with your government and with the contractor who hired them for the job."

"Good work, Sabastien."

"I also asked Veronique to cross-reference for anyone who is involved in multiple companies, their bank account information, arrest records…"

"And what they ate for lunch yesterday?" Lorraine asked.

"I am sure if they used a credit card, we could find out where they dined," Sabastien said.

"That was a joke, Sabastien. I was making a funny."

"Oh, right." He smiled sheepishly. "Anyway…" His fingers flew over the keyboard and he nodded. "Okay."

The printer hummed and Vaughn grabbed the papers as they came out and handed them to Lorraine.

She scanned the data, flipping through the pages, looking for anything that stood out. "Oh." She felt for the closest chair and sat down.

"What is it?" Vaughn asked.

"Our smoking gun. We've got our smoking gun."

❧❦

Kate and Jay reached the top of Chimney Mountain in the Adirondacks. Kate handed Jay the water bottle and Jay took a generous drink.

"Fancy meeting you here." Peter came around the corner from behind the rocks that created the formation for which the mountain was named.

"You picked a helluva place to meet," Kate said.

"I figured you two taking off in your car like a bat out of hell and hightailing it over to my place might raise a red flag or two with your FBI shadows."

"On the other hand, a nice hike on a sunny day in the middle of nowhere…" Jay let the sentence trail off.

"Exactly."

"Yeah, they didn't look happy about driving a few hours north and cooling their heels while we have all the fun."

"Hey, they should be happy. Fresh air, the beautiful scenery of Joe King's Flow with Humphrey Mountain in the distance. What's not to love?" Kate asked.

"My hamstrings. My hamstrings are not to love right now," Jay said. She lifted her leg out straight onto a rock and stretched.

"Where did you park?" Jay asked Peter. "We didn't see your car."

"I thought it might be best if I parked elsewhere so as not to raise suspicion about your motives in taking a hike. I'm parked a mile or so away. I'll wait to leave until after you guys hike down and take your friends with you."

"Never mind all that," Kate said. "What was so urgent?"

"You guys are slipping. I wondered why that wasn't your first question."

"I'm not as young as I used to be," Jay said. "I needed a second to catch my breath."

"So?" Kate persisted.

"Two things. One, we've got the connection." Peter's eyes gleamed.

"*The* connection?"

Peter nodded. "Lorraine and Sabastien have identified the subcontractor."

"That's fantastic!" Jay said. "How?"

"Never mind the 'how,'" Kate said. "Who and why?"

"Vector Research and Michael Vendetti in the pantry with a knife," Peter said.

"Very funny."

Peter removed his backpack and sat down on a nearby rock. "Vector Research was hired by Techtronic Industries on a major contract to upgrade Homeland Security's computer systems and improve the technological interface with the various agencies that are within Homeland Security's purview."

"Good cover if you're trying to get access to sensitive information," Kate said.

"Right. As it turns out, Vector Research is a subsidiary of West Technologies. Guess who owned West Technologies until his death?"

"Wayne Grayson," Kate and Jay said in unison.

"Bingo." Peter pulled out a bag of trail mix, grabbed a handful, and passed the bag to Jay. "And guess who joined the boards of all three companies, Techtronic, Vector Research, and West Technologies a few months ago when he was released from prison?"

"Let me guess," Kate said. "Michael Vendetti."

"Right again. Vendetti, the heir apparent to Wayne Grayson as head of the Commission."

"I thought you had eyes on Vendetti since he got out of jail?" Kate asked.

"I did and I do."

"How did we not twig onto his involvement before now?"

"He hasn't taken one step out of line or done anything to raise even a whiff of suspicion. And none of Lorraine's contacts turned up anything out of the ordinary in his prisoner visitors' log."

"He must've had somebody scrub it from the inside," Kate said. "And he must have a secure method of communicating with other Commission operatives that we're not seeing."

"Probably," Peter agreed.

Jay finished swallowing a mouthful of granola, raisins, and M&Ms. "Isn't it some kind of ethics violation for Vendetti to sit on all three boards? Especially since he was a convicted felon?"

"These are probably private corporations, or at least they would've had to have been at the time they procured the work at Homeland Security." Kate said.

"But these are public contracts," Jay protested.

"Techtronic and Vector most likely had the contracts before Vendetti was voted onto the boards. Very convenient."

"Can we focus on the more germane issue here? We found the link we needed," Peter said.

"And that makes me incredibly happy," Jay said. "So, how did Lorraine and Sabastien figure it out, how did they tell you that while we're in a communications blackout, and what happens now?"

"They zeroed in on which corporations Sabastien was about to investigate at the time of the leak. Then Lorraine provided the Grayson link and Sabastien's search turned up Vendetti. As for how I got the news, Lorraine gave me a very quick rundown in a scrambled call, the same way Sabastien contacted you the other day."

"Now that we have the information, what are we going to do with it? The mere fact that Vendetti sits on those boards isn't going to be enough to prove anything," Kate said.

Peter tossed her an apple from his bag. "Very true. Even as we speak, Sabastien is combing through the work Vector is doing on the Homeland Security contract. So far, we know that Vector's main, official directive is to provide new, secure cellular technology to protect sensitive conversations for top-level officials at Homeland Security and all agencies under their umbrella."

"Sounds like a bonanza for the Commission," Kate said.

"Hopefully Sabastien will be able to find evidence that proves they're up to no good."

"Wouldn't you think the Black Knight, or some other expert Vector has working for them, would have put safeguards in place to prevent Sabastien or anyone else from figuring out what they're really doing?" Kate asked. She crunched on the last bite of apple and tossed the core into the bushes.

"I have no doubt. Lorraine said Sabastien was laboriously scrubbing the data for trip wires, booby traps, and anything else that might alert Vector to his presence."

"In other words, this could take a long time," Jay said. "Besides, even if we figure out what they were up to, that still doesn't exonerate Sabastien for the leak," Jay said.

Kate put an arm around Jay. "I'm sure Sabastien is working as fast as he can."

"I know he is, and I'm really grateful. It's just..."

Something niggled at the back of Kate's mind. She turned to Peter. "You said there were two pieces of news. What's the other?"

"Sabastien was able to trace the source of the deposit into the fake Swiss bank account to what Lorraine identified as an off-the-books CIA slush fund. He aggregated a series of e-mails between an IP address connected to the CIA and one that's linked to an IP address within the IRS."

Jay gave a fist pump. "We have them! What do we need to do now?"

"Nothing. There's nothing we can do... Yet."

Jay's face darkened. "What do you mean? You just said Sabastien and Lorraine have enough to clear us."

"They have a paper trail, yes. But we don't have specific names at the moment, and, short of Lorraine getting on a plane with the information, there's no way that you and I take possession of the proof."

"So tell her to get on a plane!" Jay yelled.

"Look," Peter said testily, "we all have plenty of incentives to want this to be over. I'd like my wife back, you'd like your lives back and your good name, Sabastien, I'm sure, would like not to be a fugitive charged with treason. Our primary job right now is to take the information about Vector and use it to identify the Black Knight. Unmasking him is the only way to clear Sabastien and to prove you," he thrust his finger at Jay, "didn't have anything to do with the leak. The IRS mess will have to wait."

Jay picked up a small rock and threw it in the direction of the trees below. "That's just great."

"I'm sorry. I don't mean to be callous about your finances. I could've been more gentle with that news."

"You think?" Jay asked.

After an awkward silence, Kate stepped into the breach. "Peter, we have the data you picked up in Casablanca. It shouldn't be hard to figure out when John Robie hacked Vector. Then we would need to determine what Vector was working on at the time of the hack to try to figure out why he targeted them."

"And go back again to review Robie's profile to see what Vector has in common with other hacks he committed. If we find the pattern, maybe we find a name. He's likely hiding in plain sight on the payrolls of Vector Research, Techtronic, or West Technologies."

"Now that we know for sure Vendetti is involved, it explains why he picked the Hyland Commission Report to leak," Kate pointed out. "Bitter much?"

"It was a way for him to kill two birds with one stone," Peter said. "They get Sabastien out of their hair and they do real harm to Jay's reputation and career. Vendetti knows Jay is your Achilles heel, Kate."

Kate's stomach rolled and her heart lurched at the memory of the last time Vendetti and his cabal used Jay as a pawn to hurt Kate. Their murderous plan very nearly succeeded. She noted that Jay's face had lost all color and imagined she was remembering too.

"Oh my God! I-I'm sorry," Peter stammered. "That was remarkably insensitive, even for me. I wasn't thinking..." He made a move toward Kate, but she waved him off. He turned toward Jay, but before he could reach her, she stood up and started to pace, effectively brushing him off. He looked again to Kate, and she shook her head minutely, silently urging him to let it go.

She knew Jay. This wasn't a conversation Jay was willing to have. She didn't want to dwell back there—not again. She'd done enough of that while writing the book.

As if to confirm Kate's thought, Jay abruptly changed the topic. "Even if we can prove everything we think is true about the Commission and Vendetti's involvement in the leak, it still won't get the Feds or the IRS off my back if they think the movie discloses top secret information."

Kate checked her watch. "True, but we still have some weapons at our disposal. Speaking of which, if we hustle, we might be able to get back to Albany in time to watch Mimi Hyland's press conference. That ought to go a long way toward bolstering your case."

᠅

Mimi Hyland stepped through the door and stood off to the side of the podium. She blinked as dozens of flashes from digital cameras exploded in her face. It took a moment for her eyes to adjust. Apart from Charlie's funeral, she hadn't faced a room overflowing with journalists eager to hear what she had to say in many years. *Well, you got them here, old girl. Better put on a good show.*

Her former press secretary glanced over at her from the podium and Mimi nodded that she was ready.

"Ladies and gentlemen of the press, I give you the former First Lady of the United States of America, Mimi Hyland. Mrs. Hyland will make a brief statement. She will not be taking questions at this time. No exceptions."

Mimi walked to the podium and gazed out at the gathering. The red lights from the television cameras indicated that they already were recording. The print journalists all had their notebooks and tape recorders out and at the ready. She'd been told that some of the cable networks were carrying her remarks live. She was sure that wherever Kate and Jay were, they were watching. Although she wished Jay could be standing here with her, together they'd made the conscious decision that having Jay there would be counterproductive and a distraction. *This one's for you, kid.*

Mimi took a deep breath and addressed the gathering. "Thank you all for coming. A lot has been said and written in the past little while about events that happened during my husband's administration. Top secret documents purportedly were leaked to *Time* magazine, and accusations have been hurled around about who is responsible and what their motive might have been.

"I've read the stories alleging that Jamison Parker, a *New York Times* best-selling author who needs no help promoting or selling her books, is in some way connected to the leak. Frankly this is shoddy reporting. Just because the journalist to whom the documents allegedly were leaked once worked as an intern at *Time* when Ms. Parker was a reporter there, it does not mean that she was the source of the documents.

Mimi gripped the sides of the podium with her hands and leaned forward. She was surprised at the well of anger that bubbled up on Jay's behalf. *Maybe letting them see that indignation isn't a bad thing.*

"Let me tell you a little of what I know. First, I have known Jamison Parker and her wife, Katherine Kyle, for more than thirty years, dating back to when Charles Hyland was Governor of New York. There are no more upstanding, finer citizens and patriots than these two women."

She hadn't planned to mention Kate, but really, it was nearly impossible to think of Jay without Kate and vice versa.

"Second, Jamison Parker risked her life to report the truth when my husband and our national security were under siege. She was an integral reason why the story had a happy ending. If she had wanted to reveal classified information pertaining to that situation, she wouldn't have needed to leak any documents to do it, and she could have done so ages ago.

"Third, and I really want you to pay attention now, I have read the manuscript in question. I want to tell you a couple of things about it, no spoiler alerts required. It is a fabulous, masterfully crafted piece of writing. It is fiction. In no way could this work be construed to be a threat to national security. And, because I think we can all agree that I was an eyewitness at the time, I can safely tell you that no top secret information is revealed in the making of this work of fiction.

"There. Now I hope we can put *that* bit of fiction to bed and move on to more important stories. I do not deny that top secret documents may have been leaked. I'm not privy to that information. What I can say unequivocally is that Jamison Parker is a heroine, not a villain. And I will not stand by and watch her, and her reputation, be tarnished in this manner. If my husband was still alive..."

Mimi's voice quavered and she took a moment to compose herself. "Charlie would be appalled by these accusations. Tyranny flourishes when those in a position to tell the truth do nothing. I've remained silent on this matter for too long. Thank you for your kind attention."

Mimi let go of the podium, straightened up to her full height, and retreated via the entrance through which she'd arrived.

◈◈

Sitting at home on the couch, Jay wiped away a tear. "Wow. Did you put her up to that? I can't believe she went that far. She didn't need to do that."

Kate pulled Jay close and kissed her on the temple. "Nobody asked her to do that, sweetheart. The press conference was her idea. As far as I know, no one gave her talking points or discussed with her what she would say. I certainly didn't have a conversation with her about it."

"Do you think that's a game-changer?"

"I don't know. I certainly hope so."

◈◈

"You've got to be kidding me! Can they do that?" Dara asked.

"They're the government," her accountant said. "Who's going to stop them?"

"What can we do?"

"Under the law and per the terms of the audit, I'm required to provide them with the documentation they request."

"Seven years' worth of tax returns?"

"And the backup materials."

"I'll have everything shipped to you as soon as possible." Dara turned her neck from side to side in a vain effort to alleviate the stress. "I find it rather curious that this comes up at the same time we lose our location in London."

"About that. You know I have to advise that it would be unwise to sink money into a new location."

"I'm aware. George and I are working on a strategy that salvages the existing location. We're scheduled to meet with

British officials day after tomorrow. George's assistant is working on all the arrangements right now."

"Keep me posted. And Dara? I'm sorry I had to be the bearer of bad news."

"It's not your fault. I trust you to take care of me."

"That's my job."

"And I'm grateful that you're very good at it." Dara shook off the feeling of foreboding. There were too many coincidences. The FBI, the IRS, and the Brits? *Where there's smoke, there's fire.* The question was, what could she do about it?

"Trouble?" Rebecca asked. She sauntered into the home office and slid her arms around Dara's waist. "Anything I can do to help?"

Dara closed her eyes and breathed in the scent of Rebecca's shampoo. "You're already helping just by holding me." She nuzzled Rebecca's cheek. "I love you."

"I love you too. But you're evading the question."

"I know. I just…" Dara's throat tightened. *I just…what? Am in over my head?*

"Whatever it is, we're in it together, sweetheart. For better or worse, remember?"

"I do," Dara quipped, as much to lighten her own mood as to deflect Rebecca.

"Very clever." Rebecca kissed Dara's chin. "Don't quit your day job."

"Which one?"

"Either." Rebecca backed away and took Dara by the hand.

"Where are we going?"

"To watch television."

"You want to watch TV right now?"

"I knew you were busy, and I gathered from the tone on your end that it wasn't good news, so I didn't want to interrupt. But I recorded something I really think you're going to want to see."

When they were snuggled together on the divan, Dara filled Rebecca in on the conversation with her accountant and the mounting roadblocks they were facing.

Rebecca listened attentively, but didn't say a word, a reaction Dara thought odd and out of character.

"How are you not reacting to all that?" Dara finally asked.

"Oh, trust me, I'm hopping mad on the inside. But I think what I wanted to show you just might be a tonic for both of us."

Dara narrowed her eyes. "How so?"

"Watch." Rebecca pushed Play. Former First Lady Mimi Hyland appeared on the screen.

"Thank you all for coming. A lot has been said and written in the past little while about events that happened during my husband's administration…"

Dara watched in silence, an idea forming in her head. When the press conference was over, she ran back into the office to grab her phone. As she was about to place a call, she noticed a notification for a text message from George. She clicked to open it.

Brits now are refusing to meet with us, citing diplomatic relations with the US. Go figure. Call me when you can.

Dara clenched her teeth. That was the last straw. It was time to fight back.

CHAPTER TWENTY-THREE

P eter pushed away from the desk and stretched his arms over his head. He'd spent hours sifting through the details of John Robie's activities and he'd made good headway. With Kate and Jay's help, he had identified the date Robie hacked Vector, and mapped his subsequent hacks to confirm their suspicion that, after he'd likely gone to work for the Commission, he'd inadvertently targeted another corporation with Commission ties.

He thought of Jay with a pang. She was still sore at him, he could tell, and it pained him. He loved Jay like a sister... If only she were here now. She was so good at seeing the connections and synchronicities that most people overlooked. Peter checked his watch. By now, she and Kate should be at the airport.

He made a note to send a nice bottle of wine to Lorraine's petite blond friend, their next-door neighbor, Jessica. When he'd called her this morning and asked for her help, she'd come right over. Peter explained what he required, and Jessica enthusiastically embraced the assignment.

A short while after Jessica's arrival, Jay pulled her car into the second bay of Peter's garage, the FBI tailing not-so circumspectly in her wake. Fifteen minutes after that, Jessica drove off in Jay's car, wearing Jay's clothes. Predictably, Jay's FBI buddies followed several seconds behind. Ten minutes after that, Kate and Jay, now dressed in an outfit she'd brought with her, headed in the opposite direction in Peter's truck.

Peter scooted closer to the desk and bent once again to the task at hand. It was time to ferret out exactly who the Black Knight really was. They were close; he could feel it.

◈◈

Kate and Jay waited in the shadows of a private airplane hangar a short distance from the Million Air Terminal at Albany International Airport. Each of them carried a briefcase and an overnight bag.

"Ma'ams. If you could step back this way, the plane you're waiting for is being towed in right now."

As if on cue, an airplane tug backed into the hangar, pulling a sleek Dassault Falcon 2000EX jet. The plane was eerily quiet with the engines shut down. When it was all the way inside and stopped with the wheels chocked, the aircraft door opened to reveal Dara.

She bounded down the stairs and enveloped Jay, and then Kate, in hugs. "It's so good to see you both."

"I can't believe you're here. Riding in style, no less," Jay said.

"Ride courtesy of one of our newest producing partners. Randolph Curtain from 722 Films called me last night."

"I thought he was a no."

"He was, until he saw Mimi Hyland's press conference yesterday. Apparently, he was a major contributor to President Hyland's campaigns back in the day. He met the President and First Lady several times and was very impressed by her.

"After watching the press conference, he called me to say he had a change of heart, and he wanted to know what he could do to help. I told him loaning me the studio's plane and crew for a couple of days would go a long way. I figured the FBI couldn't follow you up in the air."

"True," Kate said. "You said you had an idea you wanted to bounce off us?"

"I do."

"And why did we need overnight bags?" Jay asked.

"You'll see," Dara said enigmatically. "I have some surprises for you. Come on board. Rebecca and George are inside, along with some other folks I'd like to introduce you to."

Kate and Jay followed Dara up the stairs and boarded the plane. The inside of the craft was luxurious with eight captain's chairs in two groupings. Five of the eight seats were taken, leaving just enough room for Dara, Kate, and Jay.

Jay and Kate dropped their bags next to two of the empty seats. "I'm so glad to see you," Rebecca said. She kissed Jay on the cheek and hugged Kate.

"Likewise," Jay said.

"Jay, since you can't come to us in LA without bringing unwanted company…" Dara smiled her megawatt smile. "I decided to bring some of our cast to you. Let me make the introductions. You know George Nelson, our director."

George shook Kate's hand and gave Jay a hug. "Good to see you again."

"This," Dara pointed to a handsome, distinguished-looking man Kate thought she recognized, "is Trevor Hanscome, who will be playing the president."

"What a pleasure to meet you in person," Jay said. "I love your work."

"Thank you. It's great to meet you. I'm a fan of yours as well."

"You've read my books?"

"I have. And I've been memorizing your lines." He pointed to the open script on his seat. "Nice to meet you also, Ms. Kyle." Trevor bowed slightly.

"Kate, please."

"Very well. Nice to meet you, Kate."

"As for the rest of this lot," Dara said with affection, "Jay, Kate, please meet our other main players, Laura Simmons, Juanita Jensen, and Richard Broderick."

Kate caught a glimpse of Jay out of the corner of her eye. She looked positively star-struck. "Nice to meet you all." Kate stepped forward and shook hands with each of them in turn.

"Yes." Jay recovered. "What a thrill to meet you all. To have all of you, whose acting I so admire, say words that I wrote… I never imagined anything like it. Thank you all for agreeing to be in this movie."

"What you created is magic, Jay," Juanita said. "I think I speak for all of us when I say, the honor is ours."

"Here, here," Laura, Richard, and Trevor piped in.

"Okay, if we're done with the mutual admiration portion of our program, let's get down to business," George said.

"Kate, Jay, have a seat." Dara pointed to the chairs next to which they'd placed their stuff. "I'll just let the pilot know we're ready to go—"

"Go? Where are we going?" Kate asked.

"That's ultimately up to you," Dara answered. "But for now, in terms of privacy, we're better off in the air than we are sitting here, so the crew assures me we can spend a little while flying around in the friendly skies before we select a destination."

"Don't Kate and I have to show our ID to anyone? We're not on your manifest, are we?"

"The beauty of flying privately. The crew only needs to report the number of passengers, not their identities." Dara retreated to the cockpit to talk to the two pilots and the flight attendant.

"And they sign a confidentiality agreement preventing them from disclosing who the passengers are, and any details of what happens on board," Rebecca added. "We thought, given the increased level of scrutiny, an airborne conference room would be most advantageous."

Dara returned. "We're all set. They're going to get us out of the hangar, then it will take them another fifteen or twenty minutes to get all of the systems up to speed before we can be cleared for takeoff."

"And we can just fly around with no destination and no flight plan? I didn't think that was even possible," Jay said.

"We can," Trevor piped in. "It's called a VFR departure—visual flight rules."

"Snore," Richard joked. "Don't mind Trevor, he has his own plane and likes to talk about flying ad nauseam."

"Hey. The lady asked a question, didn't you?" Trevor winked at Jay.

"I did."

"Don't encourage him," Juanita said.

Kate crossed her legs, got comfortable, and observed the interaction. All of the actors seemed not only to know each other well, but also to genuinely like each other. She smiled to herself. Hopefully, that camaraderie would serve them well if the going got tough.

The co-pilot closed the door and sealed it shut. "You all might want to sit down. We're about to get our push out of here. As soon as we're outside on the ramp, we'll turn on the auxiliary power unit and get the air circulating in here so you'll be nice and comfortable."

Everyone took a seat.

The flight attendant came by. "I'm Nancy." She indicated Kate and Jay's luggage. "Can I take your bags, please? I'll stow your briefcases in the overhead compartment. Would you all like me to lower the shades so you have more privacy?"

"Yes, thank you, for all that, Nancy. That would be lovely." After all of the shades were down and Nancy had stowed the bags and returned to her seat, Dara turned to Kate and Jay. "You've both told me in the past that you don't believe in coincidences. Neither do I. So let me add up a few recent developments.

"One. The FBI questioned Jay about her manuscript. Two. The FBI tried to interview me about the movie through my attorney. Three. Suddenly, after giving us full cooperation and a wonderful incentive package, the Brits have withdrawn all permission for us to shoot at our primary location, where our crew already was building the sets and prepping the site. And four, the IRS has mysteriously decided to audit me."

"At least all they're doing is auditing you," Jay mumbled.

Kate put a restraining hand on Jay's arm and gave a subtle shake of her head. It would serve no useful purpose to mention the trumped up Swiss bank account and investigation.

"As I've said many times, I don't much care for bullies," Dara continued. "I think our best course of action is to confront them. Bullies invariably back down when challenged."

"Let me get this straight—you want to take on two governments to see if they'll blink?" Trevor asked.

"This isn't some backyard pool game of chicken you're talking about," Laura said. "This is the government of the United States of America. The FBI, the IRS."

"And don't forget the British government," Richard added.

Kate watched everyone's body language. George sat back, calm, comfortable, and seemingly without a care in the world. Rebecca was focused on Dara, clearly being supportive. Richard, Laura, and Trevor displayed serious cases of nerves. Jay, of course, was intrigued.

"May I?" Kate asked.

Dara looked relieved. "Please." She addressed the group. "For those of you who don't know, Kate is the former Press Secretary to the President of the United States. Public relations, government, and dealing with the media are her areas of expertise."

"And you should hear her sing," Jay threw in.

She winked at Kate, and Kate understood that Jay was trying to loosen up the crowd.

"I'll keep it in mind in case we add a musical number," George deadpanned.

Kate smiled at him. "If you two are done joking around, I'll give you my best professional advice and judgment."

"Please," Juanita said. Trevor, Richard, and Laura nodded in agreement.

"Okay. I'm not sure if any of you had a chance to see Former First Lady Mimi Hyland's press conference yesterday…"

Dara and Rebecca nodded.

"I saw something on the evening news about it," Richard said.

Trevor, Juanita, and Laura mumbled something about being otherwise occupied and not paying attention to the news.

"All-righty then," Kate said. "The former first lady held a press conference in which she blasted the media, and indirectly went after the Feds, for investigating Jay with regard to the manuscript and the leak of classified information to *Time* magazine." She made eye contact with all of the actors and George. "Are you with me so far?"

Everyone grunted an affirmative.

"Every newspaper headline and every radio and television talk show last night and this morning was abuzz with the story." Kate drew the imaginary headlines in the air. "'First Lady Comes Out Swinging.' As you can imagine, the Feds aren't too happy with the publicity or with losing the moral high ground."

Again, Kate tried to gauge whether everyone was following her. They seemed to be. "If some very big, very popular, very influential Hollywood stars were to hold a press conference a day or two after the First Lady's event grabbed headlines, it would mean another few cycles of very ugly, very bad publicity for the Feds. Trust me when I tell you, they're not going to want that. In short, yes, I think they will blink, Trevor."

"Howdy folks, from the flight deck again. You'll need to buckle up now. We've been cleared for taxi and takeoff. It's a beautiful day for a ride. The air is nice and smooth around 17,500 feet, so we'll climb up to that altitude and have a look around until you tell us you're ready to do something else."

As the engines revved up, everyone buckled in. Kate leaned over to Dara and spoke into her ear. "There's no point trying to compete with the noise, so let's wait until we're airborne to continue the group discussion."

"Agreed."

"Am I giving you the advice you were looking for?"

"Honestly, I'm interested in your best judgment, not what you think I want to hear. Am I crazy, or is what I'm suggesting a good idea?"

"What's your desired outcome? What do you hope to gain by holding the press conference?"

"We need the Brits to back down and give us our shooting location. That's the biggest hurdle right now. I haven't done anything wrong, and I trust you and Jay, so I know I'm not in any real trouble with the Feds, and the IRS can kiss my ass. All of my tax returns are in perfect order. Although I'm annoyed as hell, I'm not worried on that front."

Kate didn't want to tell Dara what the IRS was capable of—that the agency could make her life a living hell—as they were doing with her and Jay. For now, it was more beneficial to focus on the matter at hand.

"If your primary goal is to be able to move ahead with the film and the location, then bringing public pressure to bear might do the trick."

"Last interruption from the flight deck, folks. Just letting you know we've reached our cruising altitude and everything looks beautiful up here. Please enjoy the ride and let Nancy know if you need anything."

Kate opened the shade. The sky was crystal clear with the sun shining in through the window, refracting the light and creating a rainbow on the cabin wall.

Everyone else followed suit, opening the remaining shades.

When the group was settled again, Dara said, "Listen, we've invested a lot of money and work into the sets and the location outside London. Frankly, without an approval to go forward there, we're going to be hard-pressed to move ahead with the film."

"Dara, what do you need, specifically, from us? Why are we here?" Laura asked. "Surely, you don't need us. You've got more than enough star power on your own to attract the media's attention."

Dara leaned forward and made eye contact with all of the other actors. "Yes. Laura's right. I could've called a press conference in LA by myself and pleaded our case. But here's the thing. Nothing about this movie-making experience has been conventional. George and I understand that each of you has put something of yourselves on the line in committing to this project. Attaching your names came with risks, as we spelled out to you at the outset."

"What Dara is trying, very nicely, to say here," George interrupted, "is that your asses are on the line too. We don't want to run roughshod over you on this. We'd prefer that we were all in this together. So if you have a problem with standing up for what's right here, please say so now."

Trevor and Laura fidgeted in their seats. Richard frowned. Juanita's knee bounced up and down. She addressed Kate. "What's the downside if we do this press conference? What could happen?"

"Good questions. Here are some things to consider. Because you all are widely recognizable and popular both in this country and abroad, there will be plenty of press at the event. Neither the US nor the British are going to want this kind of adverse publicity. It's possible that all you'll have to do is put out what we call a media advisory announcing your intention to hold a press conference. In the advisory, you'd explain that you want to address intentional obstructionism by these two governments."

"I don't understand," Laura said. "We would telegraph what we wanted to say? Why would the media come if we already told them the punch line?"

"I know this might not make logical sense to you," Kate said, "but it's like playing poker or blackjack."

"Now you're talking my language," Trevor broke in.

"How much did you lose to me last week?" Richard asked.

"As I was saying," Kate shot the guys a glance, "oftentimes if you show enough of your hand—"

"Your opponent folds!"

"Yes, Trevor. Your opponent folds up cards and you win without ever having to play out the entire hand."

"Do you think that's what would happen here?" Juanita asked.

Kate weighed the odds. "I think it's a strong possibility that, at the very least, the British government would back down, and you'd be back on track with your location. They're going to view this as the US's problem. They won't want any part of the fallout for keeping the world from seeing some of its favorite stars on the big screen."

"If it was your ass on the line, would you do it?" George asked.

Kate decided she liked him for his bluntness. "I would." She nodded. "The timing is in your favor. As Dara pointed out, you've invested significant resources into the project, and if you do nothing, there's no incentive for either government to make any of your current problems go away."

"What do you think they could do to us personally for going public?" Laura asked.

Kate smiled at Laura, hoping that by being at ease herself, it would calm the actress's nerves. Of everyone present, she clearly was the most timid.

"Once you step out in front of those cameras and say that the federal government is intimidating you, they can't very well go after you and prove you right, now, can they? You'll be fine."

"Shine light, heal away darkness," Jay muttered, as much to herself as anyone else.

Kate heard her and gave her hand a quick squeeze. Heaven knew Jay was paying a high price for doing just that.

"So," Dara said, "I'll take a show of hands. Who's willing to do this?"

Each of the actors looked at the others. Kate wondered which of them would take the lead. She didn't have to wonder long.

"I'm in," Juanita said.

"Me too." Richard held up his hand.

"Me three," Trevor said.

Laura shrugged. "I guess so."

Dara's eyes shone with gratitude. "Excellent. Kate?"

"Mmm?"

"If this were you, where would you hold such an event?"

"You mean we're going to do this right now?" Laura asked, a hint of panic in her voice.

"No time like the present," Dara answered. "As Kate indicated, now is the time to strike, on the heels of the former first lady's event."

Kate drummed her fingers on her leg, calculating. "If you hold the press conference in LA, you'll get the entertainment reporters to come out for sure. But what you really want here is to get as close as possible to the lion's den. I'd schedule the press conference in Washington, D.C." She checked her watch. "You want to be sure that your remarks will get the widest play in papers like *The New York Times* and *The Washington Post*, and on all the major news shows. That means you want to hold it either between 10:30 and 11:30 in the morning, or 2:30 and 3:30 in the afternoon."

"We've already missed those windows," Rebecca said.

"That's fine." Kate pulled out her laptop. "Tomorrow's another day."

"So, we're going to fly around until tomorrow?" Laura's voice went up an octave.

"No," Dara said. "We're going to ask the pilot nicely to take us to the nation's capital, where we're going to spend the night at a lovely hotel I'll be happy to book for us. And we'll plan to hold the press conference tomorrow at whatever time Kate thinks is most advantageous to us."

Kate chimed in, "I'd prefer to schedule it for tomorrow afternoon. That will give me time to secure a venue for the news conference, write the advisory, and have it disseminated to all of the appropriate news outlets."

"You can do all that from here?" Rebecca asked.

"You forget, I spent a lot of time flying around on Air Force One using much more antiquated technology than we have available to us today. You'd be amazed at what you can accomplish at 20,000 feet."

Kate extended the desk from the wall, set the laptop on it, and booted it up.

CHAPTER TWENTY-FOUR

Sabastien hunched over in his chair, squinting at the tiny code crawling across the laptop screen. In the background, Veronique was running a larger query that he hoped would yield the specifics of the Commission's plot.

"What are you doing sitting like that? Your back must be killing you," Lorraine said. She handed him a cup of fresh espresso, which he sniffed appreciatively.

"I am determined to solve our encryption issue so that we can communicate securely with your husband via e-mail. I am almost there. One more string of code, and I believe I shall have it."

"How are you going to know if you got it right without risking our exposure?"

"I set up a dummy account to which to send a nonsense e-mail for the testing."

"You're brilliant."

"You doubted this before?" Sabastien gave Lorraine a toothy grin.

"Not for a second." She pointed at the large monitor on the desk. "What's Veronique up to?"

"Ah, she is searching for trap doors..." Sabastien stopped talking when Veronique dinged. He stroked the keyboard lightly with his fingertips. "I love you so very much, beautiful Veronique. You never disappoint."

"What's going on?"

Sabastien's eyes darted left to right as he read across the screen. "Fantastique."

"What's so wonderful?"

"First, my girlfriend was able to disable a series of trip wires so that we would not alert any bad guys."

"Excellent."

"I am not finished. After that, she examined every piece of code Vector Research installed within each system they touched."

"You mean as part of their contracted work with Homeland Security?"

"I mean any command they inputted anywhere within your government's network, period. Not just Homeland Security, but anywhere."

"You could do that?"

"I am Sabastien Vaupaul. There is not anything involving technology that I cannot do. If I cannot do it, it cannot be done."

"I love how modest you are."

"When you are the best at what you do, there is no reason to hide under a tree, yes?"

"Under a bushel. The expression is, don't hide your light under a bushel."

"You say bushel, I say tree. Is the same, yes?"

Lorraine laughed. "If I say yes, will you be happy?"

"Very."

"Then, yes."

"Okay, good. Anyway, where was I?"

"You were about to dazzle me with what you and Veronique discovered."

"Ah, just so. Let us be dazzled together, okay?"

"Sure."

Sabastien clicked the mouse, hovered, clicked again, rearranged the data on the screen, and whistled.

"What is it?"

"Holy…"

"Sabastien. I love you, but if you don't explain what you see in that mess of symbols, I'm going to strangle you."

"Oh. Of course. Veronique and I, we have hit the jackpot."

"Meaning?"

"Meaning, we have proof that Vector was using their access to the system to embed tracking capability that would give them unlimited access to all of your government's most sensitive data."

"Such as…?"

"You see here?" He pointed to a string of code. "This gives Vector access to the development status of new weapons systems and designs." He glanced back at Lorraine, then returned his attention to the screen. "This here? This gives them a blueprint to your latest technology to counteract cyber-spying."

"Holy Mother of God."

"And this? This one provides them with all the codes to hack into the new encryption software protecting top secret communications between Homeland Security and all of its agencies. The pièce de résistance, of course, is the thing Vector was actually supposed to be doing, creating secure technology to protect sensitive conversations for top-level officials, except that they gave themselves a way to eavesdrop and record every conversation."

Lorraine's face paled, and Sabastien was afraid she might pass out. "Are you okay?"

Lorraine blinked. "That's…"

"Horrible. I know."

"And you can prove it? All of it?"

"Every line of code, every back door they opened, every aspect of the system with which they tampered."

"Do it quickly, before they catch onto us. Capture it, save it in several places, print it out just in case, and get out of there. Make sure you don't leave any traces behind. We don't want them to be aware that we know."

"Oh, Lorraine. What do you take me for, an amateur? Sabastien is on the job."

"Good. And as soon as you've got that squared away, finish figuring out a way to safely get the information to Peter ASAP."

"As I said before Veronique interrupted us, I am only a few keystrokes away from making us secure once more."

Lorraine jumped up and gave Sabastien a big, loud, kiss on both cheeks, and he blushed to the roots of his hair.

"I love you, Sabastien Vaupaul. You really are a genius."

She was gone before he gathered his wits about him to respond.

≪⋙

Peter paced back and forth in front of the white board. On it, he had created a timeline of hacks perpetrated by John Robie prior to, and immediately after, the Vector hack.

"What is the common thread here?" What was it Lorraine's profiler had said about Robie? *She said he had a persecution complex.* Peter stared at the board again.

He uncapped a marker and began circling the dates of each hack. Then he opened Google on his computer and typed in the name of each affected company and searched each of their websites for press releases and announcements of what projects they were working on just before John Robie hacked them. By the fifth search, he'd found the pattern. "Gotcha."

Peter's computer chirped, indicating an incoming e-mail. The sound was loud in the silence and it startled him. He clicked to open the message and his eyes opened wide when he saw that it came from one of the accounts Sabastien had set up.

Peter opened the e-mail and scanned the contents.

```
We are secure once again and we have
news. I am sending you a birthday
greeting via a new e-mail address. I hope
you will enjoy the gift. I would love to
Skype with you to wish you greetings in
person. Ping me if you are able.
```

Peter read the note again, making sure that he understood the message. Sabastien was sending him the proof, wrapped up with a ribbon. When his computer chimed again, Peter opened the new e-mail and eagerly double-clicked on an encrypted, zipped file. He saved it to an external hard drive, opened another laptop with a new IP address, connected the external hard drive to it, and opened the files.

When he'd finished reading the report and all of the attached documentation and printed all of it out, he sat back and smiled with satisfaction. Everything was coming together. Now all they needed was to finish solving the John Robie/Black Knight puzzle.

"Well, dummy, if transmissions are secure now, why are you trying to do this alone?" He double-clicked on Skype and placed a video call to Sabastien.

∽☙

"Kate?"

"Peter? What's going on?"

"Where are you right now?"

Kate heard the urgency in Peter's voice and wanted very much to know what was causing that. Had he found the Black Knight? Were Lorraine, Sabastien, and Vaughn okay? Had they found something? Could she ask Peter? Were their communications secure? There was no point in taking unnecessary chances, so she decided to be circumspect. "Where you and I were the other day. Why?"

"That's perfect."

"Because...?"

"I need you to drop whatever you're doing and meet with a friend of mine."

"Here?"

"Yes."

Kate tamped down her frustration. She wanted to be able to speak freely. How was she supposed to know who she was meeting and where to go? And was Jay supposed to come with her?

"Am I going to need any details? Like who, what, where, when, how, and whether it's a table for two or three?"

"Table for three. I hope you're hungry right now. It's a business meeting, so bring your three hundred-page portfolio. I'll arrange the details. I suggest you stand outside on the curb, enjoy the sunshine, and wait for your ride."

The line went silent. Kate scratched her head and tried to decipher the cryptic message. Table for three meant the meeting included Jay; that was easy enough. The three hundred-page portfolio... *He means the manuscript. He wants Jay to bring the manuscript.* Whoever was meeting them obviously had to have a way of tracking their whereabouts without needing any input... *Trust, Kyle. Trust Peter.*

Kate stepped back inside the hotel where they'd been sitting in the lobby when Peter called. Dara still was at the reception desk, arranging the hotel rooms so that neither Kate nor Jay's name appeared in any computer systems. Kate found Jay window shopping at the gift shop at the far end of the lobby. "We have to go."

"Why? Dara is still checking us in."

"I know. I'll let her know we have to go out for a little while. We'll be back in time for dinner."

"Where are we—"

"Sweetheart, I love you, but now is not the time for questions. Keep your briefcase with you. I'll ask Dara to have a bellman bring our bags up to the room."

Kate strode across the lobby and touched Dara on the sleeve. "Jay and I have to go run an urgent errand. Will you be okay here?"

Dara raised an eyebrow in surprise. "Of course. I've got everything under control. I'll get you your room and have the bags brought up. I'll text you the room number."

"I'm sorry. Normally I wouldn't..."

Dara squeezed Kate's shoulder. "Don't give it a thought. We'll be fine."

"It's just that this is important and unavoidable. We'll be back in time for dinner. Will you join us?"

"Absolutely."

"I'll call you as soon as I can." Kate hustled toward the front door and motioned for Jay to join her.

They'd barely reached the sidewalk when a large black SUV pulled to the curb in front of them. The back passenger door opened. "Ladies, can I give you a ride?"

Jay stepped back, her fear palpable. Kate steadied her with a hand in the small of her back.

"He's a friend of Peter's, sweetheart. We're safe. Get in."

Jay stepped into the car, sat, and hugged her briefcase to her. Kate followed behind her and sat next to her.

"I'm sorry for the cloak and dagger." The man next to Jay was beefy and balding, with a slightly bulging belly. "I'm Derek LaPointe, Deputy Secretary for Homeland Security." He held out his hand and shook theirs each in turn. Then he tapped the driver on the shoulder. "Let's roll."

Kate narrowed her eyes. The name sounded so familiar to her, but at the moment, she couldn't recall why.

"Where are we going?" Jay asked. Her left arm still clutched the briefcase to her chest.

"Someplace I know we can talk openly."

The driver made a left-hand turn, and suddenly Kate knew their destination. It had been many years since she'd been there. "I love the Willard Hotel."

Derek smiled at her. "Me too. For so many reasons."

"Anyone want to clue me in?" Jay asked. "Kate, how did you know where we're going?"

"You'll see in a minute," Kate answered.

They pulled into a garage and the SUV stopped in front of an elevator. The driver came around and opened the door for Kate and Jay.

"This is our stop, ladies. Please, I would ask you to leave your cell phones in the car."

Jay looked to Kate, and Kate nodded. She removed the cell phone from her pocket and placed it on the seat. She motioned for Jay to do the same.

To the driver, Derek said, "Wait here. We won't be too long." He walked over to the elevator and inserted a key into a keypad on the wall. The doors opened, and he motioned for Kate and Jay to step inside.

Jay's eyes were wide and she was clenching her teeth so hard that her jaw bulged. Again, Kate put a hand on her back to reassure her.

The elevator doors opened to reveal a room several steps away. Derek led the way to the room, and used a retinal scan to give them access. The three of them entered the room and the door closed behind them.

"Welcome to our SCIF," Derek said.

"Sensitive Compartmentalized Intelligence Facility," Kate explained to Jay. "This room has double-reinforced walls and blocks out all recording devices."

"One of the most secure meeting places in D.C.," Derek boasted. "I wanted to be certain we were clear."

"How do you know this place?" Jay asked Kate.

"The Willard Hotel has been here since 1850. This room was created... Well, I don't even know when, but I attended more than one meeting here when I worked for the president."

"Derek, no offense, but why are we here? And why is your name familiar to me?" Kate asked.

"Ah. I wondered if you'd remember." Derek shifted from foot to foot, his eyes on the far wall. "You never met me, but I know both of you and everything that happened back... Well, back in '89."

"You do?" Jay asked.

"Yes. At the time, I was Deputy Director of the FBI. Peter came to me and asked for my help with your...case, Ms. Parker."

"That explains it," Kate said. "How do you know Peter?"

"We served in Vietnam together. That man saved my life— dragged my ass out of a POW camp. I wouldn't be here if it wasn't for him."

"Speaking of being here, why are we here?" Jay asked.

"Peter called me a little while ago. I hadn't heard from him in years, although apparently he'd been following my career. He said he had something big and very sensitive, and he needed someone he could trust absolutely and who had access to the president. Peter will be here in the morning, by the way. He and I have a meeting scheduled at oh-seven-thirty. If the information is as vital as Peter says it is, and I've never had a reason to doubt him, then we'll take it to the president."

"We, as in...?"

"The four of us."

"Oh," Jay said.

"Not to question your authority, Derek, but how is it that the Deputy Secretary of DHS has direct access to the president?"

"You're very sharp, Ms. Kyle. Every bit as sharp as Peter said you were. You are correct that I would normally be too low on the totem pole to rate an audience with the president, except that I was, at one time, Director of the Secret Service under this president. I spent time with him every day."

"Until you were appointed to this current position," Kate said.

"Exactly."

"You still haven't directly answered the question. Why are Jay and I here?" Kate asked.

"Although Peter wouldn't go into any specifics about what he possesses, he did go into great detail about you, Ms. Parker— specifically about the scrutiny you've been under—and I did some checking. Frankly, although I'd seen some vague justifications from the FBI for surveilling you, it wasn't much of a blip on my radar until Peter brought the situation into sharp relief. On behalf of our government, I want to apologize for what the FBI has been putting you through. I want you to know, I personally had a...discussion...with the Director of the FBI, and you are no longer under surveillance of any kind."

Jay swayed with relief and Kate put an arm around her. "Thank you."

"I'm not done yet." Derek cleared his throat. "Peter asked me to do something else, and I told him I would."

"What's that?"

"He asked me to read your manuscript."

Unconsciously, Jay tightened her grip on the briefcase.

"I see that you are reluctant, and I can understand why," Derek rushed on. "But here's the thing. Remember that I know a great deal about what transpired during the Hyland situation. In fact, like you, I was one of those required to testify before the Hyland Commission. More importantly, I've seen the documents in question—the ones that were leaked. Peter assures me that if I read your manuscript, I will recognize that there is no disclosure of top secret information therein. If he's right, then I will personally bring that information to the president and have you exonerated."

"Why would I need to be exonerated if I've done nothing wrong?" Jay stiffened.

"Perhaps exonerated is the wrong word," Derek said. "You're the writer, not me. What I mean to say is that I will see to it that the truth comes out—that what you've written doesn't in any way violate national security or disclose top secret information." Derek pointed a finger at Jay. "If, and I emphasize *if* that's true. But the only way I'm going to know that is if you allow me to read your manuscript."

Kate looked to Jay. "Peter trusts this man."

"I know he does, but you'll pardon me if my recent experiences with the Feds have made me a little skeptical."

"I'd like to tell you we have the luxury of time, ladies, but we don't. If you give me the manuscript now, I will read it tonight and personally hand it back to you in the morning. I give you my word that no one but me will see it, and I will make no copies."

"Jay," Kate said gently. "Peter asked him to read it. We have to trust that, and him. We have to trust somebody."

Reluctantly, Jay opened her briefcase, removed the copy of the manuscript she had brought with her, and handed it to Derek. "You might want to vet the movie script also, since it's based on the manuscript." She handed that over as well. "Same conditions apply."

"Of course."

"I hope you're a fast reader."

"Fortunately, being able to quickly digest information is one of the requirements of my job. Besides, I love a good thriller."

⟡⟡

When Kate and Jay were safely in their own hotel room, Jay said, "What the heck just happened?"

Kate shrugged. "Sounds to me like Peter has all the proof in his possession. Sabastien and Lorraine must've isolated actionable information on what Vector and the Commission are up to and they must've found a way to get that to Peter."

"Do you think he figured out who the Black Knight is?"

"He wouldn't have risked calling Derek to meet if he hadn't solved that piece of the puzzle."

"God, I wish we could find out what Peter knows. We need our own SCIF."

Kate laughed.

"Did you notice that Derek only mentioned the FBI harassment? He didn't say a word about the IRS thing."

"Either he doesn't know about that, or Peter was saving that for tomorrow."

"Or we still don't have the physical names of who made the wire transfer and who at the IRS came after me."

"And Dara."

Jay nodded. "And Dara."

"Speaking of which, we should call her. It's almost dinnertime."

CHAPTER TWENTY-FIVE

P eter finished eating dinner at Tonic and decided to take a stroll. It was a nice enough night, though more humid than it had been the other day. The message from Derek indicated that he'd successfully convinced Jay to let him read what she'd written. Peter was glad for that; he hadn't been entirely sure Jay would go along with it.

While he was on the subject, he wondered how long it would be before his friends figured out that if he was meeting with Derek at seven thirty tomorrow morning, he must either be in D.C. by now, or at least be on his way here.

He wandered past the Vietnam Memorial, pausing to touch the wall. For a moment, he got lost in the memories of so many friends and comrades lost. Then he moved on, drawn to the Lincoln Memorial Reflecting Pool, which suited his mood.

If everything fell into place as he believed it would, by this time tomorrow night Lorraine, Sabastien, and Vaughn would be on their way home, and the Black Knight, Vector, and Michael Vendetti would be out of commission. Peter snickered at his own pun.

His phone buzzed. When he saw that it was a text from Kate asking where he was, he congratulated himself on his prescience. He typed, *If you're available, meet me at the haunted place.* He pressed the Send key, then looked up at the Lincoln Memorial in the distance.

His phone buzzed again. *Be there in ten.* He couldn't decide whether it was a blessing or a curse that Kate so easily understood the meeting place he referenced, but some things didn't bear thinking. So instead, he picked up the pace and headed for the Lincoln Memorial.

By the time he arrived, Kate and Jay were jogging up the steps. "Going somewhere special, ladies?"

"Just out for a little exercise, actually," Jay said. She gave him a big hug. "Thanks for this morning and the decoy."

"You're welcome, squirt."

"And thanks, maybe, for your friend. I'm not sure about that one just yet."

Peter nodded sympathetically. "I understand. But Derek is a good man, an honest man. He's above reproach. I trusted him with my life in 'Nam, and I trust him now."

"Why didn't we go to him sooner?" Kate asked.

"We didn't have enough evidence. If I'd gone to Derek before we'd figured out all the pieces of the puzzle, he would've told me there was nothing he could do without proof. I wanted to keep the loop as tight as possible until we had everything we needed."

"And do we?" Jay asked. "Have everything we need?"

"We do indeed."

He loved seeing the light in his friends' eyes. It had been forever since either one of them had smiled this broadly.

"Can you tell us?"

Peter checked their surroundings. There wasn't another soul in sight or likely in hearing distance. "Sure. Let's walk."

They turned around and headed in the opposite direction, toward the Washington Monument.

"Well? Come on, the suspense is killing us," Jay said.

"All right. Sabastien was able to isolate what he believes is all of the code and the evidence proving that Vector was using its contract to extract state secrets, insert commands that would allow them unfettered access to virtually every sensitive government program and communication, and expose Homeland Security and all of the agencies under its aegis to untold attacks from anyone to whom Vector sold the information."

"And he was able to send the evidence to you without tipping anyone off?" Kate asked.

"He was. He finally solved the interference and sent me everything he had." Peter put a hand on Jay's shoulder. "That includes what he was able to uncover about the wire transfer, the phony Swiss bank account, and the IP addresses involved. We've got them now. I just have to give that information to Derek and he'll be able to take care of it."

"Thank you, God."

"What about the Black Knight?" Kate asked.

"This is where it gets interesting," Peter answered. "As it turns out, we were right about a lot of things. He is hiding in plain sight on Vector's employment roster and, according to Sabastien, his ID card is swiped daily at Vector Research headquarters, right here in Chevy Chase, Maryland."

"Who is he and what do we know about him?"

"His name is Dustin Wolford. A dozen years ago, he was working for a large tech firm in Silicon Valley. He was part of a team testing new programs the company was developing under a government contract. Wolford was poking around in one of the company's products and determined that it was flawed—the code would trample all over people's privacy.

"Wolford brought this to the attention of his superiors. He argued that the information collected was illegal at the time, even in light of the emergency legislation and powers afforded the government after 9/11, and could result in damaging or embarrassing disclosures for everyday folks whose data would be swept up in the collection process. Two days later, he was fired."

"Oh my."

"Right. He brought suit against the company, accusing them of wrongful termination."

"Is that where you got all this background information? It was in the legal papers?"

"Not me. Sabastien. I just led him in the right direction. Not long after Wolford got fired, John Robie showed up. Guess who was his first hacking target?"

"His former employer," Jay said.

"Bingo.

"And that's how you found him," Kate said.

"That's how we confirmed that he was our guy. Eventually, the company in question went belly up, but our man Wolford holds a grudge and has used it to fuel his anger at corporations similar to his former employer and the government, since they're the ones offering the contracts."

"Lovely," Kate said.

"Once Sabastien figured out the technique Wolford was using to sabotage him and set traps to trip alarms, he was able to disable all of that. When he did, Sabastien hacked in and retrieved financial records and correspondence from West Industries, Techtronics, and Vector, proving that Vendetti was the one personally responsible for ordering the hack of the Hyland Commission Report and subsequent payment to Wolford."

"Now what?"

"I give everything I have to Derek, and he orders the bad guys arrested and all of their electronics and any other potential evidence gets confiscated before they can destroy the proof."

"Why are we waiting until tomorrow?" Jay asked.

"Honestly? Because I want Derek to spend the night reading your book. We need someone in a position of authority to have read it to put to rest any discussion about whether or not it reveals top secret information."

"Peter's right, honey," Kate said. "Even with every piece of proof we have confirming who the hacker was, who authorized the leak, and what the Commission is up to, none of that addresses the question of whether or not the manuscript, and now the screenplay, contain classified information, and therefore, whether you're breaking the law."

"What if Wolford or Vendetti figure out we're on to them?" Jay asked. "We risk their destroying all of the damning evidence and getting away."

"No one's going anywhere, sweetheart."

"What Kate said. Walk you two home?" Peter looped an arm through Kate and Jay's arms. "Where are you staying?"

"The Ritz-Carlton."

Peter whistled and turned them in the proper direction for the hotel. "Nice digs. You had enough cash for that?"

"No. Dara insisted on paying."

"Nice new friends. I can see Lorraine and I are going to have to up our games to keep top standing."

"Never." Jay snuggled closer to Peter.

"That reminds me. I figured neither one of you brought appropriate attire for a meeting with the president—"

"Oh my God! That's right. I can't go to a meeting with the president dressed in what I brought."

"Relax. As I said, I anticipated that you'd need something more formal than you had, so I went to your place and picked up a suit for each of you."

"You, Peter Enright, let yourself into our house, rummaged through our closets, and came up with outfits for us to wear tomorrow?" Kate asked.

Peter nodded. "I did. And I have to say, never have I seen two more anally organized closets in my life. Suits ordered by color and type? Really?"

Jay playfully punched him in the arm. "Please tell me you selected matching blouses and shoes."

"Of course."

"Why am I frightened to see what you brought?"

"You could just say thank you, you know."

"Where's the fun in that?"

"By the way, why are you two in D.C.?" Peter asked. "Last I knew, you were going to meet Dara and Rebecca at the airport in Albany."

"Dara, her director, and some of the cast members have scheduled a press conference here for tomorrow afternoon. The Feds and the Brits are throwing up roadblocks to forestall the filming. We thought a little adverse publicity might lead them to reconsider."

"Brassy."

"I'm pretty confident the Brits will capitulate, even if the Feds won't," Kate said.

"I'm sorry to have thrown your schedule off," Peter said. "You should be spending time with Dara and Rebecca and friends."

"Well, what we're doing with you and Derek is kind of important," Jay pointed out.

"And it was rather convenient that we happened to end up in the perfect place to tackle both issues," Kate added.

"All true," Peter agreed. "Listen, there's no reason for you to drag your butts out of bed at the crack of dawn to hear me rehash for Derek what I just told you. Why don't you have breakfast with your friends? I can meet with Derek, and then he and I will swing by and pick you up for the sit-down with the president."

"What about our clothes?" Jay asked.

"I'll have them delivered to you first thing in the morning." They came to a stop in front of the Ritz-Carlton. "I believe we have reached your destination."

"Where are you staying?" Kate asked.

"The Willard. I thought it would be most convenient since that SCIF is where Derek wants to meet."

⌘⌘

Kate and Jay were just finishing up breakfast in the hotel with Dara, Rebecca, and George when Kate's phone buzzed with a text message from Peter saying that he and Derek were on their way to get them.

"I'm so sorry we have to run," Kate said. "I know this has turned into a crazy trip. Jay and I expected to be available to you the entire time and—"

"Kate," Dara interrupted her. "Go. This is important, even if you can't tell us exactly what it is you're doing and why you're both dressed for some serious business. You both look smashing, by the way."

"If I said that, you all would say I'm sexist," George said.

"Right," all three women said in unison.

"Which is why I wouldn't dream of saying it," George finished.

"Smart man."

"We're not going to ask about where you're going, who you're seeing, or what you're up to," Rebecca said, "but it doesn't mean we're not curious as all get-out."

"Sorry, folks. We'll be happy to fill you in when it's all over." Kate put the napkin that had been in her lap on the table, rose, and handed Dara some bills to cover the cost of breakfast.

"I'm going to pretend you didn't just try to hand me money." Dara closed Kate's fist with the money still in it. "Get out of here. You're going to be late."

"We'll text you as soon as we're done, and then we can go over the details of the press conference, okay?" Kate asked.

"Perfect," Dara agreed. "We need your moral support and expertise. Don't leave us hanging."

"We won't," Jay said. Kate took her hand and they hustled out of the restaurant and onto the street where a black stretch SUV was idling at the curb. The door opened and they stepped inside.

"Good morning, ladies," Derek said. He and Peter sat on one bench seat. He invited Kate and Jay to sit opposite them. "You're just in time."

"For...?" Jay asked.

Derek handed her a laptop identical to the one sitting on the seat beside him. "I thought you might want to see this."

Kate scooted closer to Jay and squinted at the screen. The images were in grainy black-and-white. "What are we looking at?"

"These are four simultaneous live feeds courtesy of our FBI and Homeland Security Rapid Deployment Joint Task Force. Top left is from the spy glasses camera of an FBI agent in Chevy Chase, Maryland. He and his team are about to arrest Dustin Wolford. Top right is a collar camera from another FBI team leader also in Chevy Chase. That team's objective is the CEO of Vector Research. Bottom left is a feed from our team in the Adams-Morgan neighborhood here in D.C. Their target is Michael Vendetti. Bottom right is Rock Creek Park, where our dirty CIA operative thinks he's meeting with his IRS contact. He is, since we sent them each a cryptic message supposedly from the other. The only problem for them is that they're both meeting our FBI agents."

"Team Leader Alpha in place."

"Roger that, team leader..."

Kate, Jay, Peter, and Derek watched in silence as the action unfolded on the screens. It all happened very quickly, with surgical precision, and without a struggle from any of the suspects. Less than three minutes after the last arrest was made, Derek's phone rang.

"LaPointe... Right... Excellent... Make sure we execute all of those search warrants right away... Good... Everything from Wolford's house is secured? Make sure you triple-check. We don't want to miss anything. Keep me posted. And Todd? That was really good work out there today. I'm proud of all of you. Let the rest of the teams know." Derek ended the call.

"That was just confirmation of what we saw. All of the major players are in custody. We'll get more search warrants and make more arrests in the coming days, I'm sure."

"Good job, my friend," Peter said. He shook Derek's hand. "That was fast work."

"Are you kidding me? You're the one who did all the heavy lifting. I had no idea you were that proficient with technology issues."

Jay opened her mouth to say something and Kate surreptitiously squeezed her hand. She was certain that Jay would mention Sabastien and his hard work. As much as all of them would love for him to get the credit he richly deserved, he was the prime suspect in the leak. It wouldn't help their case for him to be known as the one who uncovered the truth. It might make all of their findings circumspect.

"I had a lot of help," Peter said.

"Do I want to know who?" Derek asked.

"Probably not."

"Will I live to regret this, Enright?"

"Definitely not. You're a hero, LaPointe."

The SUV pulled to a stop in the White House drive. "We're here." Derek got out of the SUV and buttoned his jacket. "Let's go tell the president the good news."

Derek and Peter had just finished briefing the president and his top advisors on the scope of the Commission's infiltration into the country's national security systems and the details of the just-completed Joint Task Force operation. Peter had cleared Sabastien's good name, opening the door for him to return to the United States and to the job he loved. Everything had gone like clockwork.

Jay bit her lip. She knew the protocol where meetings with presidents was concerned. She knew she should remain mum and be grateful that the good guys had won today and the bad guys were likely going away for a very, very long time. She knew all that, but...

"Mr. President, sir? I know I probably shouldn't say anything, but I can't stay silent any longer. With your permission—"

The chief-of-state waved Jay off. "The president's schedule is very busy—"

"I'd be happy to hear what's on your mind, Ms. Parker." The president gave his right-hand advisor a warning look. "I have to say, you've made quite a stir lately." He glanced at her over his reading glasses. "I read the papers, you know. And I saw what Mimi Hyland had to say about you the other day. My, that was an impassioned defense."

Jay was slightly unnerved that the president knew so much about her situation. "Mr. President, you heard firsthand just now what the Commission is capable of. This organization has its hand in every sector of our society, spreading its darkness like a stain on our democracy. Many years ago, when we first learned of the Commission and I wrote the original *Time* magazine story about the events that comprise the Hyland Commission Report, I went along with our president and his advisors who believed that to admit publicly how powerful the Commission was would weaken our country. Over the years I have come to feel differently.

"If we truly want to eradicate the darkness, we must shine light on it. The more we give in to fear and stay quiet, the more this insidious evil festers. In order to shine light, we have to speak up. We have to tell the truth. I implore you to tell the truth about what the threat really is. As you know, there have been insinuations in media reports, and frankly, in some segments of your own government, that I might have improperly disclosed top secret data in my latest work.

"This has caused me great consternation, as I would never, ever do anything to harm my country. I love my country, Mr. President." Jay's voice faltered. "I resent any implication to the contrary."

"Ms. Parker—"

"I'm not finished yet." Jay held up a hand. Next to her, she noticed a ghost of a smile on Kate's face. "What I have written— this manuscript and adapted screenplay that seems to be frightening so many people—is a work of fiction. It is fiction, Mr. President. Every good work of fiction contains elements of truth, yes. But I promise you that there is nothing the least bit threatening to national security contained in those pages. My work is simply designed to make people think, to start a dialogue, to raise awareness and shine light. That is all." Jay took in a deep breath.

"Are you finished yet?" The president asked. His eyes twinkled at her.

Jay cleared her throat. "I am."

"Good. Ms. Parker, I am well aware that your work poses no threat to national security and that you are not a traitor."

"You are?"

"Do you honestly think I'd take a meeting with you in the Oval Office if I thought otherwise?"

"Good point."

"Coincidentally, I discussed you at length with Mimi—Mrs. Hyland—when she joined us for dinner last night. Not only that, but Deputy Secretary LaPointe here read the manuscript in question and advises me that it is his best professional judgment that your work poses absolutely no danger and violates no existing statutes or regulations."

"Oh."

"I want to personally apologize to you for the troubles you've had. It wasn't my doing, but it happened on my watch, and for that I am truly sorry. I assure you, heads will roll over this."

"Sir—"

"I'm not finished yet." The president smiled at her. "You know, for a long time, I was inclined to agree with President Hyland that we should just let sleeping dogs lie and not give any attention to nefarious groups like the Commission. But this whole episode has made me rethink that strategy."

Kate stepped forward for the first time. "Mr. President, sir. If I could be so bold as to give you a little public relations advice?"

The president laughed. "You two are quite the pair. Ms. Kyle, I am well-familiar with your prowess in such matters. I yield the floor."

"Well, sir. I think you have a golden opportunity here to shine the kind of light Jay just referenced. It's to your advantage to take a strong stand against those who would threaten our national security, whether those threats come from within or without. I would urge you to hold a press conference, announce and take credit for the arrests, and put the Commission on notice that you're not afraid of them."

"Sound advice, Ms. Kyle."

"One more thing you might want to know, Mr. President. I'm not sure if you're aware, but someone in your government has asked the Brits to withdraw cooperation and support for the movie based on Jay's manuscript, and the Brits have accordingly notified the producers that they've nullified all of the permits and agreements already in place for filming. One of the film's executive producers is the Oscar-winning actress, Dara Thomas. She and her co-stars are holding a press conference here in town this afternoon to decry deliberate obstructionism. It doesn't look good for your administration—"

"Ms. Kyle?"

"Yes, sir?"

"You can stop right there. I get your gist. Assuming I can get our British counterparts to cooperate and allow filming to go forward, would you see any strategic benefit to my pre-empting Ms. Thomas's press conference and asking her to appear with me instead so that I can lend my support to the project?"

"I believe easing the way for the most popular actress in the world to make a new film is always in your best interests, sir."

"I don't suppose you know how to get her here?"

"I do think I could arrange that, sir."

"Good enough. We'll hold a press briefing in an hour in the media room." The president pointed at Jay. "I expect you to be on the podium as well."

"Yes, sir," Jay responded.

CHAPTER TWENTY-SIX

Dara straightened the collar on her blouse. Next to her, the president of the United States tugged on his sleeve and fidgeted with his cufflink. She couldn't believe they were here, and that she was about to take part in a presidential press conference. At first, when Kate had called and told her what was to happen, she thought she was being punk'd. Surely Kate was kidding.

She glanced behind her. George, Trevor, Laura, Richard, and Juanita appeared star-struck too. Only Jay appeared relatively at ease.

A sharply dressed woman standing off to the side tapped the president's arm. "They're ready, Mr. President."

"That's our signal," he said to Dara. "I imagine you're used to spotlights much brighter than this, but beware the flashes. They blind me every time."

"Thank you for the advice, sir."

The door opened, and the president walked through. Dara followed directly after, followed by Jay and the others. Once they were on the stage standing behind the president, Dara glanced around. She spotted Rebecca standing with Kate off to the side. Out front, the room was packed to overflowing. Every seat was taken, and three rows of still photographers and television videographers stood atop three risers in the back of the room. Dara recognized many of the faces seated before her. There were the main anchors of the principal network news shows, the White House correspondents she'd come to know from their coverage of the president, and...

"Good day, ladies and gentlemen of the press. I'm so glad you could make it on such short notice." The president paused and smiled as what sounded like thousands of camera shutters whirred and clicked.

"Usually, I'm standing up here alone. Today, as you can see, I've upped my game and classed up the joint. I'll introduce my guests, as if most of them need any introduction, shortly. But first, I want to say this. At oh-nine-fifteen today, members of the FBI and Homeland Security Rapid Deployment Joint Task Force conducted multiple operations in and around the Washington, D.C. area.

"These raids, along with the arrests of several individuals, were the result of actionable intelligence regarding the source of a recent leak of top secret documents to a reporter from *Time* magazine. In short," the president looked directly into the cameras at the back of the room, "we got them. We have in custody those primarily responsible for the leak. In addition, we have evidence to support our belief that the leak in question was part of a larger effort to undermine the integrity of our nation's cybersecurity and intelligence systems."

A hum of excitement swept through the room.

"In custody right now are Dustin Wolford, the person we have identified as the hacker who leaked the Hyland Commission Report to *Time*, as well as Michael Vendetti..."

The hum escalated to a buzz, and the president nodded. "I know that's a name that's familiar to many of you. Mr. Vendetti, who at one time was the Deputy Press Secretary to President Hyland, was recently released from prison. Well, I'm here to tell you that he's going right back to jail.

"We have proof that Mr. Vendetti personally ordered the documents to be leaked. We also believe that it is no coincidence that Mr. Vendetti recently was elected to the board of directors of Vector Research Corporation. That is the company that employs Mr. Wolford. In addition, Vector Research was the subcontractor on a government project to upgrade communications systems within some of our national security agencies. We have proof that Vector Research intended to use that contract and the resulting access to our systems to steal vital information and/or interfere with government operations. Vector's CEO, Lance Tractenberg, is also in custody at this hour. It's a good day for justice."

The president took a deep breath, glanced back at Jay, who was standing to Dara's left, and winked. Dara wondered if this private moment in a room full of reporters had anything to do with where Kate and Jay had disappeared to earlier.

"I want to say something more. A very wise person reminded me this morning of the value of shining light and telling the truth. When Mr. Vendetti went to prison so many years ago, several others also were convicted and sent away for treason for their roles in the plot to oust President Hyland. These persons included high-ranking government officials, heads of Fortune 500 companies, and others. What you don't know is that all of those individuals were part of a highly organized syndicate that calls itself the Commission."

The buzz turned into a roar.

"We have every reason to believe that the present-day actions of Vector Research, Mr. Vendetti, Mr. Wolford, and Mr. Tractenberg are all tied to the Commission. It's time to shine light on this insidious organization and put its members on notice." The president pointed directly into the cameras. "Wherever you are, whatever you think you can do, we will find you and stop you."

The President straightened up and put a hand on either side of the podium. "Today, I am authorizing the de-classification of the Hyland Commission Report. It's time to shine the light on a dark period in our history."

Beside her, Dara heard Jay gasp. In her peripheral vision, she watched Jay blink away a tear. She chanced a glance over to where Kate was leaning against the wall. Her eyes were closed, in relief, it seemed. It was as if a great burden had been lifted from her shoulders.

"Now, I promised you I'd introduce you to my guests, all of whom are no doubt more interesting than I am. First, I'd like to introduce you to someone who has been no stranger to the media lately, albeit not of her own doing." The president turned and motioned for Jay to step forward and stand beside the podium.

"Jamison Parker was the intrepid reporter who broke the exclusive story of the Hyland fiasco in 1989. Since then, she's become one of the world's most successful, most beloved authors.

When the leak of the Hyland Commission Report surfaced several months ago, some of you in the media, and, to be truthful, some within law enforcement circles in this government, speculated that Ms. Parker might have had something to do with that, and/or that she might divulge top secret information from that report in her upcoming novel.

"I'd like to put all of that speculation to rest right now. First, Ms. Parker's ethics and dedication to this country are above question. Second, I am told by my top law enforcement and security experts that Ms. Parker's manuscript is a fabulous read, and that it contains nothing that in any way would jeopardize national security or violate laws or regulations regarding disclosure of classified data."

From behind her, Dara watched as Jay's knees buckled slightly before she recovered her equilibrium.

"That brings me to the last item on our agenda. I don't often get to rub elbows with Hollywood royalty, so today is a special day for me." The president turned and motioned Dara forward. She joined him on the other side of the podium. "Is there anybody in this room who doesn't know who Dara Thomas is? I can't imagine there is. I want to welcome America's own Oscar-winning actress and thank her for taking time from her busy schedule to join us."

Dara nodded, unsure whether she was expected to speak.

"It is with great pleasure that I announce that Ms. Thomas is the executive producer of the movie based on Ms. Parker's work. Here today with Ms. Thomas is the film's director, George Nelson, and co-stars Trevor Hanscome, Laura Simmons, Richard Broderick, and Juanita Jensen."

The president acknowledged each of them in turn.

"Why, you ask, is this fine group here? I'll explain. It was brought to my attention a short while ago that the false innuendoes swirling around Ms. Parker's manuscript were adversely impacting the production of this movie. Filming that had been scheduled to begin in the United Kingdom was being held up.

"In the interest and spirit of international cooperation, I was able to assuage any reservations on the part of British authorities as to whether or not the contents of this film would do damage to America's national security and/or harm our much-valued relationship with one of our staunchest allies. I assured them we have no such concerns.

"On the contrary, I am a great believer that good entertainment also has the potential and the ability to educate. I hope this film does both."

"We hope so too. And thank you, Mr. President," Dara said.

"I do hope I'll get an invitation to the movie's premiere."

"You can count on it."

The president shook Dara's hand, then Jay's, then shook hands with the rest of the group and indicated that they should exit off the stage. Behind them, Dara could hear the shouts of the reporters wanting to have their questions answered.

When they were all safely through the doorway, the president shook everyone's hand again.

"Thank you, Mr. President. That was...unexpected."

"You're very welcome, Ms. Thomas. I really did make that phone call, you know. I'm sorry for the trouble. Everything should be smooth sailing for you now."

"Thank you, Mr. President. We'll resume production right away."

"Mr. President..." Jay's voice faltered.

"Ms. Parker. You taught me something today, and I'm grateful for the lesson. Thank you for your integrity. Although I didn't publicly mention the other two arrests that happened this morning, I want you to know that I have been briefed on your personal situation, and the matter has been handled. More heads will roll. I'm going to do some housecleaning at the IRS, in the FBI, and at the CIA."

"Thank you, Mr. President. Were you aware that the IRS sent Dara a notice of audit too?"

The president's eyes widened and he shook his head in disgust. "I was not. But I will take care of it." He winked at her. "I wish you much success. I can't wait to see the movie."

"Thank you, sir."

The president exited through a side door, surrounded by Secret Service agents and a gaggle of assistants.

"Now what?" Dara asked Jay.

Kate and Rebecca joined them.

"Now, we go home," Kate answered. She gathered Jay in her arms and held her close, whispering in her ear.

Dara turned away, wanting to give them their privacy.

"Well, it isn't every day the president of the United States gives your movie his personal seal of approval, eh?" George said.

"No kidding," Trevor said.

"That was cool." Juanita's eyes shown with excitement.

"All's well that ends well," Laura said.

"That's an understatement." Richard snapped a picture of the presidential seal on the door.

Rebecca slid her hand into Dara's and smiled up at her. "What a day, huh?"

"You can say that again." Dara pulled out her own phone.

"Who are you calling?"

"Our ride."

⊷⊶

Peter, Kate, and Jay shared a row on the flight home to Albany. "I think I preferred the private jet with the captain's chair that swiveled and reclined," Jay said.

"I think you got spoiled," Peter quipped. "Oh. I almost forgot. This is for you." He pulled his briefcase from underneath the seat in front of him, unlatched it, and removed the manuscript and the screenplay. "Derek gave these to me this morning. He figured you'd trust me with them."

"I'm not so sure," Jay kidded. "Thank you."

"So, Lorraine, Sabastien, and Vaughn are on their way home?" Kate asked.

"Yep. I talked to Lorraine right before we boarded. Vaughn and Sabastien are flying back to D.C. Lorraine should be home sometime tomorrow."

"All is right with the world," Jay said.

"Correction. All is better with the world," Peter answered. "There are still plenty of bad guys out there we don't know about."

"That's why we keep shining light in the dark places," Jay said. "It's why I'll never stop writing."

Kate kissed her on the top of the head. "I love you."

"I love you too."

"So, are you guys going to go to London for the filming?" Peter asked.

Jay looked to Kate and raised an eyebrow in question.

"I don't see why not. Dara did invite us."

Jay pumped her fist. "Yes."

"And our accounts are mysteriously, or not so mysteriously, unfrozen again."

"Hallelujah for that," Jay said. "I'm glad Dara's troubles are over too."

"Jamison Parker. That was pretty ballsy of you to bring that up to the president," Kate said.

Jay shrugged. "It was the right thing to do." She reclined her seat. "Speaking of the president, I can't believe he endorsed the manuscript and the movie in a press conference. He stuck his neck out and he didn't have to do that."

"He went above and beyond," Kate agreed. "Surprised the heck out of me."

"You owe Mimi Hyland a big bouquet of flowers," Peter said. "The way she told it to me, she wrangled herself that invitation to the White House for dinner so she could personally lobby on your behalf."

"Oh, my God. I love that woman. I wish I'd gotten to see her while we were in town," Jay said.

"Invite her to the movie premiere when it happens. I'm sure that will thrill her."

"We should absolutely do that," Kate agreed.

"A movie premiere. Of my film." Jay shook her head in disbelief. "Who saw that coming?"

≪๑≫

As they walked into the house, Jay's cell phone rang.

"Don't answer it," Kate said. She pulled Jay into her arms. "We're going to be very busy." She nuzzled the side of Jay's neck.

Jay peeked at the readout. "I have to answer it." Kate's lips on her throat made her purr.

"No, you don't."

Jay extricated herself and pulled the Bluetooth out of her pocket. "I really, really do. But I promise it will only take a minute. Don't lose your place."

Kate sighed, grabbed their bags, and headed for the bedroom. Jay stared at her derrière and willed her libido under control.

"Hello?"

"Jay! I've been trying to reach you. I'm so sorry I missed your calls."

"Hello, Sydney." Jay allowed the frost to come through in her voice. "What can I do for you?"

"The better question is what I can do for you. My e-mail has been blowing up and my phone has been ringing off the hook with publisher offers for the manuscript. The big six all want it and everyone is scrambling to outdo the other. I foresee a major bidding war here. We're talking multi-millions of dollars with options."

Jay's eyes flashed angrily and she took a deep breath. "Is that so?"

"You can't imagine."

"I'm glad you could find the time to take all those calls and answer all those e-mails, Sydney."

"Of course. Anything for you, Jay."

"Anything?"

"Sure. You're my favorite client."

"Good. Please forward me directly all of the offers you've received on my behalf."

"You want to look at them personally?"

"I do."

"I'll take care of it right now." Sydney sounded perplexed.

"Thanks."

Jay walked into the office and booted up her computer. Within minutes, it beeped with a series of incoming messages and e-mails. Jay checked to verify that the e-mails from Sydney included offers from the six biggest publishers in the world. Beyond that were twenty more offers from mid-range publishers.

When the last publisher e-mail had come through, she received one more message from Sydney letting her know that she had everything. Jay hit Reply.

```
Dear Sydney,
    I  hereby  inform  you  of  the  formal
termination  of  our  relationship.  You  are
no  longer  authorized  to  do  business  or
negotiate  on  my  behalf.  Please  forward
any   additional   business   dealings,
incoming  correspondence,  or  other  matters
pertaining  to  me  and/or  my  work  to:
Carolyn  Detweiler.  Her  e-mail  address,
mailing  address,  and  phone  details  are
included  on  the  contact  data  sheet
attached to this e-mail.
    Sincerely,
    Jamison Parker
```

Jay sat back and re-read the e-mail. Then she hit Send and composed a new e-mail.

```
Dear Carolyn,
    Looks  like  you're  going  to  be  a  busy
woman.  Attached  please  find  a  series  of
offers  that  have  been  made  to  me  for  the
rights  to  my  manuscript.  I  look  forward
to  working  with  you  and  hearing  your
thoughts.
    All the best,
    Jay
    PS:  Whichever  offer  we  accept,  the
publisher  must  agree  as  a  condition  of
the  contract  that  the  book  will  be  edited
by  my  former  editor  at  Black  Quill,
Jeremy Taunton.
```

Jay shut down the computer and headed for the bedroom.

"You'll never believe…"

"What, exactly, won't I believe?" Kate asked.

Jay swallowed hard. Her heart skittered and thumped in her chest. She wiped her damp palms on her pants and walked to the bed, never taking her eyes off Kate, who lay there naked and as beautiful as the first time they'd made love nearly thirty years ago.

"You'll never believe how much I love you, and how much I'm looking forward to the rest of our lives together."

Kate's eyes glistened with tears and unspent emotion. "I believe, sweetheart." She unbuttoned Jay's shirt and lifted it off her shoulders, kissing the exposed flesh. "I believe in you, and I believe in us. Through all the years, and all the hardships we've endured. Through everything, there's been one constant, one sure thing."

"What's that?" Jay slid on top of Kate, the feel of her body so familiar, and yet so new.

"Our love for each other."

"We'll always have each other." Jay ran her fingers lightly over Kate's smooth skin.

"Jay?"

"Mmm?"

"Stop talking."

EPILOGUE

J ay couldn't remember ever being this nervous. She fidgeted with her diamond necklace for the umpteenth time and smoothed the lines of her Caroline Herrera dress.

Dara leaned over and whispered in her ear. "You look radiant. Stop fussing."

"I don't know how you stand it. I'm a mess."

"I'm an actress. Don't try this at home." Dara laughed.

"Seriously. I'll take any pointers you have. This is the premiere of my first movie. What if they don't like it?"

"They're going to love it."

"But what if they don't?"

"Jamison Parker. The book spent fifty-two weeks on the *New York Times* Best Sellers list. Fifty-two weeks! You and Rebecca wrote a script that was faithful to the book. George's direction was magnificent. I gave my best performance ever, I hope..." Dara winked. "Everything is going to be fine. And if not, there's nothing you can do about it now."

Kate approached them with glasses of champagne.

"Thank you," Dara said. "Your wife is a wreck."

"Tell me about it. You should've seen her getting dressed."

"Hey!"

"Well, sweetheart. You changed three times."

"A girl needs options."

"Who needs options?" Rebecca came alongside Dara and kissed her on the cheek. Kate handed her a glass of champagne too. "By the way, I love the idea of a private pre-premiere party for the cast and crew. Genius."

"I propose a toast," Kate said. "To all the women in my life. You make this journey an adventure. To you, Dara, and you Rebecca, Jay and I are so grateful for your friendship. It's been such a delight getting to know you and to be part of your lives." Kate clinked glasses with them. "And to you, darling," Kate's eyes sparkled at Jay, "you are the love of my life, my heart, my soul, my breath. Whatever happens tonight, you're my shining star, and I love you endlessly."

"Here, here," Dara and Rebecca chimed in.

"I'll drink to that," Jay said. She kissed Kate gently on the mouth. "You're my world, Katherine Ann Kyle."

"Ladies and gentlemen, please make your way out front into the theater. The crowd is assembled and ready for your entrance."

"Oh my God!"

"It's going to be fine, Jay. You'll see." Dara squeezed her hand. She set their champagne glasses on a nearby tray. "You and Kate will sit next to me. If anyone throws rotten tomatoes, I'll catch them."

"Not helping."

They reached the back door of the theater, the area behind the screen, and paused.

"Ladies and gentlemen," the event organizer intoned, "please welcome your producers, writers, cast and crew."

"That's our cue." Dara squeezed Jay's hand one more time. She lifted her chin, looped her arm through Rebecca's, and strode into the packed theater to thunderous applause.

Kate came alongside Jay and took her hand. "Ready?"

"No."

"Good." Kate kissed her and led them behind Dara and Rebecca. George entered behind them, followed by the rest of the cast and crew.

When they were all at their seats, George turned on his lavaliere microphone. "Ladies and gentlemen, on behalf of our executive producers, actors, actresses, writers, and friends, I want to thank you all for being here tonight. Every movie premiere is special. This one is no different. Please relax and enjoy the show." He took his seat and everyone else followed suit.

The lights went out and Jay stared nervously at the screen. What if people didn't like it?

"Sweetheart?" Kate whispered in her ear.

"Yes?"

"Your thoughts are so loud I can hear them all the way over here. It's going to be fine. Everyone's going to love it, just like they loved the book. Have a little faith."

The sound came up, the opening sequence began to roll, and suddenly Jay forgot everything. She sat utterly transfixed by the story.

Two hours later, she blinked as the closing credits crawled on the screen. She reminded herself to breathe.

And then it happened. Waves of applause rolled throughout the theater, followed by shouts of *Bravo!*

Dara turned to her and smiled brilliantly. "Well, what did you think?"

"I think..." Jay cleared her throat. "I think it's magnificent. I think it surpasses my wildest dreams." Tears pricked her eyes. "Oh, my God. Thank you. Thank you, Dara. It's like seeing my inner world brought to life. I can't believe it."

"Well, I'd strongly suggest you stand up with me right now and take a bow, because they're all clamoring for you."

Jay shook her head. "No, it's you they want."

"I wouldn't bet on that." Dara lifted their joined hands together.

Jay covered her mouth with her other hand. The entire audience was standing and applauding, and looking directly at her and Dara. It was beyond anything she could imagine. There was the president, and next to him Mimi Hyland, and further back she could see Peter, Lorraine, Sabastien, and Derek. They were all on their feet, clapping and whistling.

Jay glanced over at Kate. Her eyes were gleaming with tears. Jay leaned into her. "What's wrong?"

"Wrong? Nothing's wrong, darling. In fact, everything is just exactly right."

"I love you, Kate."

"I love you too, sweetheart."

"We made it. Together."

"We sure did. We sure did."

THE END

About the Author

Lynn Ames is the best-selling author of *The Price of Fame, The Cost of Commitment, The Value of Valor, One ~ Love, Heartsong, Eyes on the Stars, Beyond Instinct, Above Reproach, All That Lies Within, Bright Lights of Summer, Final Cut,* and one of five authors of the collection *Outsiders.* She also is the writer/director/producer of the history-making documentary, "Extra Innings: The Real Story Behind the Bright Lights of Summer." This historically important documentary chronicles, for the first time ever in her own words, the real-life story of Hall-of-Famer Dot Wilkinson and the heyday of women's softball.

Lynn's fiction has garnered her a multitude of awards and honors, including four Goldie awards, the coveted Ann Bannon Popular Fiction Award (for *All That Lies Within*), and the Arizona Book Award for Best Gay/Lesbian book. In addition to the Ann Bannon Award, her contemporary romance *All That Lies Within*, was a Lambda Literary Award (Lammy) Finalist and winner of a Rainbow Award for Lesbian Romance and was additionally honored as one of the top ten lesbian books overall of 2013.

Ms. Ames is the founder of Phoenix Rising Press (www.phoenixrisingpress.com). She is also a former press secretary to the New York state senate minority leader and spokesperson for the nation's third-largest prison system. For more than half a decade, she was an award-winning broadcast journalist. She has been editor of a critically acclaimed national magazine and is a nationally recognized speaker and public relations professional with a particular expertise in image, crisis communications planning, and crisis management.

For additional information please visit her website at www.lynnames.com, or e-mail her at lynnames@lynnames.com.

Other Books in Print by Lynn Ames

Stand-Alone Romances
Bright Lights of Summer
ISBN: 978-1-936429-10-3
It's March, 1941. Captain America appears in a comic book for the very first time. New York City receives 18.1 inches of snow, its 3rd largest snowfall in history. In Holland, the Nazi occupiers forbid Jews to own businesses. In Poland, Heinrich Himmler inspects Auschwitz. World War II is raging in Europe, but America has yet to enter the fray.

And in Phoenix, Arizona, a 16-year-old scrap of a girl named Theodora "Dizzy" Hosler, takes the field to try out for the World Champion P.B.S.W. Ramblers softball team.

Set against the backdrop of perhaps the most dramatic time in US history, comes the story of Diz and Frannie, two women fueled by an unquenchable passion for the game of softball and feelings for each other that go far beyond the bounds of friendship. Will their love for the game bring them closer together or tear them apart?

All That Lies Within
ISBN: 978-1-936429-06-6
How far would you go to hide who you really are inside? And what do you do when you find the one person from whom hiding your true self isn't an option?

Glamorous movie star Dara Thomas has it all—an Oscar nomination, dozens of magazine covers proclaiming her the sexiest woman alive, and people of both sexes clamoring for her attention. She also has a carefully guarded secret life. As Constance Darrow, Dara writes Pulitzer Prize-winning fiction, an outlet that allows her to be so much more than just a pretty face.

Rebecca Minton is a professor of American Literature in love with the work of the mysterious, reclusive author Constance Darrow, with whom she strikes up a correspondence. A chance phrase in a letter leads her to a startling conclusion about the author.

What happens next will change the course of both of their lives forever.

Eyes on the Stars
ISBN: 978-1-936429-00-4

Jessie Keaton and Claudia Sherwood were as different as night and day. But when their nation needed experienced female pilots, their reactions were identical: heed the call. In early 1943, the two women joined the Women Airforce Service Pilots—WASP—and reported to Avenger Field in Sweetwater, Texas, where they promptly fell head-over-heels in love.

The life of a WASP was often perilous by definition. Being two women in love added another layer of complication entirely, leading to ostracism and worse. Like many others, Jessie and Claudia hid their relationship, going on dates with men to avert suspicion. The ruse worked well until one seemingly innocent afternoon ruined everything.

Two lives tragically altered. Two hearts ripped apart. And a second chance more than fifty years in the making.

From the airfields of World War II, to the East Room of the Obama White House, follow the lives of two extraordinary women whose love transcends time and place.

Heartsong
ISBN: 978-0-9840521-3-4

After three years spent mourning the death of her partner in a tragic climbing accident, Danica Warren has re-emerged in the public eye. With a best-selling memoir, a blockbuster movie about her heroic efforts to save three other climbers, and a successful career on the motivational speaking circuit, Danica has convinced herself that her life can be full without love.

When Chase Crosley walks into Danica's field of vision everything changes. Danica is suddenly faced with questions she's never pondered.

Is there really one love that transcends all concepts of space and time? One great love that joins two hearts so that they beat as one? One moment of recognition when twin flames join and burn together?

Will Danica and Chase be able to overcome the barriers standing between them and find forever? And can that love be sustained, even in the face of cruel circumstances and fate?

One ~ Love, *(formerly The Flip Side of Desire)*
ISBN: 978-0-9840521-2-7
Trystan Lightfoot allowed herself to love once in her life; the experience broke her heart and strengthened her resolve never to fall in love again. At forty, however, she still longs for the comfort of a woman's arms. She finds temporary solace in meaningless, albeit adventuresome encounters, burying her pain and her emotions deep inside where no one can reach. No one, that is, until she meets C.J. Winslow.

C.J. Winslow is the model-pretty-but-aging professional tennis star the Women's Tennis Federation is counting on to dispel the image that all great female tennis players are lesbians. And her lesbianism isn't the only secret she's hiding. A traumatic event from her childhood is taking its toll both on and off the court.

Together Trystan and C.J. must find a way beyond their pasts to discover lasting love.

The Kate and Jay Series
The Price of Fame
ISBN: 978-0-9840521-4-1
When local television news anchor Katherine Kyle is thrust into the national spotlight, it sets in motion a chain of events that will change her life forever. Jamison "Jay" Parker is an intensely career-driven *Time* magazine reporter. The first time she saw Kate, she fell in love. The last time she saw her, Kate was rescuing her. That was five years ago, and she never expected to see her again. Then circumstances and an assignment bring them back together.

Kate and Jay's lives intertwine, leading them on a journey to love and happiness, until fate and fame threaten to tear them apart. What is the price of fame? For Kate, the cost just might be everything. For Jay, it could be the other half of her soul.

The Cost of Commitment
ISBN: 978-0-9840521-5-8
Kate and Jay want nothing more than to focus on their love. But as Kate settles into a new profession, she and Jay are caught in the middle of a deadly scheme and find themselves pawns in a larger game in which the stakes are nothing less than control of the country.

In her novel of corruption, greed, romance, and danger, Lynn Ames takes us on an unforgettable journey of harrowing conspiracy—and establishes herself as a mistress of suspense.

The Cost of Commitment—it could be everything...

The Value of Valor
ISBN: 978-0-9840521-6-5
Katherine Kyle is the press secretary to the president of the United States. Her lover, Jamison Parker, is a respected writer for Time magazine. Separated by unthinkable tragedy, the two must struggle to survive against impossible odds...

A powerful, shadowy organization wants to advance its own global agenda. To succeed, the president must be eliminated. Only one person knows the truth and can put a stop to the scheme.

It will take every ounce of courage and strength Kate possesses to stay alive long enough to expose the plot. Meanwhile, Jay must cheat death and race across continents to be by her lover's side...

This hair-raising thriller will grip you from the start and won't let you go until the ride is over.

The Value of Valor—it's priceless.

The Mission: Classified Series
Beyond Instinct – Book One in the Mission: Classified Series
ISBN: 978-1-936429-02-8

Vaughn Elliott is a member of the State Department's Diplomatic Security Force. Someone high up in the United States government has pulled rank, hand-selecting her to oversee security for a visit by congressional VIPs to the West African nation of Mali. The question is, who picked her for the job and why?

Sage McNally, a career diplomat, is the political officer at the US Embassy in Mali. As control officer for the congressional visit, she is tasked to brief Vaughn regarding the political climate in the region.

The two women are instantly attracted to each other and share a wild night of passion. The next morning, Sage disappears while running, leaving behind signs of a scuffle. Why was Sage taken and by whom? Where is she being held?

Vaughn's attempts to get answers are thwarted at every turn. Even Sage does not know why she's been targeted.

Independently, Sage and Vaughn struggle to make sense of the seemingly senseless. By the time each of them figures it out, it could be too late for Sage.

As the clock ticks inexorably toward the congressional visit, the stakes get even higher, and Vaughn is faced with unspeakable choices. Her decisions will make the difference between life and death. Will she choose duty or her own code of honor?

Above Reproach – Book Two in the Mission: Classified Series

ISBN: 978-1-936429-04-2

Sedona Ramos is a dedicated public servant. Fluent in three languages, with looks that allow her to pass for Hispanic, Native American, or Middle Eastern, she is a valuable asset to the super-secret National Security Agency. When she accidentally stumbles upon a mysterious series of satellite images revealing activity at a shuttered nuclear facility in war-torn Iraq, somebody wants her dead.

With danger lurking at every turn and not knowing who among her colleagues might be involved, Sedona risks her life to get the information to the one person she can trust—the president.

The implications of Sedona's discovery are clear and quite possibly catastrophic. Potential suspects include foreign terrorists, high-ranking Cabinet members, and assorted others. Whomever the president picks for this mission must be above reproach.

Vaughn Elliott is enjoying her self-imposed isolation on a remote island, content to live in quiet anonymity. But when old friend Katherine Kyle brings an urgent SOS from the president of the United States, duty trumps comfort.

Time is of the essence. Vaughn, Sedona, and a hand-picked team of ex-operatives and specialists must figure out what's really going on outside Baghdad, stop it, and unmask the forces behind the plot. If they fail at any point along the way, it could mean the loss of millions of lives.

Will Vaughn and company unravel the mysteries in time? The trail of clues stretches from the Middle East to Washington. The list of people who want to kill them is long. And the stakes have never been higher...

Anthology Collections
Outsiders
ISBN: 978-0-979-92545-0
What happens when you take five beloved, powerhouse authors, each with a unique voice and style, give them one word to work with, and put them between the sheets together, no holds barred?

Magic!!

Brisk Press presents Lynn Ames, Georgia Beers, JD Glass, Susan X. Meagher and Susan Smith, all together under the same cover with the aim to satisfy your every literary taste. This incredible combination offers something for everyone—a smorgasbord of fiction unlike anything you'll find anywhere else.

A Native American raised on the Reservation ventures outside the comfort and familiarity of her own world to help a lost soul embrace the gifts that set her apart. * A reluctantly wealthy woman uses all of her resources anonymously to help those who cannot help themselves. * Three individuals, three aspects of the self, combine to create balance and harmony at last for a popular trio of characters. * Two nomadic women from very different walks of life discover common ground—and a lot more—during a blackout in New York City. * A traditional, old school butch must confront her community and her own belief system when she falls for a much younger transman.

Five authors—five novellas. Outsiders—one remarkable book.

Specialty Books - Humor

Digging For Home, By Parker & Dixie Ames (discoverable under Lynn Ames because these canine kids are too young to cash a royalty check)

ISBN: 978-1-936429-08-0

We've all done it—sat there and wondered what our canine companions were thinking while staring at the television with us during a ball game. Ponder no more! Irrepressible golden retrievers Parker and Dixie Ames have made it their mission to take you inside the dugout for a dog's-eye view of the innings and outings of the great game of softball. Assisted by their Siberian husky pal Lucy McMan-West, an obliging cast of canine cohorts, a chicken, a turtle, and a llama named LaRue, the dynamic duo reminds us that softball is not about winning or losing—it's about finding the shortest route to the concession stand.

Filled with quirky explanations and colorful photo illustrations, *Digging for Home* is a tasty ballpark treat that's packed with heart, hilarity, and plenty of doggone good fun.

All Lynn Ames books are available through www.lynnames.com, from your favorite local bookstore, or through other online venues.

You can purchase other Phoenix Rising Press books online at www.phoenixrisingpress.com or at your local bookstore.

Published by
Phoenix Rising Press
Phoenix, AZ

Visit us on the Web: Phoenix Rising Press

Here at Phoenix Rising Press, our goal is to provide you, the reader, with top quality, entertaining, well-written, well-edited works that leave you wanting more. We give our authors free rein to let their imaginations soar. We believe that nurturing that kind of unbridled creativity and encouraging our authors to write what's in their hearts results in the kinds of books you can't put down.

Whether you crave romances, mysteries, fantasy/science fiction, short stories, thrillers, or something else, when you pick up a Phoenix Rising Press book, you know you've found a good read. So sit back, relax, get comfortable, and enjoy!

Phoenix Rising Press
Phoenix, AZ

Printed in the USA
CPSIA information can be obtained
at www.ICGtesting.com
CBHW071224310524
9373CB00041B/930